"I never lied to my father before," Beverly said, regretfully, as she walked over to where Tabitha was standing.

Tabitha turned around and sized Beverly up before responding. She looked at the tall, slender girl and chuckled as she walked over to the couch. "You didn't lie to him, I did."

"But I didn't speak up, so it's the same thing."

"It's not the same thing." Tabitha sat down next to Melinda and plopped her feet up on the coffee table. "I lied and you didn't. So now, if he finds out and asks you about it, all you have to do is tell him that you didn't know."

"No way," Beverly whined, as she walked around to the front of the couch to face Tabitha. "Then I'd really be lying straight out."

"So what," Tabitha shouted. "What's a little lie once in your life…"

RISE OF THE PHOENIX

KENNETH J. WHETSTONE

Genesis Press, Inc.

Indigo Vibe

An imprint of Genesis Press, Inc.
Publishing Company

Genesis Press, Inc.
P.O. Box 101
Columbus, MS 39703

All rights reserved. Except for use in any review, the reproduction or utilization of this work in whole or in part in any form by any electronic, mechanical, or other means, not known or hereafter invented, including xerography, photocopying and recording, or in any information storage or retrieval system, is forbidden without written permission of the publisher, Genesis Press, Inc. For information write Genesis Press, Inc., P.O. Box 101, Columbus, MS 39703.

All characters in this book have no existence outside the imagination of the author and have no relation whatsoever to anyone bearing the same name or names. They are not even distantly inspired by any individual known or unknown to the author and all incidents are pure invention.

Copyright© 2006 by Kenneth J. Whetstone

ISBN: 1-58571-197-7
Manufactured in the United States of America

First Edition

Visit us at www.genesis-press.com
or call at 1-888-Indigo-1

DEDICATION

This Book is Dedicated to My Children...
Lee Kenielle Whetstone
Matthew Jerome Shields
Thomasina Anita Robinson
Vernelle Whitney Whetstone
Dasia Denise Whetstone
Also...
I want to mention some very special family members: Pearline Whetstone, Gloria Jean Whetstone, Tiney Ruth Whetstone, Patricia Straight, Frankie Whetstone, Angelon Hope Rolle, Nuraldin Abdulah Whetstone, Malcolm Aaron Whetstone, Jamillah Pearline Fatimah Whetstone, Lisa Sheilds, Vivian Gale Wilson, and Wanda Denise Hudson.
And a Very Special Dedication to the Memory of:
Matthew Walter Whetstone
July 5, 1945 – June 5, 1976
and
Ernest Whetstone
May 4, 1910 – January 17, 1994

ACKNOWLEDGMENTS

First and foremost, I want to thank God for blessing me with this, one of the many gifts that I have been able to share with you. It is His will that I bring this message to you in the form of this fable. Thank You Jesus for Your strength and guidance and for saving me!

Kenneth J. Whetstone

Special Thanks to:

Mr. Mel Seeman, my high school basketball coach, for giving me my first opportunity to coach, and for helping me to realize that coaching was my niche. Rest in peace.

Mr. Irving Falk, for showing me what it takes to participate in and run leagues and tournaments.

Mr. Barney Davis, for schooling me on how to really teach basketball, for educating me on how to educate the student-athletes, and for being there for me the many times I had nowhere else to go and no one else to turn to.

Ms. Mary Cosgrove, for trusting me, having confidence in me and making me feel needed.

Mr. Rodney Cuttino, for being one of my best friends ever; for praying for me and surrounding me with praying people. Ain't no friend loved me better, Bro!

Mr. Rodney Carr, for being a real friend, and for telling me about myself when I needed to hear it.

Mr. Robert Doss, Sr., I needed someone in my life at one time that I could talk to who was addicted to basketball as much as I was. What a great guy you are.

Mr. Michael James, you're one of the nicest guys I've ever met. Your support was instrumental in my success during the summer leagues.

Ms. Yolanda Harrell, thanks for coming back to give back. Next time will be better.

Ms. Rosheda Hopson, you came to give back, too. The girls loved you, but not nearly as much as I do.

Ms. Veronica Wright, you are truly a special woman and I love you for being who you are and what you've been to me.

Mr. Gustan O'Neal, thanks for looking out for us when we need a place to go.

I also want to remember Mr. Clyde Frazier, Jr., founder and director of the Slam Jam Women's Basketball Classic, who was taken from us by a selfish act of terrorism. Clyde was a good man who did whatever he could to help young people.

Thanks to the most loyal and dedicated members of the Imperial Crew, New Attitude and Lady Phoenix programs…

Candice Abraham
Natalie Acosta
Tamara Aponte
December Bails
Chiva Barlitier
Ionia Barrow
Elicia Bass
Karisha Battle
Christine Beau
Shaneenah Beau
Juliet Beckles
Monique Bethea
Hazina Black
Nicole Blair
Valerie Blount
Annel Bonner
Renee Bostic
Catherine Bowles
Myrtle Bowles
Paquita Braswell (R.I.P.)
Delphia Brooks
Garrianne Brown
Juanita Brown
Laneda Brown
Rona Brown
Sylvia Brown
Tondalisa Buriss
Jennifer Canty
Swenda Cepeda
Indira Ceville
Michelle Ceville
Tianni Charles
Shontell Cobb
Margo Colon
Sequana Cooke
Myriam Corbett
Taneka Cousins
Latia Curry
Tanzee Daniel
Antoinette Daniels
Latasha Davis
Tanya Davis
Raven DeLeon
Ebony Dumas
Abeni Edwards
Sharice Elmore
Natasha Ennis
Keya Epps
Ikeuchi Franklin
Tanya Gaddy

Ramona Gales
Michelle Gibson
Andrea Gee
Sharon Gifford
Ovetta Glasgow
Solieta Glasgow
Virginia Gonzalez
Letwa Gooden
Latarsha Graham
Charmaine Gregory
Ebony Haggins
Elizabeth Hall
Yolanda Harrell
Yolanda Holmes
Rosheda Hopson
Rashanna Jackson
Allison Jenkins
Tanya Johnson
Karen King
Terry King
Sabrina Knox
Nicole Latta
Roanne Lee
Amira LeGrand
Monica Lindsey
Ana Lopez
Shelly-Ann Lovell
Christine McNeil
Ronita McColley
Nicky McCrimmon
Tremell McKenzie
Rannie Miles
Denise Minto
Tamika Moore
Veronica Moses
Samantha Moulon
Latoya Moultrie
Marilyn Oates
Saudhie Oliver
Letanga Owens
Kelly-Ann Peart
Shyrene Pelzer
Shalimar Phillips
Jasmine Pierce
Kadedra Posey
Katisha Ramseur
Adia Revell
Angela Riddick
Tisha Riley
Erica Ross
Janice Rodriguez
Elba Rudder
Trica Safe
Katherine Santiago
Erica Sinclair
Rhonda Singleton
Nicole Sledge
Renee Smith
Yoneaque Steadman
Lakisha Stewart
Cherrise Strother
Amanda St. Louis
Trina Stroman
Lesley Superville
Lisa Superville
Kelshia Swanson
Regia Thomas
Katherine Thompson
Michelle Thompson
Dana Timmons
Whitney Toone
Damaris Torres
Lorraine Totten
Charleen Toussaint
Mirta Verdijo
Cinteria Webb
Raquel Welch
Tracy Wells
Ajaya Williams
Yolanda Wilson
Monique Wright

Also, to all the others not mentioned on this list. I love you all!

 The song "Oh, Lord" written by Gloria Jean Whetstone. Used with permission. Thank you, Mother!

"Kids want to dunk and shoot from deep and dribble through their legs a hundred times, and there's nobody out there who is willing to teach them the right way to play or instill better habits. AAU and high school coaches don't do it. They're too worried about getting traveling teams together and playing in the best invitational meat-markets… Half the coaches, whether it's on the high school or college level, are afraid that talented kids will leave if they discipline them."

—Oscar Robertson

PROLOGUE

Friday, January 21, 2005 – 7:46 P.M.

The bitter cold of the seventeen degrees outside clutched T.J. Stonewall's body and followed him into the home of his good friend and former junior high school basketball coach, David Martin, who was now coaching the girls' basketball team at Stuyvesant High School. David was a 52-year-old physical education teacher with thinning brown hair and a dark half dollar-sized birthmark on the left side of his neck. He grew up in the Howard Beach section of Queens before moving to his current apartment in Brooklyn Heights.

T.J. quickly shut the door and let the comforting warmth overtake him as he placed his backpack down and shed his hat and coat. The frost in the air was gone in seconds, but the numbness of his fingers and toes lingered as he followed David past the open kitchen area into the living room so that they could watch the NBA game together on television.

"It's cold outside," T.J. complained. "I hate the cold. I can't wait until summer."

"It was freezing in Jefferson's gym today, too," David said, sitting on the couch using the remote control to change the channel.

"Oh, that's right, you played Jeff today. What happened?" T.J. wanted to know.

"Well, first of all, I sat my point guard the whole game because she told me that she couldn't come to practice yesterday because she had to do something for her mother, but I found out before the game that she lied so that she could go see the boys' team play."

T.J. frowned in disappointment. "I never could understand why girls always do that."

David shrugged. "Me either. Boys sure don't duck out of their practices to go see the girls. The worst part is that she didn't even apologize or try to make amends. She just sat on the end of the bench shivering."

"It was that cold in Jefferson's gym?"

"Well, the game was close for the first one and a half quarters because it was so cold no one could shoot or even catch the ball. At the end of the first quarter, the score was 7–4. The problem was that they warmed up a lot faster than we did. The score at halftime was 27–14. They ran away with it from there. We ended up losing by twenty-something—59–32 I think."

"Wow, I thought the game would be a lot closer than that."

"So did I, but like I said, it took us way too long to warm up. But I can tell you this. They're going to have a much tougher time with us if we meet them in the playoffs. They're not going to be able to empty their bench like they did today. I'll tell you this, too. If I had one superstar, we'd beat them for sure."

T.J. got up and walked to the kitchen. "Do you plan on coaching this summer?"

"Nah, I'm going on vacation to Bermuda for three weeks as soon as school is out," David was more than happy to say. "And since you keep telling me how nice Puerto Rico was when you went there for your honeymoon a few months ago, I'm going there for three weeks, too. I'm gonna hang out on the beach all summer and get a real good tan."

"Lucky you." T.J. helped himself to a cup of water. "But you're not going to be here for the New Attitude League."

"Yeah, I know. That tournament has everybody on the New York City Girls Basketball website all fired up. It's all anyone is talking about these days, and it doesn't even start 'til May."

"Later for those people on that site," T.J. grumbled. "They should just take away the message board because the people that post there have made a mockery of it. All they do is have stupid arguments over who's the best team, who's the best player and why this person is ranked high and that one isn't. They're even ranking junior high and elementary school kids now. That's just ridiculous. I could see if they were a bunch of experts, sports writers, etcetera, but it's just a bunch of people who think they know a lot more than they actually do."

"That's for sure."

"Why do you even bother reading it, then?"

"It's funny." David laughed.

"I guess you're right about that." T.J. chuckled. "When this tournament starts, it's really going to become a circus on that site."

"Not just there, but everywhere else, too. Do you see the publicity it's getting in the newspaper already, five months ahead of time?"

"Yeah, five months ahead of time and they already have all ten teams for this region."

"They do?" David asked, surprised. "At seven hundred dollars a team? How can that be?"

T.J. guzzled his water and leaned back against the sink. "People jumped on it right away. They couldn't pass up a chance on taking their whole team to New Orleans for four days for seven hundred bucks. That's a damn good deal for whoever wins."

"Are you entering your teams into it?"

"I wasn't going to because of the entry fee, especially since they're not even giving out any jerseys but insist that every team has *full* uniforms. But the girls in my program deserve to be involved. It doesn't even matter if we get to go to the National Tournament in New Orleans. I think just playing against the competition that's going to be in this tournament will be good for us."

"I don't know." David scratched his head. "I think the same three or four teams that are always coming up short to the Roadrunners will be fighting for second place just like in every other tournament."

"Really? But they have four teams from New Jersey in this region, too."

"Yeah, but the New York/New Jersey region ain't like the Connecticut/Massachusetts region. Like I said, the same three or four teams will be fighting for second place. To me, that's just a waste of seven hundred dollars. You're going to play those same teams in every other tournament. In fact, you can add a hundred bucks to that seven hundred and pay for the West Fourth Street league, the Slam Jam Showcase and the Highland Park tournament all together. It doesn't make sense to me to spend your whole budget for four or five tournaments when the same money can get you into seven or eight."

T.J. placed his glass on the counter and rejoined his mentor on the couch, staring at him as he spoke. He knew that what David was saying had some truth to it, but he had already made the commitment and paid the entry fees for the junior and senior divisions. "The girls will get a kick out of it. I always shelter them from this type of thing so that they won't be surrounded by negative influences. This time, though, I think we'll just go in, compete hard, have some fun and get a few more looks by some of the local college recruiters in the process, since they're all going to flock there anyway."

David threw up his hands. "Okay. But I'm telling you, this is the type of thing that can be just as bad for kids as it is good. Don't let the negative stuff suck you in."

DISCOVERIES

Saturday, June 25, 2005 – 6:42 P.M.

T.J. and Sheila Stonewall had just moved into their three-bedroom house on Ninety-ninth Street near Avenue J in the Canarsie section of Brooklyn—a compromise from the respective areas they lived in before getting married. T.J. had rented a one-bedroom apartment in the not-yet-developed part of Bedford Stuyvesant. The area was making very slow, yet gradual developments, but still hadn't emancipated itself from being a part of "The Hood!" Sheila also rented a one bedroom apartment, but in a modern-renovated brownstone in the leisurely, and sumptuous area of Park Slope. Canarsie, a diversified, predominately middle-income neighborhood surrounded by the perilous, housing project-dominated streets of Brownsville; the uppity, well-to-do back streets of the Peadergaets; the subdued, out of the way community of Starrett City; and the rugged, hardcore section of East New York, was common ground for the newlyweds.

As T.J. pulled up in front of the house and parked his tan Jeep Grand Cherokee behind Sheila's midnight blue Honda CR-V, he cringed from the pain of the migraine that was antagonizing him. He was also feeling as dreary as the overcast day, a day that constantly threatened rain that never came. With his head throbbing, throat sore and muscles tense, T.J. made his way out of his car and reached the front door. He put his hand into his pocket for his keys but pulled out the note that Sheila put there reminding him to pick up a bottle of Moët to go along with the special dinner she was cooking for his twenty-ninth birthday.

Seeing his wife's exquisite cursive on the folded scrap paper brought a smile to his face and setback the agony of his headache enough for him to enjoy thinking about how much he loved the former Sheila Michelle Faison. In his eyes, she was an angel that did no wrong. She was his soul mate, and although he knew it since they were very young, it wasn't until two years earlier that she realized the same thing. For T.J., it was better late than never. He was happy to finally have her in his life the way he wanted. It was just in time, too, because he knew that if it were not for her, he would've stressed himself into a heart attack a long time ago. She saved his life, and he knew that one day soon he was going to have to start listening to her and stop letting basketball drive him crazy.

T.J. turned around and started his three-block walk to the liquor store. He couldn't stop thinking about his day. Besides watching his team struggle to pull away from a much weaker opponent, he had to deal with Mildred Negron and Charles Greene hanging around scheming on players to steal. Mildred Negron was the coach of the Roadrunners, a team based out of Washington Heights that traveled all over the country with many of the city's top players. Charles Greene was the coach of Thomas Jefferson High School in Brooklyn, public school champions for the past three years and state champions for the past two. The two of them worked together to keep each other on top. T.J. openly expressed his displeasure with the way they hung around recruiting the so-called best players in the city to their respective programs, which they both hated him for, but he didn't care. As far as he was concerned, the feeling was mutual.

As T.J. walked past Ninety-eighth Street, he noticed two girls playing on a makeshift court in the middle of the block. There was a hoop on a half-moon backboard mounted up on a telephone pole facing out to the street. It was a one-way street that wasn't very busy, so the kids on the block played in it all the time. It reminded him of the court on his old block back on Cleveland Street in East New York, where he first learned how to play basketball.

From a half-block away, T.J. couldn't tell if he knew either of the girls, so he decided to take a detour to see who they were. As he got closer, he realized that neither of them looked familiar. There weren't many players in Brooklyn, or in all of New York City for that matter, that he didn't know anything about.

T.J. walked up, rested his foot on a nearby fire hydrant and watched the two girls continue to play. They both appeared to be young, perhaps junior high school aged at most. He was impressed

RISE OF THE PHOENIX

with the taller girl. Her style was unlike most girls. The array of moves she made, her use of both hands, and her ability to stop and pull up for a jump shot showed him that she'd been playing a long time, probably always with highly-skilled boys. Although the other girl seemed to have potential also, she was nowhere near the taller girl's level. The thing that appealed to T.J. the most was that the tall girl did not try to humiliate or take advantage of her less-skilled opponent. She was teaching her friend, who seemed to be receptive and appreciative.

T.J. watched for about five minutes before he decided to introduce himself. He got the impression, however, that the girls might be apprehensive about talking to him, so he took a subtle approach to break the ice. "You girls like playing basketball a lot, huh?"

The girls just glanced at him and resumed their game. He decided to be a bit more direct. "You know, I run a program for girls that like to play basketball. You girls ever play on a basketball team before?"

The taller girl stopped and picked up the ball. She looked the well built, six-foot-two-inch stranger up and down, studying T.J.'s neck-length locks that hung around his boyish, chocolate face and the thin goatee that framed his thick lips. He wore royal blue Nike warm-up pants and a pair of grey and blue Nike 2K5's. But it was the logo of the flaming bird carrying a basketball with the words LADY PHOENIX across the top on his T-shirt that really captured her attention.

"I played for my school with the boys," she said, finally. She had a heavy Southern accent, leading T.J. to believe that she probably just moved to New York recently, which would be why he didn't know her.

"Really?" T.J. gave a friendly smile.

"Yeah, but we only played four games, two against the staff, and a home and home against another school."

"And how about you?" he asked her friend.

"No," the girl cautiously responded. "I was going to play, but we didn't have enough girls to make a team." This girl didn't have the same twang. She spoke like a true Brooklyn native.

"Oh, so is that why you had to play with the boys? The two of you go to the same school?" T.J. asked.

"Well, not anymore," the taller girl said, walking toward him to get out of the way of an oncoming car with her best friend in tow. "We're both going to high school in September, but to different schools. I'm going to Stuyvesant, and she's going to Midwood."

"I see. So why didn't both of you play for the boys' team?"

"My mother wouldn't let me play with the boys," the shorter girl whined.

"Well, maybe she'll be more comfortable with you playing with my program where there are only girls. As a matter of fact, I'd like to speak to the both of your parents about the two of you joining my program. Would you like that?"

"Yeah!" both girls replied.

"Are either of your parents at home now?"

"Yeah, my father's home," the taller girl said enthusiastically.

"So why don't you ask him to come out so I can tell him about the program? My name is Coach Stone. What's yours?"

"My name's Beverly," said the taller girl.

"And how about you?" he asked her friend. "What's your name?"

"My name's Melinda."

"So, Beverly, why don't you ask your father to come out so I can talk to him? And Melinda, you can ask your folks, too."

"I don't live here," Melinda quickly informed him. "I live on the next block. Anyway, my mother's not home."

"I see." T.J. said, and then turned his attention back to Beverly. "Well, how about it, Beverly? Can I meet your father?"

"I'll get him," she said, and then tossed the ball to Melinda and ran into the house.

Melinda started dribbling the ball out toward the chalk-drawn free throw line in the street. "Watch this shot," she said. "I can make this all day."

"Go ahead, show your stuff," T.J. encouraged as he took off his backpack and searched it throughout. He watched the fudge-colored girl with a cherubic face and big, glassy, dark eyes stand pigeon-toed with her feet too close together and holding the ball down near her abdomen. She was dressed in a yellow Ecko Red T-shirt, blue jeans that clung to her wide hips and thick legs, and a pair of all white Nikes. Her eyes beamed and a half smile turned up on the left side of her mouth

RISE OF THE PHOENIX

as she prepared to take her shot. She took a deep breath and flung the ball at the hoop, and it crashed off the side of the backboard.

"Oh-oh, we're going to have to work on that shooting form," T.J. said.

Melinda ran after the ball, picked it up and ran back to the foul line. "I can make it," she insisted. "Watch."

T.J. took his organizer from his bag and took a business card out of it. "Hold on, let me give this to you."

Melinda flung the ball at the basket again, but this time her shot fell short and missed the whole thing, then bounced over toward T.J. She ran to retrieve it, but he grabbed it first and handed his card to her.

"Whoa! Here, please take my card. Have your mother call me. You'll be making that shot and a lot more in no time."

Melinda quickly shoved the card into her back pocket, and then took the ball away from him. "I can make it," she insisted again, and turned to run back out into the street, but was held up by another passing car.

Beverly came back out with her father. "Here's my dad," she announced.

T.J. walked up the stairs to their porch and extended his hand. "How are you doing, sir? My name is T.J. Stonewall, but everybody calls me Coach Stone. I run a girls' basketball program called The Lady Phoenix."

"Hiya doin'?" Beverly's father said with an even heavier twang than his daughter's as he shook T.J.'s hand. "Burton Smalls. My friends call me Burt, but you can call me Mr. Smalls 'til we establish whether we go'n be friends or not."

T.J. couldn't tell if Burton Smalls was joking or not, so he decided to take him at his word for the moment. "Okay, well, I was just passing the block and, uh…" T.J. paused to free himself from Burton's overly firm, extended handshake.

Burton Smalls was a large man, six-foot-eight and two hundred and sixty pounds. He had an imposing posture and stood at attention like a military officer wearing a gray Champion sweatshirt, blue painter's jeans and a pair of leather house shoes. Beverly looked like her father spit her out. She was seven inches shorter, but they stood the same way. He was bald and she had professionally done cornrows braided with zigzag designs on top and hung down to the base of her neck. They both had high cheekbones, big eyes, full lips, and tanned, caramel complexions. Beverly wasn't broad like her father. She was thin and lanky with arms and legs that seemed to go on forever, and she had big feet and hands. She wore an oversized red Michael Jordan Chicago Bulls jersey over a white T-shirt, black nylon warm-up pants and black and red Jordan sneakers.

"Yes, I was just passing by when I noticed your daughter and her friend here playing a little one-on-one," T.J. continued. "It captured my attention because I have a program for female student-athletes who enjoy playing basketball and would like to be the best they can at it. I teach them the game, keep them in good physical shape, and play in numerous leagues and tournaments all year-round—"

"Now, just where all these tournaments at," Burton interrupted. "And how do you expect these gals 'posed to play all year-round when they got school and all? You know, I been workin' out with these gals for most of the spring, tryin' to get them ready to play on they high school varsity teams. I know Bev'ly's ready." He used his index finger to poke T.J. on the shoulder. "You better believe she's ready. Them gals at them other schools are gonna wanna quit playin' when my baby's done whuppin' on 'em."

"Yes, I don't doubt that one bit, but..." T.J. attempted to finish telling Burton about his program, but he found it difficult to finish a sentence.

"Now, Melinda ain't so good yet," Burton went on, lowering his voice slightly, knowing the girls were listening even though they continued playing and tried to pretend that they weren't. "She's still learning. She try real hard, though. But she can't shoot one bit. Shucks, the po' child can't throw a rock in the ocean. But, like I said, she work real hard, and she's gotta lotta potential. She's go'n be somethin' in time. Yessiree, these gals go'n play on they varsity teams and earn themselves a college scholarship."

T.J. got excited. "That's it! That's what my program is all about. We use basketball as a vehicle to help carry student-athletes through school and into college. You see, Mr. Smalls, it's like this. Just as it's required

RISE OF THE PHOENIX

to do well academically in school to be eligible for sports, it's also required to do well academically to participate in the Lady Phoenix program. Beverly told me that she's going to Stuyvesant, which is one of the best public schools in the city, so she must already be doing well academically. My good friend, David Martin, is the coach at Stuyvesant. I learned a lot from him about coaching and how this is supposed to work and patterned my program after his."

"Yeah, I heard about that coach. That's why I'm glad Bev got in. But I knew she would, she's smarter than I don't know what."

"I'm sure she is. And it just means that she'll have no problem adjusting."

"Well, long as you're sure this ain't gonna interfere with her schoolin'."

"Oh, it won't. During most of the school months, we meet only on weekends. In the fall and winter, I set up study workshops that offer tutoring, and I set up study halls. The summer months are when we do mostly basketball. We just started competing in this year's tournaments last month. They all usually start in April or May. We just finished in second place in the Slam Jam Showcase a few weeks ago. Now, we're in two other tournaments, the New York City Housing League and the New Attitude League. The New Attitude League is the big one. The winner from that league will get sponsored to travel and participate in their National Tournament."

"What's it gonna cost me?" Burton asked, and then prepared himself for an over the top answer.

"There's a one hundred and twenty-five dollar yearly membership fee and every kid has to write an essay," T.J. told him. "This year's essay title is 'Where Will I Be in Ten Years?'"

Burton managed a slight smile. "Oh, okay, that there sounds like somethin' worth considerin'. Why don't you just give me your number and let me get back to you?"

T.J. took another card from his organizer along with a small pamphlet he put together on the Lady Phoenix program and handed it to Burton. "Sure. Here, call me *anytime*. I'd like for you and Mrs. Smalls to bring Beverly down and check us out."

Burton's smile faded. "Bev's momma drowned five years ago," he lamented. "It's just me and her, now."

"Oh, I'm very sorry to hear that. Well...uh...I'm sure you will be impressed with our program, Mr. Smalls. We'll talk, and perhaps we can arrange a date for you and Melinda's parents to come and check us out. I think this would be the best thing for both girls."

"Well, we'll see about that," Burton said. "Thank you. You take care."

"Thank you, too, Mr. Smalls. I'll be seeing you."

With that, T.J. turned and headed back down the stairs. "Take care, girls," he said, and waved at them. "Melinda, have your folks call me as soon as possible."

"Okay," Melinda responded, smiling and waving back. "I'll tell my mother tonight."

As T.J. started back up the block, he heard the girls giggling with excitement.

"Y'all go to the store and get me some onions and season salt so I can start makin' dinner," Burton told them, his voice projecting like he was speaking through a bullhorn. "And don't be foolin' around. Hurry on back here."

T.J. admired Burton Smalls for being a single father raising a teenaged daughter. Apparently, he seemed to be in favor of anything that would help her get ahead. He seemed very protective of her, as well.

T.J. also felt that Beverly was a steal. He was very surprised that Mildred Negron and Charles Greene didn't know about her yet. At least, he hoped they didn't. He knew, however, that if Beverly turned out to be as good as he thought, keeping her from them would be the biggest challenge he'd face as a coach.

7:20 P.M.

T.J. entered his house, which was lit only by candlelight, and the sound of he and Sheila's favorite love songs CD played on the stereo. Sheila came out of the dining room and greeted him the way she always did, she hugged him close and gave him a deep, passionate kiss. All of the anxieties from the day usually went away the moment he looked

RISE OF THE PHOENIX

into her sparkling, light-brown eyes, which was why he always looked forward to coming home to her. As T.J. kissed his wife, he inhaled the sweet smell of Red Door perfume. He loved that perfume, and although Sheila didn't really care for it, she still wore it to please him.

T.J. looked his lovely companion over and shook his head in disbelief. He couldn't believe that it was possible for her to look even more stunning and radiant than usual. Sheila was always a sophisticated yet casual dresser. For her husband, however, she liked to be erotic. She wore a long, white dinner gown cut very low in the front, hardly containing her perfect breasts. It hung elegantly from her slender five-ten frame, with thigh-high splits on both sides. She liked to show off her long, shapely legs to him because she knew how much they turned him on.

T.J. held Sheila's hand and slowly spun her around so that he could get a good look at her, observing her from her head to toe. That's when he noticed she changed the color of the streaks in her mid-length, relaxed hairstyle from the usual goldish color to a soft auburn.

"Wow, Mama, I love what you've done with your hair. It matches your natural brown color better than the gold."

Sheila's blush was her response. "Dinner is ready, baby." Her voice was smooth and comforting. She had a beautiful singing voice, too, and T.J. loved for her to serenade him. "Now, go take a shower and get dressed. Be careful, though, the tub is slippery. We need a bath mat."

"Oh, yeah, I'll get one tomorrow."

Sheila prepared T.J.'s favorite meal, baked salmon with penne alfredo. He hurried to take a shower, and then put on the beige linen outfit that she had laid out for him. It was the same two-piece suit he wore when he proposed to her just fifteen short months earlier.

T.J. was getting dressed when the telephone rang. It was Sam Pernell, his best friend and the coordinator for the New Attitude League.

"Hey, Sam, what's going on?" T.J. answered after recognizing the number on the Caller ID.

"What's up, T.J.? I'm calling to ask you a small favor."

"Sure, what's up?"

"Well..." Sam hesitated. "The truth is that this may not be such a small favor. It may be a rather large favor for you."

T.J. didn't get worried, but there was concern because of Sam's tone of voice. "What do you mean?"

"I'd like to revise the schedule and have you play the Roadrunners next weekend instead of two weeks from now because they're going to Washington, D.C. for the Tournament of Champions."

T.J. became enraged at the suggestion. "What?! No friggin' way, Sam!" Sheila hurried into the bedroom to see what was wrong. T.J. put his hand up to let her know that he'd be okay and quickly changed his tone. Sheila left the room, and he resumed his conversation. "You know, I'm tired of Millie trying to take control of every tournament the Roadrunners play in. She thinks she runs New York City because all of you people who run the leagues and tournaments allow her to run all over you."

"Slow down, T.J. No one is running over anyone. And trust me, if it was totally up to me, I'd just proceed without her. But the Board of Directors felt that this would not affect the tournament in any way, and they like the idea of the two of your teams playing during the Fourth of July weekend. Believe me, if it was solely my decision, I'd let her team forfeit. But, once again, it's *not* solely up to me."

"This is messed up. It just isn't right." T.J. pondered for a moment, trying to think of a way to not go along with it. "What if I said no? What if I insisted on playing on the scheduled date and time?"

"I knew you'd say that, and so did the Board of Directors. We know you're supposed to be playing in the City Housing League championship that weekend, so one of the board members called and got the director of that league to change your game. You'll probably be getting a call from him tonight, as well."

"You've gotta be kidding me, Sam."

"Look, I'm sorry about this, T.J. You know you're my boy, and I'd never do anything like this to you. I fought for you as hard as I could."

T.J. and Sam were best friends since high school, so T.J. always knew when Sam was being sincere. "Yeah, I know you did. Thanks anyway."

"Okay, take care and Happy Birthday to you, bro."

RISE OF THE PHOENIX

"Yeah, thanks a lot."

Sheila came back into the room just as T.J. hung up the telephone. "Is everything okay?" she asked with a concerned tone.

"It's nothing for you to be worried about. It's just Mildred Negron finding ways to piss me off again. That woman is the absolute worst!"

Sheila came over to the bed and sat on T.J.'s lap. "Don't worry about her," she said with a sultry voice as she gently stroked his face. "Just do what you do best and things will come out favorable for you."

"Yeah, but…" T.J. started to whine some more, but Sheila's soft lips pressed against his stifled him. She removed her lips after a short endearing kiss and stood up again.

"Now is not the time to be thinking about that stuff." She took him by the hand. "Let's go. Dinner is going to be ruined if you don't come now."

T.J. followed Sheila into the dining room and held out her chair for her before taking his place at the opposite end of the table. They held hands, and he said Grace, thanking God once again for life, love, health, and most importantly, for his lovely wife. As he poured the Moët, he told her how much he loved her and that she was his priority—then the telephone rang again. T.J. started not to answer it, but then remembered Sam said someone from the City Housing League might be calling. He figured that if he could talk them out of rescheduling, it would stop Mildred Negron from having her way.

"Excuse me, Mama." He jumped up from the table and headed back into the bedroom.

"No, T.J.," Sheila called out to him. "Please, whoever it is can wait."

"No, this is important. I promise I'll turn the telephone off after this. It'll only take a minute."

T.J. heard Sheila say something else, but he didn't understand what it was because he was in the process of snatching up the receiver. "Yes? Hello?"

"Coach, this is Velvet," said a trembling voice. "I gotta talk to you—"

"Oh, Velvet," T.J. cut her off, disappointed that it wasn't who he expected. "I really can't talk now—"

"But this is important, Coach. I need to tell you something."

"What is it, Velvet?" he asked impatiently, trying to rush her off the phone.

"Coach, I can't go back home, and I don't know where else to go or what to do."

T.J. hadn't anticipated anything like this, and he became focused on the problem at hand. "What? Why can't you go home?"

"My mother found some letters and pictures I had in my room."

T.J. let out a sigh and closed his eyes, anticipating what Velvet's answer to his next question would be. "What kind of letters and pictures were they?"

"They were love letters from my girlfriend, and some nude pictures we took together."

That was only part of the answer he thought he'd get. He figured they were love letters and sexually provocative photographs, but the "girlfriend" part is something he hadn't expected.

Velvet was an extraordinarily beautiful girl. She was five-eleven with big, brown eyes, full lips and an oval face that outlined her flawless butterscotch complexion. Her hair extended down beyond her shoulder blades and was always permed and conditioned well. She wore it cut to frame her face and let it hang down her back unless she was playing basketball, in which she'd tie it back into a long ponytail. Velvet also had great posture and walked like a model with her head held high. She was always well dressed in designer dresses and skirts most of the time, very feminine and lady-like all the time. She'd smile, bat her eyes and tilt her head slightly when she talked. At sixteen years old, Velvet exuded sexiness, but always in a classy, conservative way. The boys never left her alone, but she always brushed them off. T.J. thought it was because she was so religious and focused on school, basketball and her singing career. He never fathomed the possibility that she may have been gay.

T.J. sighed again. "Where are you now, Velvet?"

"I'm sitting in McDonald's, around the corner from your house," she told him. "Can I come over and talk to you?"

"Now is not a good time, Velvet. Sheila and I are…"

RISE OF THE PHOENIX

Velvet began to cry. "Please, Coach. I can't go home, and I don't know what else to do."

"What's wrong now?" Sheila asked.

T.J. looked up and saw his wife standing in the doorway with her arms folded and an obvious look of disappointment in her alluring, almost sleepy-looking, bedroom eyes, although she was trying to be concerned.

"Hold on just a second, Velvet," he said before pressing the mute button. "Honey, Velvet's afraid to go home because her mother found out she's a lesbian. She wants to come here to talk."

"Where is she?"

"She's around the corner on Rockaway Parkway."

"Tell her to come on, then."

"But, Sweetheart, what about…"

Before T.J. could finish his question, Sheila turned away and started to walk out of the room. "Tell her to come before she goes somewhere and you won't be able to find her. I'm going to put your food in the oven and change clothes."

T.J. could only shake his head at how supportive Sheila was. He let go of the mute button and put the phone back to his ear. "Okay, Velvet, come on over."

She was still crying. "Thank you, Coach."

T.J. hung up the phone, thinking about ways to convince Velvet that going home and talking to her mother would be best. Then he thought about calling her mother before she got there, but decided to wait and hear what all she had to say first.

Sheila came back into the bedroom and walked to the dresser where she pulled out a T-shirt, socks and a pair of cutoffs and threw them on the bed. She kicked off her shoes, took off her gown and walked to the chest of drawers. As she walked past T.J., he inhaled her perfume once again while admiring the smooth walnut complexion of her bare beauty. He took in all he could, fearing that the probability of him seeing her that way again that night would be highly unlikely.

Sheila pulled out some sweatpants and a T-shirt for T.J. and tossed them onto the bed. She walked back past him without saying a word or looking in his direction and began to get dressed. Just as she pulled her T-shirt over her head, the doorbell rang.

"That must be her," Sheila said. "I'll get it and talk to her while you change your clothes."

As she headed out of the room, T.J. called out to her. She stopped and turned. He could see the disappointment in her eyes.

"Sweetheart, I'm sorry about this," he said, sincerely. "I know you did so much to make this a special night for me. I'll make it up to you, I promise."

Sheila smiled slightly and shrugged her shoulders. "What could you do, right? Sometimes things happen that we have no control over, and we have to sacrifice what we want to do to take care of what we have to do. You know what they say, 'Everything happens for a reason.'"

Sheila walked out of the room and T.J. laid back on the bed. His headache flared up again because he was mentally drained from his day: the sub-par game his team played, Sam calling him with the Mildred Negron situation, and now Velvet and her situation. The only good thing T.J. felt about the day was discovering Beverly and Melinda.

NEW ADDITIONS

Sunday, June 26, 2005 – 12:33 A.M.

T.J. knew he heard Sheila's voice coming out of the living room, but there was another voice in there, too. As he regained full consciousness, he lay still a moment and listened, trying to figure out whom she was in there singing with. Whoever it was, he thought she was very good.

He sat up, still dressed in his suit and realized he must've dozed off. Suddenly, he remembered Velvet. He jumped up from the bed and rushed into the living room.

Sheila and Velvet were sitting on the carpet in their pajamas. There were picture albums and CDs scattered about along with some dishes on the coffee table. They stopped singing when they saw T.J. standing in the doorway and looked as though they were waiting for him to say something…so he did.

"Hey, I dozed off," T.J. humbly confessed. "I didn't realize I was that tired. I'm really very sorry."

"That's okay, Coach Stone," Velvet said. "I was just kickin' it with Sheila."

"Well, we can talk now if you like."

"Come over here and have a seat, T.J.," Sheila said. "Let us fill you in."

T.J. jerked his head back and raised a brow. "Fill me in? What do you mean?"

"T.J., it's after midnight. You've been asleep for five hours. You need to just come over here so we can tell you what's going on."

"After midnight? Are you kidding me?"

"T.J., just come sit down, please."

"Sheila, she can't just stay here. I have to call her mother."

"I've already spoken to her mother. If you'd just come over here and sit down, I can tell you what we talked about."

T.J. huffed and marched over to the couch. He sat down and leaned forward, anxious to hear what Sheila and Velvet had to tell him. "Okay, what happened," he asked impatiently.

Sheila got off the floor and sat beside him. Velvet got up and sat on the loveseat facing them.

"Well, while you were *sleeping*," Sheila emphasized, "Velvet explained that..." She paused, looked at Velvet and sat back on the couch, folding her legs up. "Why don't you tell him what happened, Velvet?"

Velvet closed her eyes, tilted her head and bit the left corner of her bottom lip. She looked up and began telling T.J. her story. "Coach, me and Kim have been together for almost a year—"

"Kim? Kim's your girlfriend?" T.J. asked, once again surprised.

"Yes, ever since last summer. My mom went on tour with my oldest sister and my brother. I stayed in New York because I wanted to play basketball. My mom agreed to let me stay because Kim was staying with me in the house, and her mom checked on us."

"I remember that," T.J. recalled. "I think I checked in on you once, too."

"Yeah, that's right," Velvet said. "Anyway, me and Kim were always real cool, but I never knew she was into that lifestyle until she ran it down before she came to stay with me. She wanted me to know she was feelin' me before she stayed there so I'd know exactly what her intentions were. I'd never been with a girl before, but I was curious about it for a minute. I was feelin' Kim because we were cool already, and she was femme."

"Do Kim's parents know about her," T.J. asked. "Do they know about your relationship with her?"

"Yes, Kim's parents got no problem with it," Velvet told him. "They said they had problems with acceptance from their parents with him being black and her being white. They said they weren't going to be like that with their kids. They're going to let them be who they want to be. Kim's lucky."

T.J. and Sheila reacted to Velvet's last statement with a glance at each other.

"Well, finish telling me what happened," T.J. said.

"Well, to make a long story short," Velvet continued, "me and Kim took some pictures and video taped some of the things we were doing together. I hid the stuff in my closet in my suitcase. My mom was packing to leave in the morning, and for whatever reason, she decided she wanted to use my suitcase this time."

"Unbelievable." T.J. rubbed his forehead as his migraine once again started to surface.

"Exactly!" Velvet said. "My mom and I have the exact same luggage. I don't know why she needed mine when she's got her own. The pictures and some letters Kim wrote to me were in there, but I hid the videotape behind my bed. I taped it to the back of the headboard. If she would've found that, I'd be dead right now for sure."

"Well, what makes you think she won't find it?"

"I have the videotape, T.J.," Sheila said.

T.J. whipped his head to face his wife. "You have it? How'd you get it?"

"Well, while you were *sleeping*," Sheila emphasized again, "I took Velvet home and had a talk with her mother. Mrs. Fuller was really upset to find out that her sixteen-year-old daughter was sexually active and even more so to find out that she's doing it with a girl. But, in my opinion, she's wasn't upset to the point where Velvet should've been worried about going home."

T.J. scowled in confusion. "So what is she doing here then?"

"Well, Mrs. Fuller does not want to go away and leave Velvet without a chaperone again," Sheila told him. "She was definitely not letting Kim stay with her this time, and it was too late to make arrangements to take her. That made her even more upset, so I suggested she let Velvet stay with us so that we can watch her."

"What?!" T.J. exclaimed.

Sheila rested her hand on top of his. "Mrs. Fuller was ready to skip the tour," she said compassionately. "I didn't think she should have to do that, so I told her to go on her trip and assured her that you and I would take good care of Velvet while she's away. She agreed under the condition that Velvet studies her Bible scriptures and attends the youth counseling group at her church on Wednesday nights. I gave my word that she would."

T.J. slouched back on the couch and shook his head. "I can't believe this."

"Anyway," Sheila continued, "while I was convincing Mrs. Fuller to let Velvet stay here, she was able to go in and grab some clothes *and* the video tape."

"Yeah, luckily," Velvet said.

T.J. grinned and shook his head in disbelief. "So, how long will your mother be away, Velvet?"

"Nine weeks. Her plane leaves at six o'clock in the morning. She'll be back in New York on August 5th for four days when they play Madison Square Garden,and then for good on August 23rd."

T.J. looked over at Sheila sitting next to him. She stared back at him with pleading eyes, and he knew he couldn't say no to her. "Well, Velvet, it seems like you're stuck with us for the whole summer. I've always thought you were a responsible girl, so I'm going to trust you to go and come as you normally would if you were at home, but you're going to have to hold up your end of the deal. Your mother isn't asking very much of you, considering you spent the whole summer having sex in her house last year. I'm telling you right now; that's not going to happen here. I don't know what you and Kim have been doing since being left alone last summer, but whatever it is has got to cease. The two of you are not to be alone in *anyone's* home for any reason. Is that understood?"

Velvet lowered her eyes and softly said, "Yes, Coach."

"Good. Well, get some sleep."

Velvet got up and helped Sheila straighten up the living room while T.J. went back into the bedroom to prepare for bed. Sheila then helped Velvet get settled into the guestroom.

"Sheila, I just want to say thanks again for looking out for me," Velvet said. "I knew that you and Coach Stone would find a way to help."

"You're welcome, Velvet. Don't worry. Things will be okay. You get some rest now, and I'll see you in the morning."

"Okay, goodnight."

"Goodnight."

RISE OF THE PHOENIX

Sheila closed the guestroom door and returned to the master bedroom. T.J. had just finished taking some aspirin and was crawling into bed. Sheila looked over at the chair and saw his clothes thrown across the back of it. Without saying a word, she hung his suit up and put the rest of his clothing into the bathroom hamper. She then disrobed and climbed into bed beside him.

"Hey, y'all sounded good together in there." T.J. snuggled close behind her. "I always knew that Velvet's siblings could sing, but I'd never heard her before. She's really, really good."

"Yes, she is," Sheila concurred. "I'm going to church with her in the morning to hear her sing. She asked me to sing with her. I'm thinking about it, but I don't know if I will. Do you want to come with us?"

"No, I have to stay home to get some work done. I'll go next time, okay?"

"Yeah, okay, I'm going to hold you to that."

"You know I'm a man of my word, Sheila."

Sheila rolled her eyes up and twisted her lip. "Anyway...I never knew that Baritone and Melody Scott were Velvet's siblings. We've got all their CDs, and you've never said a word about it to me."

"I'm sorry. I assumed that everybody knew."

"How could I have known the biggest gospel artists, whose last name is Scott, is Velvet's sister and brother?"

"I don't know, Sheila. I just figured you might've heard it somewhere. Her other sister has the same last name. You did know that Harmony Fuller is her sister too, right?"

"No, I didn't know that either."

"Aw, c'mon Sheila. Not only do Harmony and Velvet have the same last name, but they look so much alike. Didn't you notice the resemblance?"

"I've heard of Harmony Fuller, but I don't remember what she looks like. You know I don't listen to hip-hop music."

"Yeah, that's true."

"So, why don't Melody and Baritone have the same last name as Harmony and Velvet? They have different fathers or something?"

"No. Actually, they have different mothers. Melody and Baritone aren't Mrs. Fuller's children, but she manages and tours with them because they sing gospel. But Harmony, who is her biological daughter, chose to sing R&B and hip-hop, so Mrs. Fuller won't have anything to do with her."

Sheila shook her head a little. "Oh, so I can understand a little more now why Velvet was afraid to go home."

"Precisely. That's another reason why I was so tentative about her staying here."

Sheila shrugged. "Well, I don't see the big deal with that. Velvet is a good girl. She just got into some freaky stuff, and her wild side got loose."

"Yeah, ain't that the truth? We're definitely going to have to keep an eye on her and Kim."

"Keep an eye on them?" Sheila echoed as she turned over to face her husband. "You know, you are something else. You allow your players to bring their boyfriends around, holding hands, hugging, sitting on each other's laps, and you don't say a word. And you have to believe that a few of them are probably sexually active with the way they carry on. But you should've heard yourself in there a little while ago." Sheila deepened her voice to mock T.J. as she quoted him. "*I don't know what you and Kim have been doing…but it has got to cease. The two of you are not to be alone in anyone's home for any reason.*' What kind of crap was that?"

"Wait a minute," T.J. said defensively. "I was just trying to help the kid comply with her mother's wishes."

"Her mother didn't say those things to her, or to me. All she said was make sure Velvet goes to youth counseling and studies specific scriptures. The way I understood it, those were the same rules she left for her last summer."

"Well, if I keep her and Kim apart, they can't get into the same kind of trouble."

"If you tell them they have to stay away from each other, it's just going to make them want to be together more. Do you want them to start sneaking around behind your back? Besides, how do you expect to keep them apart when they're both on your team?"

RISE OF THE PHOENIX

"When they're playing basketball, I can monitor their activities and bring Velvet straight home with me."

"Didn't you tell that girl she could go and come as she normally would? You have to make up your mind, T.J. Can she or can't she?"

T.J. stared into space with a confused expression. Sheila shook her head and started to turn away from him.

"Shoot, if I would've known you were going to act like this—" she started.

"Act like what?" T.J. interrupted. "I just don't want her to get into anymore trouble than she's already in. I want Mrs. Fuller to be satisfied with the way we look after her daughter."

Sheila sat up in the bed and looked into T.J.'s eyes. "I know you do. And I do, too, especially since this is all my idea. But it doesn't seem like you're looking out for her. It seems more like you're punishing her the same way she was afraid her mother would, for being who she is."

"That's ridiculous, Sheila."

"Is it?"

T.J. thought for a few moments. "Yes, of course it is. Her being a lesbian has nothing to do with anything. You know that's not how I am. I'm a very open-minded person."

"I hope so, because one day your child may decide he or she prefers same-gender involvement."

"No, not *my* child," T.J. blurted out.

Sheila shook her head. "You see, look how your attitude has changed. When you have a child, you have to be prepared for any and every thing, and you have to love that child unconditionally."

"Of course I will, Mama. Undoubtedly. When we start having children, you'll see. I'm going to be the best father ever."

"Well, we're glad to hear that," Sheila muttered.

T.J. continued to ramble. "Yeah, you'll see. Our children will have it all."

"You talk the talk, T.J. I just hope you're ready to walk the walk."

"I'll be ready. Make no mistake about that. When we start having…" T.J. paused and thought about what Sheila was saying. "Sweetheart, are you trying to tell me something?"

Sheila smiled slightly as her eyes filled with water. Her bottom lip trembled. "I wanted everything to go right tonight because I wanted to surprise you. It was going to be your birthday gift."

T.J. started to get excited. "What are you saying, sweetheart?"

"I know you had plans and wanted to wait awhile, but…"

"No, no, no, Mama." T.J. put his arm around his sobbing wife and pulled her close to him. "It's perfect. *You're* perfect. There is never a wrong time for this. Oh, Mama, this is great news. How far along are you?"

"Five weeks," Sheila whimpered.

"That's great, baby. We have so much to do. As soon as Velvet goes back home, we can turn the guestroom into a nursery. I can't wait to get started."

Sheila smiled and wiped her tears with her hand. "I know you're going to be a good father, T.J. You have a way with kids. Just to think that Velvet called you instead of any family or friends says a lot. She obviously sees you as more than a coach and mentor. She looks up to you as a father figure. I don't think that her mother would've turned her over like she did to anyone else, either. I was only able to talk her into letting Velvet stay because of you. Every third word that came out of that woman's mouth was your name. That's because of the kind of man you are. Your heart is in the right place even if your priorities aren't always."

"You're right, Mama. I haven't devoted the time to you that I should, but that's going to change, starting right now. We're having a baby. God, we are so blessed."

Sheila kissed her husband deep. T.J.'s body responded to the touch of her soft, tender lips, and then he embraced his wife, and their bodies entwined as they indulged in marital bliss.

1:10 A.M.

Velvet was still awake, thinking about all that happened and wondering what was going to happen when her mother came back home. She was scared, worried that her mother would disown her the way she had her older sister Harmony—right after she beat her half to death. Death would be better than having her family more torn apart than it already was.

Velvet sat up on the twin-sized bed in the Stonewall's guestroom, took her cell phone from her purse and called Kimberly.

"Hello?" Kimberly answered in a groggy voice.

"It's me, baby," Velvet whispered.

The sound of Velvet's voice brought a broad smile to Kimberly's face. "Hey, sweetie, what's going on?"

"I just talked to Coach Stone a little while ago. I'm definitely gonna be staying here for the summer. He was buggin' and whatnot, saying something about you and I can't ever be alone or something crazy like that. Don't worry, though, his wife promised to handle him if he tripped. She's got my back fo' sho'. She came through big time with my mom and everything."

"That's what's up," Kimberly said.

"Sheila saw the tape," Velvet confessed.

"Stop playin'," Kimberly quietly exclaimed.

"Coach Stone was still asleep when we got back here, so I let her see about three or four minutes of it. She wouldn't watch anymore after that."

"I can't believe you showed it to her."

"She was curious to see what we did. She was cool about it."

"What did she say?"

"She didn't say anything. She turned it off, took it out and told me to hide it where Coach Stone wouldn't be able to find it."

"Dayum!" Kimberly softly shrieked. "You'd better let me hold it because I don't think that it's safe anywhere close to Coach Stone."

"Yeah, you're right about that."

"So, where are the pictures?"

Velvet sucked her teeth and sighed hard. "My mother still has them. I was trying to figure out a way to get them without getting a beat down, but I came up with nothing. I think she's going to show them to my father."

"Damn! I know she's gonna wanna show my mother when she gets back. I already told my mom the whole deal, though."

"Word? What did she say?"

"She went off, of course. She was mostly upset because I told her that we never had sex—that we were just trying our relationship out to see where it goes. Needless to say, you and I will not be spending the weekend at my uncle's house in the Poconos for my birthday."

"I know," Velvet said with disappointment. "That was going to be hot, too. Anyway, I just wanted to hear your voice before I went to sleep. Are you coming to church tomorrow?"

"Of course," Kimberly said. "I wouldn't miss your solo, girl."

Velvet smiled. "Cool. Sheila is coming, too, so we might not be able to hang afterwards."

"Aw, Velvet, we were supposed to go to the parade in The Village tomorrow. You're not going?"

"Oh, I forgot about that," Velvet said, slapping her forehead. She thought for a second before making a decision. "Nah, I better just chill."

"I hear ya. I'll see you at practice tomorrow night, though."

"Yeah, that's right. I'll give you the tape then."

"Okay."

"Well, goodnight. I love you, Kim."

"I love you too, Velvet."

WHO HE IS

Sunday, June 26, 2005 – 8:42 A.M.

T.J. awakened to the telephone ringing. He turned over to tell Sheila to answer it but found that he was alone. He then remembered that she went to church with Velvet, so he reached across the bed and picked up the receiver.

"Yes?" he answered with a morning time bass.

"Eh, hiya doin'? This is Burton Smalls calling for Coach Stonewall, please?"

T.J. immediately became fully awake and sat up and cleared his voice. "Yes, this is T.J. Stonewall. Good morning, Mr. Smalls. How are you?"

"I'm okay. Look here, I was reading this pamphlet you gave me, and I talked it over with my daughter. It looks like somethin' we might wanna try, but I just a have a few questions. A coupla personal ones if you don't mind."

"Sure, no problem. What is it?"

"Well, first off, when and where y'all practice? I know a lot of these teams just run around playin' in tournaments, and the kids don't put in quality time learnin' the game."

"Oh no, the Lady Phoenix doesn't operate that way, Mr. Smalls. We practice at the Parks and Recreation center on Linden Boulevard every Saturday morning from ten o'clock until two-thirty, and Sunday evenings from five to eight. We'll be there tonight if you want to come and check things out."

"Tonight? I don't know, we'll see. Is coachin' these gals your full-time job?"

"No, I don't get paid for this," T.J. said. "I actually have to come out of my pocket a lot of times. I work for the Department of Parks and Recreation. I'm the sports and activities director."

"Oh, really? I worked for the parks department part-time back in Mississippi," Burton mentioned. "I coached in the little rec league we had there. That's when Bev first got serious 'bout playin' ball. That was five years ago."

"Five years? She got real good real fast."

"It's in the blood," Burton bragged. "Bev's momma played in Italy and for the ABL. I played overseas a little bit, too, and in the CBA, but I had to stop 'causa my heart."

"Oh, that's too bad. I'm sorry to hear that."

"Yeah, thank you. What can you do, right? Anyway, I see here you got an assistant coach. Eh, Juanita Moore?"

"Juanita was one of my first players when I started this program six years ago," T.J. said, proudly. "She graduated college two years ago, and she's working as a substitute teacher. She's coaching and tutoring our members to give back to the program. She assists me and coaches our junior team."

"Oh, that's real good," Burton commended. "Just one more question if you don't mind."

"Sure, go right ahead."

"Are you married, Mr. Stonewall?"

T.J. was happy to say, "Yes, I got married nine months ago. My wife Sheila is a college official."

"Is that her full-time job?" Burton asked.

"No, sir. She's an agent for the IRS. She does tax audits."

"Well, the reason I asked you these questions is because if I decide to let Bev participate in your program, I wanna know what type of people I'm leavin' her in the hands of."

"Oh, I know, Mr. Smalls. I totally understand."

"Good. Well, I'm gonna think about this a little more, and I'll get back to you. I gotta go. You take care."

"Okay, Mr. Smalls, you too."

T.J. hung up the telephone, sat up on the side of the bed and stretched. His locks slid away from his face when he threw his head back and he moaned aloud as he loosened his muscles. He twisted his body left then right to stretch his lower back and was about to kneel to say his prayers when the telephone rang again.

RISE OF THE PHOENIX

"Yes?"

"Good morning, T.J.," a hesitating voice replied. "This is Frances Fuller."

"Ms. Fuller? Good morning."

"Please, T.J., just call me Frances."

"Okay, Frances," T.J. complied. "How are you? How was your flight?"

"My flight was good, thanks." Her voice steadied a bit. "I'm calling to thank you for looking after Velvet for me. This is an unfortunate situation, which I'd rather be home to deal with, but it came at a compromising time. I'm thinking, now, that I shouldn't have left and perhaps should just come home."

"Well, that's up to you, but you don't have to," T.J. said, comfortingly. "I believe everything happens for a reason. I know there is a lot that you and Velvet have to talk about, but perhaps this time apart will allow you both to think some things over. Go ahead on the tour and do your job there. Velvet will be fine. Sheila and I will look after her like she's our own."

"I appreciate that." She paused. "This whole thing is weighing down on me. Velvet has always been the model child. I never expected anything like this from her."

"I can only imagine what you're feeling, but she's a teenager, and kids her age do all kinds of things that are unexpected. Most of them are easily influenced, too. It might just be an experimental phase she's going through."

"That's some kind of experiment. First, my eldest daughter with her nonsense, and now Velvet with this. God, why me?"

"Try not to let it get to you too much, Frances. I know that's asking a lot, but if you can, you'll be able to focus on the tour, and then come back and deal with this."

"Yeah, maybe you're right," she said with a sigh of relief. "Well, if you need anything, anything at all, just call me, okay?"

T.J. smiled, hearing the ease in her voice. "Don't worry, everything will be fine, but I will if I need to."

Again she paused. "Uh, what is Velvet doing now? Is she okay?"

"She's not here," T.J. told her. "She and Sheila went to church."

"Oh, okay," Frances remembered. "She's supposed to sing a solo today. She wrote the song herself."

"I know," T.J. said. "Sheila was up practicing with her last night."

"Well, I'll call back later to check on her. Thanks again, T.J. I'm praying for you all."

"You're very welcome, Frances. I appreciate that."

T.J. hung up with Frances Fuller and dialed Sam Pernell's number. After three rings, Sam answered.

"Hello."

"Hey, you runt-fink."

Sam laughed. "Stop calling me that. I'm not short, I'm just vertically underprivileged."

"Vert-? What? You ain't nothing but a tall midget."

"You know, I would tell you something, but I'm on my way out to church, and I don't want to get struck down. I'm gonna have a few select words for you tomorrow, though."

T.J. laughed. "Yo, no one from the Housing League ever called last night."

"Oh, no? Well, I'm sure it's because it's the weekend," Sam concluded. "We talked to them yesterday, so I assumed someone would call you right away. They're probably going to wait until tomorrow and call you at work."

"Yeah, whatever," T.J. said, annoyed. "Give me a call later when you get home from church."

"What's up, you're not coming to church today?" Sam asked.

"Nah, I'm staying home to do some paperwork I neglected that's due tomorrow morning. I'll be there next week for sure."

"Is Sheila still coming?"

"No, she went to church with Velvet," T.J. said. "I gotta tell you what's happening later, and I have some big news for you, too. Can you meet me tonight at Caliente's around nine? I'm meeting Glen there."

Sam thought for a moment. "Yeah, I can do that."

"Okay. I'll talk to you later."

"Later."

RISE OF THE PHOENIX

1:39 P.M.

T.J. had put on one of his many Lady Phoenix T-shirts—this one white—with a pair of royal blue basketball shorts and the same sneakers he wore the day before. He was sitting at the dining room table just finishing up his paperwork when Sheila and Velvet came home from church.

"Hey, ladies, how was service?"

"You should've been there, Coach Stone," Velvet said, excitedly. "Sheila helped me sing my song. It was great. They want us to sing again next week for the Fourth of July service, and Sheila was asked to join our church and sing in the choir."

"Wow, that's something else," T.J. said. And then he said to Sheila, "But, baby, I thought we decided to join the church where Sam goes."

"Well, I didn't give them an answer yet," Sheila said. She placed her handbag down and strolled over to where T.J. was sitting and stood behind him. She rubbed his shoulders. "I wanted to talk to you about it first. I really do like Velvet's church, though. I think we should talk about it after you come with us next Sunday."

"Yes," T.J. agreed, basking in the delight of his wife's gentle massage. "That sounds like a good idea."

After giving T.J. a gentle peck on his right cheek, Sheila said, "Well, I'm going to fix a quick lunch before the two of you leave for practice, and then I'll make dinner."

"Oh, baby, I'm going out to dinner with Sam and Glen after practice," T.J. said. He looked over at the custom-designed grandfather clock against the wall and got up from the table. "I wanted to ask you if you could come by and pick Velvet up from practice, if you don't mind."

Sheila stopped in mid-stride as she was about to pass Velvet, who was sitting on a chair in the living room, and shot T.J. a look. "You're going out to dinner with Sam and Glen, huh?" She glanced at Velvet and relaxed her tone. "Well, in that case, I guess I can pick Velvet up and we'll just go out to dinner, too."

Sheila flashed Velvet a *we got our own thang* smile, which Velvet returned.

"Sounds like a plan," T.J. quickly agreed as he stacked his papers and left them on the table. "I'll see you both later."

"Where are you going?" Sheila asked. "What about lunch?"

"I'm going to check out the games at the Dean Street Park tournament. I already ate last night's dinner for lunch." He kissed Sheila and Velvet both on the cheek and headed out the door, but then remembered something and turned around. "Oh, Velvet, your mother called this morning. She said she'd call back."

Before Velvet could respond, T.J. had pulled the door shut and was gone.

NEEDING SOMEONE ELSE

Sunday, June 26, 2005 – 3:03 P.M.

It took Mildred Negron longer than she thought to finish packing, and although she didn't have a whole lot to take, she was finally done. She'd put most of her belongings in Charles Greene's car already and came back upstairs for the rest. She grabbed her last two suitcases and was heading for the door when Terry, her companion of four years, walked in. Mildred stopped and stared at the sight of Terry standing there, still holding the front door to their luxury Upper West Side condominium open, and wearing a bewildered expression.

A quick sigh to gather herself and Mildred proceeded forward. "Please, Terry, just step aside and let me leave," she dryly requested, praying it would be that easy.

"Where are you going?" Terry asked in a trembling voice. "W-Why are you going?"

Mildred stopped, closed her eyes and took a deeper breath than before. She became angry with herself for not moving faster and getting out sooner. "Don't make things any more difficult than they already are, Terry. Just step aside and let me go so we can be out of each other's hair for good."

"I don't want you out of my hair," Terry said. "I don't want to be out of your hair. I love your hair. I love you. Why are you doing this? I mean…what's the reason? What brought this on?"

"C'mon, Terry, you knew this was coming. We're wasting our time staying together. You and I are too different. We don't share the same ideals. I can't be with someone who doesn't support what I do. I need to be with someone who's always going to be in my corner. You are not my support system, Terry. You don't believe in me."

"Not…" Terry's eyes flashed back and forth, astounded by Mildred's comments. "Not in your corner, Millie? Not your support system? I can't believe you. You know I've always been there for you through thick and thin for the last four years. Who else was there for you when you were starting your team? Who wrote your proposals? Who found you your first sponsor? Me, that's who."

"Yeah, yeah, right. Blah, blah, blah," Mildred mocked. "Whatever, Terry. What about now? Now is when I need you, and you refuse to be there for me."

"So, that's it? I tell you no about something and you walk out on me? You're choosing to throw away all we've been through because I don't do everything you ask of me? All I've done to help you means nothing now because I won't compromise my integrity and risk my career for you, is that it?"

Mildred nodded and smiled sarcastically. "That's right. Now, please step aside."

Terry looked at the cold and uncaring expression on Mildred's face, and then sidestepped so she could pass. Mildred quickstepped out of the apartment and headed down the hallway toward the elevator. Terry stepped out and watched her walk away, resisting the urge to submit to her wishes in order to keep her there.

Mildred looked up at the floor counter to see what floor the elevator was on, and then looked down the hall at her five-foot-ten lover with shoulder-length, wavy hair and a golden-brown, tanned complexion and shook her head. When the elevator finally arrived, Mildred held the door open and looked back again. Terry was still standing in the doorway staring back at her.

"You're going to miss me in the morning, Terry, when you wake up and I'm not laying next to you!" she shouted. "*¡Nunca vas a probrar más este dulce culo!*"

"*Me hace falta ahora, Millie,*" Terry responded. "Tomorrow I'll miss you more."

When Mildred came out of the building, Charles Greene got out of his white Lexus GX470 and rushed over to her to help with her bags.

"Did Terry see you?" Mildred asked.

"I don't think so," Charles answered with a shrug.

Fifty-five year old Charles Greene was a five-foot-eight, rail thin man with bushy, sandy-colored hair and light skin with brown freckles.

RISE OF THE PHOENIX

He was wearing tight blue jeans, a white dress shirt with blue pinstripes and a pair of white New Balance sneakers.

After putting the suitcases in the backseat, they headed uptown to Mildred's new apartment. When they stopped at a light, Charles gave Mildred a prurient stare as she sat quietly staring straight ahead. His tongue slithered across his bottom lip as he admired the exotic looking forty-one year old, who could easily pass for a woman in her late twenties, with her copper-toned skin and long, straight, jet-black hair. He followed her long, slender neck—decorated by a Tiffany's Heart Tag Toggle necklace—down to her muscular shoulders and arms. His eyes danced down the line of separation of her ample bosom to the imprints of her nipples fighting to push through the material of her white halter-top.

"You know, you could've stayed with me," Charles managed to say after swallowing hard to keep saliva from escaping.

Mildred rolled her eyes and shook her head. "I'll be fine, Charles, thanks."

"It'll give us a chance to get more things done," Charles said as his eyes followed her features from the long lashes of her almond-shaped, brown eyes to her straight nose and blood-filled red lips.

Mildred ignored the double entendre. "I'll get plenty done when I get a computer."

"You don't have a computer?"

"No, I was using Terry's. That's what took me so long. I was copying all of my files."

Charles smiled impishly, and then looked down at her chiseled abdomen and on past her pink miniskirt that had risen to reveal the tattoo of paw prints on her silky soft, muscular left thigh crossing over the right one. "I have two computers, one in my basement and one in the *bedroom*. If you stay with me, you could use it whenever you liked."

"Charles, please, stop the charade." Mildred huffed and looked away. "I know why you really want me to come and stay with you, but you're not my type."

"Why is that, Millie, because I'm white or because I'm fourteen years older than you?"

"Why would you think it was something like that?"

"Because Terry is four years younger than you and you once told me that you've only ever dated Blacks and Latinos."

Mildred cut her eyes at him, and then looked away out of the passenger side window at the red hand flashing on the traffic light. "No, Charles, it's neither of those things."

"Look, Millie, regardless of what you think, I'm a good man. I know how to treat a woman. With me, you would want for nothing."

"Charles, just go please?" Mildred agitatedly requested. "The light's changed."

"Fine," Charles surrendered. "Well, I'm leaving to go to Hawaii tomorrow. What are you going to do about Stacey Conyers now that you can't get Terry to help?"

"I'm going to have to find another way, that's all." Mildred was still looking away. "I'll figure it out."

"Well, do whatever it takes," Charles ordered with more authority in his voice. "We can't let her stay where she is, and not coming to Jefferson is not an option."

"I should be able to come up with something soon," Mildred promised. "Don't worry."

"And what about Jennifer?"

"Hofstra wants her, and she likes the school. The problem is that she needs Kaplan and Sylvan to get hooked on phonics. Otherwise, it's juco or Division III."

Charles nodded. "If Hofstra really wants her, and she really wants to go, I'll get her there."

THE LADY PHOENIX

Sunday, June 26, 2005 – 4:54 P.M.

Practice was about to start and T.J. was standing on the sideline reviewing some new plays he wanted to implement when Kimberly led Beverly and Burton into the gymnasium.

"There he is," Kimberly said, pointing at T.J. "Coach, somebody's here to see you!"

Kimberly went over to shoot around with some teammates. T.J. walked over to Burton and Beverly. "Mr. Smalls, Beverly, I'm glad you made it."

Burton extended his hand with a broad smile on his face. "Yeah, we decided to give this a shot and see how it works out. I figga we got nothin' to lose."

"Good," T.J. said, shaking his hand. "We're about to start, so Beverly can go change."

Once again, Burton shook T.J.'s hand with a firm grip, and it seemed as though he didn't want to let go. T.J. excused himself and freed his hand. "Trina, come here, please," he called out.

Trina Smith's face lit up when she heard her coach call her name. The mature-looking, six-foot-four center with a dusty gold complexion and medium-length, combed back hair tied back with a scrunchi trotted over to the man she most admired, wearing an ear to ear smile. "What's up, Coach?"

"Trina, this is Beverly."

"Hey, Beverly," Trina pleasantly greeted.

"Hi." Beverly gleefully smiled back.

"And this is her father, Mr. Smalls."

"Hiya doin' there, gal," Burton said, immediately taking Trina's hand and shaking it as aggressively as he did T.J.'s.

"Trina is our team captain," T.J. informed, and then turned his attention to her. "Will you show Beverly to the locker room, please?"

Trina freed herself from Burton's handshake. "Excuse me, sir," she said, politely. "Come on, Beverly."

Beverly followed Trina into an open door on the other side of the gymnasium. At that moment, assistant coach Juanita Moore came in from her game at the New Attitude League with the fourteen-and-under team and headed for the locker room.

T.J. called out, "Hey, Juanita, come here for a minute, please? I want you to meet someone."

Juanita walked over to them, unconscious of her tantalizing sashay. She wore a wide smile, showing off deep dimples, a smooth mahogany complexion, gleaming white teeth and big, round, sparkling eyes. Burton couldn't see her short, platinum-dyed, curly hair under her backward Yankees baseball cap, but he marveled to himself at her voluptuous physique in her Apple Bottoms jeans and blue Yankees T-shirt. She always wore Yankees apparel.

Burton glanced at T.J., raised his brow and gave a quick nod of approval. T.J. grinned slightly, mostly because he was used to Juanita having that affect on men.

As she approached and put her gym bag down, T.J. said, "Juanita, this is Mr. Smalls. Mr. Smalls, this is my assistant coach, Juanita Moore."

Burton took Juanita's hand and gently kissed the back of it. "Miss Moore, it's a pleasure to meet you."

"Thank you, Mr. Smalls." Juanita's voice was deep and sultry.

"Oh, call me Burt, Suga'."

"Okay, Burt, and you can call me Nita."

"Mr. Smalls brought his daughter, Beverly, to join our program," T.J. told Juanita. "She's loaded with potential."

"Really? Where is she?"

"Trina took her to the locker room to get changed."

"Oh, okay. Well, that's what I'd better do, too. I'll introduce myself to her." Juanita picked up her bag and headed across the gym. She looked back at T.J. "Hey, we won by the way."

"You're the girl." T.J. raised his thumb high in the air.

"Thanks." Juanita blushed. "Take care, Burt. Again, it's nice meeting you."

RISE OF THE PHOENIX

Burton wiggled his fingers at her. "Likewise, Nita. I'll seeya soon."

Juanita went into the locker room. Burton looked at T.J. with a grin and shook his head. "Wow, man, you got yourself one fine lookin' assistant."

"You're right about that, Mr. Smalls. But Juanita's interior is far more attractive than her exterior."

"I'm sure it is. She'd probably make a fine wife."

"Her fiancé thinks so, too. They're getting married in a few months. You're a little too late."

"Oh, I wasn't implyin' that I was interested in that way. No, my heart belongs to Bev's best friend Melinda's momma."

"Oh yes, Melinda. I was hoping that she would be here, too, or I'd hear from her mother by now."

Burton let out a hearty laugh. "Oh, no, man. Hold your breath for that and you'll suffocate yourself. That woman's tighter than spandex on a fat lady. She don't let that child go no place or do nothin'. The kid just come down the street to my house and go right on back home."

"Well, Melinda told me that she would've played for her junior high school if they had a girls' team. And you said that you were helping her to prepare for her high school team."

Burton waved it off. "Oh, man, that there's just a dream we got. Carlene Thompson don't let that gal spin around in a circle without permission. Then, she never give it, so the chile don't even know what it feels like to get dizzy."

"Well, maybe if I just had the chance to talk to her…"

"You can try, but it's gonna be like tryin' to sell fleas at a dog show. I gotta be gettin' on. I'm sorry I can't stay, but I got somethin' important I gotta take care of. Bev was beggin' to come, so I brought her, but I'm go'n sit in on the next practice."

"That'll be good," T.J. said.

"What time y'all go'n be finished so I can come back for her?"

"We'll be finished about eight o'clock."

"Okay. Well, I'll be back around seven-thirty. Take care of my baby, now, you hear?"

"She'll be fine. See you soon."

When Burton left, T.J. turned around and saw Trina return with Melva and Velvet walking behind her. Tabitha had just arrived and walked in slowly, wearing flip-flops and holding her sneakers in her hand. T.J.'s patience with Tabitha's tardiness was steadily growing thin, but still he didn't say anything to her. Instead, he ignored her and addressed the team.

"Good, everybody's here. We can start the warm-ups as soon as Beverly comes out."

"Who's Beverly?" Melva asked.

"A new girl," Trina told her. "I just took her downstairs to get dressed. You didn't see her because you were in the bathroom."

As the team formed a circle at mid-court, Tabitha slowly dragged her feet over to the bleachers and sat down to put her sneakers on. Again, T.J. ignored her because Beverly still hadn't come upstairs yet. He prayed that Tabitha would be done before Beverly came up so he wouldn't be forced into an inevitable confrontation with her.

"Today, we're putting in a new defensive zone and a few options to our man-to-man offense," he told the team. "I want this to be fluid before we play the Roadrunners next weekend."

"Next weekend?!" several players asked at the same time.

"Coach, weren't we supposed to play them on July 10th?" Trina asked.

"They changed the date," T.J. said. "It's tentative, though. I'm trying to get it changed back, but just in case I can't, I want us to be ready."

"But weren't we supposed to play the Housing League championship next weekend?" Trina asked.

"That's supposed to change, too."

"It doesn't matter, the Roadrunners are garbage," Velvet said. "We can beat them anytime."

"We should," T.J. agreed. "But we haven't been playing like we could beat anyone, and we haven't been practicing like we want to win at all."

"We'll win if I get the ball," Melva jumped in. "Nobody on that team can stop me, but I don't get the ball."

RISE OF THE PHOENIX

"How can you say that?" Trina asked her. "You're the point guard, you always have the ball."

"Yeah, but I pass the ball one time, and I never see it again. Even when I cut I don't get it back, and you know none of those bitches can hold me."

"Hey, hey, hey!" T.J. shouted. "You know that I don't go for that kind of language! Show some respect in here, you're not in the streets! I don't want to hear that anymore!" Beverly came into the gym and stood off to the side. "Melva does have a point, though," he continued. "The reason we're not playing well is because we're not playing together. All of you have to realize that you have a job to do, and each one of you must do your own. You're all trying to do everything yourselves like you have no confidence in each other. That's why, as I said before, this practice is so important. So, let's get started. Beverly, come join us over here."

Beverly joined the team at mid-court. T.J. looked over to see Tabitha still taking her time. "Get up, Tabitha," he shouted at her. "Why aren't you dressed yet?!"

"I am dressed," Tabitha shouted back.

"No, you're not. Your sneakers are still untied, so you're unprepared."

Tabitha quickly tied her sneakers with an attitude. "So, you weren't ready," she shouted again. "You said we were waiting on the new girl!"

"Girl, you know when you come into this gym you have to be fully dressed and ready to practice. We don't have time to wait for people who just feel like being lazy. Now, hurry up!"

When T.J. heard Tabitha mumble, *Don't rush me*, he became irate. "What?! What did you say?!" She just ignored him, which made him angrier. "I asked you a question!"

Tabitha gave him more attitude. "I wasn't talking to you."

"That's it! Everybody line up for suicides! Three sets!"

Juanita had just come out of the locker room dressed in her Lady Phoenix T-shirt, long, black shorts and white Adidas with blue stripes and stood next to T.J. "What happened now?" she asked him.

"That damn Tabitha is working my nerves again," he grunted in a whisper.

The team all walked angrily to the end line. Beverly joined them with a bewildered look on her face, and Tabitha slowly followed.

"I'd like to thank you for giving Beverly such a good first impression and showing her how disciplined and respectful we all are," T.J. shouted out. "I'm sure she is overjoyed about being punished for something she had no part of on her first day."

"We had no part of it, either," Melva said. "Tabitha should be running by her stupid self."

"Who're you calling stupid?!" Tabitha shouted at her.

"Both of you just be quiet!" T.J. yelled. "Now let's go!"

T.J. blew his whistle, and he and Juanita watched the team sprint the suicide drills. They all finished and waited for Tabitha, who was trotting and finished twenty seconds behind the last person. T.J. was livid. He wanted to run over to her and drag her out of the gymnasium. Instead, he took his anger out on the whole team again, hoping that by punishing everyone, Tabitha might be inclined to get her act together in fear of getting heat from her teammates.

"Now, you can all thank Tabitha for another set," T.J. announced. "Let's go!"

Trina was upset with Tabitha, but she didn't yell at her or give her any attitude. She spoke like a team captain assuming authority. "Come on, Tabitha! Hustle!"

The rest of the team, however, was not as diplomatic.

"Yeah, I don't wanna be doing this all day!" Velvet shouted.

"So, don't!" Tabitha retorted.

"We won't if you stop acting stupid," Melva said.

"Please, Melva. I'll stop acting up when you stop chuckin'."

"Chuckin? I can't believe you said that. You're the one who shoots every time you touch the ball."

"Enough down there!" T.J. shouted. "Let's go!"

Juanita walked over and whispered in Tabitha's ear as the team lined up again. T.J. blew his whistle, and they ran the drill a second time. Tabitha picked up her pace considerably, but she still finished last.

"What am I going to do with this girl?" T.J. whispered to Juanita.

RISE OF THE PHOENIX

"Just talk to her, T.J.," Juanita whispered back. "Calm down, take a deep breath, and try to find out what's up with her."

Taking Juanita's advice, T.J. huffed and said, "You're right. You go start the warm-ups."

Juanita gathered the team and led them in the stretching exercises. T.J. paused for a moment and watched Tabitha lazily go through the motions. When Juanita glared back at him, he called Tabitha over.

"Tabitha, come over here."

Tabitha exhaled hard and rolled her eyes up before walking over to him while the rest of the team continued stretching. She walked on her toes with grace and poise like a dancer. She had taken ballet from the time she was five-years-old until she was thirteen, which showed in her smooth style of play.

Tabitha Gleavy was the Lady Phoenix' starting shooting guard. She stood five-feet-nine-inches tall and weighed about a hundred and fifty pounds. She had a strong, athletic build with great muscle tone, but a hard face due to excessive frowning from being mad at the world. She had a dry, tan complexion and always wore her hair in thick cornrows.

"What's the matter?" T.J. asked as she stood before him with an agitated expression on her face as if he were disturbing her. "Is something wrong? Is there something I can help you with?"

Tabitha twisted her lips slightly and rolled her eyes up in her head. "Nothing's the matter. I'm just tired. You need to schedule better times to have practice."

"We have practice when time and space permits. I don't think it's the time we have practice that's bothering you. I think it's much deeper than that. Talk to me, Tabitha. Let me help you."

"Nothing's wrong," she insisted. "I'm just tired."

"In that case, I suggest you turn in earlier on Friday nights when you know we have practice Saturday mornings, and take a nap or something Sunday afternoons so you can be refreshed for Sunday evening practices. I can't have you sitting around and dragging behind during the drills. Show some enthusiasm. Put your heart into this. That's the only way you're going to get something out of it. You have a lot of potential. Don't waste away being lazy. You have to try and understand what all of this is about. We're your family here. Believe in us, okay? Trust me. Do you think you can do that?"

Tabitha didn't respond. She just stood there with her arms folded, staring into space.

"How about it, Tabitha?" T.J. pressed.

"Yeah," she finally responded as if she was trying to get him to shut up.

"Yeah?" he persisted, forcing her to be more mannerly.

"Yes," she said in a humbled tone.

T.J. pulled Tabitha close and gave her a comforting hug. "That's good. Now, go back and join your team."

The team finished stretching and ran through their warm-up drills. There wasn't much talking, but Tabitha wasn't lagging as much anymore, either. After they completed the last drill, T.J. walked out onto the court and called them all over.

"Okay, everybody, bring it in. I want to introduce Beverly to everyone. Beverly, you already met Coach Moore and Trina. This is Melva, Kimberly, Velvet, Tabitha, Tracy, Monica, Keisha, Tanya and Danisha. Beverly is going to be a freshman at Stuyvesant in September. Let's all see to it that she gets through this summer comfortably and productively. Agreed?"

"Agreed!" they all responded.

"Okay, let's put our hands in and get busy."

The team all put one hand in on top of Trina's and she shouted, "One! Two! Three!" to which the team yelled out, "Phoenix!"

GIRLFRIENDS

Sunday, June 26, 2005 – 8:42 P.M.

The hostess at the downtown Brooklyn Dallas BBQ raised her hand and beckoned Sheila to follow her. "Miss, table for five? Right this way, please."

Sheila, dressed in a plain white V-neck T-shirt, black jeans and loafers, trailed the line of Kimberly, Velvet, Melva and Trina, following the hostess to a table near the rear of the restaurant.

Patrons stared at the five tall females as they made their way to their table. Kimberly was the shortest of the group at only five-foot-six, but appeared taller because of good posture and her long, slender physique. She had long mirco-braids hanging loose around her face. Her form-fitting Tommy Hilfiger denim capris and red sleeveless top showed off the curves of a magnificent body. Her fair complexion made the array of tattoos on the back of her neck, side of her right shin, above her left ankle, and on her thin, well-toned arms as noticeable as her dazzling hazel eyes.

"Thanks for inviting us, Sheila," Trina said as everyone took their seats. "This is a first for me."

"I can't believe you've never been to BBQ's before, Tree," Melva said. She slouched down in her chair with her legs spread open and threw her left arm across the back. Although she gained ten pounds, Melva, at five-foot-eight, was still only a hundred and twenty pounds fully dressed. She wore her clothes too big, usually oversized T-shirts and baggy jeans or shorts, which made it impossible to see any feminine attributes on her physique. She had shoulder-length locks, which she tied up on both sides of her head. You would think she was a boy if it wasn't for the shape of her eyes and her long slender fingers. She was actually a very pretty girl with nice brown skin, but a tomboy at heart, someone who had to be forced into a dress. She did, unfortunately, have a few faint marks on her face from all the fights she'd been in over the years.

"My family can't afford to go out to restaurants and stuff," Trina shamelessly stated. "Besides, nothing compares to my momma's cooking, anyway."

"Yeah, but this is only BBQ's," Melva said, making gestures with her right hand like a performing rap artist the way she always did when she talked. "It's not expensive at all in here. Don't you just want to get out sometime?"

"Damn, Mel," Kimberly said. "Why're you stressin' it?"

"It's cool, Kim," Trina said. "My mom's doing the best she can to take care of me and my sisters. I'm proud of her and what she's made me."

"I understand that," Melva said. "But you got a man, too. Are you saying that Coach Stone's son don't ever take you out?"

Velvet interjected. "Yo, Mel, why don't you just chill?"

"Coach Stone's son?" Sheila asked, puzzled.

"His name is Daquan," Trina told her. "We just call him Coach's son because they look a lot alike: tall, dark-skinned, locks, everything. Daquan is about three inches taller, though. His real father works in the Pathmark supermarket around the way."

"Oh, I see," Sheila said, relieved.

"I'm just saying, dawg," Melva continued. "Daquan's only with you 'causa all that booty and boobs you got, anyway. I can't believe you're letting him dig your back out, and he doesn't even take you out to eat. I wouldn't be givin' it up if I couldn't be livin' it up."

Velvet's eyes widened as she flashed them toward Sheila, and then gave Melva a hard stare. Kimberly threw her head back and looked up at the ceiling in disbelief.

"I can't believe she just said that," Kimberly said.

Trina grinned and started blinking her eyes the way she always did when she got annoyed. "Okay, that's enough, stupid."

Melva looked over at Sheila and realized what she'd done wrong. "Oh, no disrespect, Sheila. I'm sorry."

Sheila waved it off. "Don't worry about it. You should apologize to Trina, though."

RISE OF THE PHOENIX

"I'm sorry, Tree. I wasn't trying to blow up your spot, but it just doesn't seem right that in 2005 you've never gotten the chance to go out because of your situation, and you got a man and nothing's better."

Blinking her eyes and rolling her neck, Trina said, "You see, that's where you're wrong. I don't have a *man*. I have a *boyfriend*. There's a difference. Daquan is only sixteen, still in school and living off his parents, just like you and me. I don't expect to get from him more than he can give."

"Well, I don't see the point in having a *boyfriend* if that's the case. Shoot, I can do bad by myself."

"Do you have a boyfriend, Melva?" Sheila asked.

"No, I don't," Melva replied matter-of-factly.

"I can see why," Kimberly said.

"What are you talking about?" Melva asked Kimberly. "I've never seen you with a man, either."

Kimberly grinned. "And you never will."

When Kimberly, Velvet and Trina all looked around at each other and broke out into laughter, Sheila couldn't contain herself and laughed aloud as well. Melva couldn't understand what was so funny to everyone, but thought for sure that the joke was on her.

"What's so funny?" Melva demanded to know.

Trina waved it off. "Nothing, Mel."

"Nah, everybody just busted out laughing when Kim said she never will. Somehow, I missed the joke, so I need someone to enlighten me."

Velvet reached over and took Melva's hand in hers. "Well, if you must know, Kimberly is my inamorata."

Melva looked at Velvet with a dumbfounded expression and said, "Your what?"

"Let's just say that we prefer each other's company over that of any man."

Melva's eyes widened. She looked over at Kimberly, who gave her a confirming nod. She then looked at Trina and Sheila and got the same responses.

"Get the fuck outta here!" Melva snatched her hand away. "You, Velvet, the prissy, high-heels wearing gospel diva? When did this happen?"

"Last summer," Velvet admitted.

"Last summer? And everybody knew about it except me?"

"Hey, I just found out yesterday," Sheila said.

"You always knew about this, Tree?"

"Yes, Mel," Trina replied. "Almost everybody on the team knows except you and Coach Stone."

"Coach Stone I can understand, but me?"

"C'mon, Mel, you know you blab everything," Kimberly said.

"No, I don't!"

"Yes, you do. You let anything come out of your mouth without thinking about it first. Velvet wasn't ready to let her mom know about her lifestyle, and if you would've known about us, it would've gotten back to her somehow in no time."

"That's not true. I don't blab."

"Mel, look at how you just blabbed all of Trina's business out in front of Sheila just now. You just let anything come out of your mouth without thinking about what you're saying, who you're saying it to, or what affect it may have on other people."

Melva lowered her eyes and spoke in a modest tone. "Yo, Tree, I wasn't tryin' to blow up your spot or nothin' like that. I was just trying to get some understanding on why you ain't never been out, even to a spot like this, when you got a man. Now that you've told me, though, I can relate somewhat. My bad. It ain't nothin' but love."

Melva held out her fist across the table, and Trina tapped her own against it.

"Yeah, I know," Trina said. "It's cool."

The waitress came over and everyone placed their orders. Melva excused herself and went to the bathroom. Velvet looked at Trina staring into space and knew that she was upset.

"What's the matter, Tree? Mel got you worked up?"

"Nah, Vee," Trina said, shaking her head. "Stuff Mel says doesn't usually bother me because I know her, and I know she just runs off with the mouth most of the time. She doesn't mean to hurt anyone's feelings. Well...unless it's Tabitha's. I'm just thinking that...well...maybe she's right. Maybe my family is in the shape we're in because we don't expect much."

"Oh, Trina, that's nonsense," Sheila said.

"No, it isn't. All we've ever known is poverty. My mother and my grandmother have so, so many stories to tell about how they struggled growing up. They both were single mothers popping out babies for whatever man that came along professing his love."

"Trina..."

"It's true. My grandmother had eight kids by five different men. My mom has five kids by four different men. My oldest sister already has two kids by two different men. It's a pattern, and I'm following suit by putting myself in a situation that'll have me dropping out of school and on welfare before I know what hit me."

Kimberly reached across and held Trina's hand to comfort her. "Don't be negative, Tree. You just got finished commending your mother on the job she's doing with you and your sisters."

"She *is* doing a good job, but she's doing it alone, and *that's* the problem. She didn't expect much from, and made excuses for, the men that came and left the same way I just did for Daquan. Shoot, I don't even like him that much. He gets on my nerves most of the time."

"If that's the case, perhaps you shouldn't be sleeping with him, huh?" Sheila said. "In fact, why are you even bothered with this boy if you don't really like him?"

Velvet and Kimberly looked at each other because they both knew the answer to that question. Trina looked into Sheila's eyes and fought back the urge to admit that Daquan was T.J.'s substitute. She was in love with her coach, but she dared not reveal it to him fearing rejection. She could not tell Sheila that she was sleeping with Daquan only because he resembled T.J. so much, and every time they did it she fantasized about making love to Sheila's husband.

Trina lowered her eyes and shook her head. "I don't really know. Maybe it's because he really doesn't expect much of anything from me, either. He's not crowding me or looking over my shoulder all the time. Sometimes, grown men come on to me and he doesn't get jealous. He's not insecure, and that's a turn-on. Other than that, he's nothing but a big kid. He's sixteen, but he acts like he's six."

"Which is probably why he doesn't get jealous," Sheila told her. "Six year olds like to say they have a girlfriend or boyfriend because it's cool and fun, and they don't know the difference between that and just having a good friend who is not the same gender. Even if this boy is as immature as you say, the difference is that he *is* sixteen, and though his mind may be child-like, his hormones are still adolescent."

"Isn't that the truth?" Trina said. "The truth is that my hormones were raging, too, when we first got together."

"And they aren't anymore?"

Trina smirked and shrugged. "Well, they're not exactly raging."

"But you do get that twitch ever so often, huh, girl?" Kimberly asked with a laugh.

Trina chuckled. "Yeah, it usually happens after a hard practice or a big game. I'll go looking for him, and when I find him, I get some."

"How often does he come looking for you for that reason?" Sheila asked.

"He doesn't. All he cares about is basketball. Basketball comes first, second, third, fourth and fifth. I'm not even in the starting line-up."

Sheila looked away and let out a sigh. "Yeah, I know how you feel."

"Don't tell me Coach Stone is like that, too," Trina said.

"Not all the time, no. T.J. loves the game. We both do. I still play sometimes, and you know I officiate. I stay involved with the game because I love it. T.J. just has a greater passion. That's why he's so animated. He was like that when we were kids, too. You could hear him talking junk all the way down the block when he was playing ball. He's a winner. He won't stop until he achieves whatever goal he has. It's how he and I finally got together."

"You didn't always like him?" Kimberly asked.

"Goodness, no," Sheila chuckled. "He was loud, skinny, nappy headed, and dirty."

"Dirty?" the girls all chorused.

"Yeah, I remember his mother would have to beat him to make him come in the house. He'd stay out all day every day playing ball, and when you're sweating all day for hours straight in the hot sun, you're not only dirty but you stink, too."

"Oh, my god, don't tell me that," Trina said as her teammates laughed aloud.

"Yeah, but things are different now," Sheila said to them all. "Look at T.J. now. He led the nation in assists for two years at South Carolina State University, plus he was in the top five in steals all four years. He rode the bench for the Sixers one season but he made it the NBA."

"Why didn't he stay in the NBA?" Velvet asked.

"When he didn't get picked up by anyone at the beginning of what would've been his second season, he decided he didn't want to play anymore. Luckily for you all, though, because if would've kept playing there wouldn't have been a Lady Phoenix program."

"Right, right," the girls agreed appreciatively.

Sheila nodded, smiled and went on. "Now, T.J.'s gainfully employed, doing a job that he loves. So you see, dirty, stinky, nappy headed, loud mouth little boys that play too much do sometimes grow up to become intelligent, handsome, successful men. You just have to let boys be boys because they'll always have the *boy* in them."

Trina nodded. "I hear you, Sheila."

"But, it still doesn't mean you have to give your goodies away, whether it's his hormones raging or yours," Sheila told her. "Making them wait is a good thing, and waiting yourself is a better thing. You have plenty of time for that stuff."

"That's the point I was getting to," Melva said as she rejoined everyone at the table. "Don't go out like no sucker, dawg. If you get knocked up or something…I don't even want to think about it."

"You should at least be using condoms, Trina," Sheila advised. "You can go down to the department of health and—"

"I got it covered," Trina insisted. "Or I should say that I'll make sure he keeps it covered."

They laughed.

Melva *tsked*. "God knows I'm glad I'm still a virgin. You know what having babies is like? Shoot, I'm never gonna have no kids. Well, unless I meet the actor Jason George, and he wants to give me a few."

"I guess you ain't never havin' none then," Kimberly laughed.

"Whatever," Melva snapped. "But seriously, though. You gotta go through all kind of pain to bring kids into the world, and then all kind of headaches to bring them up in the world."

Velvet sucked her teeth. "Please, Mel, somebody had to go through pain and headaches for you, and not just your momma either, because you're sure giving me a headache right now."

"Well, I guess I'm as close as you and Kim are gonna get because you can't have no kids doin' it the dyke way."

Velvet eyes bulged and her nostrils flared. "What did you say? Let me tell you something—"

"Take it easy, Vee," Kimberly said. "Think about where the comment came from."

"She needs to think about the comments she makes!"

Sheila touched Velvet's arm and shook her head. Velvet took the hint and calmed down.

"I'm sorry, Velvet," Melva said. "You too, Kim. Y'all are right. I'm gonna watch what I say because y'all are my peeps. Love?"

Velvet hesitated for a moment, and then joined Trina and Kimberly, touching fists with Melva across the table. Sheila, wanting to share, put her fist in as well. The gesture brought back the bright, pleasant mood to the table that they all came into the restaurant with.

"We had that big conversation about babies, and I didn't get to share my news with you all." The girls all paused with anticipation. Sheila took a deep breath and put on a big smile. "I'm pregnant. Your coach and I are going to have a baby."

As Melva, Kimberly and Velvet squealed with excitement to the news and got up to hug Sheila, Trina sat still with a painted-on smile, trying to look happy while disguising her disappointment. When T.J. and Sheila got married, Trina didn't attend the wedding due to illness. The thought of T.J. not being available for her when she would be ready to tell him her feelings made her physically sick. The news of Sheila's pregnancy caused her to start getting dizzy, but she quickly pulled herself together and made her way around the table to hug the mother-to-be.

COACHES MEETING

Sunday, June 26, 2005 – 9:03 P.M.

Sam Pernell emerged from the Christopher Street subway station in Greenwich Village onto the busy island in the middle of the cross streets of Christopher Street, West Fourth Street and Seventh Avenue. He looked around for T.J. in the uninhibited area of bars, restaurants, novelty shops and nightclubs, frequented by tourists and nocturnal residents, but known mostly for its attraction of the gay community.

Sam was five-foot-four with his shoes on, in which on this night he wore brown Kenneth Cole sandals to go with his khaki shorts and white polo shirt. At thirty years old, he was already filling out in the midsection. He had a very light, almost yellow complexion, redish-brown hair that he kept cut in a low Caesar, and a thin mustache. He finally saw T.J. walking across Seventh Avenue toward the Caliente Cab restaurant and hurried over calling out to him. T.J. stopped and waited. They greeted each other by knocking fists and with the exchange of playful repartees. After a few shots at each other about physical, mental and sexual inadequacies and deficiencies, they laughed, snorted and proceeded into the restaurant.

Glen was waiting at the bar when T.J. and Sam came inside. He stood up and waved to get their attention. T.J. noticed him, and he and Sam walked over and joined him.

"What's up, big timers?" Glen said, greeting both T.J. and Sam with a soul shake and shoulder hug. Glen Ford was the thirty-two year-old head coach at Kingsborough Community College for seven years, winning the City Universities of New York championship for the last six. He was a broad, stocky, dark-skinned man, about five-eleven with a short Afro and thick mustache. He put many in the mind of Carl Weathers. He wore an orange T-shirt with KCC BASKETBALL in large blue letters across the chest, blue nylon Adidas warm-up pants and white Adidas with blue stripes.

"Nah, I'm not the big timer," T.J. said. "You're the big timer. I haven't won any junior college national titles like you have."

"Oh yeah, that's right," Sam said, patting Glen on the back. "I haven't seen you since the season. Congratulations, Mr. Ford. You finally got that ring."

Glen held out his hand for Sam to see. "Thanks, man. You like it?"

"Oh, yeah," Sam said as he marveled at the sight of the fourteen karat gold ring with words NJCAA NATIONAL CHAMPIONS 2005 around a large blue stone. "That's real nice."

"Tell Sam how Lady Phoenix players carried you to the Promised Land," T.J. boasted.

"Oh, no doubt," Glen testified. "Patricia Henderson got the MVP because she put up big numbers, but Ruth Hope was the catalyst. The Lady Phoenix alumni rose to the occasion for us. But I didn't expect anything less. T.J. preps those girls right. Any kid coming out of his program is sure to be well-coached."

"Oh, Glen, quit while you're ahead," T.J. said. "Flattery will get you nowhere with me. I'm not a fly, so bullshit doesn't attract me."

Glen let out a roaring belly laugh. "Hey, I'm not ashamed to kiss up a little. I'm gonna need you to send me some more players."

"I'll tell you, the way Melva Fields is going you might want to start recruiting her."

"Yo, don't even get me all excited like that. You know what a player like Melva can do on the juco level, especially in our region?"

"Well, her grades have slipped a lot," T.J. let Glen know. "She may have to go to a junior college if she doesn't get her act together. Hopefully, she'll bounce back, but you should put a bug in her ear just in case."

Glen slapped T.J. five. "You ain't said nothin' but a word, bro. With the team I have coming back and Melva at the point, shoot, we'll definitely be contending for another title. That is, if I actually stay there another year."

T.J. sucked his teeth and waved his hand at Glen. "Man, you talk that 'This is my last year' crap every year. You know you're not going anywhere."

"Well, I may actually do it this time. I've been looking into some other positions on higher levels. I've applied to a few four-year Division I and Division II schools in this area. I feel good about my chances of getting in somewhere."

"It would be good if you where able to move up," T.J. agreed. "We need strong, caring, knowledgeable *brothers* like you at the helm. In the meantime, though, you should be down at the New Attitude Tournament."

"Yeah, I know. I was planning on coming down this weekend. What's up, Sam? Can I get the V.I.P. treatment now that you're big-time and running the biggest tournament ever in New York City?"

"I'm just the coordinator," Sam modestly stated.

"Yeah, but you run shit," Glen said in his usual aggressive, street-like way. "That tournament ain't shit without you."

"That would be true, Glen, if they'd let Sam do his job," T.J. chimed in. "But the tournament is heading for disaster because his higher-ups are already letting Millie Negron call the shots."

Glen threw his hands up in disgust. "Oh, no! What's that chick doing now?"

"She got the board of directors to accommodate her so that she can go away and participate in another tournament out of town," Sam explained. "Not only that, but she got the City Housing League to switch their dates on T.J."

"You're shittin' me, right?" Glen said.

"Well, the way I see it, nothing's changed with the Housing League until they call me and we discuss it," T.J. said. "I haven't heard from them, so as of right now, the dates they gave me are still the same."

"Well, I told you that they will probably wait until tomorrow to call," Sam said.

T.J. looked away and leaned up against the bar. "It doesn't even matter because I'm not going to let this happen. I read the rules, and it says that I don't have to switch my game if I don't want to."

The bartender approached. "Can I get you gentlemen anything?"

"Yeah," Glen said. "I'll have a Cranberry Absolute. What do you guys want? The evening's on me in honor of T.J.'s birthday. Happy belated birthday, my man."

"Thanks, bro." T.J. wiped away imaginary tears. "I'm getting misty-eyed. I'll have a Long Island Iced Tea."

"I'll just have a Sprite," Sam said.

"Yo, you gotta speak up," Glen told Sam. "If you let Mille influence your bosses, you may be on your way out before you know it. Or worse than that, you could end up working for *her*. She knows you and T.J. are down, so she'll do you dirty to spite him."

"That's not going to happen," Sam stated confidently.

"Don't be naïve, bro. That chick's got some shit with her."

"She sure does," T.J. agreed. "Especially now that she's in cahoots with Charles Greene."

"That's right," Glen said. "And you know that mothafucka ain't never been 'bout no good. He's just using Millie, anyway, because T.J. put the spotlight on his cheatin' ass with all the recruiting he was doing. So what did he do? He got smart and teamed up with Millie, T.J.'s biggest rival, and uses her to get kids to come to his school. She's doing his dirty work, and the Department of Education can't do anything about it."

"So, what does she get out of it?" Sam asked.

"That's what I want to know," T.J. said. "I know it's something, but what? Whatever it is, I doubt if it's anything legitimate. Shoot, they might even be sleeping together."

Sam shook his head at the notion. "Please! The likeliness of that is minimal."

"Charles Greene wouldn't start to know what to do with a woman as fine as Millie," Glen added. "That dude is barely a hundred and fifty pounds soaking wet and fully dressed. That nerdy little white boy couldn't handle a woman like that if he had two dicks."

They all laughed.

"Besides," Glen continued, "doesn't Millie play on the other side of the fence, anyway?"

"That's the big mystery," T.J. said with a questionary shrug. "But speaking of playing on the other side of the fence, you guys will never, ever guess who came out of the closet to me yesterday."

Glen sat back and reached for his drink that the bartender just put down. "Oh-oh." He rolled his eyes. "Who is it now?"

"Velvet Fuller," T.J. told him.

"What?!" Sam exclaimed.

Glen slapped his own forehead. "Oh, you've gotta be fuckin' kidding me."

"Yeah, it took me by surprise, too," T.J. related. "Her girlfriend is Kimberly James, the little, light-skinned girl on my team with the pretty eyes and all the tattoos and stuff."

"Yeah, I know that girl," Glen recalled. "She's always all over the court playing D. Her mother still plays ball, too."

"Yeah, that's her."

"That's an odd couple," Sam said.

"I know. But listen to this," T.J. said before taking a sip of his drink. "Sheila and I were in the middle of celebrating my birthday yesterday, when Velvet called crying, saying she couldn't go home because her mother found some letters and pictures that she and Kimberly took together."

"Oh, shit!" Glen blurted out. "Nothing's worse for a person than having their parents find out they're homosexual like that."

"How do you know?" Sam asked him. "Is that how your parents found out about you?" He and T.J. laughed aloud.

"Fuck you, little man," Glen jokingly retorted. "What I meant to say was that I wouldn't want to be the last to find out that my kid was having same-gender relations."

"Yeah, I hear you," Sam agreed.

"Which is something that Sheila called me out on, too," T.J. told them. "Dudes, I'm gonna be a father."

"Get the fuck outta here!" Glen shouted. "Way to go, bro!"

"Yeah, congratulations to you," Sam cheered. Then, he remembered something T.J. told him. "Hey, wait a minute. How did this come about?"

"I know I said I wanted to wait," T.J. said, "but we got our chance to fulfill our locker room fantasy last month and we couldn't let the opportunity pass. There was no time to run to the drugstore, if you know what I mean."

Glen raised his glass to toast. "Well, like I said, way to go, Big Poppa!"

"I still want to hear about what happened with Velvet," Sam said. T.J. proceeded to tell his two closest buddies of all the events that took place the previous night. They both listened, astounded by what they were hearing.

"Yo, that's some crazy shit, T.J.," Glen said. "Sounds like your wife did all that so she could test your fathering skills."

T.J. nodded and stroked his goatee as he thought out the possibility. "You know, I never thought about that, but you might be right."

"You think so, T.J.?" Sam asked. "Sheila doesn't seem like the type of woman to play games like that."

Glen held up his hand to pause Sam after taking another chug of his drink. "Hold it right there. Let me tell you something about women. There is always a method to their madness. Her brining in that kid without discussing it with T.J. first was just madness, especially for Sheila. Am I wrong?"

"No, you're right," Sam agreed.

"We all know that she's a smarter, more respectful person than that. She had to step out of character the way she did because the opportunity was too good and might've been lost if she didn't. She found out she was pregnant, but she knew T.J. had been saying he wanted to wait a few years before having a baby. What happens? She gets pregnant, and then *boom!* Along comes this situation and a light bulb comes on over her head. She starts thinking that she'll start prepping him for some of the things they might be in for as parents."

T.J. continued nodding, thinking that Glen had made a valid point.

"In her mind, the plan was ingenious," Glen continued. "She knows she's got T.J. whipped, so getting him to do whatever she wants is no real challenge for her."

"Why do you say I'm whipped?" T.J. asked defensively.

"Because you are," Sam told him. "Everybody knows it, but don't worry, it's cool."

"What makes you guys always say that?"

Glen put his arm around T.J. and gave him a firm, manly embrace. "Don't look at it as a bad thing, she's your wife. But she became your wife so fast because she whipped it on you on the first date, and she's been doing it ever since."

T.J. freed himself. "Man, I've known Sheila since we were nine years old. When I first laid eyes on her, I knew that she was the only one for me. She was beautiful, smart and she could play ball. The problem was that she didn't seem to feel the same way about me. She rejected me over and over again for years, no matter what I did or how I tried. Then, she moved away the summer after tenth grade, and I didn't see her again until two years ago. No contact with each other for twelve years, and she winds up back here refereeing games. It was destiny, guys. I saw her and fell in love all over again. This time she loved me back, though. So you see. It's not about being whipped. It's about a love that was meant to be."

Glen and Sam looked at one another and busted out laughing. "Damn, he's more whipped than we thought," Glen said.

T.J. smiled and shrugged his shoulders. "So what!"

"So, what are you going to do, T.J.?" Sam asked.

"I'm going to handle this. I can pass any test Sheila tries to give me. Right now, though, I'm just thinking about how to handle Millie's bullshit."

"Actually, T.J., you may not want to hear this, but the best thing to do with that whole situation might be to leave it alone," Glen advised.

T.J. was shocked. "Are you serious?"

"Yeah, man. Let her kids get whatever they can out of it. Remember, it's not for her, it's for them. You don't want them to miss out on any opportunities that they can get. Millie's shit will be exposed soon enough, trust me. You've always been for the kids. Don't stop now."

"The kids will get their opportunity. Just about every scout that'll be in Washington, D.C. will be here for the playoffs in the New Attitude League. Am I wrong, Sam?"

"No, you're right," Sam confirmed.

"This is not about the kids, Glen," T.J. told him. "The kids have opportunities all around them. The thing is that if the Roadrunners don't go to all these big-time tournaments, it would be a lot harder to draw all those top-ranked players from all over. Stacey Conyers is playing with them now. Not even the Long Island Tide can keep their best players because all kids want is to travel and get gear. Millie Negron, Charles Greene and everybody like them are ruining women's basketball in New York City. You'd better believe, though, that if I have anything to do with it, that shit'll never happen because I'm going to be the one to expose them all."

"You're right, T.J.," Sam said. "But what we're saying is that this isn't about Millie Negron and the Roadrunners. It's about all of us doing what's best for the kids. You know a lot of times these scouts want to see kids two and three times. What if a kid like Future doesn't have a good game, or gets sick or something? Doesn't a talent like hers need to be seen as often as possible?"

"You know it's not even about that, Sam."

"But it is about you, being my boy, trusting me and helping me out here," Sam implored. "You know I'll be right there next to you on the front line when it's time go to war. I'm going to be there with you when it's time to bring Millie and Charles down. But, for right now, I need you to be on the front line with me."

T.J. stroked his chin again. "For you, eh? Humph. I think you're being used, Sam. But for you…for you I'll let it happen. I just have this feeling that somehow it's going to end up biting me in the ass."

UNITED WE FALL

Thursday, June 30, 2005 – 4:15 P.M.

Beverly Smalls was shooting around alone at one of the six baskets, the one closest to the entrance to the handball courts, in the park next to George Gershwin Junior High School. She tossed the ball out away from the basket, catching it on the first bounce, and then turned and shot with perfect form: her eyes locked in on her target, right hand high over her head, elbow locked, wrist snapped, and left hand in the same place it started with the fingers pointing straight up at the sky. She repeated that over and over, sometimes faking one way, and then turning to the other before leaping high into the air and releasing. Sometimes she'd dribble through her legs and spin into the lane before she'd shoot.

Beverly had taken close to two hundred shots—making two-thirds of them—when she heard someone call out to her. She looked back to see her best friend Melinda walking toward her with her mother holding her hand. Beverly shook her head at the fact that Melinda was a five-foot-six, one hundred and forty-five pound fourteen year old, yet her mother treated her like a four-foot, seventy-pound nine year old. Whenever Melinda came to visit, Beverly would have to escort her from house to house, and Melinda was two months older. There was another reason Melinda's mother let her spend time with the Smalls, though, and his name was Burton.

"Hey, Bev, what's up?!" Melinda shouted.

"What's up, Melinda?" Beverly responded. "Hi, Miss Thompson."

Carlene Thompson let go of Melinda's hand long enough to give Beverly a hug. "Hey, Beverly, how are you doing?"

"I'm fine," Beverly said.

"And how's your good-looking daddy?" asked the mocha complexioned, wide hipped, thick lipped, well-endowed woman, who stood five-seven with a thick mane that she kept pulled back and wrapped.

Beverly and Melinda giggled as they made eye contact with each other.

"He's doing fine," Beverly said.

"Tell him I'm still waiting for that dinner he promised to cook for me."

"He said he was going to call you tonight because he wants to talk to you about something important."

Carlene blushed and smiled with eagerness. "Really? He wants to talk to me about something important?"

"That's what he said."

Carlene fidgeted and straightened herself up like Burton was coming to see her right then. She tugged at her white silk blouse and made sure it wasn't tucked too tightly in her long gray tiered skirt. "Well, tell him I'll be in after eight o'clock, and I'll be waiting on his call."

"Okay, I'll tell him."

Carlene took Melinda's hand again. "Come on, Melinda. I want to get downtown before it gets too late. Say goodbye to Beverly."

Melinda resisted slightly, and her voice trembled with hesitation as she spoke. "Mommy…Mommy, can I stay in the park with Beverly?"

Carlene's attitude quickly changed. "Girl, no! Come on!" She gave Melinda a tug and proceeded to walk off. Again, Melinda resisted.

"Please, Mommy. I can stay at Beverly's house 'til you get back."

"Girl, I said no," Carlene said, angrily. "I didn't ask Burt if you could stay over. What makes you think you can just invite yourself over to their house, anyway?"

"He won't mind," Beverly said. "He said Melinda's family, and she can come over anytime."

"Really?" Carlene asked, seemingly surprised. "Well, that's awfully nice of him. I don't know what to say."

Melinda got hopeful. "So, can I stay?"

"No," Carlene snapped, leading her away. "I need you with me."

Beverly waved. "Seeya, Melinda."

"Bye," Melinda whined, looking back sadly.

A few minutes after Carlene and Melinda left the park, Beverly saw Melva, Trina and Tabitha coming in from another direction.

RISE OF THE PHOENIX

"Hey, Beverly," Trina called out to her. "What's up, girl?"

Beverly smiled and waved. "Hey, wassup, y'all?"

"Yo, you live around here?" Melva asked.

"I live in Canarsie, on 98th Street."

"Word? I live on 103rd and Flatlands," Tabitha said.

"Oh, I'm only a few blocks from you."

"I didn't know you were from around here, Beverly," Trina said. "I live in Brownsville, on Dumont Avenue near Rockaway Avenue."

"Yeah, and I live over in Starrett City," Melva added.

"So, I hear you're going to Stuyvesant, Bev," Tabitha said. "Why that school?"

"Why not?" Beverly asked. "Isn't it one of the best schools?"

"Yeah, academically," Tabitha said. "But you got skills on the court. I mean, I just thought with skills like yours, you'd want to go to a school where you'll be seen."

Trina grunted and rolled her eyes up. "Oh, Tabitha, don't start that."

"Yeah," Melva said. "So what you're transferring to Saint Joseph's. It's not like they really need you, or like you're gonna help them beat Jefferson."

"What? You're crazy," Tabitha said with a grin. "Yo, Bev, let me get a shot."

Beverly tossed her the ball and Tabitha dribbled back behind the three-point line and chucked up a shot with a quick release that swished straight threw the hoop.

"Damn, my shot is wicked," Tabitha gloated. "I'mma go right in and start at St. Joe's. I guarantee it."

"I saw you run off a buncha shots like that in practice," Beverly said as she retrieved the ball.

"It's all day everyday," Tabitha said. "You'd better ask somebody."

"Let me get a shot, too, Bev?" Melva asked, moving to the opposite side of the court. Beverly tossed her the ball. She started dribbling back and forth between her legs. "You know that I can't just take an open shot," she said. "I need some D. Check up, Tab. You was talking all that junk in practice. What's up, now?"

"You ain't got nothin' for me," Tabitha replied, twisting her fingers in the air to say *later for you*.

"So, check up then," Melva pressed.

"I don't have to prove anything to you. You're just mad because you know Saint Joe's is going to the Federation Finals again, and this time we're gonna beat Jeff."

Melva laughed aloud. "Please, Tabitha. If they do, it won't be because of you. But, you did the right thing, scrub. Stay over there in your place."

"Yeah, okay. It's your world, right?" Tabitha said sarcastically.

"You're damn right about that!" Melva declared.

Tabitha threw her thumb back at herself, "That's why I'll be playing in the Federation Finals," and then stabbed her index finger in Melva's direction, "and you'll be home reading about us in the paper."

"Hey, hey, hey," Trina interjected. "You forgot that Melva and I go to the same school? Don't be hatin' on us."

Tabitha touched her heart. "You know I ain't got nothin' but love for you, Tree." She stabbed her finger at Melva. "It's not your fault your school is stuck with a whack-ass point guard. Y'all might be contenders if y'all had somebody to run the show. Look how easy Future skated past Melva in the Slam Jam championship game a few weeks ago."

"You're crazy," Melva barked. "Nobody can hold me! I scored twenty-seven points in that game with Future guarding me. What did she have, fifteen?"

"Yeah, but she did keep getting past you," Trina said, inclined to agree with Tabitha.

"And what?" Melva asked, and then answered her own question. "Passing off to Connie, that's what. That's what we should be talking about, how Connie King scored forty-one on y'all."

Trina took offense because she was the one defending superstar Connie King. "Later for Corny Connie with her overrated game. She scored all of those points because of Future. Every time Future broke you down and we stepped up to help, she found Connie somewhere under the basket for an easy lay-up. Keep Future on lock down and Corny Connie won't score as many points, because she can't create on her own."

"She can't keep Future on lock," Tabitha taunted. "She gets embarrassed every time she tries."

Melva became outraged. "Shut up, Tabitha! You hold her, then! Oh, I forgot, you're scared. You won't even step up to me for one point out here."

Beverly was a mere observer up until this point. She found the opportunity to get involved by taking Melva's challenge in place of Tabitha. "I'll play defense on you, Melva," she said with an innocent shrug.

Melva, Trina and Tabitha were all silenced as they stared at each other. Melva began dribbling back and forth between her legs again with a smirk on her face. It was the look she made whenever she felt she had an obvious advantage over an opponent.

"Nah, that's okay," Melva told her young, new teammate. "You're not ready yet."

"C'mon," Beverly pleaded. "One point, do or die."

Melva sucked her teeth and twisted her lips. "Get outta here. You shouldn't even be thinking about trying to check me."

"Check you?" Tabitha said. "I'll bet money that she'll put you on total lock down."

"You're crazy!" Melva shouted.

"So, what's up? There's your D," Tabitha said, holding her hand out to present Beverly.

After giving Tabitha a cold, hard stare, Melva tossed the ball to Beverly. "Check," she said.

Beverly tossed the ball back to Melva who faked right and quickly dribbled to her left, going toward the basket. Beverly quickly recovered, got in front of her and knocked the ball out of her hand. Melva was able to block Beverly's path and regain possession of the ball. This time she threw the ball out to her left—a soft, high dribble—and took a half step backwards. Beverly didn't go for the ball like most defenders did. She was too smart for that. She knew it was a set up and knew enough about Melva's game—her speed and ball handling skills—from seeing her in practice to be fooled into going for a steal. When Beverly didn't take the bait and reach for the ball, Melva took a hard step to her left and showed her left hand like she was about to take another dribble.

When Beverly reacted, Melva pulled the ball away with her right hand—like one of those Allen Iverson-type crossovers—and went the other direction. Beverly recovered once again, took a long stride and was able to bat Melva's shot attempt out of the air before it reached the basket.

Tabitha picked up the ball, displaying a big smile. "Dag, Mel." She shook her head. "You didn't even get a shot off. What's up with that?"

"Gimme that." Melva snatched the ball away from her. She turned around and tossed it back to Beverly. "Let's go. Try that again."

"Nope, it's my turn," Beverly said, tossing the ball back to Melva. "You check."

"Oh-oh." Tabitha laughed.

Trina was laughing, too. "It's on, now."

Melva stood there for a moment with her face balled up with anger.

Tabitha continued to taunt. "What's up, Mel? Check up. Or is your bark bigger than your bite? Step up or shut up."

Melva dropped the ball and stormed over to Tabitha, getting up in her face. "Yo, I'm tired of your mouth. What's up with you?"

Tabitha didn't flinch. "I know you'd better back the fuck up off me."

Trina ran over and wedged herself between them, her six-foot-four-inch, two hundred pound frame causing them both to stumble backwards a couple of steps. She grabbed Melva's arms and pushed her back a couple more steps. "Take it easy, Mel, we were just kidding. We can't be fighting each other. We're a team."

Melva was irate and waving her fists. "You better tell her something, then, before I whup her ass out here!"

"Please!" Tabitha smirked. "You ain't doin' a damn thing." She wasn't easily intimidated. In fact, she was used to being the intimidator. Tabitha's reputation for being a bully and a troublemaker preceded her wherever she went since she was very young.

Melva, on the other hand, wasn't considered to be a bully. She just had a quick temper that she was learning to tame. Tabitha brought out the worst in her, though. The only time anyone would see them together was when they were both with Trina.

RISE OF THE PHOENIX

"Y'all better chill," Trina demanded, to which both girls complied for the moment.

Trina never had a physical altercation a day in her life, but it wasn't because of her imposing stature. It was because people respected her intellect and integrity. She was a big girl at sixteen years old, with an overdeveloped figure that caused her to draw attention from much older men.

Melva freed herself from Trina's hold and started to walk away.

"That's right, punk out like you always do!" Tabitha shouted. "You're a sucker, Mel! You'd better stay outta my face!"

Melva swung around and stood her ground. Heavy breathing from anger made her thin chest rise and fall under her oversized white T-shirt. "You see what I'm saying, Trina! Let me hit her just once! That's all I need, one hit!"

"Come on with it then!" Tabitha beckoned.

Trina became angry and spoke more aggressively. "Hey, that's enough! Both of you need to relax! Nobody's going to do any fighting out here! I want you both to squash this mess, right now!"

"Later for it. It's squashed." Melva turned on her heels and started to walk away.

"Where are you going?" Trina asked.

"I'm going home," Melva said. "I have better things to do."

"Please stay, Melva," Beverly requested. "I wanted to play two on two."

Melva paused, but didn't turn around.

"Yeah, Mel," Trina said. "That's a good idea. Please, stay and hang out a while?"

"Don't beg," Tabitha snarled. "Let her go if she wants to." She waved her hand, shooing Melva away. "Get outta here if you're going!"

Melva turned around and started to respond, but looked at Trina and Beverly and decided against it. She then turned and left the park.

"You see," Tabitha said, snickering. "I told you she was a sucker."

Trina cut her eyes and shook her head at Tabitha. "What's wrong with you? Why do you insist on being such a miscreant? Why can't you just get along with everyone?"

"I didn't start this, Tree," Tabitha noted. "And I'm not on this team to make any friends or pretend for anybody."

"Pretend? Nobody's asking you to pretend."

"I'm just here to play ball and get a scholarship, that's all."

"Well, the Lady Phoenix is about more than that, Tabitha."

Tabitha twisted her fingers again. "Yeah, whatever."

"Well, if you feel that way, why stay?" Trina asked. "There are plenty of teams around. Just go play for someone else."

"Like I said, I want a scholarship and Coach Stone has good connections."

"Oh, so you're using us, huh?"

"Not y'all, just Coach Stone." Tabitha turned to leave. "I'll see you when I see you."

Beverly walked over to Trina, cradling the basketball under her arm. "Well, now it's just us two."

"I'm sorry for all of that, Beverly," Trina said. "Unfortunately, things tend to get out of hand sometimes. But that's what the Lady Phoenix is all about, helping us get through things like this so that we can be ready to progress to the next level. Some learn faster than others. Do you know what I mean?"

Beverly coyly shrugged her shoulders. "I think so."

"Don't worry," Trina said while getting into a defensive stance, "you'll get it soon enough."

Beverly welcomed Trina's challenge and faked a shot, causing her to raise her hand to contest it. That was all Beverly needed to take that explosive first step of hers and blow past Trina for an easy lay-up. Trina clapped her hands in frustration with herself for making the same mistake as Melva in underestimating their new teammate. Then she smiled widely, knowing that was exactly what all their opponents would do as well.

"Good one," Trina said as Beverly tossed the ball back to her. "You're exactly what we need."

5:48 P.M.

When Trina left the park that day, after losing two games to Beverly fifteen to nine both times, she headed off to see her boyfriend,

RISE OF THE PHOENIX

Daquan. She felt loneliness and emptiness and thought that being with her *true* love's substitute would provide her with some temporary satisfaction. The conversation with Sheila Stonewall and her teammates at the restaurant a few nights earlier weighed on her mind. She decided she needed to make changes, and they had to start with her not putting herself in a compromising situation such as she was doing with Daquan. After deciding that she really needed to change out of her sweaty T-shirt and shorts, she changed direction and headed for home instead of going to try to find him. She knew she had chores to catch up on anyway, which would give her some time to do some thinking. She had to get headstrong before seeing him again so that she could look into his face and the thought of sex would not sway her decision to cut him off for good.

7:00 P.M.

Trina was unfocused and disinterested in what she was supposed to be doing at the moment. She felt agitated pressure instead of the relaxing fulfillment that she hoped for as she lay in the bed staring up at the ceiling. She began comparing the boy to the man. She knew that Daquan Mitchell was nothing like Timothy Jerome Stonewall. Besides the fact that they looked so much alike they had to have had some kind of family connection, they had nothing else in common. She saw Coach Stone as strong, assertive, focused, caring and brave. Daquan was passive, uncaring and self-absorbed. Then, she thought about what Sheila said about the way Coach Stone was as a child.

Perhaps he will turn out to be a great man, too, she thought to herself about Daquan. *Sheila didn't give Coach Stone a play when they were young because he wasn't ready. Perhaps I should just give Daquan some time to grow. Everyone always says that girls mature much faster than boys. He probably just needs time to catch up.*

Just then, the pressure Trina was feeling suddenly increased, so she braced to give herself support. Its intensity continued to increase despite her attempt to relax and give herself some comfort. Then, its weight fell down upon her, causing tears of guilt and confusion to flow down her face unnoticed by the source. And although she only had to endure a few minutes of the outlandish mixture of ardor and repulsion, it was a feeling she decided at that moment not to experience again.

Finally, when the weight had lifted, Trina quickly concealed her shame and guilt. She looked into the face of her distorted reality being overwhelmed by a parasympathetic nervous response, and she broke down. She received no comfort, and wondered why she didn't follow her first thought to just go on home.

RISE OF THE PHOENIX

New Attitude Sports Association League
Game Rosters

LADY PHOENIX
Timothy J. Stonewall, Coach
Juanita E. Moore, Assistant Coach

Starters
5 – Melva Fields, Grd, 5'8", 120 lbs., Paul Robeson H.S., 2006
13 – Tabitha Gleavy, Grd, 5'9", 150 lbs., St. Joseph's H.S., 2007
22 – Velvet Fuller, G/F, 5'11", 145 lbs., Fiorello H. LaGuardia H.S., 2006
25 – Keisha Miller, Fwd, 6'2", 177 lbs., Middle College @ Medgar Evers H.S., 2007
35 – LaTrina Smith, Ctr, 6'4", 200 lbs., Paul Robeson H.S., 2006
Non-Starters
11 – Danisha Barnes, Grd, 5'7", 142 lbs., St. Joseph's H.S., 2007
15 – Kimberly James, Grd, 5'6", 144 lbs., Prospect Heights H.S., 2008
21 – Monica Johnson, Fwd, 6'0", 165 lbs., Stuyvesant H.S., 2007
23 – Tracy Williams, Fwd, 6'1", 185 lbs., St. Joseph's H.S., 2007
32 – Beverly Smalls, G/F, 6'1", 156 lbs., Stuyvesant H.S., 2009
33 – Tanya Campbell, Ctr, 6'2", 180 lbs., Boys & Girls H.S., 2008

ROADRUNNERS
Mildred Negron, Coach

Starters
10 – Rayna Cortez, Grd, 5'8", 140 lbs., Thomas Jefferson H.S., 2008
11 – Erin Saltzman, Grd, 6'0", 153 lbs., Thomas Jefferson H.S., 2007
12 – Ellen Saltzman, Fwd, 6'0", 158 lbs., Thomas Jefferson H.S., 2007
21 – Stacey Conyers, Fwd, 6'2", 172 lbs., Lawrence H.S., 2008
34 – Connie King, Ctr, 6'4", 186 lbs., Thomas Jefferson H.S., 2006
Non-Starters
13 – Angela Chueng, 5'4", 132 lbs., Thomas Jefferson H.S., 2007
22 – Illyana Santana, Fwd, 6'1", 172 lbs., St. Michael's Academy, 2006
23 – Jennifer Davis, Grd, 5'9", 154 lbs., Thomas Jefferson H.S., 2007
24 – Renee Imes, Forward, 6'0", 166 lbs., Christ the King H.S., 2006
33 – Lissette Cruz, Forward, 6'2", 185 lbs., Murry Bergtraum H.S., 2006
42 – Brittany Coles, Center, 6'2", 175 lbs., August Martin H.S., 2008

THE AGONIES...

Saturday, July 2, 2005 – 4:48 P.M.

On 145th Street in Harlem coming from Broadway was a steep hill going down. One block and it came to an end at Riverside Drive, where the Riverbank State Park entrance was bridged over the Henry Hudson Highway and looked over the Hudson River. The path on the left was for buses and permitted traffic. Walking in, one would take the path on the right and follow a long walkway that eventually forked to the left leading past the bus stops. But staying on the right one would pass a picnic area with tables and benches until he or she come upon the recreation building where the gymnasium was located. The glass doors allowed passers-by to see all of the action going on inside and there was always plenty of action. It was here where just about every major basketball tournament was held, a beautiful facility with a full-sized court and locker room accommodations for everyone. It was the ideal place for the New Attitude Sports Association to host a tournament of this magnitude.

The games in this tournament drew hundreds of fans and two dozen college recruiters every day during the open evaluation period. This day was no exception. There was standing room only for fans that came to see The Roadrunners, New York's most dominating team with their all-everything roster, take on the very talented Lady Phoenix. Both teams were undefeated up to this point, and they were both coming into this game with a new player added to their respective rosters. T.J. hoped that Beverly Smalls would be as good as he imagined. Meanwhile, everybody in the gym knew of Stacey Conyers, the forty points per game scorer from Lawrence High School, who was making her debut with the Roadrunners. The tension mounted as the two teams warmed up at their baskets, waiting for the five o'clock tip-off.

RISE OF THE PHOENIX

6:27 P.M.

T.J. stood facing his team's bench holding his clipboard behind his back as he watched his players sit before him...defeated! Trina was leaning forward with her elbows on her knees and her face buried in her hands. Tabitha sat with her back to everyone with a towel draped over her head. Kimberly and Velvet were sitting next to each other on the floor in front of the bench. Melva was covering her face with her hands so no one could see her crying. Beverly sat on the end of the bench with her arms folded, and the rest of the team stood behind the team bench with long faces.

T.J. started to pace, trying not to be upset because his head was already hurting again, but he couldn't help it. It wasn't the fact that they lost to the Roadrunners. He was upset with the way they lost. Juanita stood behind him, not knowing what to do or say because T.J. didn't bother to have a conference with her before addressing the players when the game ended like he usually did. He walked past the bench and stood off away from everyone, then let out a deep breath and spoke calmly.

"We had them. We had the game won, but we let them come back and beat us." He started to pace again. "And it's not like they really beat us. Oh, no. We gave them the game. We took this game, put it on a silver platter and catered to them like we were their servants." He turned and asked Juanita for stats. "What margins did we lead by in each of the first three quarters?"

Juanita read from her stat sheet. "We were up six after the first quarter, seven at the half, and we held on to a five point lead after the third."

"And for what?" T.J. asked, rhetorically. "To lose by ten? Ten?! They outscored us by fifteen points in one quarter, and why? Because we refuse to unite and become one machine with all of its parts working together. We refuse to lay our differences aside, handle our off-the-court problems at a more appropriate time, and get our acts together to play good, hard, team basketball for thirty-two minutes." He lost his cool. "Thirty-two minutes! That's all!"

T.J. looked over toward Juanita again. She held up her hand, gesturing him to calm down. He tried. "The new defense worked. For twenty-four minutes we were able to pressure Future and make her give the ball up early. For twenty-four minutes we boxed Connie King out and kept her from controlling the boards." His voice became hard and unnatural sounding—mechanical. "For twenty-four minutes *we* were in control! Then, in eight minutes, we fell apart at the seams! They made their run, and instead of keeping our composure and playing smart, we had people trying to be the hero, people arguing on the court, people walking back on defense, *and showing outright disrespect for yourselves, for me and for everyone who came here to see us play!* What does that say about us?! What does that say about each one of you?! I have never seen such a form of self-destruction in my life! And I don't want you to get the wrong idea. This is not about winning or losing. Noooo, not at all. This isn't even about basketball. This is about attitudes, your attitudes. You have to get them in order…"

Tabitha lifted her head and removed the towel from her face. "I do have an attitude," she admitted. "It's because people on this team think it's all about them and they be trying to show off to prove a point. Then, they have the nerve to get mad if they don't touch the ball one time down the court. That's why I have an attitude!"

"So, getting an attitude is supposed to make things better?" Trina lifted her head to ask her. "If one of us messes up, you get mad and mess up on purpose, right? That's the way to solve the problem, right?"

"Well, apparently that's the way some of us think," T.J. interjected. "That's why we're having so much trouble getting over that hump—the hump that keeps us at second best. The Roadrunners are even cockier now. They think they're always going to be better than us because no matter what happens, we're going to choke. Coach Negron is in that locker room right now telling her team how fortunate they are. She's saying to them, 'I told you it would just be a matter of time before they fell apart.' She's saying, 'They don't want to win. They don't even want to play together. They're fighting among themselves! They don't even respect each other!' She's telling her team to thank their lucky stars that we can't get our act together!"

T.J. stopped, controlled his breathing, took a step back and looked his team over. Shaking his head, he pointed to each player. "From here

RISE OF THE PHOENIX

on, whatever happens is on you. Each of you has to decide what's going to happen next for the Lady Phoenix. Go get dressed."

As the players started to gather their belongings, Juanita stopped them. "Hold up, everybody," she called out, extending her hand. "Put your hands in first."

T.J. felt bad for being so angry that he failed to initiate the thing that most teams use to signify a bond of unity, especially after all he just said to them. He marched over to them with his hand out and placed it firmly on top of the pile.

"I'm sorry, girls," he said. "It's just that I know you're much better than this. It upsets me to see you not doing as well as I know you all can. It pains me to see you come so close, and then fall short. You have the talent. You have the intelligence. Start using it. The only place for us to go is up, ladies. Let's not look down as we rise."

Trina took the cue. "One, two, three!"

"Phoenix!" the team shouted, less enthusiastically than usual.

Juanita handed T.J. the stat sheets. "I'm leaving," she said. "I'm taking Keisha, Tanya, Monica and Danisha home. Are you taking anyone?"

"Yeah, I got Beverly, Melva and Velvet. Trina, Tracy, Tabitha and Kim are going home on the subway."

"Okay, I'll see you at practice."

T.J. nodded and waved in response.

As the team gathered their things and started out to the locker room, T.J. called Melva back. "Wait up, Melva. I need to talk to you."

Melva walked over, unaware of what T.J. wanted because she still had her game face on. Her expression changed when he pulled a piece of paper from under the stat sheets and handed it to her.

"Your coach at your school sent me a copy of your report card. You know, the one you kept telling me you never got. Well, here it is. Look at it. Your grades are horrible, and you failed biology. Why?"

Melva's face dropped, and she started scratching her head through her thick locks. "My science teacher don't like me. Every time I got to his class and asked to go to the bathroom, he'd say no, so I'd just leave, and he don't let me back in. But I can't help it. I always have to go the same time everyday. And when he don't let me back in, I miss the work."

"That's a poor excuse because you can go to the bathroom during the time you're changing classes," T.J. told her.

"I don't be having to go then."

"*I don't be having to go then,*" T.J. mocked. "What kind of English is that? I see you only got a sixty-five in that class. It's ridiculous. Look at this, thirteen times absent from your Global Studies class. Why are you cutting Global Studies?"

"I'm not cutting, I be waking up late. They make you wait outside when you come late, so you end up missing first period."

"I suggest you invest in an alarm clock, then."

"I have one. I just don't hear it when it rings."

"Look, girl, you're going to have to stop making excuses for yourself and get your act together. All those letters you're getting from colleges for basketball won't mean anything if you can't make the grade. You have to make waking up on time, getting to class, and studying a habit, right now."

At that moment, Mildred Negron walked up. She held out her hand to T.J. as she approached him.

"Good game, Coach," she said, shaking his hand. "You always make me sweat. I like that, though. None of the other teams have the firepower to pose a *real* threat. We need this kind of practice to prepare ourselves for the National Tournament this year."

"Oh, is that a fact?" T.J. asked. "Well, the last I checked, you had to win this tournament, first, before you could go on to The Nationals. Don't go counting your chickens before they hatch, Millie."

"Oh, T.J., there's nothing wrong with being confident," Mildred said with a spiteful grin.

"There's a big difference between confidence and cockiness, you know."

"Whatever you say, T.J. I'll see you around." Mildred turned to walk away, and then remembered something. "Oh, yeah, you know I'm taking my team to Washington, D.C. for the Northeast Tournament of Champions, right?"

T.J. shrugged. "Yeah. So?"

RISE OF THE PHOENIX

"Well, I'm only carrying eleven players, and we're allowed to bring fifteen. I was just thinking that a few of the Lady Phoenix players would make good additions to the Roadrunners and strengthen our team enough to win the whole thing, easily. That new girl on your team would be really great. Where'd you find her? She is so good."

T.J. turned to Melva and excused her. "Melva, go ahead and get dressed. We'll finish this conversation outside." He watched Melva walk off. He knew she wanted to stay and hear the conversation, but he waited until she was gone to resume.

T.J. turned and faced Mildred again and looked her up and down. The striking six-foot woman was dressed in a white Nike polo shirt with her team's logo on the left, crimson Nike tennis shorts and white Nike Shox. T.J. cringed at the sight of her. It wasn't because she was unattractive. Her exterior was actually quite stunning. T.J. wouldn't see it, though. In his eyes, she was ugly and decrepit. He often made faces behind her back like she reeked of raw sewage. Now she stood before him with the audacity to ask to use his players. He couldn't believe it.

"Look, Millie, you already know how I feel about my kids playing outside of this program…"

T.J. paused when he noticed Connie King and Rayna "Future" Cortez coming up behind their coach. He nodded to Millie to turn around. She turned and put her hand up to stop them.

"Hold it, girls," Millie ordered. "I'll be with you in a minute."

"It's important, Coach," Rayna Cortez insisted.

"Yeah, we have a big problem concerning our trip," Connie King added.

Mildred turned her attention back to T.J. She raised a finger to him. "Hold that thought for a moment, T.J. Let me handle this right quick."

"No, Millie. We really don't have anything to talk about. You already know how I feel about that subject. My players are preoccupied doing Lady Phoenix work. They have no time for anything else." He started walking away. "Have a good day. And good luck in Washington."

Mildred glared at T.J. and turned to resume her conversation with her two star players. "What's up girls?"

"Coach, we have a problem," Rayna said. "The twins said they can't play next weekend."

"Why not?"

"They said they have to go to North Carolina with their parents for their cousin's post graduation party," Connie told her.

Mildred's face hardened. "What? Why didn't they tell me this themselves?"

"I don't know," Connie said. "They just told us about it in the locker room before they left."

Mildred was livid. "Just now, when? Right before you came to me?"

"Yeah," both girls answered.

"Connie, run outside and see if you can catch them."

"They're probably—" Connie started.

"Girl, don't give me no lip! Just do what I told you!" Mildred growled.

Connie turned and started walking out of the gymnasium.

Mildred shouted at her, clapping her hands to hurry her along. "Let's go, Connie! Hurry up!"

Connie jogged out.

"Oh, man, Coach," Rayna said. "First we lose Lissette to a family commitment, and now the twins. We can't go to Washington with only eight players. We have to get at least three more girls."

Mildred thought for a moment, staring at her longhaired, slender, underdeveloped, Puerto Rican point guard, who looked more like twelve years old than fifteen, and then smiled devilishly as an idea popped into her head. "Don't worry, Rayna. I'm working on that right now."

"Who do you have in mind?"

At that moment, Trina, Tabitha, Kimberly, Velvet, Tracy and Beverly were just approaching.

"Your question has just been answered." Millie eyeballed the Lady Phoenix players. She stepped in front of them and put on a fallacious smile. "Hey, girls, good game."

Velvet and Kimberly were walking ahead of everyone else. They just smiled cordially and proceeded out of the gymnasium.

RISE OF THE PHOENIX

"Yeah, thanks," Trina cautiously responded.

"I mean it. I thought you all played very, very well. As a matter of fact, I was just telling my players that. Isn't that right, Rayna?"

Rayna didn't respond.

Trina smiled, politely. "That's nice. Take care."

"Wait," Mildred said, again blocking the girls' path. "I'm sure you all heard about the Northeast Tournament of Champions being held up in Washington, D.C. in a few weeks. I'm taking the Roadrunners to that tournament again this year."

"Why?" Tabitha asked with a smirk. "You never win it. You didn't even make the semi-finals last year."

"That's true," Mildred admitted. Although she was a bit incensed by Tabitha's tone of voice, she was impressed with her forwardness. She knew at that moment that Tabitha was someone she needed on her side. "That's very, very true. However, that wouldn't be the case if we added players like you to our roster. The Roadrunners and the Lady Phoenix have the best players in New York on our teams. The Baltimore Lady Raiders and the Bridgeport Belles are always the best teams in D.C. They usually run through the tournament easily if they eliminate us, and we usually play one of them in the first or second round. That's why I'm trying to convince Coach Stone to let you girls join us for events like this so we can represent New York City the right way."

"I understand what you're saying," Trina said, "but we put a lot of time and work into building our program. If we took the time to play for every coach that asks us, what kind of dedication would we be showing to ourselves and to Coach Stone?"

Connie ran back into the gym. "I don't see them, Coach."

"Oh, Connie," Mildred said. "Come here." She took Connie's hand and pulled her over to Trina as if she was putting her on display. Connie stood erect and proud at six-foot-four with broad shoulders and thick, muscular arms and legs. She had a light-brown complexion with leukodermic patches all over, a square jaw, thin nose, and a short, tapered haircut with tight curls on top.

"I'm sure you already know that Connie is an All-American," Mildred went on. "She's already made up her mind to play at Baylor

University next year. Do you know how she got recruited by the defending National Champions? Not by staying here in New York, playing for the same tired ol' leagues. She got her opportunity when a coach from Baylor saw us in Washington, D.C., last year."

"Yo, that's what I'm talking about," Tabitha blurted out with a change of attitude. "That's what I should be doing."

"Maybe we should ask Coach Stone to put us in that tournament," Tracy suggested.

Mildred immediately attempted to steer her thinking in another direction. "Why? You can just travel with us. That way, like I said before, we can have a much stronger team and represent New York City the right way."

Tabitha got wide-eyed. "Yeah, that sounds real good. We can win tournaments that everybody will recognize."

"I guess if it didn't interfere with anything we're doing it would be okay," Tracy said.

Trina was not as optimistic about the idea. "But it will interfere, so let's just go."

"Hey, why don't you want a better opportunity?" Rayna asked.

Trina became defensive. "Hey, it's all good, but I can't just walk on my coach like that. Coach Stone bends over backwards to help us. We had eight players go to Division I schools in the last two years, so we must be doing something right."

Rayna submitted. "I hear you, girl."

Connie, like Millie, wasn't willing to accept that. "What's up with you, Trina?" Connie asked, giving Trina a hard stare through squinted eyes. "You act like you don't want us to win."

Trina smirked and looked Connie up and down. They matched each other in height, but Connie had more of a muscular, athletic body. Trina was all curves, but that didn't matter because she was still as strong as an ox. Connie was faster and more agile, but Trina was not impressed or intimidated.

"Listen, Corny..." Trina started, and then decided against agitating the situation. "Uh...I mean, Connie. I really don't care if you win or not. If you do, more power to you. I'll be the first to congratulate you. But, before I worry about anyone else, I have to take care of home. The Lady Phoenix have things we need to work out among ourselves. Until we get those wrinkles ironed out, we have no time for anything else, especially some other team."

"You're making a big mistake," Mildred said. "Loyalty is good and all, but I think you and Coach Stone are taking it to the extreme?"

Trina shook her head. "Extreme loyalty. Yeah, that sounds about right." She proceeded to lead her teammates out of the gymnasium. "Let's go, y'all."

Beverly didn't follow. "Bye, Trina," she said, waving. "My father had to leave before the game ended, so Coach Stone is gonna drive me home when he's finished talking to Melva."

That was Tabitha's cue. "It's okay, Tree. I'll wait here with her."

Trina hesitated, then against her better judgment, but assuming that T.J. would be back soon, she let Beverly stay around the Roadrunners in Tabitha's care and left with Tracy.

Beverly walked back to the team bench and sat down. As Tabitha followed behind her, she turned and spoke to Mildred. "You know, Coach Negron, as long as me and Beverly are still here, we might as well hear what you have to say."

Mildred and Connie smiled at one another and quickly went over to talk to Tabitha and Beverly. Rayna walked away. She wasn't like her best friend and coach, which is why T.J. always wished she was in his program instead of playing for the Roadrunners. He felt Rayna had morals and integrity, the things her coaches lacked.

A RELATIONSHIP IS BASED ON...

Saturday, July 2, 2005 – 7:26 P.M.

Burton and Carlene were in his living room having a good time dancing to old Motown songs. "I Believe in You and Me" by the Four Tops ended, and Burton took Carlene by the hand and led her to the couch, where they indulged in some freshly brewed Gevalia coffee. Carlene found it hard to stop smiling as she sipped from her cup and stared at the large bouquet of long-stemmed red roses Burton gave to her.

"That was fun," Carlene said with a slight giggle. "I haven't danced in a very long time. Dinner was fantastic, too. Thank you."

"Well, you're quite welcome," Burton pleasantly replied. He looked Carlene over endearingly and admired her simple style. She always wore solid colored blouses, long skirts, patent leather shoes and no make-up. She was the exact opposite of his late wife. His attraction to Carlene was for different reasons. She was a change of pace, slower, quieter, far less flamboyant. He loved each of them for the type of people they were. "It's quite an honor havin' you join me this evenin'."

"Well, I'm glad to be here. I must say, though, I didn't think you were going to call. I was starting to think that you weren't interested in me anymore."

"Nonsense, suga'. I was short on time, is all. Besides, I wanted to make sure I gave you my undivided attention."

Carlene gave Burton an inviting look as she slid herself over closer to him. "Well, Burt, you certainly have my undivided attention, now."

Burton leaned forward and placed his coffee cup back on its coaster. "That's good because there's somethin' very important that I wanna talk to you about."

Carlene noticed the serious expression on Burton's face, so she placed her cup back on the coffee table, as well. Her stomach started tingling as she wondered what was so important, hoping that Burton

RISE OF THE PHOENIX

was going to ask her for a commitment. Maybe she would be lucky enough to skip the courtship, and he would just drop to his knees and pop the question.

"Sure, Burt," she said as she leaned back, crossed her legs under her long white skirt and waited. "What is it?"

Burton sprung up off the couch and walked around in front of the coffee table. He seemed to be tentative about what he wanted to say, which made Carlene really think he wanted to discuss the M word.

"You know, Carlene, Bev's in this program that I got her into, and it's workin' out real well for her. She gets to spend some time away from home doin' somethin' constructive, you know?"

"That sounds nice," Carlene said. "What kind of program is it?"

"It's an academics and athletics program for young gals. You see, this here program hooks up with the schools and help the gals who like to play ball to get an opportunity to go get a college scholarship. It's real nice, and they got some great kids. A chance like this don't happen for a whole lotta kids. Any kid who's lucky enough to participate in somethin' like this should take advantage of it."

Carlene let out a loud sigh. "I know what you're getting at, Burt." She stood up and walked around to the front of the coffee table. "Melinda asked me about playing in some basketball league or something like that, but I'm not ready to loosen my hold on her, yet."

"Loosen your hold? Carlene, the poor child's chokin'."

"She's not choking. She's not ready to do things on her own. The world is rough, and she's young and naïve. If something happened to her, I'd never forgive myself. She's my only child."

"Hell, woman, Bev's my only child, too. You think it's easier on me than it is on you? I'm leapin' the same hurdles you are bein' a single parent and tryin' to raise a teenage daughter. I gotta worry about her education, who she makes friends with, and worst of all, boys. Shoot, you ain't sayin' nothin' that I ain't already read on the side of the barn. The writin's on the wall, Carlene. Yeah, we gotta be careful, but we gotta have faith, too."

"It's not that easy for me, Burt. I'm afraid."

"Woman, you think I ain't afraid? I'm as scared as an ant in the way of a stampede of elephants. But I gotta keep tryin' to find ways to survive. If I just hide under a leaf, that stampede's gonna crush it and me, too. I worry about Bev a whole lot. I worry about what would happen to her if I got so sick and couldn't take care of her; or worse, if my heart gave and I just stopped breathin' all together. She ain't got *nobody* else except me. Do you think I'd put her in a situation where she can get hurt?"

"Stop talking like that. You're forty-one years old and healthy as a horse. Nothing's going to happen to you."

"It might." Burton shrugged his shoulders. "It can. Anything's possible. We gotta be realistic about it. If somethin' does happen to me, I'm makin' sure Bev'ly's doin' all the right things now, so she'll already be on the right track when I'm gone."

"Burt, stoppit!" Carlene pleaded.

"I love Bev, and I want the best for her. The thing is that I love Melinda, too." He walked over, stood in front of Carlene and gently stroked the side of her face. "I want the best for all three of you gals." Carlene looked up into the face of the man she loved as he towered over her, bold, brave and loving. The words he spoke came across as sensitive and caring. He did love her, she concluded. And he loved her daughter too, as much as he did his own.

Burton and Carlene drew together in a passionate embrace and started to kiss when Beverly ran in with Melinda and Tabitha. They quickly broke their kiss and stepped away from each other when they heard the kids barge in.

"Daddy! Daddy!" Beverly shouted, as she ran in waving a piece of paper in the air. "We're goin' on a trip. Can I go, please?"

"Girl, you better stop all that hollarin' in this house and slow down!" Burton ordered, his voice ringing out like a boot camp sergeant. The girls all stopped in their tracks. Beverly was still holding the paper up and smiling widely. "Now, what's this you're talkin' about some kind of trip? A trip where?"

Tabitha quickly stepped out in front of Beverly and extended her hand. "Excuse me, Mr. Smalls." The tone of her voice was uncharacteristically soft and polite. "I'm Tabitha Gleavy, Beverly's teammate with the Lady Phoenix."

RISE OF THE PHOENIX

"Yeah, I remember you," Burton said, shaking her hand with his usual aggressiveness.

"We're going to Washington, D.C. to play in The Tournament of Champions. We're teaming up...excuse me." Tabitha had to stop to free her hand. "We're teaming up with some of the other top players to represent New York, and the coach thinks that Beverly can help out a lot on this trip. New York has never won before, but now that another girl from Long Island, and hopefully Beverly, will be playing, we'll definitely have a shot at the championship."

"Where at in D.C.?" Burton asked. "How much is it gonna cost, and how y'all gettin' there?"

Beverly stepped forward and handed her father the paper she was holding. "The trip is next weekend, Daddy. All the information is on this permission slip."

Burton took the sheet of paper and glanced over it. "Sounds pretty interestin'." The girls got cheerful and began squealing with exuberance. "But I don't know. I gotta look this over again and think about it, but I think it'll be okay."

Beverly grabbed her father and kissed him hard on the side of his face. "Thank you, Daddy!" She turned around to Tabitha, and the two of them began jumping up and down and squealing.

Meanwhile, Melinda plopped down on the sofa and hung her head sadly. Burton noticed her reaction and took Carlene by the arm and led her off to the side.

"Look at poor Melinda sittin' over there on that couch," he whispered as he shoved the permission slip into his pocket. "She's a good girl. She deserves to get out and have some fun. You see what kind of things these gals got goin' for them? Why not give her a chance to enjoy some of that, too?"

Carlene looked over her shoulder back at her daughter. She saw the anguish on Melinda's face and knew that Burton was right, but she still wasn't ready to loosen up. "I'm afraid, Burt," she whispered.

Burton thought for a second, and then his face lit up as an idea popped into his head. "Okay, I think I know a way we all can benefit." He walked over to Beverly and Tabitha who were still celebrating and announced his idea. "Look here, Bev. Tell Coach Stone that I said you can go only if Melinda, her momma and me can go, too."

Melinda looked up with a cheerful, yet surprised expression.

"Oh, no, Daddy, Coach Stone's not—" Beverly attempted to set her father straight, but Tabitha quickly interjected.

"Coach Stone's not gonna be able to accommodate you," Tabitha said, thinking fast. "We're staying in the college dorms, and they're full with the teams that are playing in the tournament."

"That's okay. Melinda, her momma and me can stay at a hotel."

Carlene, surprised by Burton's idea, beckoned him over to her. "Burt, come here, please?"

Burton returned to Carlene, unaware that he'd acted in haste. "What's the matter?"

"I appreciate what you're trying to do, and as much as I'd like to get away for the weekend, I don't think it's a good idea, right now. Melinda's father is coming for her next weekend. But besides that, this is something that I really have to take my time and think about very carefully. I know you mean well, and I do trust you, please believe that. But it's going to take some time."

Burton started to persist, but looked into Carlene's eyes and submitted. He sighed and nodded. "That's okay, I understand. Still, you can at least come see how this Coach Stone fella is running this program and see these gals play. I'll tell you, you'll change your mind for sure."

Carlene agreed with a smile, trying to compromise for the sake of the man she loved. "Sure, we can go to a game when the team gets back from Washington." She walked over to Melinda. "You really want to be a part of this, huh?"

Melinda stood up, excited. "Oh, yes, Mother! I really do!"

Carlene held her arms out for Melinda to come to her. "Come here, baby."

Melinda hugged her mother tightly until Burton came over and separated them.

"Okay, that's enough of that," he said. "This is my time. You gals done come runnin' up in here spoilin' our date."

Beverly quickly apologized. "Oh, sorry, Daddy. Let's go, y'all."

RISE OF THE PHOENIX

"No, no, no!" Burton protested as he took Carlene by the hand. "You gals stay right here. We're goin' for a drive. We'll be back about..." he checked his watch. "It's a quarter to eight now. I'd say about ten-thirty, eleven o'clock. By that time, Bev, you and Melinda should be in bed. Your friend got 'til nine o'clock, then she gotta get on home." He asked Tabitha, "Where you live at anyway, gal? You need a ride, 'cause I can just take you on home now?"

Tabitha's phony smile gleamed, and there was well-acted bashfulness in her voice. "No, sir, I don't live that far. I can walk home. I'll hang out with Bev and Melinda for a little while longer if it's okay."

"Okay, now. Nine o'clock, you hear?"

"Yes, sir."

Burton held out his hand to Carlene, but she stopped to give Beverly and Melinda a hug and kiss before joining him. Then, after Burton and Carlene left hand-in-hand, Tabitha walked across the room behind them with her hands on her hips and let out a big sigh of relief. "That's nice," she said, her voice now low and dry. "Your parents hooking up like this is real nice. I guess if they get married, you two will be sisters. I know you'd like that."

"I never lied to my father before," Beverly said, regretfully as she walked over to where Tabitha was standing.

Tabitha turned around and sized Beverly up before responding. She looked at the tall, slender girl and chuckled as she walked over to the couch. "You didn't lie to him, I did."

"But I didn't speak up, so it's the same thing."

"It's not the same thing." Tabitha sat down next to Melinda and plopped her feet up on the coffee table. "I lied and you didn't. So now, if he finds out and asks you about it, all you have to do is tell him that you didn't know."

"No way," Beverly whined, as she walked around to the front of the couch to face Tabitha. "Then I'd really be lying straight out."

"So what," Tabitha shouted. "What's a little lie once in your life?! You're going to Washington D.C., right?! Be happy! Besides, weren't you just jumping up and down cheering when he said you could go? Where'd this conscience come from all of a sudden?"

"Well, what's going to happen when Coach Stone finds out we played for another team?" Beverly asked.

Tabitha held up her hand and twisted her fingers. "You weren't worried about Coach Stone, either, a few minutes ago, were you?"

"Well, what if he finds out?"

"Fuck Coach Stone!" Tabitha snarled. "We're not playing for him anymore after next weekend. I'm tired of his yelling and all his stupid rules, anyway. As a matter of fact, tomorrow night will be the last time we play with the Lady Phoenix. After that, we're down with the Roadrunners."

Melinda, who remained a quiet observer, flashed her eyes at Beverly who was seemingly submitting to Tabitha's demands. Melinda couldn't believe Beverly was allowing Tabitha to control her like that. She widened her eyes at her best friend again, signaling for her to speak up, but Beverly just turned her head and lowered her eyes.

"Come on," Tabitha said as she got up from the couch and headed out of the living room. "Let's go play some video games."

When Tabitha left the room, Beverly began gathering the dishes Burton and Carlene left on the coffee table. Melinda shook her head and started helping her. Beverly had a confused look on her face. She looked as though she was trying to sort things out, but it also looked like she was scared.

"Bev, I don't like Tabitha," Melinda whispered.

Beverly breathed in and out through her nose and gave Melinda a strange look. "Me either," she said, finally. "But, I need to deal with this my way, and I need your support, if you know what I mean."

"Why, Bev, just because *she* says so? Who is *she*?"

"Some of what she's been telling me is true, Melinda. Coach Stone is cool and all, but if he's not gonna give me a chance to do more things, I gotta get with somebody who will. So, it's not about Tabitha, it's about me. I don't wanna just stay here and get overlooked. How can I be somebody if nobody knows me?"

Melinda shook her head again. "I hope you know what you're doing."

"I do. I just need you to have my back, okay?"

"Always, Sis."

THAT'S MY WORD

Sunday, July 3, 2005 – 12:14 A.M.

When T.J. got home the house was quiet and only the living room night-light was on. He went into the bedroom and found Sheila lying on his side of the bed wearing his pajama top and clutching the pants in her arms. This was one of her ways of letting him know that she wanted him to wake her up when he got home. T.J. smiled as he inhaled the Red Door perfume, and he began to disrobe. He took off his T-shirt and turned to toss it across the chair when he noticed one of his suits and one of Sheila's dresses hanging up outside of the closet. He continued to undress and threw his clothes across the chair before going to take a shower. When he came out of the bathroom, he removed his bathrobe, sat on the side of the bed and began to slowly stroke Sheila's hair while softly calling her name.

"Sheila. Wake up, Mama."

Sheila moaned and smiled at her husband as she opened her eyes. "Hey, baby, you finally made it home. What time is it?"

"It's twelve-thirty."

"Oh, it's late. Is everything okay? Velvet said you were upset after the game."

"Oh, so she already told you all about it, eh?"

"Yes."

"Nah, I'm fine. I hung out with Sam awhile talking about the game, and then I drove home and thought some things over. I realized that it's not as much the girls' fault as it seemed at first. We weren't properly prepared to beat the Roadrunners today, but I'm pretty sure we can beat them next time. We just have to practice more on the new things I implemented and get it working right."

T.J. attempted to take his pajama pants, but Sheila moved them away. He just continued talking. "The team also has to get adjusted to the new girl, Beverly. Baby, you should've been there to see this girl. She's even better than I thought."

Sheila moved closer to T.J. and wrapped her arms around his waist. "Yeah, Velvet told me that, too. But, we can talk about that tomorrow…"

T.J. continued rambling. "I was going to let Nita play her on our fourteen and under team, too, but she'd be a ringer on that level. Shoot, she's probably a ringer on the high school level. You know, I found out that her mother and father were both college All-Americans at TCU. Her mother was Nicky Nolan-Smalls. You remember her? She's the daughter of Chuck Nolan who played for the Pistons, and she played in the ABL before she died. Beverly's father played in the CBA, and *his* father was Archie Smalls who played for the Lakers. I guess the lineage is the reason Beverly has this innate athletic ability to play this game. Beverly Smalls may be the first girl to go straight to the WNBA from high school."

Sheila sat up, put her arms around T.J.'s shoulders and began to plant soft kisses on his face and neck. "Baby, I'm sure she's great, but we can talk about her and the game later? In fact, I promise I'll come to your next game. That way I can see for myself. Now, come to bed and let's, uh…snuggle."

T.J. closed his eyes and tilted his head to receive the affection that was being given to him. A broad smile came across his face as Sheila started to massage his shoulders, and her perfume began to intoxicate him. "Ooh, that feels nice," he delightedly moaned.

"I knew you'd like that," Sheila said, her words a near whisper. "Just relax and let me take care of you, because I'm reeeally going to want you to take care of me."

T.J. turned around, took Sheila in his arms and kissed her lovingly. She melted to her husband's touch as he laid her back and moved gently on top of her. Slowly, he undid the single button that kept the pajama top closed, ran his hand across her chest and moved it down over her stomach. He then moved his head down and planted tiny kisses on her neck, all over her breasts, and every part of her flesh down to her navel. He rubbed her stomach with both hands and kissed it all over, as well.

"That tickles, baby," Sheila said with a giggle. "Umm, but it feels so nice, too. Don't stop."

"I'm glad you like it, sweetheart, but I'm not just kissing you. I'm kissing our baby, too."

Sheila smiled, closed her eyes and stroked her husband's head through his locks as he continued kissing her stomach. "I'm so happy that you're happy."

"Mmm, of course I'm happy, sweetheart. What else would I be?"

"It's just that...well...I know you kept saying that you wanted to wait..."

"Sheila, hush. We discussed this already. No time is a bad time for this. Yes, I did think that waiting would be best, but we'll be fine, and God will provide. So stop all of your worrying, Mrs. Stonewall, and just relax."

"It would be a lot easier for me to relax if you left the baby alone and kissed me. Yes, like that. Go down lower. Lower. Lower. Teehee..."

7:06 A.M.

T.J. and Sheila were awakened by a tapping on their bedroom door and Velvet calling out to them.

"Coach Stone! Sheila! Breakfast is ready!"

T.J. and Sheila looked at each other with puzzled expressions and said, "Breakfast?"

"Come on, y'all," Velvet shouted, tapping on the door again.

"Uh...okay, we'll be right out, Velvet," Sheila responded, shrugging at T.J., who grinned and hopped out of bed.

"What are you waiting for?" he said. "The girl said she cooked breakfast. Let's go."

Sheila laughed and sprung up out of bed, as well. "Wait a second, I'm coming."

T.J. put on a T-shirt and his pajama pants, and Sheila quickly put some panties on and donned his top again. They entered the dining room and both dropped their mouths to the sight of the breakfast buffet.

"Oh, my God," Sheila said. "Look at all this food."

"You really outdid yourself, Velvet," T.J. said. "Look at what we've got here: pancakes, grits, fried green tomatoes, buttermilk biscuits, sausages, hash browns, scrambled eggs, and coffee."

Velvet smiled proudly as she entered the dining room carrying a pitcher of orange juice, wearing a pink cotton camisole and sky blue boy shorts. "The eggs have cheddar cheese in them. I hope that's okay."

T.J. looked at his wife and chuckled. "Is that okay? Shhi—"

Sheila put up her hand to T.J.'s mouth to stifle him. "Hey, hey, hey! Watch that in this house."

"Sorry, Mama."

Velvet placed the pitcher in the middle of the table and thought back to how T.J. scolded Melva in practice for using bad language, almost the same way Sheila did him for the same exact thing. "Uh…well, you guys have a seat," she said. "We don't want the food to start getting cold."

"Yes, you're right," T.J. said, before pulling Sheila's chair out for her to sit, and then hurrying around to do the same for Velvet.

"This is all such a pleasant surprise, Velvet," Sheila told her. "You've really outdone yourself."

"It was my pleasure. I love to cook, and you guys deserve for me to do something special for you."

T.J., who was sitting at the head of the table, held out his hands for Sheila and Velvet, who both took one and reached across to join hands with each other as well. T.J. was about to say grace when Velvet interrupted.

"Coach, can I say the grace, please?"

T.J. smiled and nodded. "Okay, Velvet, be my guest."

They all bowed their heads and closed their eyes as Velvet began to pray. "Lord, we thank You for this meal we're about to receive and all the many blessings You've bestowed upon us. Thank You for the kindness and love that You've filled this home with, and for allowing me the opportunity to share those things while I'm here. In Your Holy Name I pray. Amen."

"Amen," T.J. and Sheila echoed.

"You'd better believe that I'll be sampling a little bit of everything." Sheila reached for the plate of pancakes.

"Well, you're eating for two now, Mama. Your appetite was bound to get bigger."

"What?! You said I'm already getting bigger?!" Sheila shouted.

"No, Mama. I said, 'your appetite was bound to get bigger.'"

"That's not what you said!"

"Yes, it is," T.J. said with a defensive grin. "Tell her, Velvet."

"Is that what he said, Velvet?"

Velvet giggled to herself. She enjoyed watching T.J. humbled by his wife, who seemed to her to be the only person on earth that could come anywhere close to achieving such a thing. She saw her coach as a powerful, authority figure who did everything he could to impart values, responsibility and loyalty into every member of the Lady Phoenix program, even if it meant by using means of intimidation and fear. In that sense, he reminded her of her father. The difference, however, was that none of the women in her father's life were able to humble him the way Sheila did T.J.

"Yes, he's telling the truth," Velvet attested.

Sheila playfully raised a brow and gave her a stern look. "Are you sure you're not just taking up for your coach?"

"C'mon now, you know the sistas gotta stick together," Velvet replied, giving Sheila a hi-five across the table. "A'ight? He's on the level…this time."

T.J. didn't care that they were laughing it up at his expense because he'd discovered that Velvet was indeed a good cook as he ate pancakes and eggs with the look of delight on his face. Sheila took two empty plates and put portions of everything on them. Velvet's smile was ear to ear now, watching her temporary foster family enjoy and appreciate their breakfast.

Sheila was devouring her food, but paused to ask, "Velvet, did you ever get a chance to go to Macy's to get that dress you wanted to wear to church today?"

Velvet swallowed. "Yes. I picked it up before I went to the game yesterday. It's the bomb, too. I meant to show it to you when I got home last night, but I was so tired."

"I should've bought a new dress, too," Sheila said while chewing, "but the one I'm wearing is one of my favorites."

"Did you decide whether or not you're going to join my father's church and sing in the choir?"

"Well, T.J. and I are going to decide together after the service."

T.J. stopped eating and looked up wide-eyed. "Oh, my God."

"Don't tell me you forgot, T.J.," Sheila annoyingly asked.

"Okay, I won't tell you."

Sheila was not amused. "That's not funny. I don't see how you could've forgotten when you knew that Velvet and I were going to rehearsals all week. We discussed this, T.J."

"But, I promised Sam—"

"You promised Sam what?" Sheila's voice got sharp. "What about what you promised me? Is it okay to break your promise to your wife to appease your friend?"

"It's just that I was going to his church because we got these tickets to go see the Yankees play the Mets after the service."

Sheila got really angry, but she took a deep breath and controlled her tone. "You gave me your word, T.J. That's all I care about. My God, it's not enough that I'm always taking the back burner to basketball, but now I have to take a back seat to baseball, too."

T.J. rolled his eyes up and shook his head. "Okay, Mama, I'm sorry. I'll call Sam and tell him I forgot I made a promise to you. I'm sure he'll understand."

"You're concerned about Sam understanding, and just take it for granted that I will." She was waving a butter knife around now. "Well, I don't. I don't understand why I have to constantly be put on the back burner. Why is it that keeping your word to everyone else is more important than keeping your word to me?"

T.J. was taken aback. "I just forgot, Sheila."

"That's the problem, though, T.J.," Sheila said, her voice more stern as her patience began to grow thin. "You shouldn't have forgotten. It seems like it's so easy for you to forget what's important to me, but when it comes to basketball and your friends, you have a photographic memory."

"Honey, I said I'd call Sam—"

"And what, tell him you're sorry?" She slammed the knife down on the table, startling both T.J. and Velvet. "Did you give me the decency of a call last night before you dropped Velvet off, didn't even come upstairs, and then decided not to come in until after midnight?"

T.J. got up, walked around the table, stood behind his wife and began to rub her shoulders. "Okay, Mama, I hear you," he said, soothingly. "Please, calm down. Let's not make a scene in front of Velvet."

Sheila huffed again and looked across the table at Velvet, who kept her head down eating and pretended to be ignoring them. Still, it was easy to notice the expression on Velvet's face, which showed that she was sorry she brought the subject up.

T.J. kissed Sheila gently on the cheek. "Forget Sam. Let's just finish enjoying this great breakfast so we can get ready to go. I can't wait to hear you sing."

Sheila blew out hard through her nose and started putting more food onto her plate. "No, T.J. You've bought the tickets for the baseball game already. I don't want you to waste your money. Besides, you're a man of your word, right? I wouldn't want anyone to think otherwise of you. Go to church with Sam and enjoy the game afterwards. Velvet and I will be fine."

"Are you sure, sweetheart? I—"

"I'm absolutely sure!" Sheila roared, but then quickly regained her composure. "Your suit is hanging up outside of the closet. You should go take your shower and get dressed so you won't be late."

"I have time," T.J. said. "I want to finish my breakfast, first."

Sheila glared up at her husband and spoke through clenched teeth and tightened lips. "T.J., please...just go get dressed."

"But, Mama, I..." T.J. thought about the price he'd have to pay later if he continued to argue, especially after just getting his way, and decided that going to get dressed was best. "I'mma just go on and get ready."

After T.J. left the dining room, Sheila and Velvet continued eating without talking or making eye contact for about five minutes. When Sheila started to reload her plates once again, Velvet knew that she should say something. "Sheila, I'm sorry."

"Hm, sorry for what?" Sheila asked, still piling more food onto her plate.

"It wasn't my intention to cause friction. I just thought everything was squared away."

"Yeah, so did I," Sheila said. "But don't blame yourself. It's not your fault. This is all part of the molding process. A part of a good sculptor's skill is patience."

"Well, I don't think I have sculptor's skills because I don't see myself having that much patience," Velvet said. "From what I can see, women have way too much trouble dealing with men. I've only had one girlfriend, and maybe I'm just lucky, but being with her is nothing like what I see you going through with Coach Stone, or Trina with Daquan, my oldest sister with her husband, my sister-in-law with my brother, and especially my mother with my father. I'll tell you the truth. Whether me and Kim last forever or not, I don't ever see myself being with a man."

Sheila looked up with a half smile. "Hey, don't knock it 'til you try it."

"I don't want to try it," Velvet seriously replied.

Sheila put her fork down and rested her elbows on the table. "So, this lesbian thing is not just a phase you're going through?"

"Nope," Velvet proudly replied. "You saw us on the video tape. Did that look like we were just playing?"

Sheila shook her head. "Girl, please. Just because you fool around with sex, it doesn't mean you're serious or that you know what you're doing."

"Isn't sex the union that makes two people one? Isn't it the link that ties the two together?"

Again, Sheila shook her head. "Wow, you know so much until you know nothing at all."

"I know that I'm never, ever going to be with a man," Velvet told her.

"Well, let me ask you something, Velvet, if you don't mind?"

"What is it?"

"Doesn't the lifestyle you're living contradict your beliefs? I really don't want you to think I'm taking sides, because I'm not, but the Bible does condemn homosexuality."

Velvet rolled her eyes up and let out a loud, moaning sigh.

RISE OF THE PHOENIX

"Look, don't get upset," Sheila said. "I haven't judged you thus far, and I'm not going to start now. I just wondered, being as involved as you are in the church... I mean, you'll only sing gospel, you don't curse, and you don't do anything *else* without putting God first. Why this?"

"I do love the Lord, very much," Velvet testified. "It's just that I've never been attracted to boys, but I was afraid to get with a girl because of my parents."

"I don't understand that, either," Sheila said. "I've never met your father, but you're their daughter, and they love you. I'm sure they'll accept you for who you are, even if it hurts them at first."

"You're only saying that because my mother was putting on that calm front in front of you. If you weren't there, she would've grinded me into powder. Man, I wish my father was here. He's more understanding than my mother."

"Where is he, if you don't mind me asking?"

"He lives in California. He's a promoter, and he has another church there. He and my mom split up because she stopped doing everything he said, which is not heard of because everybody does whatever my daddy says. He's not the kind of man you defy, which is one of the main reasons why, even though she won't admit it, my mom still manages *his* kids."

Velvet put her fork down, pushed back from the table and let out a big sigh while shaking her head. "She's still struggling to come to terms with not being with him," she continued, looking off into space. "He promotes the tour, so she gets to see him for a few weeks every year. She's a hypocrite, though, because she stresses how important it is for us to do whatever daddy says, even though he's not around, because 'he's a good man, and he knows what's right.' What I don't understand is, if he knows so much, why doesn't she listen to him so they can be together and we can be a real family?"

Sheila could see Velvet's eyes start to flood as she continued staring into space, trying to hold her tears back.

"Why don't you talk to your mother about it, Velvet?"

The first stream rolled quickly down Velvet's left cheek and made its way into the corner of her mouth as she spoke. "I have talked to her…several times. But she's just like him. It's her way or the highway. My sister, Harmony, chose the highway, because she said it was the *only* way. My mom turned her back on Harmony because she chose not to sing gospel and do what she and my daddy said. I never, ever wanted to sing anything except gospel, which is why she spoils me the way she does, to make sure I don't change my mind. That's why I call my mom a hypocrite. She's not with my father because she says she can think for herself and make her own decisions, but she's not letting me and Harmony do it."

Sheila watched Velvet sit across from her with tears rolling freely down her face. "What's your father going to say when he finds out about your sexual orientation?"

"I have no idea. I don't think he's going to turn his back on me the way my mom did my sister. My dad supported Harmony even though he disapproved of the choice she made. Hopefully…hopefully, he'll support me, too."

Sheila gave a napkin to Velvet to wipe her tears. "Here, stop crying. We're supposed to be happy this morning. We have a big day ahead of us. We can't go to church to praise the Lord and sing about His goodness after sitting in here sulking and crying. Let's live for the day and cross the bridge of tomorrow when we get to it."

Velvet wiped her face and blew her nose. "You're right, Sheila. I'm going to clean up in here and start getting ready."

Sheila pulled her two plates of food and the plate of biscuits closer to herself, and Velvet chuckled at the gesture as she began clearing the table of everything else.

As Velvet was leaving the dining room, Sheila looked up. "Uh, Velvet, have you read those scriptures your mother gave you?"

Velvet paused and lowered her eyes. "Yes, I have. I haven't memorized them yet, though."

"What were they? I'd like to read them for myself."

"I'll write it down and bring it to you."

Sheila nodded. "Okay."

THIS IS HOME

Sunday, July 3, 2005 – 10:39 A.M.

T.J. and Sam looked dapper in their Sunday's best. T.J. was decked out in his olive green suit with a silk, bone-colored shirt and matching tie set. Sam was in the spirit of the holiday, wearing a blue suit with a red and white striped shirt and red tie with tiny white specks.

They were ushered through the atrium of the Believers in Christ Church to its two hundred seat overflow room because the dual-level, four thousand seat main sanctuary was at its capacity, as it was for every holiday because every member knew that there would be something extra special to look forward to. They were right. The church's drama club put together a very special Independence Day play to perform for the congregation, but that wasn't the only reason people flocked there that day. Velvet and Sheila put on such a strong performance the week before, people couldn't wait to hear them sing again.

"I had no idea this church was so big and nice," T.J. told Sam, looking around in awe at the church's plush décor. "I should've known. Velvet's family does everything big. I'll tell you, though, I heard Velvet singing around the house, and she is indeed something else. The girl is the real deal with major skills. Sheila is an outstanding singer, but Velvet…woo-wee. She's a much better singer than all of her famous siblings."

"Wow, I can't wait to hear her," Sam said, also admiring the surroundings. "You think she's going to pursue her singing career over basketball?"

"I think she wants to try to do both. Nita told me Velvet said she wants to play ball in college and record during the off season."

"Yeah, that's a lot harder than it sounds," Sam said.

"For most people, yes, but Velvet is a unique child. She's always been sort of a taskmaster."

"Yeah, well, she's going to have to be. Those are two very demanding tasks. Is she getting any college looks?"

"She's gotten interest letters from numerous schools," T.J. told his friend, "including Temple, Southern State University and Texas Tech."

"Texas Tech? How'd *they* hear about her?"

"I sent them a tape of her. Nita told me that Velvet is a huge Sheryl Swoopes fan and wants to win an NCAA championship at the same school she did."

"Yeah, she does have a Swoopes-like game," Sam recalled. "Especially the way she stops and shoots on a dime."

"Velvet has a better handle, but I wish she played defense like Sheryl and had her kind of heart and poise. Plus, Velvet needs to bulk up some. She gets pushed around too easily. She's been working out hard, though."

"So, do you think she has a real chance?"

"I think so," T.J. said. "She's talented and smart."

"What about Temple and Southern State?"

"Definitely Temple, they're all over her. I don't know for sure about Southern State, though, because their focus is on Melva, right now."

"Well, now that Velvet, Trina and Melva are all going to be seniors, you're going to have some major rebuilding to do for next summer."

"I don't think I'll have *major* rebuilding to do, Sam. Beverly will most likely be the go-to player and Danisha will replace Melva in the backcourt with Tabitha. Monica will take Velvet's spot, so Trina is the only one I'm going to have trouble replacing. I'm thinking that the two big girls I have on the fourteen-and-under team can share that responsibility, though. Nita has been doing such a great job with that team."

"Well, tell her to keep an eye on her kids," Sam cautioned. "You know the Roadrunners are going to have a fourteen-and-under team for next summer, right?"

T.J.'s eyes flashed, and the bass in his voice got deeper. "Millie better stay far away from our kids. She can pull that mess with other people, but she knows what consequences she'll have to pay for messing with us. Nita knows the deal about Millie. She knows how to handle her."

RISE OF THE PHOENIX

Their conversation was cut short as parishioners stood and applauded when Velvet was introduced. They looked up at the screen and watched as the four backup singers came out and took their places in front of the band, and then Velvet came out onto the sixty-foot pulpit to a roaring reception, wearing a pink cowl-neck dress with a flower pin on the left strap and pink jeweled sandals.

Sam looked at T.J. with a raised brow. "Wow, she really is popular."

"I'm telling you, Sam, she's got skills."

"She looks great, too, doesn't she?"

"She *always* looks good."

"Yeah, but she looks like a real star up there."

Velvet looked down and saw Kimberly sitting in her usual place in the third row on the left hand side, dressed casual in a lemon-colored babydoll halter dress, and waved to her. She then waved and bowed at the congregation until they settled and took their seats. Bashfully smiling, she greeted them in a humble tone. "Thank you, very much. You are all too kind. God is surely good, don't you all agree?"

Amens and cheers filled the church.

"Well, He's been especially good in blessing me this summer," Velvet continued. "One of my many blessings came in the form of two very special people, my summer league basketball coach and his wife, Sheila. I had the pleasure of having Sheila join me here for a song last week. Do you remember that? Wasn't she great?" The congregation once again responded with cheers and applause. "Well, she's back again, and for those of you who missed her last week, you're in for a treat. Please, welcome Mrs. Sheila Stonewall."

T.J.'s eyes widened at the sight of the love of his life as she walked onto the stage with her long legs extending down from her black buckle-strap dress into her black stiletto dress sandals and her hair lying flat down to her shoulders. "Wow, look at my beautiful wife."

"She does look fantastic," Sam noted. "You sure are a lucky man."

T.J. nodded, knowing that Sam's comment was an understatement. As Sheila took her place next to Velvet, the screen showed a close-up of her face. T.J. looked at her eyes and thought she looked uneasy. He hoped she was not nervous or stressed out and said a quick prayer for her.

Sheila didn't address the congregation. She just smiled slightly and waved. The band started playing, and T.J. held his breath as she started the song.

Sheila:
Oh, Lord
I just want to thank You today
For how You came in and washed my sins away
I'm willing to do
All You want me to
And I know my life, my life, my life
Means nothing without You
Velvet:
Oh, Lord
I'll be what You want me to be
Let Your will be done, Lord, and use me
You are my strength, Lord
You're my comfort, too
And I know my life, my life, my life
Means nothing without You
Sheila:
When my way seems lost
And I can't see clear
Velvet:
You open my eyes
Lord, Lord, I know You're there
Sheila:
You are my strength, Lord
You're my comfort, too
Velvet:
And I know my life
Sheila:
And I know my life
Together:

RISE OF THE PHOENIX

And I know my life, my life, my life
Means nothing without you

The standing ovation began well before the song ended, as worshipers were up cheering and singing praise, filled with the Holy Ghost, inspired by the stimulation of Velvet's and Sheila's singing.

T.J. stood, applauding and shaking his head in amazement. He was also moved by the lyrics of the song, feeling even though he made the effort to keep his word by coming to hear her sing, he needed to do more, much more to get his priorities in order. He closed his eyes and said another prayer. When he opened them, he saw Sam staring at him.

"There are things I have to take care of," T.J. told his best friend. "First, at home, and then with the Lady Phoenix."

Sam nodded.

8:43 P.M.
When T.J. got home from the baseball game with Sam, Sheila was in the shower. He came into the bedroom and placed her favorites on her pillow, a bag of brownies from the Fat Witch and a bouquet of tulips with a card that read:

I wouldn't have missed you singing for the world. You were as beautiful and fantastic as always. I look forward to joining with you. I love you,
T.J.

He then tapped on the bathroom door and proceeded inside without waiting for an answer. Steam clouds lingered high and the mirrors on the medicine cabinet and the space saver were fogged up. The white porcelain of the sink, tub and toilet, along with the powder blue ceramic tiles that lined the walls, all appeared to be perspiring. T.J. could see Sheila's silhouette through the shower curtain.

"It sure is steamy in here, Mama," he said. "You must've been in there a long time. I need a shower, too. You mind if I join you?"

Sheila didn't respond. She pulled the shower curtain back and reached out for her towel hanging on the rack. T.J. snatched the towel and opened it up for her. Without showing any expression, Sheila stepped out into the towel, taking it from T.J.'s hands and wrapping herself in it.

"I keep telling you the tub is too slippery," she said. "You said you were going to bring home a rubber mat or some of those little sticky things." She stepped into her slippers and made haste exiting.

T.J. reached in the shower and turned the water off. He left the bathroom and walked past Sheila sitting at her bedroom vanity applying moisturizer on herself. He attempted to talk to her again, but when she wouldn't even make eye contact, he decided to leave well enough alone and give her time to cool off.

"Your dinner is in the microwave," Sheila said, just before he left the room.

"Thank you," T.J. said on his way out.

He stopped in the living room on his way to the kitchen. He turned on the television to the Sci-Fi channel so he could watch *The Twilight Zone* marathon.

The doorbell rang and T.J. opened it to let Velvet in. She and some of the other Lady Phoenix members had gone shopping to buy a birthday present for Kimberly. T.J. shook his head at the aspiring diva as she strolled into the house like she was modeling the lavender, floral-designed Tommy Hilfiger sundress she was wearing.

Velvet flashed a huge smile and peeked at T.J. over her 14-karat, gold-framed Gucci specks as she came inside carrying bags in both hands. "Hey, Coach, what's up?"

"Hi, Velvet. What're all these bags? You went shopping for Kim's birthday or for the whole team?"

"Actually, I do have Kim's presents from Melva, Danisha, Keisha, and Trina, too. Well, we chipped in to buy her a present from Trina."

T.J. closed the door and locked it. "That was nice of you all. What'd you get her?"

"Come on, I'll show you." Velvet let out a tiny squeal of excitement as she sat on the couch and began searching through her bags.

"Wait, Velvet," T.J. said, taking a seat in his favorite recliner. "Let's talk for a minute."

"What do you want to talk about, Coach?" Velvet innocently asked.

"Well, how are you? Are you okay?"

RISE OF THE PHOENIX

Velvet, not sure of what he meant, raised her head and gave T.J. a quizzical look. "Yeah, I'm fine. Why?"

"It's just that we haven't really had a chance to talk one-on-one since you've been here. You called to talk to me about your *problem* that day, but we never got a chance to discuss it."

"You say my 'problem' like I have a disease or something."

"No, no, no, I didn't mean it like that," T.J. said, waving both hands. "In fact...we don't even have to talk about that at all. I really want to find out about you. You've been a part of this program for three years, and I don't even know why you're here. I don't know why you ever chose to play basketball, or why you love it—if indeed you do. I don't know what your favorite subject in school is or what motivates you to be the A student that you are. I know this stuff about everybody else in our program, but not you. I never sat you down just to talk, and, before the whole episode with you and your mom, you never really came to me for anything."

"Not to sound cocky or stuck up, but up until now, I've just never needed anything. All I've ever wanted, besides the worldly things that God has blessed me with, was a complete, functional family. But no one can have everything, right?"

"Girl, don't you know that dysfunctional families are in these days," T.J. quipped. "Shoot, if your family is dysfunctional, you're in style."

Velvet shyly chuckled. "Oh, Coach, you're so silly."

T.J. laughed. "I know. Seriously speaking, though, what makes you tick?"

Velvet tilted her head and looked up into space as she thought to herself. "Well, of course basketball," she said, finally. "I love Sheryl Swoopes, everybody knows that already. Ever since I saw the WNBA championship series in ninety-nine, I wanted to be just like her. That series was the bomb—Theresa Weatherspoon hitting that shot in game two—and Sheryl was doing her thang. Everybody was jocking Cynthia Cooper, but I liked Sheryl's style. I've been her biggest fan ever since."

"I hear you." T.J. smiled. "Is that when you started playing basketball."

"Yes. I've always liked to watch basketball. I was always a Sprewell fan, but when I saw women doing work like that, I wanted in."

"Yeah, the league has had an impact like that on lots of young girls, which is good."

"Singing is still my first love, though," Velvet noted. "I used to rehearse with Harmony and sing back-up for Melody and Barry. Ninety-nine was a good year for all of us. All of my siblings dropped their first album that year. Did you know that Melody and Barry's first single was a remake of one of their mother's biggest hits? Did you know that my mother was one of their mother's backup singers?"

"No, I didn't know that," T.J. answered in surprise.

"Yeah, well, that's another soap opera. You can read about it in my book."

T.J. laughed again. "You are something else, Velvet."

"For real," she insisted. "After I finish college and record my first CD—not necessarily in that order—I'm going to write a book about my life. Shoot, I already have enough material for it to be a bestseller. By then, it'll probably earn me every literary award out there."

"Well, when you do become a best selling author with a top selling gospel CD, who plays in the WNBA, don't forget us little people back here in Brooklyn."

"Coach, are you patronizing me?"

"No, not at all," T.J. assured her. "I really meant what I said. I believe you are the type of person who can accomplish all of that. You have the will, the drive, and the determination to do whatever you put your mind to, especially if it's in your heart."

"You really, honesty think I have what it takes to do all of those things?"

"I think you might have enough potential to possibly make the WNBA one day if you get stronger and continue to work on your game. As far as your singing is concerned, that voice you have is sure to make you famous."

"Humph, you've only heard me practicing around the house," Velvet said. "You've got to come hear me in church."

"I did hear you in church," T.J. told her. "Mr. Pernell and I came to see you and Sheila at your father's church today. There were so many people there we were forced to watch you on the screen in the overflow room."

Velvet's smile opened up her face. "Are you serious? Y'all were there?"

"Yes, we were there. I wouldn't have missed that for the world. You both sounded so good. I always tell Sheila that she should pursue a singing career, but she says it's not in her."

"Yeah, I told her the same thing, and she gave me the same answer."

"You are doing the right thing, though. You can play basketball well, and you'll get by doing that, but singing is your calling. When your parents named you Velvet, they must've known how smooth your voice was going to be."

Velvet closed her eyes, inhaled deeply, and then exhaled slow. She opened her eyes again and spoke softly. "I got two full scholarship offers already, but I'm not going to take either of them," she said.

"What?!" T.J. shouted.

"They're performing arts scholarships," Velvet explained, "one at Stanford and the other at Oral Roberts University. If I would've accepted either of them, I wouldn't be able to play ball. The demand would be too great."

"But, Velvet, they're full scholarships. You've already gotten what all your Lady Phoenix teammates are striving for."

"They're all striving for *basketball* scholarships, Coach Stone, which is what I want, too. I can always get a recording deal, that's not a problem."

"Yes, perhaps a recording deal, but not a free education."

"Coach, please, I know what I'm doing. I want a basketball scholarship more than anything. I know I can get a scholarship for singing. I have to do this to prove to myself the very thing you just said about me, that I can accomplish whatever I put my mind to. You did mean that, didn't you?"

"Of course," T.J. said. "Do your thing, then. Understand, though, that I'm just on the front line. When your parents find out…" When Velvet's face dropped and she lowered her eyes, T.J. knew it was time to back off. "Anyway, I'mma go get my dinner. You hungry?"

Velvet stood up and gathered her bags. "No, I ate when we were out."

"Oh, yeah, let me see what you all bought."

Velvet sat back down and reopened the bags. "You like this?" she asked him, holding up a pair of pink, silk Baby Phat pajamas. "This is from Danisha."

T.J. smiled. "That's very nice."

Velvet continued showing the gifts: a bottle of Channel No. 5 perfume from Keisha, a Bulova watch from Melva, and a personalized New York Liberty jersey from Trina.

"Those are some pretty extravagant gifts from a bunch of kids with no jobs," T.J. commented. "I know your parents just sent you a nice piece of change. What did you do, give out a bunch of loans?"

"No, let me tell you how we did it," Velvet said, enthusiastically. "We caught all of the Fourth of July sales. Melva's mother bought a watch for herself and for Melva and got one for free. We got the perfume from a store on Twenty-Eighth Street in the wholesale district. The pajamas were on sale in Century 21, and like I said, we all chipped in to help Trina get her the jersey."

T.J. gave his nod of approval. "It's good to know that you are smart shoppers."

"No doubt. I know how to work things out for my gir—"

"Well, I'm going to go eat dinner," T.J. said after an awkward silence. "We'll talk some more later."

"Okay, Coach."

When T.J. went into the kitchen, Velvet looked up and saw Sheila, who had been a silent, unnoticed observer, standing across the room. Sheila nodded her head toward the kitchen where T.J. was. Velvet knew what that meant, and she thought about the advice Sheila gave her after church. Then, she swallowed hard, closed her eyes and said a short, quiet prayer.

"Coach?" Velvet called out.

"Yes, Velvet?" T.J. answered from the kitchen.

"Coach…uh…since we don't have anything with the Lady Phoenix tomorrow night and I don't have to get up early Tuesday morning, I was thinking about going out tomorrow night...with Kim."

T.J. stepped from the kitchen and looked into the living room at Velvet. He opened his mouth to respond but all that came out was a breath.

"We...uh...I want to take her out for her birthday," Velvet continued. "We're going to see the play *Wicked,* and then to dinner. I'm just saying...you know...I know you said you want me in by eleven, but...you know I might, uh, be getting in a little later than that. More like around one or two o'clock."

T.J. did notice the one bag Velvet didn't pull anything out of was from Victoria's Secret. He wondered if its contents were for herself or for Kimberly, and then decided that it didn't matter if they planned on seeing each other in it. He hesitated to agree, not wanting to be a part of them engaging in any intimate adult activities. Then, he thought about what Sheila said about them sneaking around and gave a half-hearted nod.

"Okay," he replied. "I mean, yeah, sure. You said one o'clock, right?"

"Maybe two," Velvet said quickly. "It shouldn't be any later than that. Of course I'd call if something came up. I mean...you know...if something happened."

"Dinner and a play, right?" T.J. asked, wagging his finger.

"Yes, coach."

"And you talked to Sheila about this already?"

"Yes."

"And she said it was okay?"

"Yes."

"Okay, but the deal is one o'clock, and you have to make sure you call before you go into the theater, before you go into the restaurant, and if you make any detours."

"Okay, I will."

T.J. stepped into the kitchen and took a set of keys from the cabinet above the sink. "Come here, take these," he said. "Ain't nobody gettin' up in the middle of the night to let you in. You just...hold on to them while you're staying here, okay?"

Velvet smiled widely and hurried to the kitchen entrance. "Thank you, Coach." She took the keys, gave T.J. a peck on the cheek and hurried to her room. She looked over at Sheila standing out of T.J.'s view and raised her thumb.

T.J. was about to return to the kitchen when he heard a voice.

"Psst, I'm talking to you, Mister."

He stepped into the living room entrance to see Sheila standing on the other side near their bedroom wearing his pajama top and holding the bouquet of flowers in her arms.

"So you were there, huh?" Sheila asked. "Why didn't you tell me?"

"How long were you standing there, Mama?"

"Long enough to know that you're a great mentor, you're going to be a great father, and to remember how much I love you."

"But you were mad at me," T.J. pouted.

"Well, I'm not mad at you anymore," Sheila cooed. "I'm going to put these flowers away and get my brownies. Get your food and meet me in front of the TV."

"Okay, Mama." T.J. smiled and felt relieved to have his wife talking to him that way again.

Later, after Velvet had changed into her pajamas, she came back into the living room and laid on the floor in front of the loveseat where T.J. and Sheila were snuggled up together watching television.

ANYTHING FOR LOVE

Tuesday, July 5, 2005 – 4:30 P.M.

After fifteen minutes of staring at the computer while moving the cursor back and forth and up and down the screen, Terry pulled a card from the Rolodex and dialed the number.

"Good afternoon. Sam Pernell speaking."

"Mr. Pernell, my name is Terry Gonzalez," said a low-pitched, easy flowing voice with a Spanish accent. "I'm a friend of Mildred Negron from the Roadrunners team."

Sam breathed in through his nose and switched the telephone receiver from his right ear to the left. "What can I do for you?" he asked.

"Actually, this is about what we can do for each other," Terry said.

"Oh, is that a fact?" Sam questioned, doubtfully.

"It is, indeed," Terry told him. "I know that you have associates who want to see the demise of the Roadrunners, or better yet, of Millie's coaching career. Well, I have news that may surprise you, Mr. Pernell, so do I…sort of."

"Sort of, huh?" Sam asked with a grin. "I don't know who told you that I wanted to see the Roadrunners or Millie Negron out of the loop, but whoever it was, they led you astray."

"So, you're saying you don't?"

"I'm the coordinator of the New Attitude league," Sam stated. "I have no personal relationships with any of the teams."

Terry chuckled. "I doubt that, very much. Please don't insult my intelligence, Mr. Pernell. I didn't make this call without knowing some intricate facts about my cause."

"And what exactly is your cause."

"I told you, I want to put an end to Millie's involvement with the Roadrunners, but more importantly, with Charles Greene."

"Oh, Charles Greene too, eh?"

"Yes, Mr. Pernell, especially Charles Greene."

"Look, this is ridiculous," Sam asserted. "I'm not the person you think I am…"

"Oh, but you are," Terry insisted. "You've been best friends with Timothy Stonewall for a long time. I happen to know that Mr. Stonewall has quite a vendetta for Mr. Greene and for my fiancée."

"Your fiancée?" Sam shockingly asked.

"Yes, Millie is my fiancée—or at least she was—which is part of the reason I need your help, to get her back."

Sam fought to refrain from laughing aloud. "A lovers' quarrel? That's what this is all about? Now I *know* you've got the wrong person."

"Mr. Pernell, please, just here me out. If what I say doesn't appeal to you, then I won't ever bother you again." Terry paused a moment before proceeding. "Millie and I had plans to go to Canada to celebrate our anniversary last weekend, but she left me a little over a week ago, walked out because Charles Greene has got her mind all twisted. He's ruining her, corrupting her, turning her into something she never was. Now she's trying to do those same things to other people, including me. I used to be able to talk to her, but it's like she's possessed now. I couldn't understand why she was acting this way, but now I do. I just got a hold of something that explained the whole thing to me."

"And what's that?" Sam asked.

"I'd rather show you than tell you over the telephone."

Sam blew out hard. "I'm sorry, but I can't take part in any of this."

"Please," Terry begged. "You have a wife, Mr. Pernell, don't you?"

"Yes, but…"

"How would you feel if the woman you loved and devoted your life to just up and left because you were trying to save her from making some huge mistakes?"

"I wouldn't be very happy," Sam replied.

"I know you wouldn't," Terry said. "I need you, Mr. Pernell."

Sam pondered a brief moment. "Like I said before, you've got the wrong person. If you know that T.J. Stonewall has this so-called vendetta against your fiancée, then it's him you should be calling, not me."

RISE OF THE PHOENIX

"Well, he is the person I really need," Terry admitted. "But because he dislikes Millie so much, he may not do what I want if he knew what I now know."

"And what is it that you want him to do?"

"To use his resources to help me to expose Charles Greene without getting Millie into trouble," Terry said bluntly.

"Ha!" Sam blurted out, unable to contain himself. "Good luck with that."

"We can do it, Mr. Pernell," Terry encouraged.

"We?" Sam asked.

"Yes, we. Mr. Stonewall would never listen to me, but he would listen to you. If your friendship is as tight as I suspect—and I know that it is—then I made the right call."

"I'm sorry to have to burst your bubble, but your call was in vain," Sam said. "I'm not in a position to get involved with this. I'm sorry."

After Sam hung up the telephone, Terry sat and sulked in disappointment before composing an email to Mildred that read:

Dear Millie,

We should have been celebrating our fourth anniversary today. In the eight days since you left me, I've been thinking a lot. Mostly about us, but a lot about our last conversation, which is why I'm writing this letter to you. I still can't believe that you walked out on me because I chose to remain steadfast with my integrity. It tells me how little respect you have for me. I know you don't see it that way, or maybe you don't want to, but I wish you did. I love you, miss you, and I am absolutely miserable without you near me. I've never felt so strongly for any other woman I've been with in my life. I'm in so much pain because this all seems so very, very crazy to me.

When we first got together, all you ever talked about was finding your niche. You wanted something of your own, something that would make a difference. You said you wanted to help youth with potential to achieve their goals. I supported that and helped you as much as I could. Now, you're telling me that what I did wasn't enough because of one thing I won't do. What have you become? What has Charles done to you?

I know you think what you want to do is harmless and insignificant, but it isn't. I believe that one dishonest action begets another, thus creating a line that starts with lies and ends with people hurt. Usually, the people hurt the most are the loved ones of whomever the culprits are. I don't want to be the one hurt.

Please, think about this. Think about all I've done to help you. Think about all we've shared together. Think about how good things were before you became so obsessed with being the best. I know how much you loved the volleyball team you played on, and how hurt you were when they started having financial problems and losing all the time. You're not going to make up for those things by doing what's wrong. You wanted to be involved with something successful that was the result of your labor. But if you cheat, Millie, you haven't labored.

Please, call me so we can talk. At least hear me out. I know if you just took the time to listen, you'd see that leaving was a mistake. I still want us to get married. I can't imagine life with anyone else. I want you to come home and be with me, where you belong. I'm laboring so that you and I can be successful.

With Eternal Love,
Terry

THOSE WHO CONTRIVE

Tuesday, July 5, 2005 – 5:51 P.M.

Charles Greene entered the YMCA, looked around for Mildred and unconsciously walked past the front desk.

"Excuse me, sir. I need your membership card."

Charles looked back and saw the receptionist, a young light-skinned woman in her early twenties with a beaming smile and long box braids, beckoning him over while taking cards from two members standing in front of the desk. He didn't notice any of them when he walked in.

"Oh, I'm sorry." He walked back to the desk.

The receptionist quickly swiped the two members' cards on her computer, and then held out her hand, assuming Charles had a card as well.

"No, I'm not a member here," Charles told her. "I'm just looking for someone."

"Oh, I see," the receptionist said. "Well, who is it? Perhaps I can help."

"Mildred Negron. She's a tall, Hispanic woman with a long ponytail and—"

"Yes, I know Ms. Negron. She's in the cardiovascular center."

"Well, if you don't mind, I need to see her for just a minute."

"Of course," the woman said, still smiling. "I just need to see some identification, please."

Charles showed his driver's license and signed the visitor's book.

"Just walk straight and go to your left," the pleasant young woman told him. "The cardio center is right past the glass doors."

"Thank you, very much," Charles said, and then walked off, following her directions. He paused and raised a brow when he saw Mildred on the treadmill dressed in pink Nike low-rise workout shorts, a sleeveless seamless sport top and pink and white Nike Shox.

Mildred looked up and smiled when she saw Charles coming toward her. "Hey, Charles, when did you get back? How was your trip?"

"I got back early this morning," Charles said with his eyes darting all over her body as she continued to jog. "Hawaii is fantastic. I'm seriously thinking about moving there when I retire. I may even go back there for another week before school starts. Would you like to come with me? I would love to get you in a bikini on the beach."

Mildred rolled her eyes up. "No, thanks. I'll pass."

"Okay, well, maybe we can go for a night out on the town when we get to the National Tournament."

"We?" Mildred asked, surprised. "What do you mean 'we?' I didn't know that you were coming, too."

"Since it's being held in New Orleans and the two schools ranked higher than us in the national polls are from that area, I figured I'd go meet those coaches and talk to them face to face. I want them to come to New York to participate in a tournament at St. Joseph's during the Christmas holiday."

"I didn't know St. Joseph's was hosting a tournament."

"Yeah, we're doing it together. Jefferson's gym is too small to host an event of this magnitude, so I asked them to have it there."

Mildred tilted her head. "Wow. I never would've guessed the people at St. Joe's would want to do any type of collaboration with you."

"Well, again, that's why I'm going to The Nationals," Charles said. "I sort of promised St. Joe's those two teams from Louisiana would participate. The trouble is that I haven't been able to talk to either of those coaches. We've just been playing phone tag, and nothing's coming out of that."

"I wish you would've told me that you were working on this, Charles. I would've gotten Union Prep from Virginia to come."

Charles got excited. "Really? Is it too late?"

"I don't know. They were talking about going to that tournament in Las Vegas in December."

"To hell with Vegas. Why would they want to go to the desert when they can come to the Big Apple for the biggest eight-team shootout ever? If I get the two schools from Louisiana, we'll have eight of the top ten-

RISE OF THE PHOENIX

ranked high school teams in the country in one tournament. I'm sure we'll be able to beat any of them, especially if we get Stacey Conyers in."

"Oh, yeah," Mildred recalled. "That's a done deal. Stacey will definitely be attending Jefferson in September, *and* she's eligible to play."

"Yes!" Charles shouted, drawing looks and grunts from other members.

"Control yourself, please," Mildred scolded.

"Sorry," Charles said in a hushed tone. "You are the best, Millie. How'd you do it?"

"As it turns out, Stacey has an aunt that lives in Brooklyn."

"So, she'll be staying with her aunt to go to school?" Charles asked.

Mildred winked at him. "Not really, but that's between us."

"Damn, Millie. Won't it be quite a hike for her coming from Long Island?"

"She lives in Lawrence, Charles. She has a fifteen-minute bus ride into Far Rockaway where she'll take the A-train straight to school. The whole commute is only about an hour and forty minutes each way. All you have to do is see to it that she doesn't get any classes too early."

"Well, my P.E. basketball class is first period, so that won't be much of a problem in her first semester. What did it take to work out this deal?"

"Exactly what we discussed," Mildred said.

"Whew, we got off easy," Charles said, relieved.

"You bet your ass, we did. It was nothing like what we had to do for the Kings in order to get Connie. They stuck it to us hard."

"Don't worry." Charles smiled. "We'll get back double what we put out for the Conyers deal just for making the finals at the Nationals. Now that we have Stacey, we won't need to make a deal like we did for the Kings again."

"Don't speak too soon, we may have to. Did you hear that St. Joseph's got a new player, too?"

Charles' expression changed. "No. Who'd they get?"

"Tabitha Gleavy," Mildred told him.

"Tabitha Gleavy? Oh, I'm sure T.J. is crazy about that."

"The fact is that I hadn't heard anything from anyone about his opinion of it. You know how T.J. likes to make everything into a big production, but he hasn't said a word as far as I know."

Charles stroked his clean-shaven chin. "Getting Gleavy was a good move by them, I have to admit. It gives them another pure shooter and makes it difficult for anyone to play zones against them. She handles the ball pretty well, too, which helps them break presses. Yes, it's a good move."

"Well, I made the same good move because she's going to be playing with us in Washington, D.C.," Mildred bragged.

Charles took a step back and gave Mildred a disbelieving stare. Then, he smirked and grinned. "Yeah right, you're pulling my leg."

"No, I'm not. She told me she wants the chance to get away so that she can be seen, and she doesn't like playing with the Lady Phoenix, anyway."

"So she can be seen, eh?"

"Yeah. I know she thinks she's better than she is…"

"Well, she did average thirty points a game last season," Charles noted.

"Yes, she did. But she's still just second best at that position on my team. I still think that Erin is better, but we'll see. Now, she did get this other girl from her team to come, too. I don't know where T.J. got this girl from, but she is the real deal."

Charles laughed. "Wow, you're taking two of T.J.'s kids? I don't think you're going to be on his Christmas card list this year. What do you think he's going to say about this?"

"It doesn't matter," Mildred said, seemingly agitated as she raised the incline and picked up speed on the treadmill. "T.J. can say whatever he wants. He can't kick my ass, so I really don't care."

Charles put up his hands defensively. "Okay, I hear you."

"I'm telling you, Charles, this new girl is the next great player to come out of New York City," Mildred reiterated. "Maybe even the greatest."

"Who is she? Where did she come from?"

"Her name is Beverly Smalls. She moved here from Mississippi last year. She's going to be a freshman at Stuyvesant. This girl is only fourteen, and I'd bet my last dollar that she's good enough to play at any college in the country, right now."

RISE OF THE PHOENIX

Now it was Charles who seemed agitated. "I don't understand, Millie. These girls are going to be playing with you, but they're going to all these other schools. One's a transfer and the other's a freshman, yet they're both going elsewhere."

Mildred held up her hand like a traffic cop. "Slow down, Charles. Don't get your pressure up. I found out about Tabitha going to St. Joseph's *because* I was talking to her about transferring to Jefferson. She said she chose St. Joseph's because you have too many players playing the same position as she does."

"They're the exact same players she'll be playing with on your team."

"Them, and if this Beverly girl comes, her too. The truth is that this Beverly kid can play any position. She almost beat us by herself the other day when we played the Lady Phoenix. For whatever reason, they froze her out in the fourth quarter, and we made a run to win."

Charles folded his arms and started tapping his foot. "Well, lucky you. You win the game *and* get the players. What about me? What do I get?"

Mildred stopped the treadmill, picked up her towel and started wiping the sweat off her neck and shoulders. "What are you talking about, Charles? You know how hard I had to work and what I had to do, besides the obvious, to get you Stacey Conyers? And I did it without any help from Terry. You didn't even thank me for that, yet."

Charles stepped closer to Mildred and got right in her face. "Thank you? You forgot about all I've done to keep your program going? You wouldn't even have a program anymore if it weren't for me. You've been thanked enough, dammit. I saw to it that you got what it takes to draw the players that'll make sure nobody around here could beat you. Get off your ass and see to it that nobody has a chance of beating me, either. If this girl, Beverly, is as good as you say, I want her at Jefferson."

Unfazed by Charles' aggressiveness, Mildred looked down at him and said, "Well, start gathering your resources together then, Charles. Getting this girl may require a *King*-sized deal."

Charles backed off. "She's really that good?"

"I have a DVD of our game against the Lady Phoenix in my bag in the locker room. If you can wait about twenty minutes until I finish my workout, I'll let you hold it."

7:32 P.M.

Mildred took the number one train home, uptown to 181st Street in the Latino dominated community of Washington Heights. She ran up to the top of the four-story walk-up, dropped her bag by the door and began to disrobe, leaving a trail of her gym bag, sneakers, socks, and workout clothes through the living room and kitchen of her moderately furnished railroad apartment. She went into the bathroom and filled the bathtub with hot water and Epsom Salt, slowly dipped herself in, rested her head back, and closed her eyes. Just as she began to clear her mind of anything relating to work or basketball, her telephone rang. She slowly opened her eyes and reached over to her bathroom vanity to pick up the receiver.

"Hello?" she answered, annoyed.

"Millie, it's me, Charles."

"*¿Qué quieres ahora, tu pequeña comadreja?*"

"I don't know what you said, but it sounds like I caught you at a bad time. Don't worry I'll make this quick."

"What is it, Charles?"

"I was watching this DVD. You were right. This girl Beverly is the real deal."

"I told you that."

"I want to start working on trying to get her into my school as soon as possible."

"Charles, I told you that I'd work on it."

"Your working on it is not good enough," Charles snapped. "I'm still going to need your help, but I want to talk to her parents myself. This kid needs a double-team."

Wanting to get him off the phone, Mildred said, "That's fine with me. I'll give you the number, but you're gonna have to wait. I'm taking my bath right now."

Charles started grinning and changed his tone. "That's a lovely vision."

"Goodbye, Charles." Mildred hung up the telephone and went back to soaking. She rested her head back, closed her eyes and let her fingers massage her muscles under the warm water. With a lonesome sigh, she thought about Terry, whom she was desperately trying not to miss. She

121

RISE OF THE PHOENIX

explored within herself, trying to fill an emptiness that no one except her former fiancé was capable of. She was satisfied with herself for the moment, but she yearned for more.

8:34 P.M.

Mildred had a taste for something sweet, so she put on a T-shirt, shorts and sandals and went to one of the many New York City's all-night fruit stands, where she bought some green apples and bananas. When she returned to her building, there was a surprise awaiting her.

"What are you doing here, Terry? How'd you find me?"

"C'mon, Millie, you know it's not hard for me to find people." Terry smiled.

"I see. So, it's okay to use your connections at your agency to stalk me, but not to do what I ask you?"

"*No empieces, Millie.* Please, can't we just move on from that? I came to get you back. I don't want to be without you."

"It would've been so easy for you to just pull a few strings," Mildred snapped. "It was just a measly little hook up and a few dollars. People do it all the time."

"Not this person, Millie." Terry began walking toward her. "Honesty and integrity are things I hold sacred, and so should you. Didn't you get the email I sent you this morning?"

"Yeah, I got it. So what! Since you're so damn—" Mildred's indignation was halted as a woman and small boy approached. She and Terry stepped aside and let them pass to enter the building. Mildred looked down the deserted, dimly-lit street, and then back at Terry. He was dressed in a red muscle shirt, gray sweat pants and red and silver running shoes. He was staring at her. The look of love in his dark, glassy eyes tugged at her heart, but only for a moment. When the woman and child disappeared into the building, Mildred cut her eyes away from him and went on with what she was about to say. "I still say that since you're so righteous, you should've wanted to help a family in need. That kid's mother needed a job and a place to live."

"She already has a job and a place to live. You just want her to move to the city so her daughter can play for your team."

"This is not about Stacey playing for the Roadrunners," Mildred said sternly. "She can come back and forth by herself in the summer. What we needed was for her to live here in the city so she can go to school at Thomas Jefferson."

"What's wrong with the school she's going to now?" Terry asked, innocently.

"She'll be a much bigger star and get a lot more looks playing at Jefferson instead of at Lawrence High School. What have they ever won?"

Waving it off dismissively, Terry said, "I don't know. I don't keep up with that stuff."

"But that's just it, Terry. You should've. If you supported me one hundred percent, you would know everything there is about what I do."

"About what you do, Millie?" Terry asked with raised brows. "You send and receive information about trades and securities at an investment bank, *that's* what you do."

"That's what I do from nine to five, Terry. Don't be a smart ass. You know I'm talking about basketball."

"Oh, well, as far as I knew, you were supposed to be volunteering your time to coach a rec team because it's fun, and it helps you to relax. Isn't that what you told me? It was supposed to be a little hobby, and a way for you to give back to the community, but instead, you've turned it into a way of using kids for prestige and financial gain."

"No, I just discovered that there is a way for everyone to win," Mildred remarked. "The kids get to play basketball on, not one, but two top-ranked teams and travel around the country. Meanwhile, I get to have the number one summer team in New York, Charles gets the number one high school team, and we both get a few things extra that we can share with their parents. A lot of parents can't pay the five hundred dollars to have their kid play for my team, and that used to be a problem. Now, with the deal I hooked up with Charles, the real good ones won't have to worry about that anymore. This kid Stacey, however, is a different case because she lives out on Long Island."

"And to you, this is worth our relationship?" Terry asked. "This Stacey kid is so valuable to Charles—not you, because you've already said that she can commute by herself to play with the Roadrunners—that you'd sacrifice our relationship and move out? Okay, I get it now. You don't, and never did, give a shit about me."

"It ain't about you, Terry," Mildred barked. "It's about me! You're supposed to be keeping *me* happy! Isn't that what you promised you'd do when we first got together? Guess what? I'm not happy with you! Now, please, just leave me the fuck alone!"

Mildred stormed up the steps leading to the front door of her building, but Terry hurried up to block the doorway.

"Dammit, Terry, move!" Mildred ordered.

"No," Terry said, looking lovingly into her eyes. "I'm here to get you back and I'm not leaving without you."

Mildred's eyes were beginning to flood. She tried to push pass to go inside, but Terry grabbed her in his strong, muscular arms and held her close. Their lips met, their tongues touched and her arms clamped around his neck.

11:33 P.M.

Mildred watched as Terry got dressed. She wrapped the sheet around herself and sat up on the bed.

"Why are you taking so long?" she impatiently asked.

"Millie..." Terry started.

"Please, Terry, don't say anything. It's too much for me, right now. You got your shit, now just leave!"

Again, Terry tried to speak but was cut off.

"Just go!" Mildred screamed.

Terry turned, slowly walked to the bedroom door, hesitated, and then left.

When Mildred heard the front door of her apartment close, she jumped out of bed, raced through the house and quickly locked it. She then collapsed on the spot, and as her bare skin folded in the fetal position on the cool tiled floor, she wept uncontrollably.

Terry, who was leaning up against the door on the opposite side, heard and cried as well.

ALL EYES ON US

Wednesday, July 6, 2005 – 7:19 P.M.

It was the last day of the New Attitude Tournament regular season at Riverbank State Park. The Lady Phoenix's game was against the last place Ravens. All of the players got together and went ahead of T.J. and Juanita because they wanted to see the game before theirs, which was a battle for the last playoff spot between the Imperial Crew and the Lady Panthers. Some of the Roadrunners were there, too, even though they'd already played all of their games. The players from the Lady Phoenix and the Roadrunners had a love-hate relationship. They weren't exactly enemies off the court, but their on-court rivalry provoked constant trash talking and taunting between them.

It was an open period, so college coaches and recruiters were at the game as well. The coach from Southern State University, Vincent Bellows, along with his assistant coach, April Harley, was there to see the Lady Phoenix play. They sat directly behind the players, taking in all that was said and done.

"Hey, look," Beverly said, pointing toward the gym entrance. "My dad's here and he brought my best friend, too."

"Yo, Tree, Daquan just walked in, too," Melva said, alerting her best friend.

Trina looked down toward the gym entrance and saw Daquan walking up the stands with his headphones on, looking for a place to sit. He never liked sitting with her when she sat with her teammates. He saw her looking at him and just lifted his chin to her before sitting down. Trina twisted her lips and rolled her eyes away from him.

Burton and Melinda found seats near the entrance. Beverly tried to get their attention by waving her arms, but they didn't see her because they were watching the game being played as they walked.

"Come on, Lady Panthers, play some defense! Close up that middle! Let's GO!" Tabitha was standing up shouting onto the court as she rooted for her friends on the Lady Panthers team. "Damn, I can't believe the Imperial Crew is winning this game."

"You don't sound sick to me, Tabitha," Kimberly said. "How is it that you're too sick to play tonight, but you're here yelling and screaming? Explain that for me, please, because I don't get it."

Sounding innocent, Tabitha said, "Explain what? I already told you my stomach hurts."

Of course if Tabitha was the target, Melva wouldn't miss a chance to take aim and fire. "Yeah, Kim, her stomach hurts, not her throat or her big-ass mouth."

Tabitha's tone quickly changed as she retaliated. "Why do you always have something to say, Mel? Why can't you just shut the fuck up?!"

Melva laughed, knowing she hit a bulls-eye. "Okay, you're right. I'll shut up, because I know you'll try to make me if I don't. Honestly, I think you might even be *man* enough to do it."

Trina quickly intervened. "Hey, why don't both of you just stop?"

Melva put her hands up to surrender. "Don't worry about me. I'm cool."

"You two have got to understand how important it is for us not to be carrying on like that."

"Oh-oh, Miss Righteous is about to preach again," Connie King interjected.

Velvet quickly came to Trina's defense. "Yo, Connie, you need to be minding your own business and stick to helping the Roadrunners dodge coyotes, you big Looney Tune."

The girls all laughed.

"Look," Rayna said, pointing to the scoreboard. "The game's tied up."

Tabitha jumped up and started clapping. "All right, Lady Panthers! Let's go!"

Melva quickly jumped up and started clapping and shouting louder. "Come on, Imperial Crew! Get it back!"

"I know you're not cheering for the Imperial Crew like they're really going to win?" Rayna asked Melva.

"I don't care who wins, really," Melva said. "I just like to root for the underdog."

"Ohhh," Connie said. "So, that's why you're always cheering for your team when y'all play my team, huh?"

The Lady Phoenix players all sneered as Connie and Rayna gave each other high-fives.

"Oh, now see, you didn't have to go there," Melva said.

"We went there, so what's up?" Rayna challenged.

Melva smiled mischievously. "Yo, Tree, the Roadrunner scrubs sound like they wanna go 'Head Up.'"

Trina grinned. "Nah, they don't want to go there."

"Oh, yeah, we want to go there!" Connie assured her.

"What's up, set it off," Rayna dared them.

Trina turned the challenge back on her. "You set off. You started it."

The girls all started chanting "Hey! Hey! Hey! Hey!" until Rayna stood up, waving her hands and rolling her neck as she broke out into a battle rap:

"I swear, my dear, you thought you were hype
But this pair right here must say to you, psych!
The way you come across is like you got it goin' on
But I heard a gong, and that means you're wrong
Yo, you gotta know my style's 3,000 A.D.
Rayna C, the F-U-T-U-R-E
Cut you so much your coach will get fed up
And sit you on the bench because you tried to go Head Up!"

Rayna sat down as Melva quickly stood up to take her turn:
"Child, please, your mouth flows like diarrhea
Always running, but if it didn't it just wouldn't be-ya
Think you got it goin' on 'cause people say that you're fast
But you need a mask, 'cause yo, you're gassed!
You do a lot of talkin', but what can you tell
Everybody knows you can't mess with Big Mel
I shot the sheriff when he just wouldn't shut up
And did the deputy, too, when he tried to go Head Up!"

RISE OF THE PHOENIX

Melva sat back down, and everyone in that section of the bleachers had turned their attention away from the game and focused on the players as they battled. Connie couldn't wait to go next:
"If I may, let me say that Connie King is the queen
To your dismay, you're getting played when I step on the scene
I am the highest, you peasant, so kneel to honor me
All hail with a cheer; scream, "Her Majesty"
An All-American girl is how I was voted
Number one in the state in case you didn't know it
Behold; don't hold your head down 'cause you're fed up
I'll stick pins in your chin to make sure you go Head Up!"

Connie sat back down and Trina immediately stood up prepared to cap things off:
"You're deceivable, unbelievable; you lie around like a rug
Goodness gracious, you're outrageous; walkin' 'round like a thug
Miss Thang, sittin' pretty on your media throne
But I still have yet to see you score a point on your own
You and your buddy are just too gassed
You're Corny Connie and she's a thing of the past
One-on-one you're done, Tree schools with no let up
Next time it's on, (with Lady Phoenix) *WE'RE GOIN' HEAD UP!"*

They all laughed and gave each other hi-fives. With them all carrying on so much, none of them noticed that T.J. and Sheila came in and walked over to their side of the gymnasium.

"Look at the score," Tabitha said. "Fifty-four to fifty-one and two seconds left in the game. The Lady Panthers are about to seal this victory."

"All right," Rayna cheered. "The ultimate comeback!"

Melva remained hopeful. "The Imperial Crew ain't out of it, yet."

"Aw, c'mon," Connie said. "Admit the game is over. It'll take a miracle for the Imperial Crew to win. They're inbounding from all the way under the Lady Panthers' basket, too."

"So what," Melva said. "We believe in miracles."

"Look," Kimberly said, drawing everyone's attention. "They're inbounding the ball."

"I bet they give the ball to number twenty-two," Beverly said.

"No way!" Tabitha quickly discarded the notion.

Velvet agreed. "That girl hardly ever gets into the game."

Beverly smiled. "Why else would they be putting her into the game now? She must be in to shoot."

Connie wasn't buying it. "Get outta here. That girl is not getting the ball."

"Hey, Beverly, you're a good player and all, but you're still learning the game," Rayna added. "The ball's going to number eleven or number twelve."

"Okay," Beverly said as she grinned with confidence, "we'll see."

"They're checking the ball," Kimberly announced.

The girls watched as the Imperial Crew ran a play setting screens and made a long pass past half-court.

Beverly jumped up from her seat and shouted, "They passed it to number twenty-two!"

They all watched as the girl caught the ball a few feet before reaching the three-point line and immediately turned and launched it toward her basket. Everyone in the gymnasium watched the ball in flight, and then jumped up with screams and cheers as it entered the basket just as the buzzer sounded to end the game.

"What did I tell y'all?!" Beverly shouted.

"Oh, my god," Tabitha said as she plopped down with her hands over her face.

"The Imperial Crew is playing good," Kimberly noted.

"Well, you know this game will determine the last playoff spot," Rayna told them.

"No," Velvet said. "If the Imperial Crew wins, it'll be a three way tie with them, the Lady Panthers and the Lady Tigers."

"So how will they know which two teams to take for the playoffs?" Kimberly asked.

"They'll probably have to have them play it out," Velvet assumed.

"Nah, I doubt if they do that," Trina said. "They'll probably go by their head-to-head meetings."

"That'll be hard, too," Rayna said. "The Lady Tigers beat the Imperial Crew and the Lady Panthers beat the Lady Tigers."

"Oh, they'll probably go by point spreads then."

"We were there when The Lady Panthers beat the Lady Tigers," Tabitha mentioned. "The Panthers weren't supposed to win that game."

"Didn't the Lady Tigers get blown out by the Lady Panthers?" Connie asked.

"Yep, by twenty-two points—70–48," Tabitha answered.

"The Lady Tigers blew the Imperial Crew out, though," Kimberly stated.

"That's right," Velvet added. "The score was 66–45—twenty-one points."

"Let me get this straight," Melva said. "If the Imperial Crew wins this game, the Lady Tigers will be eliminated because of point spreads, and the Imperial Crew will end up in third and the Lady Panthers in fourth?"

"Yeah, but it's messed up," Tabitha said. "I feel sorry for the Lady Tigers because three of their starters were away when they lost to the Lady Panthers."

"I don't feel sorry for them," Rayna said, "because we would've had to play them in the playoffs, and we only beat them by twelve the last time."

"We beat the Lady Tigers by fifteen," Trina said, "but it wasn't as easy as the score indicated."

"So, if the Imperial Crew does win, does that mean we'll play them and The Roadrunners will play the Lady Panthers?" Beverly asked.

"That's right," Trina said. "That's why I don't understand why Connie and Rayna are cheering for the Lady Panthers when things will be easier for the Roadrunners if the Imperial Crew wins."

"Because the Lady Panthers are our peeps," Connie replied.

"Yeah," Rayna added. "They're our homegirls from around our way."

"So, why don't you just play for them instead of going all the way uptown to play for the Roadrunners?" Trina inquired.

"Because the Roadrunners are better," Rayna told her.

"The Lady Panthers don't go nowhere," Connie said. "They just play in these local tournaments here in the city. Even your team goes to

Philly or Boston sometimes. With the Roadrunners, we've been to Puerto Rico, Toronto, Washington D.C., Chicago, Alabama, Florida, North Carolina, and wherever the Nationals take us. We go on at least four trips every year with the Roadrunners and at least two more every year with our school. We get all kinds of gear and stuff, too."

Kimberly sucked her teeth and rolled her eyes. "That's your problem. All you think about is how many trips you can go on and what kind of gear you can get. All the teams that use things like that just to attract players are only thinking about themselves. Both of y'all are spoiled by that crap. You get it at Jefferson and with the Roadrunners and you think it's helping, but it's not."

Connie got offended. "How can you say that? You know that's not true. What's wrong with being on the best teams and looking fly? We *should* look nice when we travel, especially since so many scouts are out there watching us."

"C'mon!" Melva jumped in. "Y'all don't even win when you go to the big tournaments."

"Yes we do!" Connie said.

"You do *sometimes* with Jefferson," Melva said, "but not with the Roadrunners. All that talent y'all got, and y'all got your asses cracked the last two summers. And don't even get me started on your coaches. Oh, my god! I'd like to see Coach Negron make a weak team better. I bet she can't do it. And Coach Greene can't coach at all. He just has money and connections. All they care about is winning."

Connie stood up and put both hands on her hips. "Hold up, I know you're not talking. All your coach thinks about is winning, too. That's why he's always yelling and going crazy in the games."

"He's not yelling because he only thinks about winning," Melva told Connie, "he's yelling because he *is* crazy."

Tabitha didn't hesitate to toss her two cents in there. "He sure is crazy, that's why I can't stand him."

Trina immediately came to T.J.'s rescue as always. "You can't stand him, but you're willing to use him to get what you want, right?" she asked Tabitha with blinking eyes and a rolling neck. "You should watch what you say, Tabitha. You know that Coach Stone will be right there for you when you need him."

RISE OF THE PHOENIX

Tabitha sucked her teeth and waved Trina off. "I don't need him for anything."

"That's not what you were saying in the park the other day," Trina said.

Tabitha shrugged her shoulders. "So, now I have other options."

"Good," Melva said. "Why don't you just go ahead and take those other options and stop wasting everybody's time?"

"I am," Tabitha said. "The first chance I get, I'm outta here."

"Don't wait, go now," Melva egged on. "We don't need you."

"I don't need y'all, either!" Tabitha angrily shouted.

T.J. was sitting, chatting with Glen Ford about players but heard enough commotion coming from that part of the stands and decided to go over and make his presence known. He got up and left Sheila to talk to Glen and started over toward the players. That's when Kimberly looked and saw him coming. "Hey, cool out. Coach Stone's heading this way," she warned.

Tabitha sucked her teeth again and blew out hard. "Oh, brother!"

T.J. played it cool as he walked up the bleachers. "Come on, girls," he said, calmly. "Let's go to the other side and wait for this game to be over." The Lady Phoenix players began to slowly gather their things, moving leisurely. T.J. clapped his hands to hurry them along. "Come on, now. Let's go."

The Lady Phoenix, with the exception of Tabitha, all made haste and hurried down from the stands.

Trina filled T.J. in right away. "Coach Stone, Tabitha says she's not playing tonight."

T.J. looked at Tabitha sitting there and gave her a cold, hard stare. That was usually enough to get any of them to jump, but she was unfazed.

"Tabitha, what's wrong?" T.J. asked with a stern tone. "Why aren't you dressed to play?"

"I'm not playing," she grunted.

"Why not?"

"I don't feel well."

T.J. wouldn't have normally cared about making a scene, but he thought about it and submitted. He turned and addressed the team before speaking to Tabitha again.

"You all can go on over to the other side and sit behind the Imperial Crew's bench. I'll meet you over there. Tabitha, go with them. I still want you with us even if you can't play tonight."

Now, Tabitha wouldn't even look at him. She was trying to look around him to see the game as the overtime period had just begun.

"I don't want to go over there," she snapped. "I'm fine right here."

T.J. was fuming, but he did his best to hold it together. "Please, do as I ask? I want the whole team together."

Tabitha ignored him and moved over so that she could see the court.

T.J. surrendered. "Fine, have it your way. You won't be playing the next couple of games."

Tabitha just shrugged her shoulders, so T.J. left her alone and moved up the bleachers to talk to the Southern State University coaches.

Head Coach Vince Bellows was a thirty-three year old, well-built, Brooklyn-born Italian, with full, dark, slicked back hair, a square jaw and a dimple in his chin. He used to coach in New York City at St. John's University for three seasons before moving on to Southern State U. Assistant Coach April Harley, a twenty-five year old, slender woman with a red-dyed, short haircut and a sandy complexion with freckles, grew up in Riverdale, NY and was a star when she played at Fordham University. Coach Bellows wore a burgundy, cotton vest with "SSU COACH" embroidered in gold on the left breast over a white T-shirt to go with his cream khakis and white Adidas. Assistant Coach Harley wore the same style Adidas with her burgundy mesh basketball shorts and gold T-shirt with "SOUTHERN STATE UNIVERSITY" printed across the chest. They both greeted T.J. as he approached them.

"Hey, T.J.," Coach Vince Bellows said. "How've you been, my man?"

"I can't complain," T.J. said, shaking his hand. "Things could be worse. How are things going with you guys at SSU?"

RISE OF THE PHOENIX

"We look pretty good for next season, actually," Vince was happy to say. "I have high expectations from the group we have. My concern is for the following season because three of our guards and two of our post players are seniors now. We're looking to try and fill most of those positions in the first signing period."

"Well, you got the tape I sent to you, right?"

"We sure did," Assistant Coach April Harley replied, enthusiastically. "Melva Fields looked great."

"If you think she looked great then, you should see her now," T.J. said. "She's gotten so much better."

"So, what other leagues are you in?" April asked. "I want to see more of her while we're here."

"Right now, just the City Housing League," T.J. told her. "We have a championship game there against the Imperial Crew this weekend."

"So, you're doing a little scouting right now, eh?"

"Yeah, something like that," T.J. said. "I have to, since my team really hasn't been playing up to their potential. We're seven and one in this league but we've just been holding our own. Hopefully, we'll fare better here tonight against the Ravens."

"You said your championship game is next weekend?" Vince asked.

"Yes, Millie Negron managed to get the dates changed so she can go to Washington, D.C. and play in the Tournament of Champions. Those are her two players sitting right there, Connie King and Rayna Cortez."

Coach Bellows looked. "Yeah, we know King. Who doesn't? We heard a lot about Cortez, but we've never seen her play."

T.J. smiled in adoration. "Ah, Rayna. That's the kid they call 'Future.' She's a good kid. I like her a lot. She's only going into her sophomore year, but she is, in my opinion, by far the best point guard in this part of the country. She'll probably be the best in the entire nation after next season. She just does everything right."

"That's what we keep hearing," Vince said. "We'll be in D.C. this weekend, so we'll be able to see her then."

"Why don't you ever take your team to the Tournament of Champions, T.J.?" April asked.

"I was actually thinking about trying to go next year if I can get a sponsor," T.J. told her. "They always send me an invitation, but that tournament is so expensive. We've been in a financial rut, and with transportation, hotel and everything else, we'd have to give up our whole summer of activities just to go. We're only in this tournament because it's right in our backyard. My team is usually too busy doing stuff that our players really need, anyway."

"T.J., who is the kid from your team sitting with King and Cortez?" Vince Bellows asked, pointing to Tabitha.

T.J. ran his hand through his locks and took a breath. "That's Tabitha Gleavy."

"Oh, *that's* Tabitha Gleavy," April repeated. "I've been hearing a lot about her. She's transferring schools, right? What year is she in? Does she shoot as well as people say?"

April Harley was known for reeling off a series of questions all at once. She loved her job and wanted to be good at it so she worked hard.

T.J. giggled a bit before answering her. "She's going to be a junior next season. She's loaded with potential, and yes, she can really shoot the ball. She averaged over thirty points a game in her first two years at Park East, but she was her team's only player and they never went to the playoffs. Now, she's transferred to Saint Joseph's, so she thinks she's on top of the world. She actually can be a really special player if her attitude improves."

"Yeah, we noticed that you were having a bit of trouble with her just now," April said. "She doesn't seem to get along well Melva Fields, either."

"You know, her and Melva started out as very good friends. Now, for whatever reason, they're always at each other's throats."

"That's too bad," Vince said. "Teammates need to do their best to get along. We won't deal with that kind of stuff. Anyway, how is Melva doing in school?"

T.J. knew one of them would ask that question sooner or later. He thought it would've been more sooner than later. Never the less, it came and he had to be honest with them.

RISE OF THE PHOENIX

"Melva had a tough year," he admitted. "She slacked up in her school work and got involved with hanging out, partying and whatever else..."

He was interrupted by a roaring cheer from the fans.

"Wow, that was a great move," April shouted. "Did you guys see that?! The Imperial Crew's number eleven broke her player down, split two defenders and made a reverse lay-up around a third! *And* she got fouled! She took the whole team!"

"That girl's really good," Vince Bellows said. "I've been watching her the whole game. Who is she?"

"That's Yolanda Hopson," T.J. told him. "She'll be a sophomore at Prospect Heights High School. Number fifteen on my team, Kimberly James, goes to the same school."

"Got it," April said as she wrote the information down.

"So, you think Melva's going to come around?" Vince asked.

T.J. nodded. "She just started summer school, yesterday. She passes, and she'll have the credits she needs to get back on track for graduation."

"What about her S.A.T. scores?"

"She scored nine-seventy, or something around there. She'll be a qualifier if she passes all of her classes."

"Well, I really like what I saw of her on the tape you sent. If she gets it together, she'll have a home at SSU. We really liked Trina Smith, too."

"Oh, we sure did," April eagerly agreed.

"Has she decided where she wants to go to school yet?" Vince asked.

"Trina scored fourteen-fifty on the S.A.T.," T.J. proudly informed them. "She's trying to get an academics scholarship to an Ivy League school, which I think will happen. She's even taking the test again because she feels she can do better."

"Well, we'd still love to have her come down south for a visit," Vince said. "We have some great programs that cater to students with strong academic skills. On the flip side, we also have programs that cater to students like Melva who may need more attention. We have it all down there."

"Okay, I'll definitely let her know that you're interested," T.J. promised, and then asked, "Hey, what about Velvet Fuller?"

"We liked Velvet, too," Vince told him, "but we're not sure where we could use her. She's not big or strong enough to play forward for us, and she's not really a true guard, either. She's a good player, but she'd be a project."

"I hear ya," T.J. said. The game horn sounded, and he looked up at the scoreboard. "Oh, look, the Imperial Crew pulled it out. The Lady Tigers are probably out of the playoffs. Oh, well, such is life. Are you sticking around for our whole game?"

"Most likely," Vince said.

"Well, if you do, I'll get you Trina's information."

"I'll stay!" April blurted.

T.J. couldn't help grinning at April's exuberance. "Okay, I'll talk to you later." He stood up and started down the bleachers.

"Good luck, Coach," Vince said.

WHAT ABOUT ME?

Wednesday, July 6, 2005 – 8:56 P.M.

The game had ended and the Lady Phoenix cruised to a 77–36 victory over the Ravens. Burton and Melinda left the gymnasium before T.J. and Juanita finished talking to the team and waited for Beverly outside of the front entrance. After a while, Sheila came out with Velvet and Kimberly.

"Hi, Mr. Smalls," Kimberly said.

"How you gals doin'?" Burton responded.

"Fine," Velvet and Kimberly both replied.

It became apparent to Velvet that Burton hadn't met Sheila yet, so she seized the opportunity to introduce them. "Sheila, this is Mr. Smalls, Beverly's father. Mr. Smalls, this is Sheila Stonewall, Coach Stone's wife."

"Oh, Mrs. Stonewall," Burton said, extending his hand. "It's a pleasure to meet you."

Sheila shook Burton's hand, noticing his gold number nine Lakers jersey and remembered T.J. told her his father was the Lakers' great power forward, Archie Smalls. She could see the resemblance to the man who scored over forty points four games in a row five times, but died of a heart condition at the age of thirty-six. Burton was broad and statuesque like his father, Sheila thought. He was definitely his father's son.

"Likewise, Mr. Smalls," she said.

"Hey, now, the name's Burt. You don't have to be so formal."

"Well, that's nice," Sheila politely replied. "You can just call me Sheila."

Burton's smile gleamed. "Sheila. That's a really nice name."

"You know what else would be really nice, Burt?"

"What's that, Sheila?"

"If I could have my hand back."

Burton roared with laughter as he returned Sheila's hand to her. "Sorry, about that."

"It's okay," Sheila said with an amusing smile.

"This here's Melinda," Burton said, pulling Melinda's hand so that she could step forward.

Melinda smiled and waved at Sheila and Velvet but looked Kimberly over from head to toe, repeatedly. Kimberly didn't pay it any attention.

"So, you're a referee, eh?" Burton asked Sheila.

"Yes," Sheila said. "I just moved up to the college level last year."

"Tough job for a pretty little lady. You're the person people love to hate, everybody's enemy."

Sheila chuckled. "Yeah, I know, but I don't mind. Fans, players, and even some coaches don't really know all the rules or rule differences, and they don't know much about what we do to control a game and keep it flowing with the best spirit and intent. No one realizes that of all the people in any gymnasium or on any field, referees are the only ones who have to get certified, and then pass an exam every year in order to participate in the game."

"Yeah, that is true," Burton said. "I always thought that coaches, particularly on this level, should have some sorta sport-specific training and certification before being allowed to deal with kids."

"That's right," Sheila agreed. "In these summer leagues especially, anybody can gather a group of kids and call themselves coaching them. A majority of these people never get child abuse training or child safety training. A lot of them don't know CPR. There's nothing on morals and ethics for them to refer to. And most of all, they know nothing about the sport outside of what they see on television. That's why I don't do any officiating in the summer outside of the camps. I feel everyone involved in the summer leagues, as well as in high school and college, should be mandated to get training and attend rules interpretation meetings."

Burton nodded in agreement. "You're one hundred percent right, Sheila. Maybe you and me should bump heads and see if we can contact the right people about setting a certain criteria to be able to coach in the summer leagues."

"We should," Sheila agreed. "Give me a call, and we'll talk about it some more."

"I sure will," Burton said.

"Well, take care, Burt. Melinda." Sheila said. Velvet and Kimberly both said goodbye as Sheila led them off.

"Take care, y'all," Burton replied, and watched them walk away toward the parking lot. Sheila's hair was pinned up in the back with a large brown butterfly comb. She wore an ivory fitted top and a long stylish brown to cream faded tiered skirt. Burton turned down his lips making a "not bad" gesture, giving T.J. kudos for his taste in women.

Melinda continuously stared at Kimberly, as she walked away dressed in her crop spaghetti strapped tank top and low riding denim mini-skirt. Velvet wore a matching ensemble, but Melinda's focus was on Kimberly.

At that moment, the rest of the Lady Phoenix players came out, but Beverly was not with them. Burton walked back to the entrance of the recreation center and looked inside, but didn't see anyone.

Trina had walked away from her teammates and over to Daquan, who was sitting on a bench waiting for her. Burton noticed her and led Melinda over to them.

Trina saw Burton and Melinda walking toward her and gave them a pleasant smile. "Hey, Mr. Smalls. How are you?"

"Eh…excuse me, y'all," he said, politely. "I don't mean to impose, but…" Burton squinted his eyes at Daquan and jerked his head back. "Wow! You related to the coach, young fella?"

"Nah." Daquan twisted his lips from being disgusted with always being asked that question.

Burton grinned at his reaction. "Oh, sorry. You gotta admit the resemblance is uncanny," he said, and turned his attention back to Trina. "I was wonderin' if y'all seen my daughter Bev'ly?"

"Beverly was standing by the bathroom talking to Tabitha and a couple of The Roadrunners' players when I came out," Trina told him. "I think she was waiting for Coach Stone."

"Where's your coach at?"

"He was still in the gym talking to Coach Moore, Coach Ford, Mr. Pernell, and some other people."

"Okay, thank you. C'mon, Melinda, let's go back inside."

"Take care, Mr. Smalls," Trina said.

"You too," Burton responded, and then led Melinda back inside of the facility.

"Yo, Tree!" Melva shouted from up the path. "What's up, you comin'?"

"Go ahead," Trina yelled back. "We'll be right behind you."

As soon as Burton and Melinda entered the building, they passed Connie and Rayna on their way out. Beverly walked up right after.

"Hey, Daddy, I thought y'all were still inside."

"Naw, baby girl, I told you to always meet me outside after the games."

Beverly thought for a second. "Oh, yeah, I'm sorry, Daddy."

"That's okay, baby. But you have been a little unfocused lately. What's goin' on with you?"

Beverly looked at Melinda, who turned her head away. "Nothin', Daddy. I'm just tryin' to get it together with this team."

"Whatcha talkin' 'bout, gal? You played great tonight. Wasn't she great, Melinda?"

"Yeah, girl, you were all that," Melinda agreed.

"C'mon, y'all, I just did what Coach Stone told me to do," Beverly modestly stated. "I didn't even play that much."

"You didn't need to play that much, baby girl. You was whuppin' on them gals so bad when you got in the game, Coach Stone had no choice but to sit you back down. Besides, y'all won the game by forty-one points."

"I played a lot in the other games, though."

"Well, that was because they needed you more."

"I think I didn't play that much tonight because I played so much against the Roadrunners and we still lost, and then last night we managed to beat the Imperial Crew, but I didn't score. I sat for most of tonight's game, and we won by a lot."

Burton put his arm around his daughter's shoulders and pulled her close to him. "Bev, didn't you have a triple double last game without even scorin'? That's amazin'. How often do you see that? I know it was the first time I ever saw such a thing in my life. Besides, most of them other gals sat tonight, too, didn't they. Trina and Melva, and what's the other gal's name, the one who's always all dolled up?"

"Her name's Velvet," Beverly said.

"Yeah, well, all y'all was sittin' right next to each other. But that wasn't because y'all was bad, it's because y'all was good, and your coach was lettin' the gals that don't play as much get some more time. If y'all would've played the whole game, y'all might've really embarrassed the other team. Coach Stone was showin' good sportsmanship."

"You think that's it, Daddy? I mean…Coach Stone said I played so well in the first two games, but Tabitha sat out tonight so I can take her spot, and he still didn't start me. She told me that he has his favorites already and—"

Burton got annoyed and turned Beverly around to face him. "Look here, gal, you know how this works. This ain't your first time bein' on a team. This was only your third game, how can you expect to be startin', especially on a team with so many good players? Don't start gettin' beside yourself. That's not how you was raised."

Beverly pouted her lips and rolled her eyes up. Burton saw her reaction and started to get upset.

"What the hell was that?" he asked, his voice getting louder and stronger. "What was that face for?"

Beverly didn't respond. She turned her head, and her eyes met with Melinda's, who was glaring at her.

"I asked you a question, gal. I want an answer," Burton demanded.

Beverly glanced at Melinda again and quickly changed her attitude. "I'm sorry, Daddy. I guess I just felt like I wasn't contributing as much as I can."

Melinda could see through Beverly's front and shook her head to herself. Burton, however, bought into it.

"That's okay, baby girl," Burton said, softening his tone and giving his daughter a comforting hug. "Just watch how different the rotation in the playoffs is gonna be. Everything's gonna be fine, you'll see. In fact, we can wait here and talk to your coach if you want."

"No," Beverly quickly responded. "That's not necessary. Let's just go."

"You sure, baby girl, 'cause he's right in the gym…"

"I'm sure, Daddy. Coach Stone is busy talking to college coaches about Melva, Trina and Velvet."

Burton raised a brow and peeked into the gym at T.J. and everyone standing around him. He was impressed at the scene, appreciating the time T.J. was putting into helping his players. "Oh, really? That's good. That's, uh…that's real good. Well, uh, we'll have a talk with him another time, then."

Burton escorted Beverly and Melinda out of the recreation facility with each of them holding on to one of his arms. Burton honored Carlene Thompson's wishes to hold onto Melinda's hand, but so he wouldn't make her feel uncomfortable, he walked arm and arm with her instead. Beverly would balance things out by holding on to her father's free arm just as she was doing then.

When Burton, Beverly and Melinda got outside, they saw Trina and Daquan still sitting on the bench.

"Goodnight, Beverly and company," Trina called out and waved to them as they passed.

"Seeya, Trina," Beverly shouted, waving back.

"Bye," Melinda said.

Burton smiled, nodded and proceeded to escort the girls out of the park. They walked about thirty feet when Trina called out to them again.

"Hey, if you catch up to the rest of the team, please tell them to go on without me."

"Okay, I'll tell them," Beverly shouted back.

Trina sat with her back to Daquan until Burton and the girls were out of her view. As she turned to face her boyfriend again, her facial expression changed from cheery to serious. Daquan sat slouching with his head thrown back looking up at the sky.

"So?" Trina said.

"So what?" Daquan asked.

"So, what do you think about what I just said?"

Daquan lifted his head and gave her a blank stare. "What am I supposed to say? If that's how you feel, what can I do?"

Trina sucked her teeth and rolled her eyes. "I don't know why I was thinking that you'd care."

RISE OF THE PHOENIX

Daquan sat up, leaned forward, rested his elbows on his knees and tried to rationalize what was going on. "Let me get this straight," he said. "You tell me that we can't have sex anymore, and when I say okay, that's not good enough because now I don't care. Does that sum it up?"

Trina cut her eyes at Daquan sitting there with a carefree expression wearing his royal blue T-shirt with the orange lettering "Brownsville Jets" over a ball going through a basket displayed on his chest and baggy RockaWear jeans hanging low off his hips. *What a typical child,* she thought, but still admired the way he tied his locks in the back but let the front hang loose, draping over his mature-looking, chocolate face. His thin sideburns were attached to his goatee and framed his face and mouth. Yes, Daquan Mitchell was quite handsome, almost as handsome as her true love. But he wasn't her true love. She had to keep reminding herself of that.

"I just thought you'd want to talk about it more," she said.

"Talk about it? What's there to talk about? You're breaking up with me, aren't you?"

"No, that's not what I was doing..."

"Why?" Daquan interrupted, raising his shoulders. "What's the use of being together if we're not going to be doing it?"

"We can try to work on having a *real* relationship and try to connect with each other. We need to bond on a non-physical level."

"No, you just want me to beg for the booty, but I'm not gonna do that. I don't need to beg to get some ass."

Trina was mortified. She swallowed hard, and her eyes started blinking. "No, I don't want you to beg, Daquan. You're right. I was trippin' for a sec. Something in me thought that the intimacy we were sharing meant something."

"Meant something like what?" Daquan asked with an attitude.

Trina smirked at his response, and then surrendered, deciding that he was not worth the trouble. "Nothing. Like I said, I was trippin'. The truth is, actually, that it doesn't mean anything to me, either."

"Oh, no? Why are we having this conversation, then?"

"The conversation is over, Daquan," Trina said, using her index finger to cross her throat. "You go your way and I'll go mine."

"Fine," he said, and then stood up. "Bye."

"Bye," Trina responded, and then looked away.

Daquan took his headphones from around his neck and put them back on his ears and walked off, leaving Trina sitting alone. She felt like crying but dared not.

After a while, all of the coaches finally came out of the gymnasium and headed away from the path where Trina was sitting. They were on their way to the lower-level parking lot, so Trina quickly got up and tried to walk away before being noticed. It was too late, though. She saw Coach Glen Ford look in her direction, and then point her out to T.J.

"Yo, T.J., look over there. Isn't that Trina?"

T.J. looked over and called out to her. "Trina? Why are you still here? Is something wrong?"

Trina's first thought was to tell him that everything was okay and walk away, although she knew it wouldn't be that easy. She'd been a part of the Lady Phoenix program for the past five years, since she was eleven years old, and her infatuation for her coach built more every year. What attracted her to him so much was his caring nature. She understood him better than any of her teammates, or so she believed. She knew T.J. wouldn't let her off the hook that easily, but she felt she had to try.

"No, Coach," she yelled back. "I'm fine. I'll see you on Saturday."

Trina motioned to turn away when she saw T.J. edging toward her.

"Well, why are you still here?" he asked. "Why didn't you leave with the rest of the team?"

When Trina became tentative, T.J. knew something was wrong.

"Hey, I'll talk to you all later," he told his colleagues. "I'm going to go over and see about her."

"Wait, T.J.," Juanita said. "You can go on home, I'll see about her."

"Nah, I'll go," T.J. said, waving his loyal assistant off as he picked up his pace toward his star center. "I haven't had an opportunity to talk to her in a while. This will give us an opportunity to reconnect."

"Don't forget to talk to her about us," April Harley said.

"Oh, don't worry, I'll put in a good word," T.J. assured her.

With that they all left, and T.J. went to see about his team's captain.

RISE OF THE PHOENIX

"Coach Stone, I told you I'm fine," Trina insisted as she watched T.J. walk toward her. She admired his well-toned, athletic body covered in his Michael Jordan gear from head to toe, including the white headband that kept his locks off his face, white oversized tank top, and black basketball shorts. His white, red and black Jordan Work'm sneakers completed the ensemble. Trina liked the fact that her coach was fashionable and trendy. It made him seem cool. He seemed to be floating on air as he walked, and her breathing shortened as he got closer to her. When he finally got close enough to reach out and touch her on the arm, she gasped.

"Oh, my God, Tree. You're so tense. What's going on with you?"

"I'm okay, Coach. Daquan and I just broke up, that's all."

T.J., in an attempt to console, pulled Trina close in a comforting hug. "Oh, I'm so sorry, sweetie."

A broad smile came over Trina's face as she hugged him back, tightly. "It's no big deal. I'm glad it finally happened."

"What?" T.J. asked, surprised. "I thought the two of you had something special. I thought you two were going to get married one day."

"Yiil, no! I don't like that boy!" Trina said in a high-pitched voice.

T.J. broke their hug, took a step back and laughed at Trina's reaction. "Oh, you're just saying that because you guys are having some problems. You'll be back together in a day or two."

"No, we won't, Coach. Being with Daquan was a mistake. I was just using him to…"

Trina was about to reveal her feelings, but once again decided against it. She stopped herself and turned away.

"Using him to do what?" T.J. asked.

"No, never mind. Just forget it."

"Let me tell you something, Trina," T.J. said, as he took her by the hands. "Look at me, please."

Trina turned her head and looked at her coach, staring directly into his eyes as they stood there with her hands in his. His dark eyes were soothing and compassionate. Even when he was barking at the team, she could see his passion for what he was doing and how much he cared about them all, and she appreciated how much of himself he was giving.

Regardless how much Daquan resembled T.J., when Trina looked into his eyes she saw nothing. She knew it was because Daquan was young and immature, and she didn't blame him for that. She needed something more from a man, though. Something a boy could not give to her.

Right then and there, Trina decided to take what she wanted from the man she loved. She stepped forward, threw her arms around T.J.'s neck and pressed her lips against his. He began to resist, but Trina, who stood two inches taller than her coach and matched his two hundred pounds, held on tighter and kissed him harder. Finally, T.J. submitted and kissed her back. Their tongues wrestled and their hands probed. T.J. lifted her T-shirt and let his fingers dance across her back as he pulled her closer to him and began kissing and sucking on her neck. Trina threw her head to the side and closed her eyes as her coach continued to devour her flesh…

"Trina?" T.J. said, snapping his fingers. "Are you listening to me?"

"Uh…yes, Coach," Trina responded, awakening from her fantasy.

"There's nothing you can't talk to me about," he told her. "I'm here for you, always. I told you many times before that this is about more than basketball. It's about life, and no one lives their life alone. Everyone needs someone, and we all need each other."

"Yes, Coach, I know," Trina muttered, not wanting to hear that speech again. "It's not a big deal, though. It was just time to move on, that's all. I want to be focused going into my senior year, and having a boyfriend was a distraction."

"Yeah, I understand. Sometimes they can be. Perhaps things will work out later and you two will get back together. Anything's possible, right?"

Trina smiled at T.J.'s last statement as she quickly replayed her daydream over in her mind. "Yes," she said with a smile. "Anything's possible."

Seeing Trina smile made T.J. smile, as well. "That's my girl. C'mon, I'll drive you home. You were one of the main topics of discussion among the recruiters tonight. I'll tell you all about it in the car."

RISE OF THE PHOENIX

NEW YORK DAILY NEWS
Thursday, July 7, 2005
SUMMER LEAGUE BASKETBALL

With playoffs starting, Roadrunners are favorites!
BY PEARL McBRIDE
DAILY NEWS SPORTS WRITER

    THE NEW YORK/NEW JERSEY region of the New Attitude Sports Association League is winding down. The final four of ten teams will do battle next Wednesday in the semifinals, with the winners playing in the finals for the prize of being sponsored to travel and compete in the National Tournament in New Orleans, LA, July 21-24.
    The first semifinal game (6:00 P.M. at Riverbank State Park) will feature the Columbus Avenue Lady Panthers (6–3) against the Bronx based Roadrunners (9–0). The heavily favored Roadrunners, coached by three time Division I volleyball All-American Mildred Negron (Wake Forest) is expected to run away with the game and the tournament. Negron's team, which consists of some of the most highly touted players in the area, boasts a 78–4 record over the last two spring-summer seasons and are undefeated in local play.
    The Roadrunners defeated the Lady Panthers, 65–48, in season play, and that was before Negron added Lawrence High School's superstar Stacey Conyers to their roster. Conyers, a fifteen-year-old sophomore who recently moved from Long Island to Brooklyn and will now attend Thomas Jefferson, is arguably the best all around player to ever come out of New York. The addition of Conyers, a 6–2 power forward, paired with Jefferson's 6–4 first team All-American Connie King, could prove to be the best front court tandem ever in girls high school basketball. Sophomore Rayna "Future" Cortez, who has been called the consummate point guard, completes the team's "Big Three" and will make it easy for King and Conyers to stand out. That is definitely bad news for the Lady Panthers, who ended up in fourth place after losing 57–53 in overtime to the Imperial Crew last night.

The Roadrunners will be tested before next week's playoffs, though, when they go to Washington, D.C. for the Northeast Tournament of Champions. Although they've competed well the last three years, the Roadrunners have never gotten past the second round in the nation's capital.

"This is my year," said Negron, when asked of her chances this year in D.C. "I won't have three of my key players because of family obligations, but I've already found more than suitable replacements. I have no doubt that I'll return home with the championship trophy in my hand."

The New Attitude League's 7:30 semifinal game will match up the second place Brooklyn Lady Phoenix (8–1) against neighborhood rivals, Imperial Crew (6–3). The Lady Phoenix won the season contest, 66–59, and the two teams will face off again before the NA playoffs in the championship of the City Housing League, July 9, 2:00 P.M., at the Chelsea Center.

MISREAD

Friday, July 8, 2005 – 2:03 P.M.

Melinda was sitting outside on her stoop listening to her Ipod and bobbing her head to the music as she waited for her father to come pick her up for the weekend. When she saw Kimberly walking toward her on the other side of the street, she remembered where she knew her from. They went to the same elementary school and were in the same fourth and fifth grade gym class. Kimberly had changed a lot since then. Melinda remembered her to be much like herself, common, quiet, and kept.

As Kimberly got closer, Melinda began to admire her style. She wore all black: a cropped tank top that showed off her navel ring and the tattoo of African artwork on her lower back, cargo shorts that hung down off her waist enough to reveal the top of her thong, and a pair of Timberland work boots. Her three pairs of earrings, four necklaces, twelve bangle bracelets, and rings on every finger were all sterling silver. She had her long burgundy micro-braids tied up in pigtails. She also wore black sunglasses, dark cherry lipstick, eyeliner and black fingernail polish. All of that black made her yellow skin seem extra light.

"Hey," Melinda yelled out.

Kimberly looked in her direction and kept walking.

"Hey," Melinda yelled again. "You play for the Lady Phoenix, right?"

Kimberly slowed her pace and looked over to see who was trying to get her attention. "Yeah, I play for them. What's up?"

"My best friend is on your team."

Kimberly stopped and dropped her hands into her back pockets. "Really? Who's your best friend?"

"Beverly Smalls," Melinda proudly announced.

"Oh, okay," Kimberly said. "I remember you. You came to our game with Bev's father, didn't you?"

"Yeah, the day before yesterday," Melinda replied. "I was looking at you that day because I knew I knew you from somewhere else, and then it came to me. You and I went to the same elementary school—P.S. 72 on Shepherd Avenue."

Kimberly smiled and started across the street toward her. "Oh, yeah, okay. My mom always says that it's a small world."

"Yeah, mine too," Melinda said. "Y'all played a good game. That other team couldn't hang. They were whack."

"They weren't whack, they were...well..." Kimberly searched for the right word to show good sportsmanship.

"They were whack!" Melinda reiterated.

Kimberly shook her head and laughed as she leaned up against the short iron fence in front of the Thompson's house, removed her shades and hung them on the front of her shirt. Melinda marveled at her big, almond-shaped hazel eyes topped by thin sculpted eyebrows.

"You played good," Melinda said, her words coming out in a breath just above a whisper. "You were really doin' your thang out there."

"Thanks," Kimberly said, extending her hand. "My name's Kim."

Melinda admired the flaming bird carrying a basketball on Kimberly's right shoulder as she gave her a soul shake.

"Yeah, I remember. I'm Melinda."

"I was just on my way to see if I could catch up with Beverly. The team is having a slumber party at Melva's house tonight, and we're gonna have a basketball movies marathon. Trina, our captain, thinks it'll be good for us to bond before our championship game tomorrow in the City Housing League. The game ain't 'til 4:30, so we'll be able to hang."

"That sounds cool. What movies are y'all watching?"

"Well, we're gonna start off with *Space Jam*, and then *The Air up There*, *Fastbreak*, *Jawanna Mann*, and *Love and Basketball*. All of those movies have females playing ball in them."

"That's cool. I like that." Melinda was smiling and staring admirably at Kimberly.

Kimberly returned a similar smile. "Well, if Beverly comes, I guess you can come, too, if you want. Have you seen her? We've been trying to call her at home and on her cell, and she hasn't gotten back to anyone."

Melinda's expression changed, and she hesitated as she had to think of something to say to divert Kimberly from her attempt to reach Beverly. "Oh…well…uh…Beverly's not home. She went away for a few days."

"What?" Kimberly asked with a surprised and confused tone.

Melinda didn't want to lie, but she felt she had no choice. "Oh, uh, it was a family thing. It was an emergency, and she had to leave in a hurry."

"Aw, she's gonna miss the game tomorrow," Kimberly said, disappointedly. "She didn't say anything to anyone after the last game. Man, we're gonna miss her. The Imperial Crew gave us a good game the other day. And Coach Stone suspended Tabitha, so we're really gonna be shorthanded."

"Oh, Tabitha's suspended, eh?" Melinda asked with a scowl.

"Oh, I see you've met Tabitha already."

"How'd you guess?"

"Because, everybody makes that face after meeting her or Melva for the first time. The difference between them is that Melva will grow on you because at least she's sociable. Tabitha's just a bitch who pretends to be people's friend just to get what she wants outta them."

"Yeah, I could tell that about her."

"Bev seems to get along with her, though," Kimberly said. "She'd better watch her back, though."

"Yeah, well, I've already told her that."

There was a short silence. Kimberly watched Melinda watch her for a second before changing the subject. "So, Melinda, are you a baller? I mean, Beverly's got mad game, don't you ball with her?"

"Of course," Melinda said. "We play ball together all the time."

"Why didn't you join our program, too, then?"

Melinda pouted her lips and her eyebrows turned down. "Because my mom's a possessive, overprotective control freak. All she does is keep me on lockdown. She treats me like I'm a baby."

"I'm sorry to hear that," Kimberly consoled.

"I can see that you don't have that problem?"

"What makes you say that?"

"Well, look at you. You have all those cool tattoos and stuff."

"What's that have to do with anything?"

"Aw, c'mon. How old are you?"

"I just turned sixteen. Why?"

"You're sixteen and have tattoos on your arms, legs, neck and back. And what's that, a teardrop tattoo under your left eye?"

"Oh, that one ain't real," Kimberly confessed with a guilty smirk.

"Still," Melinda said, "your parents obviously let you do what you wanna do, be who you wanna be and don't sweat you too much."

Kimberly giggled and nodded in agreement. "I guess that's true to an extent. My parents are cool, and they don't sweat me too much. I do have limits, though: eleven o'clock curfew, my bank account monitored, stuff like that."

"You got a cool nose ring, tongue ring, a navel ring. I would die to have a navel ring."

"Well, my mother's got a lot of tattoos and piercings, too," Kimberly said. "I mean, she's only thirty-three, and she's still pretty cool."

"Well, my mother is thirty-five, but she acts like she's sixty-five. There's nothing cool about her what-so-ever."

Kimberly started to feel for her new friend. "Like I said, I still have a curfew and I still have to check in to let my moms know where I am and stuff like that."

"I would be cool with that if I at least had an opportunity to get out sometimes," Melinda said.

"So, why won't she let you play basketball?"

"She's so scared something is going to happen to me," Melinda told her. "She won't let me go anywhere or do anything. The only time I get to go anywhere without her is when my father takes me, or when I'm with Bev and her father, and that's only because she wants to marry him."

"So, why can't you come with Bev? Her father usually brings her or picks her up."

"I told you, my mother thinks that I'll get hurt or something."

RISE OF THE PHOENIX

"Oh, well, I know people like that," Kimberly recalled. "We had this girl on our team last summer who could only come to practice and games when her mother brought her, which wasn't often. She twisted her ankle in a game, and that was the last time we saw her. Then, we had this other girl whose mother would come to games and ride her the whole time. The girl is good and all that, but she was under mad pressure. Once, Coach Stone didn't start her because she didn't come to practice, and her mother came outta the stands, took her off the bench and left. Now, she's just another team-hopper and plays for whoever her moms can get along with for any period of time."

Melinda lowered her eyes and shook her head. "Yo, that's a trip. Some parents be buggin'."

"You have no idea," Kimberly said with a laugh. "I said my mom's cool, but she's still a mom, which automatically makes her bugged. It comes with the job, you know."

"I do wish my mom would let me grow up," Melinda said, sadly. "I want to play basketball *so bad*. I get good grades, I don't get into any trouble and I don't talk back to her. She's got no right to treat me like this."

"What about your father?" Kimberly asked.

"My father doesn't treat me like that, he gives me breathing room. I only get to see him like twice a year, though. He's in the military and lives in Europe with his wife and my two half-brothers."

"Wow, my father is in Europe right now, too," Kimberly said, laughing at the coincidence. "He had to work in London for six months. He'll be back in September."

"You got any brothers or sisters?"

"I got a twelve-year-old sister. She plays on our fourteen and under team."

Hearing that made Melinda feel worse. "Really? Dang, it's not fair. I can be good. Bev and her pops taught me a lot. I wish I was *his* daughter."

At that moment, Melinda's father drove up in his rented Expedition with her stepmother and two half-brothers and honked the horn.

"I'm coming, Daddy," Melinda yelled out. "I just gotta tell Mommy you're here and get my bag." She got up to go into the house and reached out to give Kimberly another soul shake. "Well, I gotta go."

Kimberly smiled. "Cool. Have a good weekend. I'll come back around here next week and catch up with you and Bev then."

"Okay," Kimberly said. "Good luck in your game tomorrow."

3:58 P.M.

Burton sat on his sofa reading Charles Barkley's book, *I May Be Wrong but I Doubt It*, as he waited for Carlene to arrive. He turned off his house phone and cell phone so that there would not be any disturbances. He had another phone in his office in the basement and a cell phone he used for business, which he put the numbers to on the consent form for Beverly to go to Washington, D.C., and instructed her to use only in the case of an emergency.

The doorbell rang, and Burton quickly put the book down and hurried to answer it. When he opened the door, Carlene was standing there holding white and pink roses in one arm and a bottle of Courvoisier in the other. She was wearing a long, white, low-cut dress that complimented her dark, mocha complexion. It hung elegantly on her size fourteen frame and put the cleavage of her 38DD cups on display. She wore her hair out instead of pinned up, which was something she never did.

Burton gasped at the site of Carlene standing in his doorway. "Hey, suga. You look fa-bu-lous."

"So do you." She checked out his teal sport shirt, blue dress slacks and black leather square-toe loafers.

"Is Melinda gone?" Burton asked.

"Yes," Carlene cooed, wearing a seductive smile. "Her father came and got her about an hour and a half ago. With her gone and Beverly away playing basketball, we have the weekend all to ourselves."

"That there is exactly what I've been waitin' on," Burton said as he moved aside. "Come on in."

Carlene handed him the flowers as she proceeded inside. "These are for you," she said. "Beautiful roses for a beautiful man."

RISE OF THE PHOENIX

"Thank you, suga'. They are beautiful, indeed. But, between the two of us, you're the one that compares to them best."

Carlene giggled. "Oh, Burt, you don't have to flatter me."

"I mean it, suga'," Burton assured her as he closed and locked the door, and then followed Carlene into the living room. "I wouldn't tell you that if I wasn't bein' sincere."

"I know you wouldn't."

Carlene sat on the sofa and placed the cognac on the coffee table.

"Let me get a couple of glasses for that," Burton said.

"Yes, please do."

Burton went into the kitchen, and Carlene leaned back and crossed her legs. He returned, seeing her sitting there, and shook his head at the sight of her. "My, my, my, you are truly a vision of loveliness. Whatever am I gonna do with you?"

Carlene smiled and batted her eyes in response. Burton blushed slightly at the implication.

"Here you go, darlin'," he said, handing her a glass. He placed his own down and picked up the bottle to open it.

Carlene held her glass out and Burton poured her portion, and then some for himself. He sat on the couch and put his arm around her.

"Let's make a toast," he said. "To us, finally havin' a chance to spend some real quality and quiet time together."

"Yes," Carlene replied. "We certainly couldn't let this opportunity go to waste. I want to tell you something else, too."

"What's that, suga'?"

"I've been thinking about letting Melinda play for that team Beverly's on. I think it'll be okay, especially since Beverly will be there with her."

"Hey, now that there's some good news. That's some real good news, darlin'."

"I knew you'd be pleased."

"Well, you know, Melinda is a good girl, and I know we can trust her the same way we can trust Bev."

"Well, Beverly is an angel," Carlene said.

"So is Melinda. We got ourselves two wonderful gals. We're lucky. You see how some kids are these days. They coulda turned out to be much worse, you know."

"That's true," Carlene agreed. "Well, another toast. To our daughters for being the little angels they are."

Burton and Carlene raised their glasses together and sipped on their drinks.

Burton picked up the remote control to the stereo and started the Mighty Romancer's *Old School Love* CD. He held out his hand for Carlene and led her to the middle of the living room floor. He then placed one hand on the small of her back and drew her to him. He placed the other hand between her shoulder blades and held her close as she put her arms around his neck and rested her head against his chest. They danced through five songs, holding on to each other without saying a word. When "I Believe in You and Me" came on, which had become their favorite song, Carlene lifted her head to speak. Before she could, though, Burton's lips met with hers, and they kissed lovingly.

"I got somethin' special I wanna do, but I don't wanna do it here," Burton said softly into Carlene's ear. "Since both our girls are away, I think it'll be fun if we picked up and went to Atlantic City for the weekend. We can hit the casino, take in a show, and get into whatever's there. What do you say?"

Carlene looked up endearingly at the man she'd grown to love. "I'll go anywhere with you, Burt," she said. "When do you want to leave?"

"There's no time like the present, suga'. When we get there, I'm gonna give you what I know you've been waitin' on."

BETRAYAL

Sunday, July 10, 2005 – 4:59 P.M.

It was hazy, hot and humid for the first day of the Highland Park tournament, but despite the muggy ninety-four degrees the games went on as scheduled. Sam accompanied T.J. to drop off a check for the Lady Phoenix's entry fee into the league. The three-thirty game between the Lady Tigers and the Flushing Flames had not too long ago ended, and the five o'clock game between East Point and the Long Island Tide was about to start.

T.J. and Sam entered the park at the entrance on Elton Street from Jamaica Avenue and followed the path in front of the park house. They were walking past the children's playground up to the higher grounds where the four regulation-sized basketball courts were, when a couple of players rushed past them. The two girls removed their backpacks, took out their tournament jerseys and worked them on and their tops off from underneath, all at once without revealing anything too far above their navels.

"It always amazed me how girls do that," a new goatee wearing, freshly clean-shaven head Sam commented.

"They wouldn't have to be changing in the street if they made it their business to get to the game on time," T.J. stated, looking at his watch. "It bothers me when kids come running in just before tip-off or after the game has already started. I don't think there's really an excuse for that."

Sam shrugged. "You know how the subways are on the weekends, T.J."

"Don't make excuses for them, Sam. These aren't ten year olds we're talking about. I'm talking about the fifteen, sixteen and seventeen year olds who've been playing in these leagues for years. They know all about weekend travel, the subway service delays and detours, as well as the heavy traffic. A lot of times these kids are coming from another tournament somewhere where they played for a different team."

Sam twisted his lip and grunted a little. T.J. saw his reaction and shook his head.

"You know, Sam," he said. "There really *is* a problem with kids running around jumping from here to there like that. You may not think so because the New Attitude League has open rosters and whatnot…"

Just as they came upon the main court, T.J. saw some Lady Tigers players exiting the park on the far end and noticed one of them looked like Tracy Williams, his second-string power forward, leaving with them and wearing the same color tournament jersey. Immediately, he detoured from his path to the basketball courts to pursue the group and find out if it was indeed Tracy and why she was there playing with another team. He speed walked out behind the Lady Tigers players, leaving Sam standing there unaware and bewildered. He kept his focus on the girls, examining the tall, stocky, copper-complexioned girl with brown curly extensions wearing Tracy's trademark multi-colored knee-high socks.

"That better not be her," T.J. kept repeating as he increased his pace.

Suddenly, the girls took off running down the hill through the grass. T.J. gave chase.

"Tracy!" he screamed several times, but to no avail. The girls were too far ahead to hear him as they ran to catch the Q56 bus approaching the stop at Ashford Street. "Dammit!" he exclaimed, stopping and stomping his foot in frustration as he watched the girls board the bus, and it pulled away.

"What happened, T.J.?" Sam asked, seeing his friend return with anger in his eyes and disappointment on his face. "Where'd you go running off to?"

"That was Tracy," T.J. growled through his teeth.

"Tracy?" Sam asked. "Tracy Williams from your team?"

"Yeah. She was with the Lady Tigers' players wearing the same color jersey."

RISE OF THE PHOENIX

"Get outta here. No way," Sam said in disbelief. "It was probably just somebody that looks like her."

"I'm gonna see right now." T.J. marched across the court to the scorer's table. The referees, players and coaches all stared at him, wondering why he was parading across the court with the game about to begin.

T.J. approached the scorer's table and stepped between the two late players who were signing themselves in and addressed the scorekeeper. "If it's not too much to ask, may I see the scorebook? I want to check something from the last game."

"I'm sorry, but I can't right now," a girl with a tiny voice responded politely. "This game is about to start. You'll have to wait until half-time."

T.J. started to insist, but then looked up and noticed he was being a distraction. "Fine," he said, and walked away behind East Point's team bench.

"Is everything okay?" a concerned East Point coach asked him.

"Yeah," T.J. said. "Sorry about that."

The league director, Rhonda Charles, met T.J. as he came back around the court to rejoin Sam. "Hey, T.J., what's going on?" the short, heavy-set woman with her hair combed back and gray streaks throughout asked, extending her hand.

T.J. shook her hand and forced a courtesy smile. "Hey, Rhonda, how are you?"

"I'm fine. What about you, though? You seem like something is bothering you."

"It is," he told her. "In that last game, was…"

T.J.'s cell phone rang. The ring tone let him know that it was Glen Ford calling. "Excuse me," he said.

Rhonda nodded and started talking to Sam.

"What's up, Glen?" T.J. answered.

"Yo, bro, I wanna ask you something," Glen said. He was shouting and T.J. could hear a lot of noise in the background.

"Where are you, at a game somewhere?" T.J. asked.

"Yeah, I'm down in D.C. at the Tournament of Champions," Glen told him. "There are so many teams here. I just watched the Roadrunners play for the first time."

"How did they do?" T.J. wanted to know.

"They did real good, especially with Tabitha Gleavy and Beverly Smalls playing with them."

The silence on T.J.'s end was loud and clear.

"I didn't think you knew," Glen said. "They kicked the team from Newark's ass, and now Millie's walking around like she's too cool to shit because they're playing in the championship tonight."

More silence.

Glen sighed hard. "I'm sorry about this, man. I should've kept my big-ass mouth closed and let you fight this chick the way you wanted to. Yo, I'mma step to her and find out what's up with this shit."

"No, don't say anything," T.J. said, finally.

"You sure, bro? I'll shake her ass up right quick."

"No, Glen. I'll do all the talking and shaking up when they get back here. Thanks for the heads up."

"No doubt," Glen said. "I'll talk to you when I get back."

T.J. put his cell phone away and stared blankly into space.

"You don't look so well, Coach," Rhonda said. "You sure everything's okay?"

"Actually, no," T.J. admitted. "I don't think the Lady Phoenix is going to be able to participate in this tournament, Rhonda. There's a lot going on right now, and I need to focus and try to make things right."

"Aw, T.J.," Rhonda disappointingly whined. "I was really looking forward to your team being a part of our first league here. I want sponsors to see that we have eight well-rounded, responsible teams."

"Then you should kick the Lady Tigers out and find two other teams. I'm sorry but I just can't do it. I gotta get my program back in order."

Rhonda sucked her teeth and said, "Fine, T.J." and then walked away.

"I really am sorry, Rhonda," T.J. said again.

Rhonda held up her hand, gesturing that it was okay.

"What's up, T.J.?" Sam asked.

"Glen just called me from D.C. and said Millie has Tabitha and Beverly down there playing with the Roadrunners."

Sam's eyes widened and his mouth hung open.

"C'mon," T.J. said. "We're going to pay someone a visit."

5:31 P.M.

T.J. pulled up in front of the Smalls' house and left Sam in the car as he hurried to the door and rang the bell. Repeatedly he rang and knocked while trying to call the house, Burton's cell phone and Beverly's cell phone to no avail. He kept getting voicemails at all three numbers, but he didn't leave any messages at either. Disgusted, he returned to his car.

"Agg, I can't believe this," he shouted in frustration.

"Take it easy, man," Sam told him.

T.J. began massaging his temples as his migraine began to flare up. "I told you, Sam," he said. "I told you and Glen both that if I gave Millie an inch it'll come back to bite me in the ass. I can't wait until they get back. I'm gonna leave some teeth marks in her ass, too."

KENNETH J. WHETSTONE

NYC GIRLS BASKETBALL WEBSITE
MESSAGE BOARD
From: Roadrunners Fan
Date: Monday, July 11, 2005
Time: 10:12 A.M.
Message: Roadrunners are CHAMPS!
The Roadrunners finally did it. They've proven that they're not just the best in New York, but in all of the east. They won the Northeast Tournament of Champions by beating the defending champs Bridgeport Belles 71–65. They also beat Philly's Lady Falcons 63–54 and Newark's Benny's All Stars 67–50. Stacey Conyers got the MVP of the tournament. Way to go Coach Negron, you are the best coach in NYC.
From: Coyote
Date: Monday, July 11, 2005
Time: 10:21 A.M.
Message: RE: Roadrunners are Champs!
I heard the Roadrunners stole 2 players from another team. They couldn't win with the players they had (or perhaps the coach they have) so Coach Negron played dirty, again. The fact is that her dirty deeds won't go on forever. Sooner or later, somebody's going to stop her, Coach Greene and the others like them.
From: jay boogie
Date: Monday, July 11, 2005
Time: 2:07 P.M.
Message: RE: Roadrunners are Champs!
yo why coyote always haten? you just mad because you or your kid or whatevr is not down with the roadrunners. don't be mad because you not good enuff. roadrunners rule!
From: Mighty Isis
Date: Monday, July 11, 2005
Time: 2:22 P.M.
Message: RE: Roadrunners are Champs!
Hey, jay boogie, don't sweat what the haters say. We know can't nobody come close to the Roadrunners. The same people who hate on Jeff hate on the Roadrunners because they got the best players and they

win. Losers hate not being able to compete. Let them cry if they want. Congratulations to Coach Negron and her team!

> From: Coyote
> Date: Monday, July 11, 2005
> Time: 2:30 P.M.
> Message: RE: Roadrunners are Champs!
>
> I know for a fact that Coach Negron tried to get players from the Imperial Crew and Lady Panthers to jump ship. The players she did get were from the Lady Phoenix. My question is if she gets all the top players to play for her team, why even play in local tournaments? The Roadrunners played in the Slam Jam tournament, they're in the West 4th Street League, and they're about to be in the Shootout in Basketball City. They know they're going to blow every team out, so why bother? I think parity is much more fun. If the Lady Panthers, Lady Phoenix and the Imperial Crew are the only teams that can come within twenty points, maybe the Roadrunners should only play in the big time tournaments around the country. Obviously, they've stolen enough players to win outside of NYC. Why not just get in their bus and keep traveling to play the so-called better teams? I would have no problem if they took players to certain tournaments outside of NYC to represent this city right. Those other top teams around the country do it when they go to the big tournaments. But the Roadrunners don't ever want to give the players back. Their roster changes from tournament to tournament more than anyone's. The only loyalty they have is to Jefferson players and that's because everybody that plays for the Roadrunners eventually end up at Jeff, too. I root for the Lady Phoenix because they at least have a good coaching staff and you never, ever see them asking players from other teams to run with them in different tournaments.

> From: jay boogie
> Date: Monday, July 11, 2005
> Time: 3:01 P.M.
> Message: RE: Roadrunners are Champs!
>
> coyote just proved how much of a hata she or he is. if your team win everything you would say something different. stop being a soar loser. the lady phoenix and the imperial crew and the lady panthers will never be able to beat the roadrunners.

From: CrossOver
Date: Monday, July 11, 2005
Time: 3:08 P.M.
Message: Did you know...
...that the 3 players from the Lady Tigers' 14-under team didn't play in the playoffs because they were too old? One girl is 15 and the other 2 are 16.

From: Jiggy
Date: Monday, July 11, 2005
Time: 3:15 P.M.
Message: RE: Did you know...
The Lady Tigers always use ringers. This shouldn't come as a surprise to anyone. I don't see why they think it's going to help them when they always get caught or just lose.

From: Mighty Isis
Date: Monday, July 11, 2005
Time: 3:19 P.M.
Message: RE: Did you know...
I don't see why tournament directors don't check and double check the Lady Tigers roster. They have a history of using illegal players, and now other teams are trying to get away with it too.

From: Kramer
Date: Monday, July 11, 2005
Time: 3:25 P.M.
Message: The Roadrunners and who else?
If most of the Thomas Jefferson High School players also play for the Roadrunners but not all, then who does the rest of the them play for?

From: Roadrunners Fan
Date: Monday, July 11, 2005
Time: 3:26 P.M.
Message: RE: The Roadrunners and who else?
The 5 Jefferson players that don't play for the Roadrunners play for the Lady Panthers.

THE COMPANY WE KEEP

Monday, July 11, 2005 – 3:34 P.M.

Beverly and Melinda were sitting outside on the porch in front of the Smalls' residence playing chess. Scorching heat and high humidity rose to ninety-six degrees on the second day of the heat wave.

Kimberly walked up with her sterling silver jewelry shining, wearing sandals, short shorts, her new Bulova watch, and her personalized New York Liberty jersey tied up on the side to expose her midriff. Melinda's chubby-cheeked smile extended from ear to ear at the coincidence that she was wearing her Crystal Robinson Liberty jersey.

"What's up?" Melinda greeted cheerfully.

"Hey, Kim," Beverly said. "Hiya doin'?"

"What's up, fam?" Kimberly responded as she walked up the stairs to the porch and stood directly behind Melinda. "Can I play the winner?"

"Sure, just stand right there so you can take Melinda's seat in a minute," Beverly said.

"No, no, no," Melinda objected. "She's gonna be taking *your* seat. I'm gonna win this time."

"She's buggin'," Beverly told Kimberly. "Oh, Kim, you remember my best friend Melinda, right?"

"Yeah," Kimberly said. "We were kickin' it the other day."

"Yeah, me and Kim went to the same elementary school," Melinda told Beverly.

"Word?" Beverly said. "Small world."

As Melinda proceeded to make her move, Kimberly interrupted her by loudly clearing her throat. "Oh, excuse me," she said as Melinda looked back to her for assistance and Beverly gave her the evil eye.

Melinda looked over the board briefly and started to make another move. Kimberly cleared her voice louder this time, sounding like she was coughing up a fur ball. Beverly glared at her and tightened her lips.

Melinda moved the chess piece back and once again looked back to Kimberly for help.

"I must have something caught in my throat." Kimberly rubbed her neck. "I think it's something I ate last *night*."

Melinda smiled widely as she picked up on the hint and moved her knight. "Checkmate!" she squealed.

Beverly threw a piece at Kimberly, and they all burst out laughing.

"You see, Melinda," Kimberly said, patting her on the back. "Patience and careful decisions win games every time."

"That's right," Melinda said. "And some good coaching is always helpful."

"Good coaching? Y'all cheated," Beverly said.

Kimberly and Melinda laughed at Beverly's pouting. Then, as Kimberly and Beverly traded places, Kimberly noticed the logo on Beverly's T-shirt.

"Hey, Bev, where'd you get that shirt? Isn't that from the Tournament of Champions?"

Melinda looked at Beverly with her eyes bulging, knowing that they'd been busted. Beverly saw her reaction, and then looked at Kimberly and knew that she couldn't lie her way out of this one. Instead, she didn't respond at all and turned away.

"Wow," Kimberly said. "There was no doubt in our minds that that's where Tabitha was, but we never guessed that you would stab us in the back."

"I wasn't stabbing anyone in the back," Beverly muttered. "I just wanted to go away because I never get to go anywhere."

"Coach Stone doesn't know yet, does he? He was asking for you and trying to call your father all weekend."

"He was?" Beverly asked, nervously. "Shoot, I gotta do something to keep him from talking to my dad. I can't let either of them find out about this."

"What? Your father doesn't know about this, either? Where was he?"

"My dad was with her mom all weekend," Beverly said, nodding her head toward Melinda.

RISE OF THE PHOENIX

Kimberly looked up at Melinda with disappointment on her face, knowing she'd been deceived. She shook her head at her. "Damn, you can't trust nobody."

"Yo, I was just covering my girl's back," Melinda said. "I didn't know if you'd dime her out or not."

"Nah, that ain't me," Kimberly told her. "I don't dime people out, that's not how I get down." She changed her attitude. "But, I feel you, though. You just met me and you didn't know. I can't hate on you for covering for your girl. I would've done the same thing."

"It was just as well, though," Beverly said. "I didn't have much fun on the trip."

"Why?" Kimberly asked. "Y'all didn't win?"

"Yeah, we won."

Surprised, Kimberly jerked her head back. "You did? First place?"

"Yeah, but I still didn't have that much fun."

"Why not?"

"Well, if I tell you, you both have to promise not to tell anybody."

Kimberly and Melinda both raised their right hands and promised.

Beverly lowered her eyes as she searched for the right words. "It's just that...well...things happened...things I didn't expect."

"What kind of things?" Kimberly asked, impatiently.

"Just things. Things that I've never thought about before."

"Like what, Bev?"

"Well...there was this girl, Stacey, from Long Island."

"Stacey Conyers, the girl from Lawrence? I know her. She plays like a dude and she can grab the rim with both hands. That girl's got serious game."

"You're sure right about that," Beverly attested. "Whew! But...she did some...some things when we were together."

Kimberly slapped her leg, saying, "There you go talking about *things* again. Tell us what kind of things."

Tentatively, Beverly said, "Well...on the way to Washington, she kept saying things like how cute she thought some of the girls on the team were and stuff like that."

Suddenly, it became apparent to Kimberly what Beverly was talking about. Melinda, however, was still waiting for some clarity.

"You mean she was going around telling everyone that?" Kimberly asked.

"No, she was just saying it to me. And she kept telling me how pretty she thought I was, and how much she liked me, and how we should be special friends."

"So what?" Melinda said, still naïve to what was going on. "What's wrong with that?"

"You don't understand, Melinda. She wasn't talking about being special friends like you and I are. She meant like a guy and girl would be."

"Are you sure that's what she meant?" Kimberly asked. "Maybe you misread her."

"No, I didn't misread her. She did other things, too."

"Come on, Bev, don't start with the *things* again."

"She was touching me all the time," Beverly blurted. "It was freaky. It made me uncomfortable."

"Did you tell her how you felt and ask her to stop?" Kimberly asked her.

"Not until I had to make her get out of the bathroom when I was taking a shower."

"Why was she in there?"

"She was fixing her hair or something."

"Oh, so the two of you were roommates?"

"Yeah."

"I still don't see what made you so uncomfortable," Kimberly said, using a small towel to wipe sweat from her face due to the sweltering heat, while trying to dissuade Beverly's thinking. "From what you're telling me, she didn't do anything that you haven't seen or done in our locker room."

"Yeah, Bev," Melinda related. "You and I are in the bathroom together all the time."

"This is different. When we're in the bathroom or the locker room, y'all don't be gettin' all up in my space, touchin' me and whatnot. Some of the other girls noticed how she was acting towards me, too. Tabitha and the twins kept saying stuff to her and telling me to stay away from her."

RISE OF THE PHOENIX

"I thought the twins couldn't go to Washington D.C.," Kimberly said.

"They came. They're the ones that started picking on Stacey first, and Tabitha almost got into a fight with her."

"What did Stacey do?"

"She didn't do anything. She didn't talk to anyone the whole time except me and to Future sometimes. She only talked to me when we were alone in our room, though. That's why I hardly stayed in there. I didn't want the rest of the team to think that I was like that, too."

"Like what, Bev?"

Melinda was clear about the matter and had heard enough, so she answered for her best friend. "You know what! The girl's a dyke!"

"Well...yeah," Beverly confirmed.

"I see," Kimberly said. "Well, it seems to me that you were uncomfortable around Stacey because of what the other girls were saying, not because of anything she did."

"That may have been part of it at first, but the last night there, before we went to sleep, she told me that if I gave her a chance, she'd show me how good we were for each other."

"What?!" Melinda exclaimed. "Argh, that's nasty! Two girls together?! Yuk!"

"You're right, Melinda," Kimberly said. "Most people say that it's nasty, or unnatural, or sinful, but people do a lot of things in life that's displeasing to others. The thing is, they don't always get judged, or laughed at and scorned. People are funny that way."

Melinda squinted her eyes and rolled her neck. "Well, if God intended for us to be homosexual, He would've just made us all the same sex!"

"So, you think all homosexuals are bad?" Kimberly asked her.

"Yes!" Beverly and Melinda responded in unison.

"I see," Kimberly said. "So, what did you say to Stacey when she came on to you like that, Beverly?"

"I told her that I don't go that way."

"What did she say?"

"She said that she understood, she respected me for it, and she hoped that we could still be friends."

"Did you talk to her anymore after that?"

"We talked some on the bus on the way back home."

"Did she mention anymore about the two of you having a relationship or anything like that?"

"No."

"But did you believe her when she told you and she respected you?"

Beverly lowered her head, feeling a bit guilty. "No."

"And still you have this perception of her, even though she was true to her word. Why? Is it because those other girls made such a big deal of it? Did the negative things they were saying appeal to you more than Stacey's word?"

"It's just nasty, that's all to it," Melinda said. "I wouldn't have even talked to her. Why were you talking to her anyway, Bev?"

"I didn't know she was like that at first," Beverly justified.

"So, when you found out you shouldn't have talked to her anymore," Melinda told her. "They're all nasty. They want to be men. You'll never catch me talking to a dyke."

"You know, I feel like you're dissin' me to my face, Melinda," Kimberly said.

With a puzzled expression, Melinda flashed her eyes from Kimberly to Beverly and back again. "Dissin' *you*? How is that dissin' you?"

"Because, I'm in The Life," Kimberly said.

"The Life?" Melinda asked, even more confused. "What's that?"

Beverly was stunned. "Ooh, that's what I heard Stacey and some other girls in the tournament talking about, The Rainbow Life. It means they're gay."

Melinda jumped up and moved away from Kimberly. "Yiiil, Kim! You're a freakin' dyke?!"

"What, Melinda? Does that mean I'm nasty and filthy, too? You're not going to talk to me or be my friend now, either?"

"Well, I don't want anybody to think I'm like that, too," Melinda said as if it were obvious. "That's why Beverly should've just stayed away from that girl…"

RISE OF THE PHOENIX

"I couldn't," Beverly explained. "We shared the same room. I stayed away as much as I could, though."

"Look, both of you," Kimberly said. "I'm the same person I was a moment ago before you knew that I was a lesbian. It shouldn't matter to you who I'm attracted to or what I do behind closed doors. I keep my personal business to myself."

"You didn't keep it to yourself," Melinda shouted. "You told us about it!"

"What I mean is that I'm not pushing my lifestyle off on you or anyone else. I wouldn't do that, and I wouldn't want it done to me. I tell my friends about it because I'm not ashamed of it. I don't want to be hanging out with somebody and some guy comes along, and they try to set me up with him. And I don't want some guy to keep trying to come on to me, either."

"So, you wouldn't try to persuade a girl that's not gay to be with you even though you're attracted to her?" Beverly asked.

"If I met a straight girl I liked and she told me she wasn't down, I'd leave her alone," Kimberly told her.

"Well, Bev told that girl she wasn't down..." Melinda started.

"And she left her alone," Kimberly concluded. "When Bev said no, Stacey dropped it."

"Yeah, but I bet if they had more time together, she definitely would've tried again," Melinda insisted.

"Melinda, I doubt..." As she spoke, Kimberly attempted to reach out to Melinda while trying and reason with her, but Melinda jerked away and turned in her seat. Kimberly shook her head, and a saddened look came over her face. "I see," she said. "So, it's like that now, huh?"

"Melinda!" Beverly shouted.

"Nah, it's cool, Bev. I don't get stressed over things like that. I gotta go." Kimberly stood up and started down the steps from the porch. "I'll see you around, Melinda."

Melinda, still with her back to Kimberly, looked up at the sky and ignored her.

"Fine," Kimberly submitted, and then walked over to give Beverly the Lady Phoenix handshake. "Bev, I'll see you tomorrow at practice."

"Tomorrow?" Beverly asked. "Tomorrow's Tuesday."

"Yeah, Coach Stone scheduled practice for tomorrow. We had a hard game against the Imperial Crew on Saturday, and we play them again on Wednesday in the semi-finals of the New Attitude League."

"Okay, I'll be there. I just have to tell my father."

"Cool. We're starting at six. I'll see you there."

As Kimberly walked away, Beverly called out to her.

"Kim! Maybe it's just a phase you're going through. You're only sixteen, how do you know you're really gay?"

Kimberly turned around and stuck her fingers in the back pockets of her shorts. "What do you mean by that?"

Beverly came down from her stoop and walked over to her.

"I mean, we're almost the same age and I haven't even considered dating or anything like that."

"Girl, please. You're one in a million, then. Most girls our age aren't just dating. They're doing a lot more than that, too. When I first got to high school I was shocked to see how many fourteen, fifteen, sixteen-year-old girls there were pregnant or already had a kid—some of them more than one. Yet, with all that, people still find time to point fingers at me."

"So, you think that being gay is the way to avoid that?"

"No, Bev. Being gay is just what I am."

Kimberly walked away and Beverly went back and sat on her stoop. Melinda sat down beside her.

"Why do girls that play basketball think that they have to act like guys?" Melinda asked.

"At first I thought the same thing," Beverly said. "But, maybe it's not like that. Maybe it's the other way around. Or maybe it doesn't matter. Anyway, what they do is their business. I'm not down with that."

"You're not afraid that what happened with Stacey will keep happening? You're thinking about asking your father to let you transfer to the same school that girl Stacey's transferring to, right? I mean, even if she doesn't push up on you again, there are other girls like that who might. What do you do when they don't take no for an answer? How do you handle the persistent ones?"

RISE OF THE PHOENIX

"I'll handle them," Beverly said. "I know how to say no and stick to it."

"What about Kim?"

"What about her?"

"You still gonna be down with her?"

"Of course. Kim is cool."

Melinda bawled up her face and shook her head. "I'm not down with that, Bev."

"That's you, then," Beverly told her. "She's never pushed up on me, and if she never does, we'll always be cool."

"Whatever." Melinda rolled her eyes. "Let's play another game of chess."

"Yeah," Beverly said, and led her friend back up on the porch. "I owe you since you cheated last time."

KENNETH J. WHETSTONE

Monday, July 11, 2005 – 4:38 P.M.
Answering Machine: Hello, you've reached the Ford residence. Unfortunately, no one is available to answer your call at this time. But please, leave your name, number and the time and nature of your call and I'll be sure to get back to you as soon as possible. Thank you and have a great day.

-BEEP!-

Incoming Message: Hello, Coach Glen Ford? My name is Samantha Rudder. I am the Athletic Director at Hofstra University. I received your resume yesterday for the position of women's head basketball coach and I was very impressed. I would like to set up an interview with you, perhaps later this week. Please, give me a call back at (516)555-3690. I'll be looking forward to hearing from you.

TEAM HOPPERS

Tuesday, July 12, 2005 – 6:24 P.M.

T.J. and Juanita walked into practice and saw the team paired up doing various drills, all except Kimberly and Velvet who were off to the side talking. Everyone was there early except Tabitha and Beverly, including the players from the younger team.

"Hey, did anyone find out what happened to Tabitha or Beverly?" Juanita asked.

"I saw Beverly yesterday," Kimberly replied. "She said she was coming to practice today."

"Did she say where she was all weekend?" T.J. asked.

"She said she'd talk to you about that when she comes," Kimberly said.

T.J. bit his bottom lip and cut his eyes back and forth from Juanita to the team. He waited, listened and inspected every face.

"And no one has seen Tabitha, right?" he finally asked.

"Come on, Coach," Melva said. "Everybody knows where Tabitha was last weekend, and who she was with. The same people she's probably with right now if we're lucky."

T.J. started to get upset and in frustration shouted, "Everybody over here, right now!"

Juanita followed him onto the court and met the team at the center circle. As the players all came over and sat on the floor, Carlene walked in with Beverly and Melinda. Seeing Beverly walk in gave both coaches some relief. Seeing Carlene and Melinda temporarily changed T.J.'s mood.

He walked over to greet them. "Well, well, well, look who's here."

"I'm sorry I'm late, Coach," Beverly said. "My father is away at a convention in Maryland, and he won't be back until tomorrow night, so he asked Miss Thompson to bring me to practice."

"Ms. Thompson," T.J. said, shaking her hand. "I'm Coach T.J. Stonewall, and this is my assistant, Juanita Moore." Carlene and Juanita shook hands as well. "I've been waiting to meet you. I wanted to talk to you about the possibility of Melinda joining our program. Mr. Smalls told me he's been talking to you about it. Have you decided to let her participate?"

"Well, we talked about it, and I thought about it, and I decided to let her give this a shot," Carlene said. "I figured it wouldn't hurt to see what this program is all about."

"That's great. Well, you just make yourself comfortable, and we can talk in a minute. I'd like to address the team first about an important matter, if you don't mind."

"Oh, no problem," Carlene agreed.

"Thank you," T.J. said, and then turned his attention to the team. "Will someone please get Ms. Thompson a chair so she can sit with us while we talk, instead of all the way over there on the bleachers?"

"I'll get it," Kimberly said as she sprung up off the floor and trotted over to the supplies closet.

"Melinda, you can sit on the floor with the rest of the team," Juanita instructed.

Beverly and Melinda sat on the floor, and Kimberly jogged back over with a metal folding chair. She opened the chair and placed it down for Carlene Thompson to sit.

T.J. began his speech. "There are a few things that need to be addressed, but first, I would like to ask Beverly about her whereabouts last weekend."

Beverly spoke softly. "I'm sorry I missed the championship game in the City Housing League. I went to Washington, D.C., with the Roadrunners."

With the exception of Kimberly and T.J., total shock came over everyone in the gymnasium. T.J. could see that Carlene was just as shocked as everyone else from the look on her face. Melinda was also surprised because she was unaware that Beverly was going to confess.

"You went where with whom?" Juanita asked with a shaky voice. She looked at T.J. and saw he had a blank expression. "T.J., did you know about this?" T.J.'s unchanging expression and failure to respond gave her, her answer.

"I didn't think it would be such a big deal," Beverly muttered. "I got the opportunity to go away and play, so I took it. Besides, I came back to the Lady Phoenix. I didn't stay with the Roadrunners like Tabitha, and I only missed one game."

"Yeah, a championship game!" Melva snapped.

"I mean...we still won, didn't we?"

"No, *you* didn't win anything. *We* won!" Melva said that pointing at Beverly, and then opening her arms to present her teammates.

"Yeah, by one in double overtime," Velvet added.

"Hold on," T.J. interjected, his voice flat and face still unchanged. "All of you can keep quiet and let me give the lecture here, because a few of you have been less than perfect yourselves." He took a deep breath and wiped his face with his hand. He paced away from the circle, and then back again. Juanita walked over with her arms folded and stood beside him, anxious to hear more.

T.J. bit his lower lip, rubbed his temples one time and looked around at everyone again. He lingered on Tracy, who made a point not to make eye contact. He said, "Now, before anybody here made a commitment to join this program, you were told about the team-hopper rule. The rule is that no one plays outside of our program under any circumstances. The reason for that is if you go around playing for every Tom, Dick and Coach Negron, then basketball is your number one priority. Basketball cannot be our first priority because we are *not* a basketball team. We are an academics through athletics program, and basketball is just the sport we play. We are all here because you want to go to college and continue your athletic careers, hopefully on scholarship. I am proud to say that every student-athlete who has participated in this program in the last four years have *all* gone to college and are doing well on the court *and* in the classroom. That's what's important, and not winning or losing."

"So, why when we're losing you start yelling and screaming at us?" Melva asked.

"That's not true. I yell and scream whether we're losing or not, but that's just me. It is a fact that I get really emotional during the games, but that's because I'm a very, very tough competitor. And yes, I would like to win every time out just like anyone else, but I know that's not reality. No one wins all the time, and I don't expect us to. What I do expect is for you to give your all every time out. I want you to give a hundred percent of effort each time you compete. If we lose, at least know that we've done our very best plus a little extra. Understand, also, that I am not just talking about playing basketball. I'm talking about in school, at work, and with anything else that you do. That means we strive for excellence without sidetracking or distractions, and achieve our goals despite them."

"Yeah, that's all good," Melva said. "But isn't doing as much playing as we can making us better? And isn't playing for different coaches helping us learn the game better?"

"Yes, in some cases that can be true," T.J. admitted. "That's definitely true if we're just talking about playing basketball, but once again, we're not. First, it depends on who the coaches are, but I won't get into that now. My question to you is, why become the world's greatest basketball player without learning the importance of commitment, dedication and loyalty? For example, last weekend in the City Housing championship, you all played hard and you played well..." He cut his eyes at Beverly for a moment. "...those of you who were present. We won with the firepower we had in double overtime after Melva fouled out in the fourth quarter. We won because we were finally able to stick to our game plan, and we have a more poised team than the Imperial Crew. But we could've lost because our team was not at one hundred percent. Some of our firepower was not present. They weren't absent because of family obligation, illness or some other emergency. They were absent because of the lack of dedication and loyalty to this program—this same program that is dedicated and loyal to them. I would never bring in players from other teams just to help us win. That's not fair to any of you. It's not fair to the time and effort you put into this. All the work that you've done to earn your playing time compromised for me to bring in an outsider who has never practiced with us, never done homework with us, never eaten a meal with us, and who won't even be around for more than one weekend, if that long. I just couldn't do that. We bring in new student-athletes all the time, but we

RISE OF THE PHOENIX

don't solicit players from other teams. I know that other teams are always approaching Velvet, Melva and Trina, and now they're after Danisha and Keisha, too. I also know that Tracy played in a game with the Lady Tigers the other day in the Highland Park tournament."

Tracy felt like her skin was being singed from all the surprised eyes beaming at her. She began stuttering from nervousness as she attempted to justify herself. "Coach...I...uh...I was there watching b-because the tournament is close to my house. The Lady Tigers only had four players when game time came and... and they were going to forfeit. Their other players got s-stuck on the subway or something like that."

"That was a very noble and considerate gesture on your part, Tracy. But helping them out cost us a chance to participate in that tournament. Playing with the Lady Tigers obligated you to their team, and I was not going to have you playing against us."

"I-I wouldn't have p-played against the Lady Phoenix," Tracy said, honestly.

"Well, I don't want to play without any of you if I don't have to. It was a good thing I didn't commit to that tournament and pay the entry fee, because then I would've had no choice but to play without you."

"Coach, what if our team is not going to participate in a tournament? Why can't we play with another team, then?" Melva asked.

"Once again, you're missing my point. This cannot be about how many tournaments you play in. Stop acting like you live to play basketball. Love the game. Strive to be the best at it and hunger to win, but don't let it control your lives. Don't let those coaches for those teams out there make you think that basketball is all there is to live for, because, God forbid, you can get an injury that'll prevent you from ever playing again. Don't let your pursuit of excellence subside, but don't lose focus, either. Remember what's important. Also, you run into conflicts when you're a team-hopper. If you're playing with team-A and team-B, and team-A has practice and team-B has a game, which do you go to?"

"The game, of course," Melva quickly replied.

"Okay, so what if both teams have a game at the same time in different places? You can't be in two places at once. Which do you go to?"

"I'd play with the team that needs me most," Tracy said.

"What if they were both playoff games?" T.J. asked everyone.

There was no reply from anyone.

"You see? That's exactly what I mean. That's what happened last weekend. Do you see how frustrated you all were when Beverly and Tabitha didn't show up? You were all cursing Tabitha because, even though she was suspended, you knew she purposely abandoned us to play with the Roadrunners. You're angry with Beverly, now, for doing the same thing. You feel betrayed. Think about that feeling. Think about this discussion long and hard. This is going to be your essay assignment. Title your paper, *The Importance of Dedication and Loyalty*. We'll spend some time after practice on Thursday in the library so you can complete it, but your theses are due tomorrow. Now, get up and get ready to run."

As the team got up and walked to the other side of the gym, T.J. took Beverly by the arm. "Wait a minute, Beverly." He called Kimberly back, as well. "Kim, come put this chair back, please."

Carlene stood up so Kimberly could take her chair and noticed her hair.

"Ooh, look at your hair," Carlene said, stroking Kimberly's braids. "This looks really, really nice."

Seeing that made Melinda rush over and try to pull her mother away. "Mommy, come on. I gotta get changed. Come so you can see the locker room."

Carlene jerked away from her daughter. "Girl, what's wrong with you? Stop pulling on me."

"I want to go downstairs," Melinda impatiently told her.

"Just wait!" Carlene ordered.

Kimberly, aware of the reason for Melinda's actions, shook her head and walked away to put the chair back. Juanita noticed both of their reactions, and before going to join the team, made a mental note to ask Kimberly about it later. T.J. was still unaware of the situation, so it all just slipped past him. He wanted to talk to Carlene about Melinda joining the program but wanted to get to the bottom of the situation with Beverly, first, while Carlene was there and since Burton wasn't.

"Ms. Thompson, I want to talk to you before you go downstairs, but I want to talk to Beverly with you present, if you don't mind."

RISE OF THE PHOENIX

"No, not at all," she said.

"Beverly, I don't understand how you, of all people, ended up going to Washington with the Roadrunners. I tried calling you all weekend, but I couldn't get through to you or your father at your house or on his cell."

Beverly just held her head down and didn't respond. Carlene spoke instead.

"Beverly's father spent some much needed time resting this past weekend. Beverly came to her father with another girl. I think it was that girl Tabitha you were talking about. They made Burt and I both believe that they were going on the trip with you."

"I wasn't going to lie at first." Beverly's voice trembled and tears began to build up in her eyes. "But Tabitha lied, and I followed her up because I thought that if I told the truth, I wouldn't be able to go. Daddy would've wanted to meet Coach Negron and check out what the Roadrunners were all about, and that would've taken too much time. We couldn't have done all of that in time for the trip, so I just let him think that I was going with you."

T.J. tightened his lips and rolled his eyes in disappointment. "So, to you, sneaking away was worth facing the consequences of being punished by your father, suspended by me and losing the trust of your Lady Phoenix teammates who embraced you and accepted you from the moment you met. Not to mention if, God forbid, something would've happened to you. The good thing is that nothing did happen and your teammates here won't turn their backs on you. The bad thing is that I have no doubt that when your father finds out you'll be put on punishment, which means you probably won't be playing in the New Attitude playoffs. Was going to Washington, D.C. worth all of this?"

Again, Beverly just lowered her head and didn't respond.

"I can't tell you enough how disappointed I am in you. Do you have any idea how much this has affected all of us?"

"Yes, I do now," Beverly mumbled.

T.J. frowned in disappointment. Then, at a loss for words, he dismissed her. "Okay, you can go downstairs now."

Beverly took her bag from Carlene and headed to the locker room. Melinda took Beverly's hand and gave a gentle squeeze as she passed.

"Ms. Thompson, I want you and Melinda to know why things have to be the way they are around here," T.J. said.

"Oh, I understand, totally," Carlene said. "I think it's great because kids now-a-days need as much discipline as they can get. Things like respect, honesty and loyalty are basic values that are practically extinct. I think your program, from what I've witnessed here today, is just what our kids need to get some of the things back that they don't get at home or in school, or forget about once they leave those places. Beverly's father tried to explain that to me, but I had to see for myself. I like what you're doing, mostly because of your emphasis on education and integrity. I would be honored for my daughter to be a member of the Lady Phoenix."

"That's great news," T.J. said as a slight smile broke free.

Melinda smiled, too, as she embraced her mother tightly.

"Melinda," T.J. interrupted. "The question is, do you understand?"

"Yes," Melinda replied, eagerly.

"Okay, because this isn't easy. Anything worth having requires hard work."

"I know. I'm ready."

"Mr. Stonewall," Carlene said. "I was wondering about the other girl, Tabitha."

With raised shoulders and hands T.J. said, "I don't know about her. I have to talk to her and hear what she has to say." He lowered his head and shook it a bit. "I have to talk to her parents, too. I really don't think she wants to be here anymore. We'll see. It's going to hurt us to not have Tabitha or Beverly for the New Attitude playoffs, but we have Melinda now. That'll give us another hard working player."

"Melinda is going to be able to come in and play even though it's the State Finals playoffs?" Carlene's question had a surprised, yet flattered tone.

"Well, if she's going to play in this tournament at all, it'll have to be with us in the playoffs," T.J. told her. "What I mean is, she'd be best suited playing with our fourteen-and-under team, but they've already finished their season in this tournament. They won the championship last Sunday, and it's too late to add players now."

"I don't quite understand how that works," Carlene said.

RISE OF THE PHOENIX

"The New Attitude League allows teams to have open rosters," Juanita explained. "That's not something leagues usually do, but teams in this league can add anyone onto their roster up until the championship game. We're all allowed fifteen players, and we can keep adding until our rosters are full."

"Hmm," Carlene pondered. "That sounds kind of strange."

"It is," T.J. said with a nod. "It's very strange, but those are the rules. They say it's because they want teams to be able to strengthen themselves enough to 'compete' in the National Tournament. But yes, Melinda will be able to participate."

"Well, the only problem with that is that she won't be able to travel with you if you win," Carlene let T.J. and Juanita both know.

"Why, Mommy," Melinda whined.

"I understand, Ms. Thompson." T.J. held Melinda's hand to comfort her. "Melinda, you'll be able to participate next weekend. I don't know how much playing time you'll get, but I want you to be there. If we win, we'll still recognize you at the Nationals. Then, when we get back, you can participate in everything else we'll be doing this summer, but it'll most likely be with the fourteen-and-under team, okay?"

"Yes," Melinda agreed, still disappointed, but happy to finally be involved.

"It's too bad about Tabitha." Carlene was still concerned. "She needs the kind of guidance you're giving these kids."

"Well, Tabitha knows right from wrong," Juanita said.

"She also knows where we are and what we're about," T.J. added. "If she wants to face the consequences for her actions and return to this program, the doors are open."

"Coach Stone, can I go downstairs now?" Melinda asked again.

"Yes, Melinda, you may."

Melinda and Carlene walked hand-in-hand across the gym into the open doors on the opposite side. T.J. turned and looked at Juanita. She saw the look in his eyes and knew what he wanted.

"Don't worry," she said, "I'm going to call Tabitha as soon as I get home."

KENNETH J. WHETSTONE

Baltimore, MD – 7:52 P.M.

Room service had just arrived and Burton Smalls had just sat down to eat dinner when his business cell phone rang. The successful Pharmaceutical Sales Representative worked a long, hard, productive day and was wondering why any of his colleagues or clients would be calling at that hour. It was the first opportunity he had in to spend some quiet time alone, and the thought of having to go back out made him cringe. Annoyed, he looked at the screen on his cell phone to see who was interrupting his dinner. His expression turned into curiosity when he didn't recognize the number coming in with the New York City area code.

"Yeah? Burton Smalls speakin'," he answered.

"Hello, Mister Smalls," replied a raspy, nerdish-sounding voice. "You don't know me, but my name is Charles Greene, and I'm the girls' basketball coach at Thomas Jefferson High School."

"What can I do you for, Mr. Greene?" Burton asked, puzzled.

"My call is regarding your daughter Beverly," Charles Greene said.

Burton became defensive. "What about her?"

"I understand that she's going to Stuyvesant High School in the fall, is that right?"

"Yeah. Why?"

Like a practiced speech, Charles said, "Mr. Smalls, Stuyvesant is one of the best schools in the city, academically. However, I've seen your daughter play basketball, and I think a talent like hers needs to be played on a national stage for all to behold every time she laces up her sneakers. It would do her a world of good if she was at a school that is nationally ranked, where all the major recruiters come to for players because they know we produce the best."

Unimpressed, Burton sort of grinned. "Before you go on any further, Mr. Greene, let me just tell you that Bev'ly's been gettin' letters from major recruiters for the last two years. I got letters right now from Louisiana Tech, TCU, and Mississippi State in a cabinet in my office at home, and that's just from her playin' in itty bitty lil' camps back home when she was twelve years old. She don't know about them because I don't want her to lose focus, or think that she ain't got a whole lot more to learn. Shoot, you know how these kids are."

RISE OF THE PHOENIX

"Yes, I do," Charles said, and then went on with his speech. "But even with all those looks, wouldn't you want her to be involved in the highest level of competition every single day? If she attends Jefferson, she'll have to prove herself in practice every day, and the games would be easy."

"Bev'ly don't need *hard* practices, Mr. Greene," Burton said, speaking as if his intelligence had been insulted. "She needs *good* practices. I hear Coach David Martin at Stuyvesant can give her real good teachin'. And if she has to work hard in games, that's good for her, too. You know what they say, don't you? You gotta beat the best in order to be the best. I figga if she can stand out playin' *against* teams like yours, it'll get her more recognition than she'll get playin' *with* you."

"Mr. Smalls, schools like Tennessee and UConn are always looking to us for players…"

"I don't think Tennessee and UConn care as much about what high school these gals go to as much as they do about whether or not they can actually play. I don't think the school she attends will have any bearin' at all as to who all is go'n be recruitin' her. I have to admit that one of the reasons for us movin' to New York was because there is a plethora of talent here, and I wanted her to be able to compete *against* high-level talent everyday. But, Mr. Greene, Bev's a very, very smart girl, so the way I see it is that she's gettin' the best of both worlds at Stuyvesant. They're one of the best public schools in the city for academics, and they got a real good coach. I understand you think it's your job to win at all costs, but would you want anything less than the best for your child?"

Charles let out a loud sigh as he thought of what to say to change Burton's mind. "I understand what you're saying, Mr. Smalls. It's just that I thought that when you allowed Beverly to go to play in the Tournament of Champions with the Roadrunners, you were interested in letting her be a part of dynasties."

"No, Mr. Greene, Bev didn't go to that tournament with the Roadrunners, she went with the Lady Phoenix." Burton thought he was setting Charles straight.

"Excuse me?" Charles asked, confused. "My associate coaches the Roadrunners and she said Beverly played with them. In fact, the Lady

Phoenix didn't go to the Tournament of Champions. They had a championship game in the City Housing League that weekend."

Burton became speechless as he remembered T.J. telling him about that City Housing championship game. He was baffled at first, but then thought that it was obviously a misunderstanding.

"Something's wrong," Burton said. "Coach Stone did tell me about that championship game, but they must've changed things around because Bev came to me with another gal from their team and gave me a permission slip from Coach Stone to sign."

"I'm sorry, Mr. Smalls," Charles said, realizing what had happened. "I'm sure the other girl you're talking about is Tabitha Gleavy."

"Yeah, Tabitha!" Burton remembered. "That's her!"

"Oh, well, Tabitha is no longer a member of the Lady Phoenix. She and your daughter both played with the Roadrunners in Washington. The coach of that team is the one who gave me your number."

It was at that moment that all the pieces fell into place for Burton, and he realized that he'd been deceived. Charles Greene had called his business cell phone, which proved he was telling the truth.

"I can't believe this," Burton muttered, angrily.

"Mr. Smalls, I know how you must feel at this moment, but I still want you to consider what I'm asking you. Obviously, Beverly does want to be involved with a more prestigious team than the Lady Phoenix, or she wouldn't have gone to these lengths. And if that's the case, she'll definitely want to play at Thomas Jefferson, too. Most of the Roadrunners team is compiled with players from Jefferson. Don't you think Beverly should play where she's most comfortable?"

Burton's face was flushed from anger. His breathing became heavy and beads of perspiration gathered around his forehead.

"Right now, Mr. Greene," he said, "where Beverly plays basketball, if she does at all, is the last thing on my mind. Thank you for calling."

"Mr. Smalls," Charles quickly said before Burton could hang up. "Please, give this some more thought. I know for a fact that I can make it very much worth your while, and I'll see to it that Beverly won't have to want for anything."

Burton's left brow raised. "What are you saying, Mr. Greene?"

RISE OF THE PHOENIX

"I'm saying that if you need it, or if you want it, there's something a little extra you and Beverly can both benefit from. All you have to do is think about it for a few days, and then we can meet and discuss it further. What do you think?"

Burton hung up the phone without responding. He looked over at his dinner tray, upset that he'd lost his appetite. Sitting on the side of the bed, he shook his head, wondering what would motivate such betrayal from his own daughter. Unable to find an answer, he cursed, screamed and cried.

8:38 P.M.
"Hello."

"Hello, Mrs. Gleavy?"

"Yes. Who's calling, please?"

"This is Coach Juanita Moore from the Lady Phoenix. May I speak with Tabitha, please?"

"Tabitha hasn't come home yet. She had a game tonight. Didn't you say you were the coach? Isn't she with you?" Mrs. Gleavy's tone of voice was accusatory.

"No, we haven't seen Tabitha since last Wednesday," Juanita reported.

"Last Wednesday?" For a moment Tabitha's mother thought her child had deceived her. Then, she remembered something. "Wha... Oh, wait. What team did you say you're the coach of?"

"I coach with the Lady Phoenix," Juanita told her, "Coach Stone's program."

Now, Tabitha's mother was glad Juanita was on the phone so she could say, "Oh no, Tabitha isn't playing with that team anymore. She said y'all were too hard on her and she doesn't need all that added pressure. She's playing with some other teams. She said y'all wouldn't let her play where ever she wanted, either."

"Ms. Gleavy, we try to help our members and keep them focused. We don't allow them to play on other teams because—"

"What do you mean you don't *let* them play on other teams?" Ms. Gleavy snapped, cutting Juanita off. "Why not? Tabitha can play basketball wherever she wants. You can't stop her from playing. Other teams want her to play because she's one of the best. That's what the best players do. They play all the time. You can't tell these kids they only have play for you. How selfish is that? Everybody wants to win. She played with that other team last weekend in Washington D.C., or where ever they went, and they won. They beat all those other teams from other states. That's what she needs to be doing."

Juanita knew very well whom she was dealing with. Not only wasn't Tabitha's mother involved with her daughter's favorite pastime, she never showed any interest what-so-ever. Ms. Gleavy never attended any of Tabitha's games or Lady Phoenix parent meetings and never inquired about her progress. Yet, she constantly complained about how Tabitha was being treated badly or unfairly. Still, Juanita Moore, T.J. Stonewall's prized protégé, tried to explain things to her. "Ms. Gleavy, we don't just focus on winning all the time. We want our players to be the best student-athletes they can be."

"Well, you're not doing a good job if all the best players are on Tabitha's *new* team," Ms. Gleavy spewed. "What I'm hearing is that you're keeping these kids from playing on other teams by telling them that you're going to make them the best, which is a lie because you are *not* the best."

"We see to it that the members of our program study often, practice often and learn how to read, write and play basketball the right way," Juanita patiently informed. "Sometimes, learning how to do things right comes at the expense of taking a loss. Eventually, doing things the right way will pay off. It may not be while we're competing as a team on this level. It may not come until our members are in college, or until there's a situation where it's a life's lesson. That's when we win. I'll take that over a trophy any day."

Ms. Gleavy spoke to Juanita condescendingly. "Please! These kids want instant gratification. They need to know that they're accomplishing something *now*. That's all that matters to them. Tabitha wants to win, so I'm going to support whatever she has to do to get what she wants."

THE TURNING POINT

Wednesday, July 13, 2005 – 5:29 P.M.

Burton was pacing back and forth in front of the couch, his nostrils were flaring and his eyes were bulging. Beverly, who was sitting on that couch, was noticeably afraid.

"What in the hell were you thinkin'?!" Burton shouted. "I can't believe you did somethin' so underhanded, sneaky and down right stupid! What were you thinkin'?!"

"I don't know," Beverly whimpered.

"What in God's name do you mean, you don't know?! Ain't you got your own mind?!"

"Yes."

"So why the hell you let that Tabitha gal do your thinkin' for you?!"

"She wasn't thinking for me. I was thinking for myself," Beverly said, sounding sassy.

Burton raised his hand to slap Beverly. She jumped back and guarded her face. "Girl, don't you talk back to me!" he hollered. "You lost your mind or somethin'?!" He decided against hitting her and calmed himself down a bit. "Don't be trying to be grown before your time. My God! I am so outdone with you I don't know what to do. I just knew y'all was gonna beat that team in the State Finals and go to the National Tournament. But noooo! You had to go sidin' with them and runnin' off to Washington, D.C. behind our backs. For what? What did it get you? I hope you're happy. Are you? Are you happy?!"

Beverly dropped her head and didn't reply.

"Gal, you better answer me!"

"No, sir," she mumbled.

Burton moved his head, darted his eyes around and waved his arms like he was in shock. "No?! No?! I don't know what to tell you then, because this here's gonna devastate you. You won't be going no place for the next three months!"

KENNETH J. WHETSTONE

"Three months?" Beverly repeated, her voice loud and sharp.

"That's right," Burton shouted. "That's what them three days in Washington cost you, one month for each day. Be glad you didn't stay a week. You won't be goin' outside, havin' no friends over, nothin'. Plus, you gonna make a formal apology to Coach Stone and your teammates."

"I already apologized," Beverly sassed.

"Do it again!" Burton roared, which caused him to crouch over and grab his chest in pain. "Argh!" he screamed.

Beverly jumped from the couch and rushed to his side.

"Are you okay, Daddy?" she asked, holding onto his arm.

"I'm fine!" Burton said, still grasping his chest. "Just listen to what I'm tellin' you! You apologize to Coach Stone and your teammates, and be grateful you still on the...Aggg!"

Burton clutched his chest with both hands and fell to his knees. Beverly panicked and started to cry while trying to hold him up.

"Daddy!" she screamed in fear. She couldn't hold her father up as he collapsed on the floor. "Hold on, Daddy! I'm gonna call 9-1-1."

Burton started coughing as he was trying to speak.

"Hold on, Daddy!" Beverly screamed. Tears streamed down her cheeks as she fumbled with the telephone and began to dial.

When the ambulance arrived, Burton was gasping for air and clinging to life. Beverly was crying uncontrollably, blaming herself for her father's condition.

5:41 P.M.

T.J. got to Riverbank State Park a short time before the first semifinal game between the Roadrunners and the Lady Panthers. He saw Millie and Charles standing near the vending machines engaged in a quiet, private conversation. "They're probably scheming on some other unsuspecting kid whose parent isn't aware of all the dirt they do," he said to himself, and then marched right over to them without looking at, or speaking to anyone else.

"You know, Millie, some people are low and deceitful, but you are the absolute worst," he said, waving his finger at her.

RISE OF THE PHOENIX

"Get your finger out of my face," Mildred responded, slapping his hand away. "Don't ever disrespect me like that."

"What?! You have the nerve to talk about disrespect?!" T.J. roared.

"Take it easy, T.J.," Charles said as he stepped between them. "What's this all about?"

"This is about none of your damn business," T.J. snarled. "Now, you need to step out of my way so I can talk to Millie!"

"Now just wait a minute…" Charles started, but was cut of by Mildred.

"That's okay, Charles," she said, and then stepped in front of him. "What's the problem, T.J.?"

"How could you go behind my back and take Tabitha and Beverly to D.C. with you?"

"What do you mean, 'behind your back?' You're not either of those kids' father. Their parents gave them permission to go with me on that trip, and I took them."

"Beverly tricked her father into letting her go. He thought she was going with me."

"I didn't know that at the time, and I had nothing to do with it," Mildred honestly, but apathetically stated.

"Oh, so the fact that they're committed to the Lady Phoenix means nothing to you?"

Millie and Charles looked at each other and laughed.

"Committed?" Millie said. "Get the hell outta here. If they were so committed, they would've stayed here with you last weekend instead of going to D.C. with me. These kids don't care what team they're on, just as long as they're playing basketball. No matter how much you lecture and preach, they're gonna go where the action is, and the Roadrunners have all the action."

"You see, just by you saying something stupid like that lets me know you don't give a damn about these kids. All you're doing is using them to try to make yourself look good and to build up your team's reputation. It's the same thing your boy here is doing at Jefferson. You are two peas in a pod. But both of you are only as good as the talent you have, and sometimes that talent is more than either of you can handle. Without those kids, you're not worth a dime."

"Yeah, and we're still worth nine cents more than you," Charles retorted.

"Come on, T.J.," Millie said. "I have sponsorship, great facilities, a bus, my players, your players, and any other players I decide I may want. You need to stop trying to run these kids' lives and let them be kids. There is nothing wrong with them playing as much basketball as they can. They need the exposure."

"Exposure?" T.J. asked. "What are you exposing them to? What are either of you teaching your players? How much have your players learned?"

"They've learned plenty..." Charles started.

"Plenty of what?" T.J. cut in. "What have you taught them that they didn't already know when they came to your teams? You both go after the best players you can find and turn your backs on the kids that need help. That's where I'm different from the both of you. The Lady Phoenix turns no kid away, despite their athletic ability or academic strengths or weaknesses. All you so-called big time basketball programs swear you're doing so much to help these kids, but all I see is you helping yourselves."

"Our players go places and get recognition," Charles said. "Connie King is the third All-American we've produced in as many years. Why can't you understand that we do things differently, but it's all for the good of the kids?"

"Yeah," Millie added. "You keep them here and preach loyalty and all that crap to them. I'm gonna take them away and let them see new places and new faces. Either way, they still get to do what they want to do most of all, play basketball. What's wrong with letting them experience both things?"

"What's wrong with it is that what you're having them spend *all* their time doing is taking away from what they need to spend *most* of their time doing," T.J. explained. "All play and no work results in nothing. These kids are supposed to be preparing to go to college to get an education, not just to play basketball. What about helping them prepare for life after basketball?"

RISE OF THE PHOENIX

"Look, T.J., you do things the way you want, and I'll do things the way I want," Mildred said, waving her hand at him. "I don't tell you how to run your team. Don't tell me how to run mine."

"Fine. Just run your team and do what you want without influencing the members of the Lady Phoenix."

"I'm not influencing anyone. Any kid that tries out for my team and makes it can play. If I invite them, I'm playing them. It's between me, the kids and their parents. Not you."

"Yeah, I've heard about the type of relationship you both have with some of your players' parents."

Mildred and Charles shot a look at each other.

"What are you implying, T.J.?" Charles asked.

T.J.'s sudden step forward caused Charles to jump and step back. "Don't play coy with me, you sonofabitch." T.J. flexed his chiseled arms as he towered over him. "I know *exactly* what you've been doing to get kids to transfer to your school. Buy any new players lately?" T.J. saw Mildred and Charles' reaction and grinned. "That's right, Bonnie and Clyde, get tight-lipped. I see you turning red, Chuck."

Charles put on a fake smile in an attempt to discard to notion. "Come on, T.J., do you hear how you sound? What you're saying is obtrusive, ridiculous and outright absurd."

"Is that right? Well, I guess we're going to have to just see about that, huh?"

T.J. walked away, and Charles and Mildred stared at each other with perturbed expressions.

"You think he really knows anything?" Mildred asked her rattled cohort.

"That's what I was about to ask you."

"Maybe Connie and Stacey have been talking?"

"They're not even supposed to know anything, Millie."

"Yeah, well, families do talk and confide in each other." Mildred paused and gave Charles a suspicious look.

"What are you looking at me like that for?"

Mildred stepped closer to him and looked down into his eyes. "Did you make Burton Smalls some kind of an offer?"

"Hell no!" Charles lied as he turned his head and stepped away. "You know the rules. We make them comfortable enough to ask, but we never offer."

5:45 P.M.

Melva and Trina were just walking into the park when Melva happened to look back and noticed Tabitha walking up about a half-block behind them.

"Yo, Tree, you go ahead," Melva said. "I'll catch up to you."

"What's up?" Trina asked.

"Nothing. I'll be right there."

"Okay, see you inside."

Trina walked off and Melva waited on the walkway for Tabitha to catch up. When Tabitha got close enough and noticed Melva standing there, she walked on the other side of the path and picked up her pace.

"Yo, Tabitha!" Melva called out.

Tabitha turned her head and proceeded to walk away.

"Yo, hold up a second," Melva shouted. "I wanna ask you something."

Tabitha reluctantly stopped, knowing she wouldn't be able to avoid her. "What do you want?" she asked impatiently.

Melva walked up to her smiling and hoping Tabitha would give her the answers she was looking for. "What's up with you? Where've you been? Why don't you come to practice?"

Tabitha smirked and answered proudly. "Because I'm not on your whack-ass team anymore."

"Yes!" Melva cheered.

"I'm down with the Roadrunners."

"Thank you, Lord!" Melva said, raising her hands and looking up to the sky. "Now, maybe somebody else will be able to touch the ball."

Tabitha clinched her jaw at the statement. "You're always talking that shit, and you're the biggest chucker in the world."

"Yeah, okay. I'm just glad you finally left. Maybe now our team can play like we're supposed to."

Tabitha waved her hand and started to walk away. "Later for you, Mel."

RISE OF THE PHOENIX

"That's right, run away like you always do."

"What's that supposed to mean?"

"You know exactly what it means." Melva told her.

Tabitha walked up on Melva toe to toe. Melva dropped her gym bag, pulled her baggy jeans up on her skinny hips and braced herself, prepared to fight if she had to.

"Let me tell you something," Tabitha said, while getting in the face of the person she hated the most. "I don't run away from nothing or nobody. I'm tired of Coach Stone with his stupid rules and essays and stuff. This is supposed to be a basketball team, not school. I get enough school at school. I pass my classes. I don't need him to keep preaching academics to me. I'm not you!"

Insulted, Melva took a step back. "Yeah, well, so what. Passing classes ain't no problem."

"Then do it!" Tabitha challenged. "Stop cutting all the time and pass."

"You cut classes, too!" Melva said.

"Why don't you get it?" Tabitha asked, raising her hands in confusion. "I pass! Cut or not, I pass! If I do skip a class, it's not everyday, and it's not so much it'll cause me to fail. You talk about this college is recruiting you and that college is sending you letters, but you probably won't even get outta high school."

"That's what you think, but watch me graduate on time," Melva said, confidently. "And just because you pass all your classes, it doesn't mean you're gonna automatically get a scholarship. You gotta have skills, too. I'll pass, and I'll get into college. Coach Stone don't let no Lady Phoenix players get stuck."

"Coach Stone can't go to school for you," Tabitha told her. "Don't sweat him. He thinks he's all that and he can control everybody because he's got little hook-ups here and there. He ain't controlling me. I do what I want. I know I can get my own hook-ups traveling with the Roadrunners and getting seen."

Melva laughed. "You're crazy. You think you're going to get a scholarship because you travel with the Roadrunners? That weak little jump shot ain't gonna get you over. You ain't got no skills. There are plenty of players that shoot like you, or better, playing low-level Division III ball. I don't like Coach Stone that much either, but I'd rather play for him and let him teach me something instead of running around with a team full of so-called all-stars and not getting any better. Too many wanna-be stars on the Roadrunners. Most of them don't go where they think they're going because somebody told them that they were better than they are. All they do is play ball. No school, no job, nothing."

It was Tabitha turn to laugh out loud. "Hold up! I know you're not talking."

"I'm gonna pass my classes, you'll see," Melva insisted. "Just to prove you're a bigger dummy for leaving us."

"Okay, when I see that mystical, magical moment, I'll believe it."

"You're gonna believe more than that on Sunday when you're playing with the Roadrunners and I'm scoring in your face."

"You'd better worry about beating the Imperial Crew today, first," Tabitha warned. "I heard Yolanda Hopson had your number in the Housing League championship game."

"We'll take care of business," Melva assured her. "Just make sure y'all beat the Lady Panthers so I can skate on your ass all game on Sunday."

"Yeah, right. You are *not* going to beat us."

Melva shrugged. "Maybe, maybe not. Whatever happens, I'm gonna embarrass your ass every chance I get. And if we do win…"

"You won't!" Tabitha said, cutting her off. "So seeya!"

Melva shook her head as she watched Tabitha stroll off down the walkway and into the gym. "We can't lose," she told herself. "Not now. Not to her."

5:48 P.M.

Carlene Thompson left Melinda sitting in the stands and went to the bathroom. Melinda proudly looked down at the new Lady Phoenix jersey she was wearing and smiled. She leaned back, and her smile faded as saw Kimberly walking past. Kimberly was looking for Velvet, and smiled and waved at Melinda when she noticed her. Melinda turned her head to ignore her. Seeing Melinda's reaction, Kimberly frowned a little bit and walked off.

RISE OF THE PHOENIX

"I can't help it," Melinda said to herself. "I get this sinking feeling in my stomach when she's around. She makes me nervous. I used to think she was so cool. Why does she have to be that way? Why?"

Kimberly continued looking for Velvet but thought about Melinda...and herself. *Why is Melinda trippin' like this? I'm a human being—a girl preparing myself for womanhood. I go to school to prepare for college so that I can make something of my life. I go to church to pray and learn how to do the right thing. But, what is the right thing? Going to school? Playing basketball? Who knows? I'm just me, and that's all I want to be.*

5:53 P.M.

Tabitha and Rayna were the first of the Roadrunners out from the locker room and walked to their team's bench together dressed in their crimson and white uniforms and matching black Nikes.

"I'm glad I'm down with The Roadrunners now," Tabitha said as she placed her bag underneath the bench. "After we beat the hell outta the Lady Panthers today, I'm going to look forward to killing the Lady Phoenix."

"True," Rayna agreed, also placing her bag under the bench. "None of these teams stand a chance against us. I think this is the best team the Roadrunners has ever had."

"I'm just wondering, though...I mean...I know this team is the best by far, but why aren't we having any practices?"

"Everybody can't always make it to practice," Rayna explained to her new teammate. "Connie is playing with the Lady Panthers in the Fly Girl tournament. The twins are playing with East Point in Highland Park, and Stacey is playing in some tournaments with the Long Island Tide."

"Stacey? That gay chick?" Tabitha grimaced. "Why'd you have to bring her nasty-ass name up?"

"Gay or not, she can play," Rayna said. "She's the real deal. When we had her and Beverly both playing with us, I'd bet money we were good enough to beat a lot of college teams. We're gonna need her when we go to the Nationals."

"Well, she'd better not step to me with no bullshit," Tabitha went on. "I'll punch that bitch right in her face."

At that moment, a six-foot-two, muscularly defined girl with a smooth coffee bean complexion walked into the gym. She wore a blowout hairdo and gold earrings shaped like her home island of Trinidad. She had on a pair of white, seventies-styled go-go boots, a short white mini-skirt and a gold-colored tunic. It was Stacey Conyers. She was running late and looked around to see if the game was about to start. When she saw the Lady Panthers on the court warming up and only Rayna and Tabitha from the Roadrunners standing by the bench, she figured that things must've been running behind schedule. She started toward the locker room and looked over at Rayna and Tabitha again. Just then, she saw Erin and Ellen walk in and over toward them. Thoughts of how she'd gotten into confrontations with Tabitha and the twins in Washington resurfaced in her mind.

I don't care what people say, she thought. *I do what I want. Why do I have to be like them to be accepted? If that's the case, I'd rather not be accepted. Humph, on the other hand, I'd better watch myself. I don't think my mom will take it too well if things blow up. I shouldn't have come on to Beverly so strong in Washington, either. Word can get out and rumors can start. I know that certain people already have issues with it.*

5:56 P.M.
Kimberly still hadn't found Velvet, so she sat on the bottom row of the bleachers and waited for her. Stacey walked past, and they made brief eye contact and gave each other a cordial wave. Juanita walked over to Kimberly and sat down.

"'Sup, sista girl?" Juanita said, playfully. She had her white pinstriped Derek Jeter jersey on.

"Hey, Nita," Kimberly dryly responded.

"What's goin' on, girl?"

"Nothing. I'm just waiting for Velvet."

"I see. Sooo...um...what's happening with you?"

Kimberly looked away. "Nothing."

"I think something is going on. It looked to me like something was up between you and Melinda in practice."

RISE OF THE PHOENIX

"It's no big thing, Nita. Forget about it."

"You sure?"

"You should be talking to her, not me. I'm fine. I don't have a problem with her, she has one with me."

"Why?"

"Because she's homophobic."

Juanita gave Kimberly a "you must be kidding" look. "You're letting that stress you? I can't believe that."

Kimberly shrugged.

"You need to stop," Juanita told her. "You're bigger than that. Get your head outta the dirt and come back to ground level. This ain't you, so don't let it be you."

Kimberly tucked her lips and leaned back. "I hear you, Nita."

"Be easy, Kim. Don't stress out over one person's pettiness."

Juanita patted Kimberly on the knee and walked off. Kimberly sat several minutes staring into space and knew Juanita was right. *I don't care what people think or say, I'm not going to hide what I am for them. I'm not hurting anyone. If people choose not to speak to me because I'm a lesbian, that's on them. I don't judge them, so they shouldn't judge me.*

Velvet walked up. "Hey!" she shouted, awakening Kimberly from her thoughts.

Kimberly jumped from being startled. "You scared me," she whined.

Velvet laughed. "That's because you were sitting here in a trance. What are you thinking about so hard?"

"I was thinking about you, and me, and everybody like us."

"What's up?" Velvet inquired.

"I'm just happy," Kimberly said. "Happy to be me, and happy to have you."

Melinda looked over and saw Kimberly stand up and embrace Velvet. She watched them as they walked up the bleachers and took seats up near the top. She noticed how they both wore matching outfits. Kimberly had on an army-green midriff top, camouflage short shorts and camouflage-designed sneakers. Velvet wore an army-green sleeveless blouse that tied in the front, a camouflage mini skirt and army green clog-heeled sandals. They both carried their game gear in matching black backpacks.

Melinda shook her head, then leaned forward, rested her elbows on her knees and put her face in her hands. She thought back to the last game she came to and how Kimberly and Velvet wore matching outfits that day, too, and came up with the obvious conclusion.

"I don't know why I'm thinking about it so much," she said to herself. "I don't even know why I care. I should be concentrating on our game. Wow, my first game and it's the playoffs. I hope I do well. That is if I get to play. I did pretty good in practice yesterday. I just hope that sinking feeling in my stomach goes away."

"I mean it," Tabitha said as Ellen and Erin walked over to her and Rayna. "She'd better not approach me with that nonsense. I'm not Beverly. I'll knock her ass out."

"You talking about Stacey?" Ellen asked.

"Yeah," Tabitha replied.

"She just went into the locker room," Erin said.

The twins both had solid athletic bodies. They were pretty girls with hypnotic blue eyes and long blonde hair they both wore in a Dutch braid when they played. They wore smaller, tighter uniforms with much shorter shorts than ball players usually wore, drawing more teenaged boys to the girls' games than usual.

"I'm telling you, something's wrong with her," Tabitha insisted.

"Yo, forget about it," Rayna said. "You just have to play together, not live together."

"You mean to tell me it doesn't bother you at all," Tabitha asked her.

"Why should it? Did it bother you that some of your Lady Phoenix teammates are lesbians?"

Tabitha stepped back and looked at Rayna displaying a puzzled frown. "Who? What are you talking about?"

"Come on, Tabitha, you had to know about Kim and Velvet," Ellen said. "It's not like they even hide it anymore."

Tabitha remembered seeing Kimberly come into the gymnasium and looked around for her near where other Lady Phoenix members were gathering. She didn't see Kimberly or Velvet with the rest of the team and didn't notice them sitting high on the top of the stands. "No, I didn't know about it," she said. "Are you sure?"

"Just as sure as I am about Stacey," Ellen said as she began to stretch.

"Anyway, it doesn't matter," Rayna said. "As long as Stacey doesn't approach me that way, we're cool. Actually, I think she's a nice person. She's always cool when she comes around. I've got no beef with her."

Tabitha thought for a second. "Yeah, I guess you're right. I'm just hyper because I want to get this game over with. I don't just want to beat my old team. I want to blow them out. They'd better not fuck up and lose to the Imperial Crew."

"I don't think they'll lose," Erin said, joining her sister in stretching. "They want to get at you as bad as you want to get at them."

"I hear ya," Tabitha said, thinking about her recent conversation with Melva.

5:55 P.M.

Stacey finished changing into her uniform and picked up her bag to head out of the locker room. Mildred had just left after rushing her and the other Roadrunner players out. Stacey was the last to leave.

"I'm ready for this game," she said to herself as she walked into the gym. "I'm not going to worry about anything or anyone. I'll be careful what I say to people because I don't want any trouble, but they'd better not disrespect me, either. I won't stand for it."

6:02 P.M.

"Hey, what if the Roadrunners lost this game?" Melva asked. "Wouldn't that be funny?"

When Trina didn't respond and just continued to stare blankly out onto the court, Melva nudged her in the side to get her attention. "Hey, you heard what I said?"

"What are you doing? Why are you fuckin' pokin' me in my side?"

Melva was taken aback by the way Trina snapped at her. She knew right away that something was wrong. "What's up, Tree? You a'ight?"

"Just don't poke me, that's all," Trina said.

Melva lifted her palms. "Yo, I ain't mean nothing by it. Dang, my bad."

Trina pulled her arms into the sleeves of her oversized white T-shirt, wrapped them around herself and began to slightly rock back and forth. "Mel, I'm going to tell you something, but what I'm about to tell you has got to stay between us."

Melva nodded in agreement and asked, "What is it, Tree?"

"You have to give me your word, first."

Melva held up her right hand. "Word. It doesn't leave this spot."

Trina hesitated. She watched as Connie King won the tap, slapping the ball into Erin Saltzman's hands, who pitched it to "Future" Cortez on the right wing. Future hit a streaking Stacey Conyers for a high-flying finger roll.

Melva watched Trina closely and waited to hear what she had to tell.

Trina looked over at Melva and wished she hadn't said anything. But she was so scared she had to tell someone, hoping that person would say something back to make her feel better. She looked up to her left and saw Kimberly and Velvet sitting together and wished she would've waited to bring this up to Velvet, instead.

"What is it, Tree?" Melva pressed. "C'mon, you can tell me."

Trina choked out the words. "Um...I, uh...I'm late."

Melva threw her head back and sank in her seat. "Aw Fuck, Tree! No! Not you, dawg! Aw, fuck!"

Trina turned her head and started rocking again. Seeing her reaction, Melva sat up and held her hand to console.

"I'm sorry. How late are you?"

"A week," Trina whispered.

"A week? Damn. You tell Coach and Nita, yet?"

Trina shook her head.

"Your moms know?"

"No," Trina said. "I don't know if I am for sure. I haven't told anyone because I'm hoping it's a false alarm."

"Yeah, I hear you. But damn, Tree, y'all weren't using protection?"

"The condom broke on us," Trina said and threw up two fingers, "twice!"

RISE OF THE PHOENIX

"Well, we need to go get you one of those home pregnancy tests after the game," Melva suggested. "You can take it at my house if you want. Wait, you gonna play today?"

"Yeah," Trina said. "I'm playing. It's cool."

"I'm sayin', you were buggin' just now when I poked you in the side."

"I was trippin'. Sorry. I want to do what you said, take the test at your house. We can't do it tonight, though. Tomorrow."

"Whatever you want, Tree. You're my dawg."

Trina nodded to her friend.

9:43 P.M.

Velvet was so elated after the game she didn't even bother to change. She took off her jersey and sneakers and replaced them with a T-shirt and flip-flops. She sat comfortably reclined and chitchatted away during the ride home as T.J. dropped off Melva, Trina and Kimberly before bringing her home.

Velvet couldn't wait to tell Sheila about the game and the twenty points she scored to lead the way. T.J. pulled up in front of the house, and she jumped out of the car and rushed to the front door. She always made a production out of using her own key to enter the Stonewall's residence. It made her feel more at home. She was especially dramatic this night as she flung the door open whooping with joy, chanting, "We won! We won! We blew them chicks out! We won! We won! Was there ever any doubt?!"

Velvet dropped her bag in front of the couch and trotted to the master bedroom and knocked on the door.

"Sheila, are you home?" There was no answer, so she knocked again. "Sheila? Sheila, are you in there?"

She gave up and turned to head back toward the living room, but then heard a noise. She turned around and put her ear to the door. There was a loud crashing sound that made her jump from being startled.

"Sheila?!" she cried, and then pushed the door a bit.

Velvet looked back to see if T.J. was coming into the house and wondered what was taking him so long to park the car. That's when she heard moaning. She opened the door all the way and stepped inside. She looked around and didn't see Sheila anywhere, but then noticed the shower in the master bedroom was running. She heard more moaning coming out of the bathroom that sounded like Sheila was in pain. She began to worry and sprinted across the room to see about her. When she got to the bathroom, she looked inside and screamed.

 T.J. had just come into the house and heard Velvet's scream. He ran into the bedroom and to the bathroom, and then cried out as well.

THE FEAR OF LOSING YOU

Wednesday, July 13, 2005 – 11:14 P.M.

Carlene and Melinda sat in the waiting area of the hospital with Beverly. They were all in anguish, waiting for a word on Burton's condition. Beverly's eyes were red and her face flushed due to the headache she acquired from her constant crying. She said silent prayers to herself, vowing that if her father was spared she'd take care of him and never give him a reason to be angry with her again.

Carlene repressed her tears, trying to stay strong for the sake of Beverly and Melinda. She kept her arms around Beverly and held her close to keep her from shaking, but also to keep herself from going into a frenzied state. She thought about her and Burton's weekend in Atlantic City. They took in some shows, did a little gambling, had romantic dinners, and strolled along the boardwalk. They got engaged there.

Melinda sat in the seat on the other side of her mother, crawled up in ball with her head rested on Carlene's shoulder. There hadn't been any words spoken in the last half-hour while they all sat without moving the whole time.

This was Burton's second heart attack in four years. He was diagnosed with an enlarged heart and was supposed to be taking it easy and trying to remain stress free. A less demanding job, exercise and a healthy diet, in addition to being strong for Beverly, were all positive steps he'd taken. But he constantly worried about his condition, which brought on anxieties that kept him at risk.

In the main emergency room, the doctor was just approaching T.J. and Velvet.

"Mr. Stonewall, your wife is going to be just fine. She took five stitches and suffered a mild concussion, but she'll be up and around doing what she usually does in a matter of days."

T.J. and Velvet both sighed with relief and clutched hands.

"Unfortunately," the doctor continued, "it appears that she was in the middle of having a miscarriage when she fell."

T.J. felt like his heart had fallen down into his stomach. He got cold as his whole body froze and his skin started feeling tight. He could feel every pulse in his temple and a migraine surfaced that felt like a sharp object was being driven into his head.

Velvet's face dropped with grief, and her whole body went limp. Her bottom lip trembled, and her eyes started flooding. She grabbed her coach and embraced him tightly, burying her face into his chest.

The doctor rested his hand on T.J.'s shoulder to console. "I'm sorry."

T.J. gathered himself enough to hug Velvet back. He asked the doctor, "Where is she? Can we see her? We need to see her."

"Yes, come with me," the doctor said, beckoning them.

T.J. put his arm around Velvet and escorted her as they followed behind the doctor. When they got to Sheila's bed in the trauma unit, she was lying with her eyes closed and covered up in a sheet to her neck. T.J. started to fret over his wife's pale complexion. He hurried over and kneeled at her bedside and combed her hair back with his fingers. When Sheila opened her eyes and saw him, she forced a smile.

"Hey, baby." Her voice was scratchy and hoarse.

"Hey, Mama, how're you feeling?"

Sheila looked into the grief-stricken face of the man she loved and began to cry. "Oh, T.J., our baby is gone. It's gone."

"I know, Mama," he said as he put his arms around her and hugged her tightly.

Velvet came over, sat on the edge of the bed and wrapped her arms around the both of them.

Juanita came running into the hospital from the emergency room entrance and saw Carlene, Beverly and Melinda sitting in the waiting room. She rushed right over to them. She saw Beverly and Melinda crying and started to panic.

"Hey, y'all, what's up? Where's T.J.? Is Sheila okay?"

They all looked at her with puzzled expressions.

"Sheila? I don't... We haven't seen Coach Stone," Carlene said.

"Well, where's Velvet? What's happening?"

RISE OF THE PHOENIX

"We haven't seen anyone since we've been here," Carlene told her. "And we've been sitting here the whole time, since they took Burt in for surgery."

Now, Juanita had a mystified look. "Burt? Surgery? What are you talking about?"

"Burt had a heart attack."

Juanita's head and shoulders dropped. "Oh, my God. This isn't happening. Velvet called me and said that Coach Stone's wife slipped in the shower and hurt herself pretty badly. She said something about Sheila busting her head and a lot of blood and something else."

Beverly lifted her head and shouted, "What?!"

Juanita gathered herself, and then touched Beverly's knee to calm her. "Wait, take it easy. You have your own situation here to deal with. I'm going to go find Coach Stone and Velvet and see how things are going with them, and then I'll come back to check on y'all. Just sit tight and be strong. Everything's gonna be all right."

"Thank you," Carlene said.

Thursday, July 14, 2005 – 8:02 A.M.

T.J. stayed by Sheila's bedside all night, and Velvet and Juanita spent the night in the waiting room. They sat and prayed with Carlene, Beverly and Melinda until a nurse came and got them around three-thirty in the morning, and they left to see about Burton. Juanita and Velvet stayed behind just in case T.J. would come looking for them.

"I'm starving," Velvet said.

Juanita pulled some money from the pocket of her jeans—a blue Matsui T-shirt to go with them—and handed it to her. "There's a coffee shop across the street. Go get yourself something to eat and bring me back a cup of tea with honey and lemon."

Velvet took the cash and left. When she got outside, she turned her cell phone on to check if she had any messages. As soon as the phone came on, it rang. Velvet knew this particular ring tone. It was from the person whose voice she felt she really needed to hear at that moment.

"Hello, Daddy."

"Booby, what's going on?" His voice was firm. "Your mother just showed me something of yours, something she found in your suitcase that just knocked me out. Is this for real, baby girl? Have you been having sex with another girl? Are you gay?"

Velvet took a breath. "Yes, Daddy."

Her father's voice saddened. "Oh, Booby, what happened? I know that more and more females are doing that sort of thing these days, trying to keep up with some sort of sick fad or whatever, but I would've never thought that you would get into such a thing. What brought this on?"

"Daddy, I..." Velvet's voice started to tremble as she searched for words.

"Take it easy, Booby. I didn't call to jump all over you about this over the phone. We do need to talk, though. I'm in New York, right now. I'm on my way to pick you up so I can bring you back to California."

"Daddy, no!" Velvet shouted. "You can't take me away now!"

"I have to. Your mother and I are suffering a great deal over this. It's making us both crazy. I know you want to stay so you can play basketball, but this is important. I set up appointments for you, me and your mother to get some spiritual counseling and also to see a psychologist. I'm on my way to your coach's house to pick you up, right now."

"Daddy, please..."

"No more discussion, baby girl, is that clear?"

"Yes, sir."

"Now, I suggest you start packing up your things. I'll be there in about thirty minutes, I guess."

"We're not home, right now," Velvet said.

"Where are you?"

"At the hospital."

"The hospital?" Now there was worry in his voice. "What happened? Did you get hurt in a game or something?"

"No, Daddy, I'm fine," Velvet told him. "It's... It's Sheila, Coach Stone's wife. She slipped in the shower."

Her father's voice changed from worry to concern. "Oh, my God, Booby. Is she alright?"

"No, Daddy. When she fell she was in the middle of having a miscarriage. She slipped and tried to grab the shower curtain, but it fell on her and she hit her head on the faucet."

"Oh, my God! I'm so sorry to hear that. What hospital are you at?"

RISE OF THE PHOENIX

"Brookdale Hospital, on Rockaway Parkway and Linden Boulevard."

"Okay, I'm coming there. Just sit tight and wait until I get there."

"Yes, sir."

Velvet put her phone away and stood in front of the hospital, staring across the street at the diner. The thoughts of her father coming to get her added to the grief she was already feeling, and she leaned up against the wall and slowly slid down to the ground crying openly.

8:50 A.M.

"There he is," Velvet told T.J., who stood beside her waiting for her father to arrive.

T.J. looked out and saw a stocky, clean-shaven, brown man sporting a wavy, close-cropped haircut with specks of gray on top, and a wearing a beige Armani suit. He walked erect, taking long, slow, powerful strides.

Reverend Douglas Scott came through the sliding doors. It was the first time Velvet saw her father face-to-face in two years. Although they spoke on the telephone every week and visited via their webcams and instant messaging since he moved to California, their conflicting schedules prevented them spending any time together. Even on holidays, Velvet was either playing basketball in some holiday tournament, or Reverend Scott was touring or both. But that was due to change the upcoming Thanksgiving, when the whole family would attend the premiere of Velvet's sister's first movie.

"Hey, Booby." Reverend Scott opened his arms to embrace his youngest daughter. His face lit up, and it was obvious how much he missed her. His expression changed, though, when he saw her puffy eyes and her dressed in a wrinkled basketball T-shirt, shorts and flip-flops. He realized that meant she had probably been at the hospital all night.

"Hey, Daddy." Velvet's voice was dry. She always thought she'd jump up and down with joy the next time she saw her father, but the present circumstances brought on different emotions. She hugged her father back affectionately, while wishing he wasn't there.

T.J. approached. "Hi, I'm T.J. Stonewall, Velvet's basketball coach."

"Yes, we met before," Reverend Scott said, releasing one arm to shake his hand. "Velvet told me about your wife. I'm sorry. Is she going to be okay?"

"Yeah, she'll be as good as new in no time," T.J. was relieved to say. "She's far more hurt emotionally than she is physically."

"I can imagine," said Reverend Scott as he looked at Velvet. "It's tough for anyone to lose their child. But God doesn't give us anything we can't handle. Just stay in prayer and everything will work out."

"Thanks, I will. Listen, my wife is sleeping right now, and I want to get back up to her before she wakes up, but I want to talk to you a little bit, first."

"Sure, we can talk. Um, excuse us for a minute, Booby."

"Okay, Daddy." Velvet let go of her father to go take a seat and glanced over at T.J. as she walked off, knowing that he wasn't his usual self, but hoping that he could come up with the right things to say.

"What's up, Coach?" Reverend Scott asked.

"I want to talk to you about taking Velvet back to California."

Reverend Scott inhaled and tucked his hands into his pants pockets. "What about it?"

"I know you made the trip all the way out here, but I want to ask you to please let her stay."

Reverend Scott shook his head. "I'm sorry, Coach, I can't do that."

"Wait, just hear me out, please?" T.J. requested. "Now, I can't say that I wouldn't be doing the same exact thing you are, right now. In fact, my wife and I talked about this the first night Velvet came to stay with us. Although she opened my eyes to some things, I still think I'd be hurt and disappointed if I found out that my child was gay."

"Oh, so you do understand how I feel?"

"Absolutely," T.J. said. "You know, I have a connection with all of the members in the Lady Phoenix program, past and present, but I've been able to connect with your daughter in the past couple of weeks on a level that I've never had with any of the others."

"Well, that was bound to happen with her living in your house," said the proud father. "Velvet is a lovely and lovable girl. I've never known anyone to meet her and not take to her right away."

RISE OF THE PHOENIX

T.J. was inclined to agree. "You're right. I know she and my wife hit it off real well. They're shopping together, having girl talks and singing together. You should've been there to see them sing in church. They were like nothing I've ever seen before."

"Yeah, Booby can really blow. God's got great things planned for her."

"God is doing great things with her, Reverend Scott, especially among her teammates and around my home. The girl's got talents oozing out of her ears. The thing is that the talent she wants to prove she has most of all is on the basketball court."

Reverend Scott removed his hands from his pockets and folded his arms across his chest. "Coach, you may not understand this, but there are things in this world more important than basketball," he said, sarcastically.

"I know that," T.J. said. "I've realized it even more over the last twelve hours. But this is not about simply letting Velvet play basketball. It's about letting her play because it's a fulfillment for her. She's trying to accomplish something: her goals and dreams outside of the music world that are within her reach."

"And they'll still be within her reach," Reverend Scott said. "She has more than enough time to reach her basketball dreams when she returns from California." Reverend Scott replaced his hands into his pockets. "But I have to be honest with you, Coach. Basketball isn't very high on my list of things I want my daughter to do. There are just too many negative influences in women's sports these days. This lesbian craze is way out of control. When Velvet told me that she wanted to play, I thought about the kinds of things she'd be exposed to. I know all about it because my sister played basketball, my niece played tennis and two of my female cousins played softball. I remember all the stories they all told me about what went on in the locker rooms and such. They were terrible, disgusting stories. But I okayed Velvet playing, thinking that since she's saved and was raised in the church she wouldn't be apt to submit to any such influences. But the devil is a liar and a trickster that plays on the desires of man. Basketball is getting to be all she thinks about and talks about. She's putting God on the back burner for it, which makes *it* her god. Velvet has to refocus and get her priorities straight. She has to get away from this kind of environment so that devil can be cast out of her."

"Reverend Scott, you know how psychology works?" T.J. asked, rhetorically. "If you believe that Velvet's sexual preference is the work of the devil, do you think snatching her away kicking and screaming is not part of his plan? Don't you think this could be a ploy to cause separation and conflict? You know how kids are. Rebellion is their nature. They do things *because* we say they can't. That's what the devil uses to get to them. Snatching her away is not the answer. She just needs constant guidance. Education is the key."

"Which is why I'm taking her away, to educate her. I should say to give her a refresher course on something she already knows very well. I believe everyone living that lifestyle knows."

"Let me emphasize again that I don't approve of that way of living either, but..."

"But what, Coach? Did you see those photographs my daughter took with that other girl? Did you see what acts they were engaging in?"

T.J. slowly shook his head. "No, sir, I didn't."

"I wish you had. Because if you really don't approve of the lifestyle, it would've affected you the way it has me, and we wouldn't even be having this conversation."

"We're having this conversation because of what you said a moment ago. I'll be honest with you. Velvet has had an affect on my wife and I that probably no one else could. We've taken to her. She...she just fits. My wife just lost a child. This would be like losing two. I know it is for me."

Reverend Scott empathized. "I know how you must be feeling. It was hard for me when each of my children left home to be on their own. Shoot, I didn't even let them go away to college. They all commuted. I said I'd bend for Velvet because of her basketball dreams, but I don't know about that now. It was extremely hard for me to move away and leave her behind when her mother and I split up." He rested his hands on T.J.'s shoulders. "You and your wife will both get through this. Just stay in prayer. I'll be in town until Sunday morning. I'll make sure Velvet gets a chance to visit you again before we leave. Until then, I'll be praying for you."

COMPROMISING SITUATIONS

Thursday, July 14, 2005 – 12:22 P.M.

Trina and Melva sat in the bathroom waiting for the results of the home pregnancy test. Neither of them had heard the news about Sheila or Burton yet because they were out all morning and hadn't spoken to anyone else. To try and make her feel better, Melva treated Trina to breakfast at the Galaxy Diner on Pennsylvania Avenue before they visited the pharmacy.

"What does it say?" Trina asked. She was sitting on top of the closed toilet seat with her leg bouncing from nervousness. Her hair was wrapped in a scarf, and she wore the same oversized white T-shirt and fitted black jeans from the day before.

Melva looked down at the pregnancy test and shook her head. She had a serious look on her face, which led Trina to believe that it wasn't the news she wanted to hear.

"I think you should still go see a doctor today if you can," Melva suggested. "I mean, this thing can be wrong. You should go check and see."

Trina wrapped her arms around herself and began to rock. "They're usually right, though."

"Well, you'd better hope so," Melva said. "Because this says you're *not* pregnant."

Trina sprung to her feet and rushed to Melva's side. "What? It says what?"

Grinning, Melva handed the test to her. Trina read it and shouted, "Hallelujah!"

Melva chuckled at her. "Like I said, though, go see a doctor."

"Yes, yes, I will. I'll call the gynecologist," Trina promised.

"And you need to visit the clinic and get tested," Melva told her. "If the condom broke on you, it could've broken on someone else, too."

"Yes, I'll do that. Right now, though, I just want to dance." Trina did a little two-step in front of the bathroom mirror.

Melva laughed at her. "Yeah, you go on." Then she got serious again. "I haven't said anything up until this point, but you get through this you better count your lucky stars and do the right thing. You sure didn't look like you were ready to do the time, and that's because you're not, so you shouldn't be doing the crime."

Trina nodded. "I know, Mel. I broke it off with Daquan last week, and I haven't seen him or spoken to him since. I'm not doing it with him or anyone else until I get myself right. This was scary as hell, and it taught me a lesson that I won't soon forget."

"That's what I'm talkin' 'bout, dawg. Keep it tight, a'ight?"

Trina hugged Melva close. "A'ight," she said.

1:57 P.M.

Mildred Negron had just come back from having lunch, and as soon as she sat down at her desk, the telephone rang.

"Thank you for calling Deutsche Bank. This is Mildred Negron. How may I help you?" she answered in such a routinely professional voice it almost sounded automated.

"Millie, this is Sam Pernell," he said in a slow dragging, doleful voice.

"What's up, Sam? You sound like you're melancholy."

"Well, Millie, I don't really feel like jumping for joy, right now," Sam sardonically replied.

Just then, Millie remembered why. "Hey, how're T.J. and his people holding up?"

"That's sort of what I called to talk to you about," Sam said. "Things are not well, so I want to postpone the championship game until the twentieth at six o'clock."

"Sorry, can't do it," Mildred abruptly responded.

"What do you mean, you can't do it?"

"Just what I said, Sam. The National Tournament is the next day. That doesn't give us enough time to get ready."

Sam began to get annoyed. "First of all, you're assuming you're going to win this tournament."

RISE OF THE PHOENIX

"I don't have to assume, Sam, I know it. And I'm not going to play Wednesday night, and then probably have to fly to Louisiana the same night, just in case I'll have to play Thursday morning. My girls will be too tired. If you're going to postpone the championship game, it'll have to be Monday the latest."

"That's too soon. Didn't you hear what happened? T.J.'s wife busted her head and lost their baby. And one of the players' father had a heart attack."

"Yes, I heard, and my heart goes out. But I still have to look out for my own best interest. I'm sorry."

"I can't believe you said that!" Sam was livid, and began involuntarily raising his voice. "You made a big fuss about having your game against the Lady Phoenix changed so that you could go to D.C., and now when they need you, you're talking about your best interest?! What makes you think it's all about you and what you want?!"

"I didn't say that…"

"You didn't have to say it! I'm telling you, not asking you! The game is next Wednesday! If you don't show up, that's on you!"

"Hold up!" Mildred quietly shouted back into the phone. She had to keep her voice down because she was at work, but she still spoke aggressively. "I don't have to play next Wednesday if I don't want to, and I'm not going to. I asked you to ask your people to work things out for me and you did. You didn't have to do it."

"That's a lie and you know it. You made the board of directors feel like their backs were against the wall by selling them some bull. You knew I wasn't going to buy your crap, and that's why you went over my head. You never said one word to me until *after* the board of directors told me that I *had* to find a way to work things out for you. You should know, however, that I fought it as hard as I could, but your charming personality won the right people over, as usual."

"Say whatever you want, Sam, but I'm still not waiting until Wednesday night to play. I'll call the national office and complain if I have to, and insist they follow the rules and play the game on the scheduled date. The rules are specific. I have them right here. I can read them to you if you like."

"I don't need you to read anything to me, Millie!" Sam growled.

Mildred ignored him and read anyway. "It clearly states right here that 'No team shall cause a delay or postponement of a game's time or date without the combination of consent from the league's directors and coordinators, and approval from the opposing team.' When I wanted it, you all granted it to me. I feel bad that I can't do it for you, but unfortunately, I can't. I'm sorry."

Sam laughed in disbelief. "This is a trip. You really don't care about anyone except yourself. You are a narcissistic ruffian without a heart or a soul who is suffering from acute megalomania. It's your fault you don't have a life. Stop taking it out on everybody else."

Before Mildred could respond, she heard a loud click followed by a dead silence. She repeated "Hello? Hello? Hello?" until the dial tone started. *"Coño, pequena rata gorda. Tus días a cargo de esta liga estan contados."*

6:06 P.M.

The mood in the gymnasium was sadness turned to anger as Juanita tried to explain to the team what was happening.

"Oh, my God!" Melva shrieked. "I can't believe this is happening!"

"It's not fair," Trina said. "We had to wait on them when they went to D.C."

Juanita spoke calmly in an attempt to settle things down. "I know, but we can't let it get us down. It's got to pick us up. I know you all may feel like it's a big jip and you should because it is. But you all know that you have to be ready for any and everything. Remember, the date wouldn't change, either, if we had a bunch of injuries. Beverly's not playing, Tabitha's playing against us, and I don't know what's happening with Velvet, but I don't think she's going to be there, either. What does that mean? It means that we may only have the eight players here now. So, we all are going to have to just dig a little deeper within ourselves and pull out something extra. I know you can do it. You did it to beat the Imperial Crew twice last week."

"Yeah, easier said than done," Kimberly whined.

"Don't be pessimistic, Kim," Juanita said.

"Word," Melva said. "Don't nobody start trippin'. There ain't no way I'm tryin' to lose, especially to no team Tabitha's on."

RISE OF THE PHOENIX

"You can't make this a personal battle, either, Melva," Trina told her. "If you come to the game with the *I* instead of *we* attitude, we're gonna lose for sure."

"No, I ain't tryin' to lose!"

"We heard what you said, Melva," Juanita said. "The problem is that you keep saying, 'I.' The only way we're going to be able to compete at all is by having a *team* mentality. We have to be willing to do everything together. Like Tree was saying, this game is not a duel between you and Tabitha."

"I feel you," Melva agreed.

"Hey, we can do this," Juanita told the team. "Everybody just free your minds of any doubts."

6:58 P.M.

Sam entered the lobby of condominiums on Central Park West and One Hundred and Tenth Street and rang the bell for suite 302. After several tries and no response, he tapped on the glass door to get the doorman's attention. The buzzer sounded and Sam entered and approached the security desk. There sat a Middle Eastern man in his late fifties whose diminutive size made Sam seem massive in comparison.

"Excuse me, sir," Sam said. "I'm here to see Terry Gonzalez."

The doorman hesitated, and his speech was tentative. "Uh…well, um…Did you say Gonzalez?"

Sam noticed the man's eyes flashing over at the group of people waiting for the elevator. The person who stepped out of the small crowd wearing a black business suit walked toward him and said, "I'm Terry Gonzalez. You're Sam Pernell, I presume?"

"Yes," Sam replied. "I was afraid you weren't home. I thought I was being stood up."

"No, I just had to run out a minute," Terry said, holding up the plastic grocery bag for Sam to see. "Sorry about that. Come on up so we can talk."

Sam sat on the ivory leather sofa in the living room of the small Neo-Italian furnished, one bedroom apartment and waited while Terry quickly changed clothes and put groceries away.

"Would you like something to eat or drink," Terry asked, calling out from the kitchen.

"No, thanks," Sam politely shouted back.

"You sure? I'm having a fresh green vegetable shake."

Sam was glad Terry couldn't see him bawl up his face and stick out his tongue in disgust. The tone of his voice remained the same, though. "No, thank you. I'm fine."

Terry entered the living room wearing a yellow T-shirt and gym shorts, carrying a large glass filled with the thick green substance and sat on the wingback chair across from the sofa.

"So, what changed your mind about meeting me?" Terry asked, then slurped some of the green drink through a straw.

"I had enough of Millie's crap," Sam said. "That woman doesn't care about anything or anyone but herself."

Terry nodded and took another slurp. "What happened to you wanting to stay out of it?"

"Let's just say that desperate times call for desperate measures," Sam answered.

Terry's eyes squinted. "Revenge, just as I suspected."

"No, it's not just that," Sam insisted.

"Oh, but it *is* that," Terry said. "Mr. Pernell, I was willing to share some things with you before, but now I don't think it would be such a good idea."

Disappointment showed on Sam's face. "So you have a change of heart. Have you and Millie gotten back together?"

"No, not exactly," Terry said, regrettably. "I know Millie loves me, she's just going through some things right now. She's under all this pressure to do what Charles Greene wants her to. She does what he wants because he's helping her live her dream. Millie grew up poor, living in the not so pleasant areas of the South Bronx, sometimes in shelters. Sports, especially volleyball, were her refuge. She's a winner, and winning is everything to her. It means accomplishment to her."

"Yeah, but winning isn't what sports is all about," Sam said. "At least not when it comes down to who scores the most points. It's about learning, achieving dreams, personal bests, making something of yourself, and stuff like that."

RISE OF THE PHOENIX

After another slurp, and then a tiny burp, Terry said, "Yeah, well, that's what people always say. I'm on the outside looking in because I've never played sports. I'm into fitness, not athletics. But looking in from the outside, I see everybody in sports doing what Charles does, what he has Millie doing and what she wants me to do. I won't have any part of it, though. I was brought up by parents who are law advocates. My father is a hearing examiner in family court, and my mother is a children's lawyer."

"So you're telling me for sure that Charles and Millie are definitely doing something illegal?" Sam asked.

"What I'm telling you is that I'm not telling you anything," Terry answered. "I think that I will be able to get to Millie, and she'll come around."

Sam ran his hand over his bald cranium. "I don't understand," he said. "Why'd you agree to see me if you've changed your mind?"

"I didn't change my mind until you got here," Terry told him. "You came in here talking about getting revenge on the person I'm trying to help—the person I'm in love with. I didn't go directly to Mr. Stonewall because I knew he'd respond the way you're doing now. Now that I know you're not the right person to deal with either, I'm going too say good day to you."

Sam looked away, thought for a moment, and then said, "Okay, let's make a deal."

"No deals," Terry said before taking another slurp. "I'm sorry you wasted your time coming over here."

Sam felt he couldn't let Mildred get away with anything anymore. In his mind, she'd crossed the lines of selfishness and insensitivity for the last time, and he was determined not to leave Terry's condo without getting what he came for. He lost his composure and spoke strictly out of anger. "You're so in love and so loyal to a woman who shows you no loyalty at all. She's gone! Left you over something petty and selfish, but you're sniffing at her tail like a lost puppy."

Taken aback by Sam's aggression and tone of voice, Terry slammed the glass of green shake on the glass-top end table and sprung up from the chair.

KENNETH J. WHETSTONE

"That's enough, Mr. Pernell!" Terry snapped, motioning toward the door to lead Sam out.

"No, it's not enough," Sam spat, unmoved. "Let me tell you something that very, very few people know about. Not even T.J. knows about this. Mildred Negron, the woman you love so much, had a partner last year, a woman named Rose Armstead."

Hearing the name made Terry chuckle. "What, are you going to tell me about all the rumors of Millie and Rose having a so-called fling? I've heard all of those terrible rumors already, Mr. Pernell, and none of them are true. Rose Armstead was just a good friend, that's all. Millie loves me and would never do anything with anyone behind my back. *That* I'm sure of."

"No, you're probably right, Terry. The rumors about Millie and Rose probably were untrue. The truth is that Rose wouldn't like Millie because Millie's not young enough. No, thirty-eight-year-old Rose Armstead likes kids: thirteen, fourteen, fifteen year olds. She was brought up on charges in Missouri six years ago for allegedly having sexual intercourse with a fourteen year old boy. There was a similar case with her three years ago in Ohio involving two thirteen-year-old boys and a twelve-year-old girl. Somehow, every time she got brought up on charges they were dropped, and she'd relocate.

"Rose is not around here this summer because two girls from the Roadrunners, a fourteen-year-old and a sixteen-year-old, accused her of making advances toward them. Millie knew this woman's history, and she let her get involved with the Roadrunners anyway. Why? Because Rose Armstead is loaded, that's why. She bought her way out of trouble. The story that was told to me was that Millie and one of the Roadrunners' players caught Rose in the act having sex with the girl's fifteen-year-old brother. Yes, Millie did dismiss Rose, but not before Rose paid her and all of those kids off.

"So, where is Rose Armstead now? She's an assistant coach at Central College. How'd she get there? Mildred Negron, your precious Millie, got her the job there in a package deal with a player named Ebony Waters. That's the same Ebony Waters, the McDonald's All-American, who was trying to make a choice between UConn, Duke and Notre Dame, and then out of the blue went to Central College, who hadn't had a winning season in eleven years. Millie worked out that deal to get Rose Armstead out of her hair. She convinced Central to give a girl named Coretta Pullman a scholarship. Now, Pullman is a mediocre Division III player at best, but she was also Waters' best friend. Millie sold Central on giving Coretta Pullman a scholarship and hiring Rose Armstead as an assistant so that they can get Ebony Waters, and they'll also get one of the Roadrunners top post players this year."

Terry was aghast and mortified, but kept a poker face and began to clap, deciding that sarcasm was the medicine for the sick feeling. "Quite a story, Mr. Pernell. You should write a book."

"You think this is a joke?!" Sam exclaimed.

"I think it's a fantastic story coming from someone who seems quite desperate," Terry retorted.

"And you haven't been acting out of desperation?" Sam threw back. "Isn't that why you called me in the first place, out of desperation to get the love of your life back?" Now, Sam saw anguish rush across Terry's face, so he humbled his tone before speaking again. "I could get T.J. to help you steer Millie away from Charles Greene. We could all work together and put an end to whatever they're doing so that no one else gets hurt as a result of it. Isn't that what you want?"

Terry sighed. "What I want, Mr. Pernell, is for you to leave. Now."

Again, Sam briefly looked away in thought. Then he pressed his palms down on the couch and pushed himself up. "Fine," he said. "Goodnight."

KENNETH J. WHETSTONE

NYC GIRLS BASKETBALL WEBSITE
COMMUNITY MESSAGE BOARD
From: Roadrunners Fan
Date: Friday, July 15, 2005
Time: 11:00 A.M.
Message: REMATCH
Did anybody see the brackets on the New Attitude website for the National Tournament in New Orleans? It was just posted this morning. There's going to be a rematch between the Bridgeport Belles and the Roadrunners. New York and Connecticut were bracketed against each other in the first round next Thursday at 5:30pm.
From: Mighty Isis
Date: Friday, July 15, 2005
Time: 11:11 A.M.
Message: RE: REMATCH
Those 2 teams should not be playing each other in the first round. Either the National Tournament is stacked with super good teams or somebody got jipped.
From: CrossOver
Date: Friday, July 15, 2005
Time: 12:31 P.M.
Message: RE: REMATCH
How could those teams be matched up? That's impossible because the New York and Connecticut tournaments aren't even over yet. Once again, people on this site are counting Roadrunner eggs before they're hatched.
From: Roadrunners Fan
Date: Friday, July 15, 2005
Time: 1:16 P.M.
Message: RE: REMATCH
To answer CrossOver, the Roadrunners just added Jillian Thorne and Shaniyah Banks to their roster. That gives them 2 more DI bound players, whereas I heard the Lady Phoenix will be playing without Velvet Fuller and Beverly Smalls. There's no way the Roadrunners can

RISE OF THE PHOENIX

lose. The Bridgeport Belles play tonight, and it's doubtful that anyone in their region can beat them either.

From: Coyote
Date: Friday, July 15, 2005
Time: 3:17 P.M.
Message: You must be kidding!

So, the Roadrunners have stolen another 2 players. I can't see how the Staten Island Angels let those girls get away. Coach Negron's brain washing machine must be on full power. I wouldn't be surprised to see them commuting from Staten Island to Brooklyn to transfer to Jefferson in the fall. I'm glad the brackets are the way they are because the Lady Phoenix is undermanned, which means they probably will lose to the Roadrunners, unfortunately. But the Roadrunners won't beat the Bridgeport Belles again because the Belles are too well coached. If the Roadrunners had a good coach, they'd be the best team in the country hands down, but they don't.

From: jay boogie
Date: Friday, July 15, 2005
Time: 3:28 P.M.
Message: RE: You must be kidding!

what's wrong coyote? did you get fired by acme so your spending all your time haten on the roadrunners? get a life and stop trippin.

From: Roadrunners Fan
Date: Friday, July 15, 2005
Time: 4:04 P.M.
Message: RE: You must be kidding!

For everyone's information, Jillian Thorne will remain at McKee Tech and Shaniyah Banks will remain at Curtis H.S. They both will play for the Roadrunners in the big tournaments and play for the S.I. Angels in the local stuff.

EVE OF DESTINY

Saturday, July 16, 2005 – 9:00 P.M.
Mildred:
    Mildred didn't know that Charles had originally made reservations at the popular La Grenouille Restaurant for another woman who called to stand him up the night before. He told her that he pulled some strings that same day to get them in.
    Charles, dressed in a blue Brooks Brothers suit, moved his head to look around the waiter, who was putting his dinner on the table. It was hard for him to take his eyes off Mildred, who sat across from him wearing a red, low-cut dinner dress that revealed the tattoo of a rose on her left breast; her great grandmother's diamond bracelet, earrings and necklace, and her hair up in a French bun. Charles stared lustfully at her full lips covered with red lipstick, which were complimented by the rest of her flawlessly applied makeup.
    Mildred had the veal kidney with mustard, flambé with cognac.
    Charles ordered calf's liver pan seared with sherry vinegar and dates.
    After the waiter sat Mildred's dinner plate down and left, she and Charles raised their wine glasses together, causing a gentle chime.
    "Now, isn't this better?" Charles asked, smiling from ear to ear as he beamed at his collaborator.
    Mildred made a face and shrugged her shoulders. "Better than what?"
    "Better than doing nothing, which was what you were doing before I invited you out on this date."
    "This isn't a date, Charles. I only agreed to come here because I was indeed bored, and you said this was a celebration."
    "And it is. We're celebrating your victory in D.C., and the victories we will both have in New Orleans."
    "So, you're sure you can get those schools to come to New York?"
    "Hey, getting them to do what I want is like doing anything else."

RISE OF THE PHOENIX

Mildred cut a bite-sized portion of her veal kidney. "Good ol' Charles," she said. "You think you can buy anything or anyone."

"That's because everything and everyone's for sale," Charles stated. "You should know."

Mildred cut her eyes at him. "You haven't bought all of me, Charles. Certain parts of me are out of your price range."

"I don't want to buy your love, Millie," Charles said, sincerely. "That's not how I want it. When you give it to me, I want it to be of your own volition. I'll wait until then to have it."

"Your ass'll grow old," Mildred spewed. "I have no intentions of letting anyone get that close to me anymore."

"Stop with the façade," Charles said, unfazed by her attitude. "You're capable of love, everyone is."

"Of course, I am. I love myself. I have more love for myself than I've ever had for anyone, and no one can love me as much as I do."

"Please, spare me the clichés, Mildred. You'd have to give someone a chance to know for sure."

"Pst, I'm tired of giving chances to people. No one's dedicated or loyal, so why try. I need a full commitment and total respect, and I don't think anyone's capable of that."

"I am." Charles stuck out his chest.

"You?" Mildred asked, amused. "How can you be committed to anything when you have respect for nothing?"

"I respect you, and I'd be totally committed if you gave me the chance."

"If you respected me you wouldn't be hitting on me all the time."

"I can't help it. I am so attracted to you it hurts. Do you think I would go out of my way to help anyone else?"

"Oh, so it's for *me*?"

"Of course. Who did you think it was for, those spoiled-ass kids? Their money grubbing parents? Those people don't give a damn about you or me. They're using us the same way we're using them, to get what they want. That's what it's all about."

"I can't deny that," Mildred agreed with a sideways nod.

"You need someone like me, Millie. I could be a pleasant change of pace for you if you gave me the chance."

Mildred just shook her head a bit and began to eat.

Connie:
"Hey, Ma, I'm home," Connie announced as she came into the house.

"Hey, Connie. Where've you been?" her mother asked.

"Coach Negron had practice today, and then I went to the movies with Erin and Ellen afterwards." Connie plopped down in a chair at the kitchen table across from her mother and watched her scratch off lottery tickets.

"Why're you always hangin' out with those white girls?" Mrs. King asked with a smirk.

Connie shrugged. "I don't always hang out with them. I hang out with Future, too."

"Future ain't nothing but a white girl that speaks Spanish."

"C'mon, Ma, stoppit."

Her mother laughed. "You know I'm just playin'. I like Future and the twins a lot. Ellen and Erin are the only white girls I know who ain't afraid to take the subway from their home in Bay Ridge to go to school in East New York."

"They want to win," Connie stated as if it was obvious.

"Humph!" Her mother twisted her lips, figuring it probably took a whole lot more to get the twins' parents to let them go to a school in a low-income, black neighborhood sitting next to housing projects, than it did for her to let Connie travel there from Rosedale, Queens.

"It's the same reason I travel from as far as I do," Connie said. "I'm glad it paid off."

"Speaking of paying off, I know you said you were going to commit to Baylor University, but your coaches have been telling me that we can gain a lot if you waited and visited a few more schools."

"I don't want to visit any other schools," Connie whined. "Baylor is my first, second and only choice. When I go for my visit there this fall, that's going to be it."

"Just be a little bit more open-minded, please?" her mother pleaded. "I'm not saying you have to commit to any other school, just take the

RISE OF THE PHOENIX

visits. It'll help Coach Greene and Coach Negron with their connections, and it'll benefit us all."

"I don't know, Ma. I'll think about it, but I really don't want to lead anybody on."

"Don't look at it that way. If you go on a couple of other visits, even if you don't want to go to the schools, it'll keep a good rapport between your coaches and those schools. Think of all your teammates coming up who're gonna need your coaches to have those connections."

"I don't know, Ma."

Mrs. King got up and went to the refrigerator. She returned with a large slice of cherry cheesecake and a fork and placed them down on the table. "I know you can't say no to this," she teased, making Connie smile. "Besides, you owe it to your coaches to give back to their programs since they've given us so much."

"Fine, I'll go on the visits," Connie agreed before taking a bite of the cheesecake. "But my mind is made up about going to Baylor."

Rayna:
Rayna's aunt Amaryllis squirmed outside of the bathroom and banged on the door.

"Ray Ray, that's you in there?"

"Yes, *Titi*," Rayna called out from the shower.

Amaryllis rushed in, sat on the commode and sighed aloud as she was finally able to relieve the tension from her bladder. Rayna pulled the shower curtain back and stuck her head out.

"Dang, *Titi*, you a'ight?"

"Ooh, I've been holding it since I got on the subway at Broadway-Nassau Street. That's fifteen stops to Ninety-Sixth Street on the C-train. I was counting the whole way home."

"You better be glad it was me in here and not Luis," Rayna said, referring to her thirteen-year-old brother.

"I don't know, Ray Ray. I might've had to come in anyway. I changed your brother's diaper. I've seen his ding-a-ling before."

"Dang, *Titi*!" Rayna squealed. "But has he seen your middle earth?"

"Oh, my goodness," Amaryllis said, covering her mouth. "The poor boy would probably faint."

They both laughed.

Rayna turned off the water and stepped out of the tub. As she pulled her towel off the rack, her aunt noticed something on her back just below her left shoulder.

"Hey, what's that on your back?" Amaryllis asked.

"Oh, a girl elbowed me in the back when she came down with a rebound," Rayna told her.

"Oh, my God, Ray. It's all black and blue," Amaryllis said as she stood up and straightened up her clothing. "Why didn't you tell me about this? Did you ice it?"

"The trainer at the game iced it when it happened," Rayna said while drying herself. "It doesn't hurt."

After quickly washing her hands, Amaryllis started to examine the bruise. "You got a little lump. Go in your room and sit on the bed. Don't put your top on, I'm going to put some ice on this."

Rayna wrapped the towel around herself and did as she was told. Amaryllis came into her bedroom a short while later with a Ziploc bag full of ice cubes and another towel.

"You gotta tell me when something likes this happens, Ray. Hold your arm up."

"Ayy," Rayna squealed.

"I thought you said it didn't hurt," Amaryllis said, placing the ice on Rayna's back.

Rayna jumped a bit from the cold. "It just hurt a little bit when I raise my arm."

"Aye, Rayna. You might not be able to play tomorrow."

"Oh, I'm playing," Rayna snapped. "I can't miss the championship game."

"But somebody might hit you there again."

"It's cool, *Titi*. I swear. I'm gonna be alright."

"You know, Ray, you gotta take care of your health, first. I know it's a championship game, but you'll be in a lot more championship games. You got the skills to go far, but you can mess it up real easy by not taking care of yourself. Besides, you know your team is gonna win, anyway."

Rayna cast her eyes down. "I don't know, *Titi*. We had practice today and only five of us showed up, and we got fourteen girls on the team now. The Lady Phoenix is good, better than people give them credit for. The last time we played them we were losing the whole game, and we came back in the end and won. I got this funny feeling that if they jump ahead this time, we won't be able to come back. I gotta make sure that don't happen."

"Listen to you," Amaryllis said, snapping her finger across the air. "You sound like the team won't be able to function without you."

"Nah, they don't need me to function," Rayna said. "But they do need someone *like* me to *keep* functioning."

Tabitha:
Tabitha was heading out the door when her mother walked up behind her and asked, "Hey, where are you going?"

"Outside," Tabitha responded.

"Outside, where?"

"Nowhere, just hangin' out on the block."

"Hangin' on the block with who?"

"Whoever's out there, Ma."

"No, I want you to stay in the house," Mrs. Gleavy said, standing in front of the door. "A'int nobody outside except those rough-necks who's always gettin' into trouble. Me and you can watch TV or something."

"I a'int going to hang out with no roughnecks, Ma," Tabitha frustratingly told her. "I just wannna get outta this hot house, geez. We'll probably just be shooting some hoops or something."

"When them fools start shooting it ain't gonna be at no hoops. Why can't you pick a better class of friends to hang around?"

"There ain't nothing wrong with my friends, Ma. C'mon, why're you sweatin' me?"

Mrs. Gleavy took her daughter's hands into her own and spoke pleadingly. "Tabitha, you ain't never in the house. You're always running around to this place and that place. You're gonna burn yourself out the way you be going."

Tabitha rolled her eyes. "Why don't you ever ask Anthony and Damon to stay home with you?"

"I hardly get to see your brothers," her mother sadly stated. "They're always out chasing women…just like your father."

Annoyed, Tabitha pulled her hands away. "Ma, please, just let me go. I'll be back by midnight."

"Is it gonna kill you to stay here with me, Tabitha? You need to rest, anyway. You have a championship game tomorrow."

"My game ain't 'til two o'clock. I'll have plenty time to rest before then. Now, can I please go?"

Mrs. Gleavy looked away. "You can, uh…you can go to your room."

Tabitha became enraged. Her first thought was to leave anyway as she took a hard step toward her mother. Mrs. Gleavy stood firm, so Tabitha turned around, stormed down the hallway and slammed her room door shut behind her.

Stacey:

Stacey was in her bedroom watching the Seattle Storm versus the Los Angeles Sparks on television. When a commercial came on, she decided to go to the kitchen for some iced tea. Passing through the living room, she noticed her mother asleep on the couch.

"Mommy. Mommy, wake up," Stacey said, shaking her mother's shoulder.

"Hmm, what?" Dawn Conyers answered, awakening from her slumber.

"You need to get up off this couch and get in the bed. Your head is hanging off the side all crooked."

"No, I'm okay. I just want to lay here a while longer."

"Well, I'm going to get you a pillow."

"No, Stacey, I'm not going back to sleep," her mother said as she slowly sat up. "I have to go to work tonight."

"Tonight? Why?"

"Somebody called out sick, so my boss called and asked me to come in. Don't fret. It's a whole night of overtime."

Stacey stood over her mother, shaking her head for a moment. "What time are you going in?"

RISE OF THE PHOENIX

"I have to be there at ten-thirty," her mother told her. "I'm going to leave here at ten."

"Ma, this is crazy. You can hardly stay conscious when you're home, and your snoring sounds like the men are drilling on the street. Why won't you let me get a job?"

"No, you focus on school. Working will cut into your study time, especially now since you're going to have to travel so far to go to school."

"I don't have to go to that school, you know," Stacey said, slowly.

Her mother twisted her lips. "What are you talking about? You begged me to let you go to Jefferson."

"I know, I know," Stacey said and sat on the couch next to her mother. "But I don't have to if it's going to make things harder on you. I can stay in Lawrence and get a job in the off season."

Ms. Conyers laughed off the suggestion. "No, you can't. As soon as the school season is over, you'll be back playing in tournaments with the Tide or the Roadrunners."

"I don't have to play in the leagues."

"No, no, no, I don't want to keep you from playing basketball. That's why I'm doing all this overtime in the first place. I found out that I can get a transfer to Brooklyn, so, if I can earn enough money, we can move and you won't have to commute so far."

"I don't want you to go through all of this for me, Mommy. For what? After two years I'll be going away to college, anyway. What are you going to do then? You might not even like living in Brooklyn."

"I'm sure I won't, especially in the areas that are in my budget. Lord knows I don't want to work the graveyard shift out there. But for you, I will. You're my only child, Stacey. I want to make sure that you do well in life. I don't want you to have to struggle like me. Every parent wants their children to be better off than they are."

Velvet:

Reverend Scott knocked on Velvet's room door as he stuck his head inside. He saw her sitting up in bed watching a Storm-Sparks game on television, wearing her number twenty-two Houston Comets jersey. "Hey, Booby. You mind a little company?"

Velvet glanced at her father, and then resumed watching the screen. "No. You might not want to stay, though. I'm watching women play basketball."

Reverend Scott proceeded inside, sat on the bed and began rubbing his daughter's feet. "I don't mind," he said affectionately. "I just want to spend some time with you. We haven't seen each other in two years, and it seems like you're avoiding me. I thought you'd be happy to see me, and we'd be having a whole bunch of fun."

"I'm just not in a good mood, that's all," Velvet said, dryly.

"Why? Is it because you haven't been able to see that girl you took those pictures with?"

Velvet huffed. "No, sir."

"Why, then?" Reverend Scott pressed.

Velvet looked at her father. "Because since you've been here, you think that everything I'm happy about, sad about or whatever, has to do with Kim."

"You're telling me it isn't?" Reverend Scott asked.

"No, it isn't," Velvet assured. "Not everything."

"What is it, then? You're worried about the coach's wife?"

"Yes, but she's doing fine. I spoke to her earlier. She went home from the hospital today."

"That's good, I was praying for her. How's your teammate's father doing?"

"I don't know. I haven't heard anything."

"I've been praying for him, too."

"So have I."

Reverend Scott affectionately squeezed his daughter's feet. "Don't worry, you'll feel better tomorrow when you see Melody, Barry and your mother. The whole family will be together in church tomorrow evening."

"Is Harmony going to be there?" Velvet wanted to know.

"No, I don't think—"

"Then the whole family won't be there."

"I can't make Harmony come, Booby. You know how stubborn that girl is. She's just like your mother."

RISE OF THE PHOENIX

"Everything is just all messed up," Velvet whined. "First, Mommy and Harmony stop speaking. And now Mommy doesn't want to talk to me, either. There's too much separation in this family."

"You know why that is? It's because sin is running all through our lives, corrupting it with worldly things and lies. Look what's happening to you."

"Daddy…"

"What?"

"There you go again."

Reverend Scott grabbed the remote control and turned the television off. "What do you expect, Booby. This thing is a major blow. It's bad enough that you're fornicating and you're supposed to be saved, but you're doing it with another girl. It hurts. I feel like the walls are crumbling around me."

"I feel almost the same way," Velvet said. "Only instead of crumbling walls, I feel like my heart and soul is being torn from me."

"Over that girl?" His voice raised several octaves.

"No, Daddy. It's not about her, it's about me. Why can't I be the person I want to be and do with my life as I please?"

"Well, first of all, your life is not your own yet," he told her. "Until you're an adult out on your own, your life belongs to your mother and me. Also, you have to remember that everything you do affects everyone in the family. And this family is always in the public's eye, which also means we're always under the microscope."

"I'm not trying to tarnish the family's image, Daddy. I never planned on coming out of the closet or anything like that. My intention was to live a very discreet, very private life, while doing my music and playing basketball."

Appalled, Reverend Scott stopped rubbing Velvet's feet and slapped his hands down on his lap. "Coming out of the closet? Discreet? Who are you and what have you done with my daughter?"

"You see, that's it. You don't want to accept who I am."

"That's right, Booby. I don't want to, I don't have to and I'm not going to. You better get your head right, girl. Don't you know the story of Sodom and Gomorrah? God destroyed those people behind the craziness you're mixed up in? The Bible says, 'Flee from sexual immorality. Every sin that a man commits is outside the body...'"

"'But he who sins sexually sins against his own body,'" Velvet said, finishing the quote. "Yes, I know, 1 Corinthians 6:18-20. That's one of the scriptures Mommy gave me to study; along with Romans 1:26-29."

"So, you're choosing to sin? Is that what you're telling me?"

"I don't really believe that it is a sin."

Reverend Scott's face hardened and he began waging his finger. "You see, that's what sinners do. They pick and choose what they're going to obey. If God's Word interferes with what they want to do, they try to find justification for it. Your mind has been poisoned by all those left-wing liberals with their pagan politics who try to get people to believe that there's nothing wrong with homosexuality, or that God approves of it. The vile and unnatural things that go on among women in sports have corrupted you. I think you should just leave basketball alone and focus on school."

"I am focused on school. I'm focused on basketball, too, though. I want to play basketball in school...in college. I want to be on TV and experience the glory of winning a championship."

"Yeah, but what about experiencing the glory of God, Velvet?"

Velvet reached forward, took her father's hand and pulled him back to sit closer to her. "Every time I win, every time I accomplish something, every goal I reach and every dream that comes true—that's when I experience His glory."

"Then you have to thank Him by praising Him," Reverend Scott preached. "You're not praising Him, though, if you're not obeying His Word. And you'll never see the glory of His Kingdom if you don't stop living in sin."

"I hear what you're saying, Daddy. But still, playing basketball doesn't have anything to do with anyone being gay."

Kimberly:
Kimberly got home and went straight to her room. When she opened the door, her mother was laying across her bed watching the videotape of her and Velvet.

"Ma!" Kimberly exclaimed, her eyes bulging from shock and shame.

RISE OF THE PHOENIX

"Come on in, Kim," Mrs. James said, beckoning her by tilting her head. "I was looking for my videotape of *Living Single* that you borrowed when I found this."

"Why couldn't you wait until I got home to get your tape?" Kimberly nervously asked, not knowing what to expect.

"Because I didn't want to," Mrs. James said, firmly. "In case you forgot, this is my house, and you're my child. That means nothing in here is off limits to me."

"So, I don't have a right to privacy?"

"You do, but I have the power to invade it when I feel it's necessary. I was in the mood to watch *Living Single*, so it was necessary. Needless to say, my interest changed when I saw this tape. You weren't even trying to hide it, huh? You had it labeled and everything."

Kimberly walked in and placed her bag down beside the bed. "Like I said, I didn't expect you to be in here snooping around."

"You better be glad it was me snooping. What if your sister would've found this? You've got to be more responsible."

Kimberly marched over to the television and reached for the VCR. "Fine, I'll hide it!"

"Don't touch it!" her mother snapped. "Come back over here and sit down."

Kimberly turned around slowly and did as her mother told her.

"Anyway…" her mother continued. "You girls must've been having sex and taping it everyday. There's a lot of footage here. Why'd you lie? First, you told me you weren't having sex, and then you told me you only did it once. Why?"

Kimberly kicked off her sneakers before sitting on the bed and pulling her feet up. The tape was still playing, and she looked at the screen and shrugged. "I don't know."

"I thought we were closer," her mother said. "I thought we had a better relationship than that. We've always shared everything, haven't we?"

"Yes," Kimberly softly replied.

"I don't get it, then. You came to me to let me know you liked girls. Why couldn't we have shared this?" Mrs. James asked, pointing at the screen.

"I don't know," Kimberly repeated. "I just didn't think it was something you really wanted to know. I thought that maybe you'd be looking over my shoulder all the time and thinking that I was sleeping with every girl that came around."

"Well, what do you think is worse, thinking you were oversexed or thinking that everything you say is a lie? People can say a lot of things about me, and I'm sure they do, but no one could ever call me a liar. *My momma always told me that there is nothing worse than a liar and a thief*, and I think she was right. Baby, you need to understand that as your parents, your father and I need to know what you're doing and whom you're doing it with. It's our job to look after you and protect you."

"Aw man, what's Daddy going to say when you tell him about this?"

"I'm not going to tell your father anything, you are. When he gets home, we're going to have a family discussion and lay everything out on the table. Do you know why?"

Kimberly shook her head.

"Because that's the relationship we need to have," her mother told her. "I don't want there to be anymore secrets or lies in this house. We're tighter than that. We love each other too much for that. Okay?"

"Yes, Ma," Kimberly replied. She then laid beside her mother and told everything about her and Velvet while the tape played on.

Melva:

"Melva!" Mrs. Fields shouted from the living room. "Girl, quit bouncing that ball in the house!"

Melva quickly grabbed her basketball and made a guilty facial expression from being caught. She was lying on her bed next to her father, and they were tossing the ball up to each other.

"That wasn't me, that was Daddy!" Melva shouted back.

"Melvin, if I don't want the kids doing it, I don't want you doing it, either! Now both of you cut it out in there!"

Melva started laughing so her father plucked her on the forehead.

"Ow, that hurt," she whined.

"That'll teach you to lie on me," he said.

"I wasn't lying. You threw the ball when it fell."

"Then it'll teach you not to tattle."

When Melva stuck her tongue out at he father, he grabbed her and they began to playfully tussle. Her mother heard the commotion and started fussing as she marched toward Melva's room.

"Why can't I leave the two of you alone for a minute without some craziness going on?" Mrs. Fields asked as she approached.

Mr. Fields heard her coming and sat up straight on the bed, trying to look innocent. "I told her to stop, Gloria, but you know how hardheaded this child is."

"Oh, no you didn't!" Melva said, unable to believe her ears.

"Yeah, that's how it feels," her father whispered to her.

Standing in the doorway, Mrs. Fields folded her arms and gave her husband and daughter the evil eye. "I'm gonna take out the strap for both of y'all in a minute if this foolishness doesn't stop." With that, she turned to walk away from the room and cut her eyes back at them before leaving.

"You got us in trouble," Mr. Fields said, shaking his fist.

"No, you started it. If you knew how to throw, she wouldn't have had to come back here."

"Please, girl, there was nothing wrong with the way I threw the ball. It was your butter fingers. You'd better be able to hold on to the ball better than that tomorrow if you want to win the championship and go to New Orleans."

Melva sat up and got serious. She looked at her father and shook her head. "It's gonna be tough, Daddy."

"Don't worry, sweetie. You're just going to have to finally become the leader I know you're capable of being. Your team is going to need that from you now more than ever."

"Trina is the leader of this team, Daddy. She gives the pep talks and motivational speeches and whatnot."

"You can't leave it up to her, Melva. Yes, she's the captain, but you're the point guard, and that gives you just as much responsibility as a leader, if not more."

"Oh, I can lead on the court—" Melva started.

"No, Melva," her father cut her off. "You have to do it on and off the court. Your teammates need to have every bit of confidence in you.

When they see you, there should be one thought in their minds, that you're there to take them to the Promised Land."

Melva wrinkled her nose. "Yiil, Daddy, you're starting to sound like Coach Stone."

"Let me tell you something.. You know why you and your coach clash the way you do? It's because you're so much alike."

"No we ain't!" Melva snapped.

"Yes, you are. Both of you get so passionate and so hyper that it sometimes affects your decision-making. He's a very good coach—as well you are a very good point guard—but you could both be great if you took a chill pill."

Melva's tone softened. "I don't think he likes me that much, Daddy. That's why he's always on my case. He gets up in my face about every little thing."

"Did you ever stop to think that was because he *does* like you? You know, being a teacher or a coach is a lot like being a parent. You think your mother and I are always on you too, but you know it's because we love you. Nobody puts so much into someone they don't care about."

Melva thought about the things she said to Trina when they went to the Dallas BBQ. She thought about the way she scolded her best friend, even when she was helping her with the pregnancy scare, but did it out of love. She realized her father was right.

Trina:

Trina hurried home, wanting to get an hour of reading in before going to sleep. She approached her building in the Samuel J. Tilden housing projects and greeted the crew of teenagers in the lobby, some fooling around with each other while others were just idly congregating. The elevator alarm was ringing out of control—as usual— so Trina took the six-story hike up the scarcely lit staircase. She reached her apartment door and went inside.

"Auntie Trina!" her three-year-old niece shouted as she ran up and hugged her around the legs.

Trina picked the child up in her arms and kissed her on the side of the face. "Hey, Quinetta. Have you been a good girl today?"

RISE OF THE PHOENIX

"Yes, I been good," said the little, proud voice. "Mommy ga'e me some money."

Trina smiled. "Oh, yeah? How much money did she give you?"

"She ga'e me dis much money." Quinetta held up three fingers.

"That's nice," Trina told her. "Put it in your piggy bank, okay."

"I did," the child was proud to say.

"Good girl."

"Trina, come here," her mother called out from the living room.

"Yes, Ma." Trina put her niece down and went to see what her mother wanted. She stopped in her tracks when she pulled back the curtain covering the living room entrance.

"Hey, baby. This is my friend Luther."

"Oh...hi," Trina grunted, seeing her mother snuggled up in the loveseat under the arm of the stranger.

"How're you doin', Trina?" the thugged out looking, out of shape, in badly need of a shave, young enough to be her older brother looking Luther asked.

"Okay," Trina answered coldly. "Uh, Ma, I'm going to bed. I'm real tired."

"Okay," her mother said, and then remembered, "Oh, wait. Nakia's got company in y'all room."

Frustrated, Trina turned and stormed out of the living room. "This place is a damn brothel," she said under her breath and bumped into Quinetta, almost knocking her down. She quickly grabbed the little girl's hand and apologized to her. Just then, her mother came rushing out behind her.

"LaTrina, what's the matter? Is something wrong?"

"I'm tired, Ma," Trina said with attitude. "And my period is making me even wearier. Why can't Nakia entertain her company in the living room with you and your company?"

"She's not going to have him in there all night. Go ask Vaniqua if you can share her bed until he leaves."

"Why can't I just lay in your bed?"

A guilty look came over her mother's face. "Huh? Uh, well, I may need some privacy myself in a little while."

Trina became more annoyed. "Dang, Ma. Vaniqua's got the baby in there, and Quinetta needs to be going in there to go to bed, too. And I'm not sleeping with Kayla and Sharona 'cause they'll be messing with me the whole time. Why don't you go get your privacy now so I can lay on the couch?"

"Okay, I can do that," her mother agreed. "I know you want to be well-rested for your game tomorrow."

"Thank you," Trina said, somewhat relieved. "Are you coming to the game?"

"Yes, of course. Me and all four of your sisters will be there."

"How's Vaniqua going to come?" Trina wanted to know. "Her son is only two months old."

"Her baby's daddy is taking him to see his other grandmother."

"She's bringing Quinetta, though, right?"

"Yeah, I think so. She really doesn't have a choice if we all are going to be there."

"You hear that, QQ?" Trina said to her niece in a playful voice. "You're coming to see me play basketball."

"Can I play, too?" Quinetta asked.

"I'm going to teach you how to play, sweetie," Trina promised.

"You think y'all gonna win?" Trina's mother asked.

"We're going to do our best," Trina said. "We're not going to have a couple of our key players."

Her mother kissed her on the cheek. "Well, we'll all be cheering for you."

Beverly:
Visiting hours at the hospital had just ended and Beverly, Carlene and Melinda were preparing to leave. Burton was slipping in and out of sleep, and when Beverly kissed his forehead he opened his eyes.

"Hey, y'all leavin'?" Burton managed to ask, his words broken and his voice scratchy as he forced the words out through his oxygen mask.

"Yes, Daddy," Beverly regretted having to say. "They're puttin' us out."

"Why?" he asked after pulling the mask off.

"It's nine o'clock, Burt. Visiting hours are over," Carlene told him.

RISE OF THE PHOENIX

"Oh...I see," he said.

"Don't worry, we'll be back in the morning after church," Carlene assured him.

"Church?" he asked. "Oh...tomorrow is Sunday, ain't it?"

"Yes, Daddy," Beverly answered. "We're going to the sunrise service, and then we're coming straight here."

Burton smiled as much as he could. "Okay, baby girl."

An announcement was made asking visitors to leave.

"Well, we've got to go." Carlene kissed Burton on the top of his bald head.

"Take care." Melinda kissed him on the cheek.

They were leaving the room when Burton called Beverly back.

"Baby girl, hold on a minute," he grunted.

"We'll be waiting for you in the hall," Carlene told Beverly before leading Melinda out of the room.

Beverly went back and stood beside her father's bed. "Yes, Daddy?"

"How're you holdin' up?"

"When you get better, I'll be better," she told him. "I'm so, so sorry for what I did, Daddy."

"Okay, baby girl. It's done...and...we've dealt with it. As long as you've learned a lesson from it...we can move forward."

Beverly lowered her eyes and sort of pouted.

"Well, have you learned anything, baby girl?"

Beverly nodded.

"Use...your voice, gal."

"Yes, Daddy," Beverly muttered.

"What...what've...you learned?"

First, Beverly shrugged and shook her head. Then, she bit her lip and answered, "Lying to you was bothering me the whole time. I don't want you to not be able to trust me. Momma used to tell me that trust is a hard thing to earn, a harder thing to keep and the hardest thing to get back."

"Did she ever tell you...how...easy it was...to lose?"

"No, sir. I found that out by myself. Everybody started talking to me different and looking at me funny when they found out what I did."

"It felt...pretty cold, eh?"

Beverly nodded. "Yes. But I'm gonna find a way to make things up and to get that trust back. I promise."

"Okay, baby girl. That…that makes me feel better. Remember…always…do the right thing."

Carlene was standing in the doorway and heard everything. She made a decision at that moment.

T.J.:

T.J. was in his living room with Sam and Glen surrounded by Get Well cards and flowers for Sheila. T.J. and Sam were both drained, T.J. from Sheila's accident and Sam from working hard on the tournament. Glen was the bright spot since he was the lone bearer of good news.

"So, that's it," Glen said. "That's what Hofstra's offering me."

"Congratulations, man," Sam said. "You deserve it. You've worked hard for eight years building a successful program at Kingsborough with a paper-thin budget. It's about time somebody recognized your skills."

"Thanks, man," Glen said. "The good thing is that my athletic director wants *me* to interview and hire a replacement."

"Won't one of your assistants be your successor?" T.J. asked.

"Nah, man. I move up, my staff moves up. All this time they've worked hard and stayed loyal while working for peanuts. I ain't gonna leave them behind. But I do know who I want to take my place. The only person I know who'll take care of the players and keep the program on top is you, T.J."

T.J. looked up with a raised brow from the surprise. "Me?"

"Of course," Glen said, "who else?"

"Oh, Glen, I don't know about that."

"What's there to know?" Sam asked. "You're the perfect choice. It'll be just like running the Lady Phoenix, but just on a different level."

"Cut the bull, T.J.," Glen said, "You know that program needs you. You can bring in struggling kids like Melva Fields and set them on the right track. And don't forget that you already have two kids there."

"Yeah, but I have twenty-five kids who need me here," T.J. said. "You know if I coach a college team I couldn't work with the Lady Phoenix. It would be a recruiting violation."

RISE OF THE PHOENIX

"Yo, when are you gonna stop limiting yourself," Glen asked. "You gotta think about yourself for once. Those kids will be all right. They'll graduate, go to college and have whatever career they choose, and you'll still be here doing the same thing."

T.J. shrugged. "I don't see the problem. Somebody's got to be here for them. If I leave the Lady Phoenix to coach a college team, where would they go? You want to see more good kids fall prey to the Roadrunners? Or would you like to see them play for a team like the Lady Tigers and get kicked out of tournaments after they've worked so hard because their coach can't stop cheating and using ringers?"

"I just think your talents would be best served this way," Sam said. "More people in more places would recognize and be able to appreciate you this way."

T.J. pondered for a second. "Uhhh...I'm going to have to decline. I'm pretty satisfied doing what I'm doing. Besides, I've worked too hard building the Lady Phoenix program and establishing its reputation just to drop it on a moment's notice."

"Hey," came a soft voice from across the room.

The three men looked over to see Sheila standing in the doorway, wearing her housecoat over her nightgown and her hair tied up in a scarf. Her arms were folded and she was drawn up like she was cold even though the thermometer read seventy-five degrees. T.J. quickly jumped up and rushed over to her.

"Hey, Mama. What's up, you okay?"

"Yeah, I'm okay," Sheila said. "What's going on in here?"

"Nothing, Mama. We were just talking."

"Hey, Sheila, how're you feeling?" Glen asked.

"I'm doing just fine."

"That's good to hear," Sam said. "I'm looking forward to hearing you sing again."

Sheila gave a slight smile.

"Well, I think we'd better get going." Glen stood up and stretched.

Sam quickly agreed as he stood up as well. "Yeah, it's getting late. I have to get up early tomorrow and get things started."

"Okay, y'all." T.J. escorted his friends to the door.

"Goodnight, Sheila," Sam said.

"Be well," Glen added.

Sheila waved. "Goodnight, guys."

"Yo, at least think about it some more," Glen pleaded as he walked out.

"All right, man," T.J. said. "I'll sleep on it and we can talk about it tomorrow after the game." He gave both men a brotherly hug before they left. He turned around, and Sheila was walking up behind him. "You okay, Mama? You don't look so good."

"I don't really feel that great," Sheila said, "but I'll be fine."

"You wanna go lie down?"

"Perhaps in a little while. What were you guys talking about?"

T.J. put his arm around his wife and escorted her back to the sofa where they sat together. "Glen got the job at Hofstra University and wants me to take his old job at Kingsborough."

"Oh, I see. Are you going to do it?"

"I don't think so. I can't."

"Why?"

"Because I'd have to let go of the Lady Phoenix, and I'm not willing to do that."

"I think it'll be a good opportunity for you," Sheila told him. "You'll get your foot in the door and be on your way to bigger and better things before you know it."

"And what about you?" T.J. asked her. "Kingsborough is in Region XV, and you just started officiating in that region. It'll be a conflict of interest."

Sheila waved a hand dismissively. "I don't have to officiate there. I can just keep doing high school and wait to get picked up by another region."

"No way, Sheila," T.J. said, adamantly. "You worked hard to get to where you are. I'm not going to let you take steps backwards to accommodate me. No, those days are over for good."

THE GAME

Sunday, July 17, 2005 – 1:48 P.M.

The site for the championship game moved from Riverbank State Park to Pace University in lower Manhattan. The school sits at the heel of the Brooklyn Bridge and directly across the street from City Hall. It was much easier for everyone to get to with dozens of subway and city bus lines all around and an abundance of parking garages on the surrounding streets.

Inside, the sub-level gymnasium seated over two thousand spectators, an incredibly large number for a girls' summer league game. Every player and coach from each of the other eight teams that participated in the tournament were all present, as well as a recruiter from every local college on every level. The tension from the anticipation loomed throughout the stands as fans for both teams were split on both sides by an imaginary line that extended from the division line on the court. It was obvious who the Roadrunners supporters were by the hundreds of crimson T-shirts with an illustration of a speeding bird running across the words "Beep Beep! Clear The Way!" on the front, or the orange and blue of Thomas Jefferson High School. Although there were a good amount of Lady Phoenix supporters on hand, they weren't as easily identified. The only people wearing royal blue T-shirts with the gold and red flaming bird logo were some of the family members of the Lady Phoenix players.

Lady Phoenix Locker Room:
Juanita was standing, facing the Lady Phoenix and holding her clipboard. No Yankees gear this day. Her curly close-cropped, platinum hair freshly shaped up and tapered, she was dressed in a royal blue fitted top with cropped sleeves, a pair of white linen pants and white thong sandals. She wore no makeup on her lovely dark skin, as usual, aside from some eyeliner and shiny lipgloss.

The twenty-five-year-old coach stared at the Lady Phoenix members for a while, watching faces and looking into their eyes to see if they had the fire. She knew the level of importance of this game and wanted to feel that the players knew it as well. *If only I was eight years younger,* she thought to herself. Her mind wandered back to when she first started playing and reminisced about the big games her teams faced. The attitudes seemed different back then, even though it wasn't that long ago. She didn't worry about *her* Lady Phoenix teammates because she knew they were always up and ready for whatever challenge they'd face. This generation of kids didn't seem to have the same type of heart, determination and focus as they did. Trina was the only exception. She could've fit in with the teams of the past with no problem.

Juanita looked across the bench from left to right at each player in their royal blue, reversible top mesh uniforms with silk screened gold lettering that read "LADY PHOENIX" over their numbers. Kimberly, Trina, Melva, Tracy, Tanya, Keisha, Monica, and Danisha, were all sitting in straight line and holding hands with the person next to them. They were bonding to pay tribute to the pain they were suffering from Burton clinging to life and Sheila's miscarriage. T.J. called Juanita a short time earlier, saying he would not be at the game because Sheila wasn't feeling well, and he feared leaving her alone.

The Roadrunners Locker Room:
The Roadrunners, being the higher seed, wore their home white uniforms. The crimson "ROADRUNNERS" lettering across the chest above their numbers were in italics to make the word appear to be moving fast. The Nike logo was on the upper left of their jerseys and lower left of their shorts.

All the players' moods were laid back and assuring. They were better than the Lady Phoenix player for player, and they knew it. They also knew that Beverly and Velvet would not be playing, and without the two of them, they would not only win, but overwhelm the Lady Phoenix in a way that no one had ever done before.

Mildred walked in wearing a crimson Roadrunners T-shirt, a pair of denim cutoffs and Nike sandals. She was smiling with confidence as she looked at her team chanting and cheering with anticipation. She clapped her hands and called out for them to settle down.

"Okay ladies, this is it," she said. "This is the final step before the National Tournament. We should feel real good going into this game. This is the best team that we've ever had, so I'm expecting you to put this game away early. The Lady Phoenix will play hard, and they're relentless, so we have to get a big enough lead to make it hard for them to come back. Hopefully, we can take the fight out of them and cause them to lie down. Future."

"Yes, Coach," Rayna replied.

"How's your shoulder?"

"It's good. I'll be fine."

"I'm looking for you to exploit Melva, or whoever is guarding you, as much as possible. We're going to pound the ball into the post as often as possible in the first quarter. Connie."

"Yes, Coach," Connie answered.

"I want you to set up on the right block as usual. I want Stacey on the left side with Tabitha..."

"Whoa, hold up," Connie interrupted. "Renee and the twins aren't starting?"

"Yes, one of the twins will," Mildred replied, moving her finger back and forth at both sisters. "Uh...Ellen will start at small forward. Erin will come off the bench today."

Rayna, Connie, Renee and the twins whined and moaned, displeased with the change in the line-up.

"Hey, now don't start that," Mildred said in a stern voice. "Get it together. Don't start crying about who's starting. You'll all get to play, what does it matter who starts? I just told you that I want to put the game away early, so I'm starting the five that I think will be able to do that.

The Lady Phoenix Locker Room:

"How is everyone doing?" Juanita asked.

"I'm doing good," Trina said, excitedly. "Let's go, I'm ready."

"Oh, I know you're ready, Trina. How about everyone else?"

"You know I'm ready, Coach," Melva replied.

"Me, too," Kimberly said.

"Good," Juanita said. "I'm glad to hear that because this is it. We're here in the championship game of the first ever New Attitude State Tournament with a chance to go to the National Tournament. This is our chance to earn our respect. You know that no one in that gym is expecting us to win today. The Roadrunners brought in some hired assassins, and they're out to get us, but that doesn't matter. I hope they're overconfident. I hope no one out there is betting on us. I like playing against the odds, personally. All we have to do is bet on ourselves and go out there and do the job. Teamwork, ladies. Let's not make the same mistakes we made when we played them during the season. I think we've learned from that and we've grown. So, here's what we're going to do. We're going to start with that match-up zone we've been working on the last few practices. I know they're expecting us to go man-to-man, so we're going to show them something different and see how long it takes for them to make the adjustments. As soon as they do, that's when we'll match up and play first pass denial. Melva."

"Yeah, Coach?" Melva answered, sweat beading up around her forehead and her leg bouncing. "Wassup?"

"Well, first, calm down and relax," Juanita told her. "I like that you're hyped up, but I don't want you to be too anxious and go out there and make mistakes. Take it easy, okay?"

"I'm good, Coach," Melva said more calmly, but still hyped. "I'm good. Don't worry 'bout nothin'. It's a wrap."

"On offense, I want to start off playing you, Kim and Trina in our gold thirteen play. That means you're going to have to dribble up the left sideline."

"Oh no, Nita," Melva protested. "I gotta come up the middle. I can take Future to the hole all day."

"I know you want to penetrate, but I want to attack Connie and see if we can get her into foul trouble early. Make her play some defense against Trina on the post."

"Come on, Mel, we can work this," Trina said, giving her best friend's hand a gentle squeeze.

Melva paused, and then nodded in agreement. "Word. Let's do this. Kim, you'd better be ready to knock down that shot from the corner."

"Oh, don't worry," Kimberly said. "I'm gonna be cashing in. Count on it."

The Roadrunners Locker Room:

"Okay, girls, let's get up and take care of business," Mildred said. "Remember, we gotta put this game away early."

"Yeah, y'all, let's make a statement from the opening tip," Tabitha encouraged. "Let's shove this game down their muthafuckin' throats."

Again, the Roadrunners, with the exceptions of Renee and Erin, all cheered, and then huddled and put their hands in together.

Connie counted off. "One, two, three…"

"Beep-beep! Clear the way!" the players all shouted.

RISE OF THE PHOENIX

All the players ran out of the locker room cheering, leaving just Mildred and Renee behind. Mildred looked at her player sitting on the bench sulking and rolled her eyes and walked out.

In the hall, just before entering the gym, Mildred came face to face with Terry.

"What the hell are you doing here?" Mildred snapped.

Terry's gleaming smile started losing its glare. "I wanted to support you."

"Don't come around trying to be supportive now."

"I was just hoping we could talk after the game." Terry's smile still fading.

"We don't have a damn thing to talk about, Terry."

"But...what about the other night? You know...two weeks ago?"

Mildred looked around and pushed Terry off to the side back near the staircase. "C'mere," she said through her teeth. "That night was a mistake, okay."

"A mistake? Millie, listen..."

"No, Terry, dammit, you listen. I'm about to go in here and win this game so I can get ready to go to New Orleans, and I don't want you upsetting me and fucking this up."

"You've got the wrong idea, Millie," Terry said. "I'm here to support you, not upset you. I want to help you."

Mildred stepped back and looked Terry over. "Help me?" she said with hopefulness. "Help how? Are you gonna pull some strings for me like I asked?"

"I thought about it long and hard," Terry said. "And I came to the conclusion that you don't really want me to do those things, nor do you want me out of your life. You're not just going to throw away four years like that. You love me just as much as I love you."

With a grin, Mildred said, "Don't fool yourself, Terry. I don't want another day, another hour, another fuckin' second to pass without knowing for sure that I can get anything I want from you. I want to have *everything* I deserve, and I'm gonna fuckin' get it."

"I heard you crying that night...after we made love. I was on the other side of the door. I know that you miss me, Millie. Please, I'm begging you, stop this madness and just come on home? We can work this all out."

Mildred lowered her eyes, sighed hard and took a step back. "Work it all out, eh? Humph, you work this out, Terry. If you come around me again, I'm gonna get a restraining order against you. *¿Me oyes?* Pop up on me one more time, and I'll have your ass served."

Terry watched Mildred walk away, and then saw Renee slowly coming out of the locker room and make her way into the gymnasium.

Sam, on his way from the trainers' room to the gym, had witnessed the whole episode. He walked up right after, saw Terry standing there and said, "Third time's a charm?"

The Lady Phoenix Locker Room:
"Okay, team, let's bring it in," Juanita said.

The Lady Phoenix all stood up without letting go of hands and formed a circle with Juanita. At that moment, Velvet walked in dressed to play. Kimberly smiled for the first time that day as she let go of Juanita's hand so that her companion could join the circle.

"My father decided to stay in New York until the tour gets here next month," Velvet announced. "He's out there, and I've got a lot riding on this, so we gotta show him that this is real."

All the players shouted, "Yeah! Yeah! Yeah!"

"I have another surprise for y'all, too," Velvet said, and then shouted, "Come in!"

Melinda and Beverly walked in dressed to play with Carlene behind them. They all joined the circle.

"I'm sorry we're late," Beverly said in a soft, trembling voice. "I'm also sorry for sneaking away and abandoning you, and for all the trouble I've caused. If you'll have me, I'm here."

"What do you mean, if we'll have you?" Melva said. "Of course we'll have you. We all make mistakes, Beverly. Sometimes we mean no harm, but they happen."

"That's right," Trina added. "We can't let mistakes hold us back. We've got to keep moving forward. Isn't that right, Nita?"

"It certainly is," Juanita agreed. "We're happy to have Ms. Thompson and Melinda here, as well."

"Thank you," Carlene said. "So much has happened in all of our lives. We thought that if we came here today and were able to somehow make a difference, perhaps things would start to pick up. Perhaps...maybe a win today...well, good news may be what Burt needs. Maybe knowing Beverly and Melinda helped, he'll..."

"Say no more," Melva said, seeing Carlene breaking down. "This game is a done deal. I'm taking a stand right now to guarantee victory."

RISE OF THE PHOENIX

Again, the team cheered with enthusiasm. Then, they joined hands again and bowed their heads as Juanita led them in prayer.

"Lord, we come to You with bowed heads and humbled hearts to thank You for this opportunity and for all of Your blessings. We're asking that You look down upon us and give us strength and courage so that we can go out and perform to the best of our ability. We know that with You on our side we can enjoy the thrill of victory, whether or not the score is in our favor at the end of the game. We just pray to You for guidance, tolerance and endurance. Most of all, we ask You for forgiveness and patience, hoping that You will be merciful to us. In Jesus' Name we pray. Amen."

"Amen!" everyone echoed, and then huddled around Juanita and put their hands in high over their heads.

Trina led the cheer and the team responded.

"What're we gonna do?!"

"Focus!"

"What're we gonna do?!"

"Win!"

"Because the Phoenix is whaaaat?!"

"Hot like fire!"

The girls all ran out of the locker room, shouting and cheering, leaving Juanita and Carlene behind. The two women embraced, letting their emotions flow freely. Then they gathered themselves together and joined the team in the gymnasium.

Mildred nearly choked when the Lady Phoenix came running in and Beverly and Velvet were with them. The Roadrunners all looked over, and their overconfidence slightly dwindled. Beverly stared back at them with a look of wrath in her eyes. She wanted them to know that she was there for business.

3:02 P.M.

The noise coming from the gymnasium was deafening. You could hear the cheers from the crowd two floors up in the main lobby.

Juanita was pacing back and forth like a nervous wreck. She was intense, and kept thinking, *If T.J. was here we wouldn't be losing this game.*

The scoreboard read 57-52 in favor of the Roadrunners with twenty-four seconds remaining in the third quarter. Stacey Conyers had the ball on the left wing. Tracy Williams was guarding her. Stacey took a hard dribble to her left—Tracy reacted—and then she stepped back and pulled up. Tracy fought to recover and contest the shot, but it was too late. The three-pointer extended the Roadrunners lead to eight.

Kimberly James quickly grabbed the ball out of bounds and threw a long pass to Beverly Smalls streaking up the left side of the court. Beverly caught the ball and saw Ellen Saltzman racing to get ahead of her, and also saw her teammate, Velvet Fuller, filling the lane on the opposite side. Two on one. Beverly knew what Velvet would do, so she advanced the ball, drawing the defense to her.

Velvet flared out to the three-point line.

Beverly whipped the pass to her.

Three!

The Roadrunners were up 60–55 with sixteen seconds remaining.

The Lady Phoenix immediately applied full court pressure. Connie King's inbound pass to Future Cortez was high and deflected off her fingers out of bounds. The turnover gave the Lady Phoenix an opportunity to run the last play of the quarter with fifteen seconds left. Melva Fields looked to Juanita for a play. Juanita raised her finger and made a circular motion. "Continuous!" she shouted.

Melva relayed the instruction to her teammates, and then looked over at Tabitha sitting on the Roadrunners' bench with a towel over her head, wearing an agitated frown. Melva smiled devilishly at her former teammate as she walked past. Mildred saw and complained to the nearest official.

"Ref, their players are taunting," she ranted. "That's a tech!" The official—who didn't see what Melva did—glanced at her and looked away. "Aw, c'mon!" Mildred cried.

Beverly was jogging to get into position when she looked into the stands and saw Carlene on her cell phone with head down and her hand over her face.

"Continuous!" Juanita shouted again. "Look! At ten!"

"No, Future, stay home!" Mildred shouted from her bench. "No help! Everybody contain!"

Velvet inbounded the ball to Melva in the backcourt, and she held the ball there until the game clock read ten seconds. When Melva put the play in motion, Juanita clutched her fists and moved her head and body as she watched the play transpire. With four seconds remaining, Trina Smith caught the ball under the basket with Connie and Stacey closing in on her. She looked up and saw Beverly spotting up behind the three-point line and pitched the ball out to her. When Beverly released the

RISE OF THE PHOENIX

shot, Juanita crouched down and watched the ball in flight, and the horn sounded just as it swished threw the net.

Juanita leapt up shouting, "Yes! Yes! Yes!" along with the players on the bench as Melva, Trina, Tracy and Velvet ran off the court pumping their fists in the air with the score now reading 60–58.

Beverly lingered behind, still standing in the spot she released the shot from with her eyes closed, pointing up to the sky. She opened her eyes and looked into the stands for Carlene. She couldn't find her, so she ran off the court to join her team. When she reached the bench, Juanita grabbed her and hugged her tightly.

"Way to go, girl," Juanita said. "Way to stay focused."

Over at the Roadrunners' bench, Mildred stood facing her team with her hands on her hips, shaking her head.

"I can't believe you let them back into this game," she said. "Look at the score. We lost a nine-point halftime lead. You let them go on a run, and now they have the momentum. But we can't let them keep it. We have to go out there and start the fourth quarter by scoring some points. Tabitha, go in for Ellen. Let's see if you can hit a couple of three-pointers when they collapse on Connie and Stacey."

"Coach, if you take Ellen out, I'll have to play Trina," Connie noted.

"So," Mildred said, lifting her hands.

"I have four fouls," Connie told her.

"We should go back to the half-court trap anyway," Rayna suggested. "They're shooting right over the 2–3 zone, and they're causing match-up problems when we play man-to-man with so many people in foul trouble. Connie and Ellen have four fouls, and me and Stacey both have three."

"Stacey can play Trina," Mildred said. "We'll double down and give her some help. We need fire power right now, and I want to open up our perimeter game."

"Okay, girls, this is it," Juanita told her team. "This is the final eight minutes. Defense is the key. We have to continue to keep the ball out of Future's hands and make Stacey and Erin handle the ball more. It's their ball now, so we're going right into our triangle and two. Melva, you have to deny Future hard. Make sure she works hard to get the ball." She looked over to the Roadrunners' bench. "I see Tabitha's going back in, so Beverly will deny her."

Beverly got wide-eyed and jumped up from the bench. "Yeah, good!" she said, enthusiastically. "Let's go!"

The game horn sounded, and the referee blew her whistle. Two of the three officials approached each bench area and instructed the respective teams to come out of their huddles to start the fourth quarter.

"It's time. Let's go," Trina said.

"Come on, y'all. Let's get this done," Rayna encouraged.

"Word, y'all. We're not going to lose to this game," Melva said.

"Tabitha, you gotta focus," Connie demanded. "You were getting burned by Melva *and* Beverly in the first half."

"Buckle down, team," Kimberly said. "Let's play tougher D."

"If we lose, it won't be because of me," Tabitha commented. "I want to beat them too badly."

"I feel good, and I've got a good feeling," Velvet told her team. "We're gonna do this."

"Look for me when I'm roaming the baseline," Stacey said. "I'm open, and nobody can stop me down there."

Beverly was still looking around for Carlene, but she couldn't find her. She looked over to Melinda, who was smiling with enthusiasm along with their teammates. Beverly knew something was wrong, and she started to ask Melinda if she knew where her mother went but didn't want to upset her. She turned her attention to the team instead. "Let's just keep playing together. We came here for one thing, so let's go out there and get it."

The second game horn sounded, and the Roadrunners got up and walked out onto the court. The Lady Phoenix put their hands in with Juanita.

"Melva, Trina and Velvet all have three fouls and Keisha and Danisha both have four," Juanita informed. "So, we're going to have to play smart help defense."

"Focus on three," Trina shouted. "One, two, three!"

The Lady Phoenix all shouted, "Focus!"

RISE OF THE PHOENIX

3:20 P.M.

Thirteen seconds remained on the game clock with the Roadrunners in control of the basketball and leading by three points. Keisha and Danisha had fouled out for the Lady Phoenix, as did Ellen for the Roadrunners. Melva was at the scorers' table waiting to go back into the game. She had four fouls and had been out of the game for the Last three minutes, while Beverly played the point guard position.

Tabitha, who was frustrated from the tenacious defense that Beverly was playing on her, took a long shot from way beyond the three-point line, which crashed off the backboard and hit off the front of the rim. Kimberly and Rayna, fighting for the rebound, came crashing to the floor, both tugging on the basketball. A unified "Oooh!" came from the crowd as Kimberly cried out in pain and one of officials blew her whistle and raised both thumbs into the air. The possession arrow pointed in favor of the Lady Phoenix, with now just nine seconds remaining.

Juanita quickly ran out onto the court. "What's the matter, Kim?"

"I twisted my ankle," Kimberly whined.

Sam ran onto court with the athletic trainer. After five minutes of tending to Kimberly, Sam and the trainer helped her up and escorted her back to the team's bench. The crowd applauded in support.

Kimberly sat on the end of the bench. The trainer put her feet up and took her sneaker off to ice her ankle.

"Are you going to be okay, Kim?" Juanita asked.

"I think so. It hurts pretty badly, though."

Juanita looked down the bench and called Tracy to substitute. The official beckoned both Melva and Tracy into the game and prepared to resume play.

70-67 in favor of the Roadrunners.

Juanita called time out. "Listen team, we need to make this good," she said in the huddle. "Velvet, you will inbound. Get the ball to Trina in the middle of the court, and then trail the play. Trina, you hit Melva on the weak side. Melva, if you can't make the next pass to Beverly going long, I want you to attack the middle of the floor. You'll have Trina filling the lane on your right and Tracy on your left. Beverly will flare out to the right corner. Velvet will go to the left wing, giving us a three-point shooter on each side. We need this one."

"We have to hold them down, ladies," Mildred told her team. "There are nine seconds left in this game. We can't let them get a good look at the basket. We're going to match-up and deny everything. Erin is in and Tabitha's out."

"Why are you taking me out?!" Tabitha asked angrily. "Do you know what the hell you're doing?!"

"First of all, you'd better change your tone," Mildred snapped back. "Don't forget who the coach is here. I put in and take out whom I please, whenever I please. Now, sit down and shut up."

"You were having trouble staying with your girl anyway, Tabitha," Rayna added.

"For real," Connie said. "Melva keeps blowing by you, and Beverly is just making you look stupid."

Stacey threw in her two cents by mocking game show host, Anne Robinson. "In other words, 'You are the weakest link!'"

Tabitha could take the comments from Rayna and Connie, but she didn't like or respect Stacey, so she lashed out at her.

"You need to mind your business, you fuckin' bull dyke!" Tabitha barked, and then shoved Stacey out of her way.

Stacey had enough of Tabitha's taunts and the shove was the last straw, especially since everyone heard and saw, including her mother who was sitting directly behind their bench. Humiliated and angry, Stacey resorted to violence.

Tabitha never saw Stacey's punch coming, but its impact on the right side of her face caused her to see a blue flash before her eyes, which was followed by a throbbing sensation from the knot that was forming. A collective "Ooh!" came from onlookers as they sprung to their feet. Tabitha stumbled a few steps before regaining her composure. Connie and Rayna were able to grab her before she could retaliate, and Mildred quickly stepped in front of Stacey.

"Let me go! I'll knock her ass out!" Tabitha screamed, fighting wildly to get free of Connie and Rayna's hold.

"Bring it on, then!" Stacey challenged.

"Both of you stop this nonsense right now!" Mildred shouted. "What's wrong with the two of you?!"

"There's nothing wrong with me," Stacey said. "She hit me first."

"And I'm gonna do it again when I catch you!" Tabitha bellowed.

"You're not going to do anything except give me back my uniform and get outta here!" Mildred roared.

Tabitha broke free of Rayna and Connie and picked up her bag from under the bench. "Get off me! I don't need y'all! Later for this!"

RISE OF THE PHOENIX

"Then leave!" Mildred told her. "You've been nothing but a liability anyway!"

Tabitha stepped out of her uniform shorts, and then pulled her top off over her head and threw it in Stacey's face before heading out in her biker shorts and sports bra. Stacey attempted to go after her, but was held back by her teammates. She then heard her mother screaming to her to stop.

"Take it easy, Stacey," Rayna told her. "Don't stoop to her level."

Mildred picked up Tabitha's uniform and tossed it on the bench.

"That's right," she told Stacey. "Just get your head together so we can finish this game."

"I can't believe what just happened over there," Trina said, looking over at the Roadrunners' bench.

"I can," Melva said, smiling. "Hey, Velvet, didn't Judas end up hanging himself in the end, too?"

"He sure did," Velvet replied. "And the resurrection of the Man he sold out is still being celebrated today, two thousand years later."

"We know what we gotta do then," Melva told her teammates. "It's time for the Lady Phoenix to rise!"

At that moment, the referee notified Mildred that she'd been assessed a technical foul for lack of bench decorum, and, as per league rules, both Tabitha and Stacey were ejected from the game. Mildred argued intensively, but to no avail. The result was security escorting Tabitha out of the building and Stacey out of the gymnasium into the care of her mother.

Velvet hit two free throws as a result of the technical foul to pull the Lady Phoenix to within one point, 70–69, while regaining possession of the basketball. Now, it was Mildred's turn to call time out.

"She was probably trying to sabotage us anyway," Connie said of Tabitha. "It's her fault they caught up. She better not show her face around here again."

Mildred patted her on the back to calm her down. "Take it easy, Connie. Come on, girls. We're still up by one, and we're still going to win this game. Let's go out there and do it."

Juanita gave the Lady Phoenix players new instructions, setting up a play for Beverly. She knew that with Stacey out of the game, no one else could match up with the youngest player on the court, who had already scored twenty-one points.

Both teams took the court, and Velvet set up to inbound the ball. She made a quick pass to Trina near the three-point line. Trina pivoted on her left foot, looking for Beverly to be running toward the basket, but both Connie and Erin were covering her tightly. Trina had a defender all over her and knew she needed to do something quickly, so she turned to find Melva, who had just broken free of Rayna's coverage, and passed her the ball. But Rayna was able to reach in and knock the ball away. Melva, Rayna, Trina, Velvet and Erin all dived on the floor after the loose ball and Melva was able to bat it away in Beverly's direction. Beverly picked up the ball near the left elbow of the free throw line and jumped high into the air, releasing her shot over Connie's outstretched hands.

Every movie and television show about basketball had that famous last shot with the ball sailing through the air or bouncing around the rim in slow motion as time counted down at a seemingly much slower pace. This was no different, as the ball seemed to stay in the air forever, and the game clock counted down at a snail's pace. Mildred gasped, Reverend Scott stood and clutched his fists and Juanita twisted her body, trying to will the shot in. All of the players on both teams watched with their hearts pounding.

The game-ending buzzer sounded.

Just as at the end of the third quarter, and so many other times in her short career, Beverly Smalls had done it again.

The ball snapped the twine of the net from within.

Game.

Juanita leapt high in the air. The Lady Phoenix players ran out onto the court and jumped all over Beverly. The Roadrunners players all froze, and Mildred dropped to her knees, overtaken by the agony of defeat.

Fans of the Lady Phoenix rushed onto the court to join the celebration. Beverly saw Melinda jumping up and down cheering, but still didn't see Carlene anywhere. She wanted to look for her, but was shackled by hugs.

Juanita was finally able to get in and pull the Lady Phoenix players away so they could line-up and shake hands with their opponents.

CHERISH THE MOMENT

Sunday, July 17, 2005 – 3:41 P.M.

Whoops and hollers filled the Lady Phoenix's locker room once they finally made their way there after being bombarded by family and friends at the end of the game and after the awards presentation. For the first time in many days, members of the Lady Phoenix wore smiles on their faces. Things quieted down when Rayna Cortez walked in.

"Hey, I just wanted to come congratulate you all, again," Rayna said. "That was one of the best, most exciting and strangest games I've ever played in my life. Y'all should be able to do real good in the Nationals. Go out there and represent."

Melva walked over and hugged her biggest rival and longtime friend as the rest of the team expressed their appreciation. Rayna whispered into Melva's ear, "We need to talk. I'm gonna call you." Melva nodded. Rayna then left and the Lady Phoenix cheers erupted once again.

Beverly pulled Melinda away.

"Melinda, come here a minute."

"What's up, Bev?" Melinda was beside herself with joy and she had worked up a sweat just from jumping up and down celebrating.

Beverly didn't want to bring Melinda down from her high, but she had to ask. "Did you see where your mother went?"

"No, I didn't," Melinda said. "Why?"

"I saw her in the stands talking on her cell phone, and then she ran out," Beverly said, biting on her left thumbnail. "She looked a little upset."

"She probably couldn't hear with all the noise," Melinda told her.

"Yeah, but she left after the third quarter, and she still hasn't come back."

Seeing the worry on Beverly's face caused Melinda to become concerned as well. The smile on her face immediately faded. "You wanna go look for her?"

"No, I'm scared," Beverly told her. "What if she left because something happened to Daddy?"

Melinda tried to stay positive. "Oh, Bev, he was doing a lot better when we left the hospital last night."

"I know, but I can't help worrying. This was his second heart attack."

Melinda took her best friend by the hand. "C'mon, then. Let's go look for her."

Before they could walk out, Juanita closed the door and started gathering the team together. "Hey, everybody, let's bring it in." The team settled. "Well, we did it y'all!"

Cheers erupted again.

"Yeah, that was some game," Juanita continued. "It was very exciting. And although we never led the whole game, I never got worried. I didn't think for a second that we were going to lose. I just kept wondering why we weren't winning yet. The time didn't come until the end of the game, but the point is that it came. All of you stepped up nicely. Everybody brought their A-game today. And we had to, because the Roadrunners weren't trying to lose. But we weren't trying to let them win, either. I'm very proud of y'all. Coach Stone is going to be so happy when I tell him."

"Well, I dedicated this game to him," Trina said. "Coach Stone is the reason we had a chance to be here at all."

"That's true," Melva agreed. "But I gotta say that Nita showed everybody today that she's a real coach, and that our junior team didn't win just because they had better players. You got skills, Nita. That's what I'm going to tell Coach Stone."

Juanita's ovation was accompanied by chants of her name and team members dousing her with the water cooler. She squealed from the cold of the water running down her body, but she also felt refreshed by it.

"Hey, let's not forget that this ain't over," Juanita told them all while wiping water off her face. "Don't forget this feeling, because we have to keep this momentum and take it with us to THE NATIONAL TOURNAMENT!!!"

Pandemonium describes what the people waiting outside of the locker rooms were hearing. It brought broad smiles to the faces of family and friends, relief to the people who were there wishing and hoping to finally see the Roadrunners' reign come to an end, and looks of pain and confusion to the Roadrunners supporters.

RISE OF THE PHOENIX

4:09 P.M.

Beverly and Melinda were the first players to come out of the locker room. They were met by their teammates' families and friends with hugs and pats on the back. Finally, they saw Carlene making her way to them through the crowd. They both rushed over to her and the three of them embraced.

"I'm so proud of you girls," Carlene said. "Burt is going to be so happy to hear about this."

Hearing that, Beverly felt as if a huge weight was lifted from her, and she was finally able to exhale.

"Where did you go, Mommy?" Melinda asked.

"Your daddy called," Carlene Thompson told her daughter. "I couldn't hear with all the noise, and the reception was bad, so I went upstairs. He wanted to come and bring his family, but he went to the wrong place. Pace University has a campus somewhere upstate, and he went there."

Melinda's eyes widened. "Oh, I didn't know he was coming."

"He called early this morning, and I told him about it," Carlene said. "He wanted to surprise you."

"Is he still coming?" a hopeful Melinda asked.

"No, but he said he'll come see you tomorrow before he leaves town."

"Well, let's go," Beverly said. "I want to see *my* father."

"Yes, I know he's waiting to see us, too. I can't wait to see the look on his face when he finds out that you girls played and your team won. He's going to be so happy when he sees those trophies."

As the rest of the team made their way out of the locker room, Velvet and Kimberly stayed back with Juanita.

Juanita changed out of her wet clothes and into her denim shorts, blue Yankees "Giambi" T-shirt and flip-flops. The two players also had changed into street clothes and sat on a bench across from their assistant coach.

"I need to tell y'all something," Velvet said. "My father was supposed to take me back to California with him this morning. I had to make a deal with him in order to get him to stay and to be able to come and play today. I'm going to accept an arts scholarship I was offered from Stanford and…" She closed her eyes and put her hands over her face. Then, she looked up and sighed. "Well, since I'm not going to college on a basketball scholarship, there's really no need for me to keep playing, especially for the Lady Phoenix."

While Kimberly was rendered speechless, the look on her face showed her shock and anguish.

"What?! No!" Juanita exclaimed.

"It's okay," Velvet said. "It'll be cool. I'll work it out somehow and probably tryout for Stanford's team. I'll be fine."

"I'll talk to him," Juanita said. "You belong here. Nothing will be the same if you're not involved with this program. Why does he want you to quit?"

Velvet looked over at Kimberly and choked out the words. "He doesn't want me to be around Kim anymore since he found out that she and I are seeing each other. He already thinks that women's sports is a cesspool for lesbianism. Now, in his eyes, I'm a product of my environment."

"Oh, that's just crazy!" Juanita shouted. "I'm not a lesbian. Trina and Melva aren't lesbians. Shoot, even Sheila used to be a ball player, and she's not a lesbian either. I'm going to talk your father, because he's got the wrong idea."

Juanita stood up and started toward the exit, but Velvet jumped up and stood in front of her.

"No, Nita. Please? It'll just make things worse. I'm already afraid he's going to make me come live with him for good. At least I'll still live here and finish my senior year before moving to California. I can still come out and support the team, and I'll tutor some of the younger players if you need me to. But if you go say something to him now, it's going to ruin things. Let's just finish enjoying our win and cherish this moment."

"You're not coming to New Orleans with us, either, are you?" Kimberly asked.

Velvet shook her head. "It was hard enough getting him to agree to let me play today. He'll never let me go away with y'all. He'd be too scared that we'll spend the whole time having wild, lesbian sex parties. I played today so that we'd have a better chance of winning. I didn't want y'all to suffer because of me. You know it doesn't really matter if you win in New Orleans or not. You just have to go there, play hard and let the recruiters know that the Roadrunners aren't the only representatives that New York City has. Show them that there are good kids here who do their school work and are learning how to play the right way."

Kimberly stood up, grabbed Velvet and kissed her softly on the lips. Then, she stepped away, picked up her bag and trophy and limped out of the locker room.

Velvet hugged Juanita, then picked up her things and left the locker room, as well. She met her father standing by the elevators, and the two of them embraced and held each other tightly.

When Juanita finally came out of the locker room, the hallway was deserted. She dialed T.J.'s number on her cell phone.

"Yes?" T.J. answered.

"We did it," Juanita told him. "We won the championship."

"We did?! What was the score?"

"We won by one, 72–71. Velvet showed up and hit five three-pointers. Beverly showed up, too. I let her play."

"That's good," T.J. said to Juanita's surprise. "How did she do?"

"Oh…uh, she got the MVP," Juanita said.

"Good. That's exactly what she needed. I was hoping she'd be there, it proves that she was really sorry about what she did and wanted to make up for it. I'm glad you let her play."

Smiling, Juanita asked, "How's Sheila?"

"She's doing better. I'm in here waiting on her hand and foot. If she had a bell, I'd be in serious trouble."

Juanita laughed. "Tell her I asked about her."

"I will. Congratulations, Coach."

"Thanks, T.J."

"Call everyone from both teams tomorrow and tell them to be at practice on Tuesday."

"Okay, I'll see you there."

Juanita hung up thinking about whether she should've told T.J. about Velvet. Then she thought that not telling him right away was best. He deserved to be able to cherish the moment, too.

KENNETH J. WHETSTONE

NEW YORK DAILY NEWS
Monday, July 18, 2005
SUMMER LEAGUE BASKETBALL

Rise of the Phoenix!
BY PEARL McBRIDE
DAILY NEWS SPORTS WRITER

THE MYTH SAYS that the Phoenix is a great bird that is consumed by flames every five hundred years and rises from its ashes to become a mighty force of immortality. Yesterday, at Pace University, the appropriately named "Lady Phoenix" showed their immortality by overcoming adversities in recent days that could've taken all of the fight out of them and made the championship game in the New Attitude Sports Association League a blowout. Instead, like the mythical bird, when their fuse was lit they swooped over the heavily favored Roadrunners and rained firebombs on them to take a 72–71 victory.

After cruising to a 16 point win over a good Imperial Crew team in the semifinals last Wednesday, Lady Phoenix members got up the next morning to learn that Sheila Stonewall, the wife of the team's founder and head coach, T.J. Stonewall, had fallen in the shower, causing her to receive five stitches, a concussion, and the loss of her seven week pregnancy. If that news wasn't bad enough, they also found out that Burton Smalls, the father of the team's young new player, Beverly Smalls, had suffered a heart attack the same night.

When the Lady Phoenix took the court Sunday afternoon, it was without the leadership of their coach, who stayed home to be by his wife's side. With a championship and trip to New Orleans for the New Attitude National Tournament hanging in the balance, assistant coach Juanita Moore took over. Moore, a former Lady Phoenix player, who scored 1,508 points at James Madison High School, and was a standout at St. Peter's College, led the Lady Phoenix's fourteen-and-under team to a championship a week earlier. Moore found out two hours before game time yesterday that Stonewall would not be present and said that she didn't expect to see Smalls either. But Smalls did show up and recorded her third triple-double of the tournament scoring 23 points, grabbing 13 rebounds and handing out 10 assists.

It's been two years since anyone from New York City has defeated the Roadrunners, and the sea of crimson worn by their fans yesterday

RISE OF THE PHOENIX

saw no reason why things would be any different. The Roadrunners sped through the tournament untested, winning by an average margin of 26 points. All-American Connie King (Jefferson H.S.) played her usual game of being a force in the post, scoring 20 points and pulling down 11 boards. Rayna "Future" Cortez (Jefferson H.S.) scored 15 points and was near perfect, even with a bruised shoulder, shooting 5 for 6 from the field, 3 for 3 from the free throw line, and handing out 13 assists without committing any turnovers. Stacey Conyers, Thomas Jefferson High School's newest star, led all scorers with 24 points and 11 rebounds.

But the Lady Phoenix played patient and poised by controlling the tempo of the game, moving the ball a lot, and using a balanced attack to take over as New York City's number one girls' basketball team. Even after trailing by as many as 9 points at half-time, the Lady Phoenix put together a series of runs using long distance shooting as their weapon as they hit 11 of 18 3-pointers for the game, including five in a thrilling third quarter in which they scored 30 points. Smalls, who hit four 3-pointers, also hit the game-winning basket from near the free throw line. It was the Lady Phoenix' only lead of the game.

Velvet Fuller (LaGuardia H.S.) hit 5 of 6 from downtown, scoring 17 points for the Lady Phoenix. Paul Robeson High School's LaTrina Smith (11 points, 11 rebounds) and Melva Fields (10 points, 6 assists) also contributed for the winners.

NYC GIRLS BASKETBALL WEBSITE
MESSAGE BOARD
From: Coyote
Date: Monday, July 18, 2005
Time: 2:13 P.M.
Message: Not a peep!
It's amazing that there hasn't been a single message posted on this website today, the day after the Roadrunners lost! There hasn't been a peep out of anyone. Well, let me be the first to say congratulations to the Lady Phoenix. I knew they could do it if they had their full team. It was a real good game, especially in the third quarter, and I'm sure the scouts were impressed with the way all the young ladies from both teams played.
From: Mighty Isis
Date: Monday, July 18, 2005
Time: 2:34 P.M.
Message: RE: Not a peep!
I want to say congratulations to the Lady Phoenix as well. It was the best game I've seen in a long time, which is what a championship game is supposed to be. If the LP can play like that in New Orleans, they'll win it all.
From: Roadrunners Fan
Date: Monday, July 18, 2005
Time: 2:40 P.M.
Message: RE: Not a peep!
I really didn't expect the turnout to be the way it was, but I'm glad I got to see such a great game. The lone downside was the fight on the Roadrunners' bench. They'll have to regroup so they can come back and reclaim their spot at the top.
From: Coyote
Date: Monday, July 18, 2005
Time: 3:12 P.M.
Message: RE: Not a peep!
The fight on the Roadrunners bench was between Stacey Conyers and Tabitha Gleavy, both of whom the Roadrunners stole from other teams. What do you think is going to happen if new players keep running thru your program? They all think they're stars. All they want out of playing is to win, which is what is instilled into their minds by a lot of coaches. They don't practice together or anything, so the only

RISE OF THE PHOENIX

time they get together is for games. These kids don't know each other, and they don't get a chance to bond. Something like the fight yesterday was destined to happen.

From: Kramer
Date: Monday, July 18, 2005
Time: 3:29 P.M.
Message: RE: Not a peep!
I have to agree with Coyote. Too many teams take advantage of kids to the point of making them believe that success only comes from winning tournaments. In sports, it's important to learn responsibility, discipline, teamwork, loyalty and respect! None of those things apply when you tug on kids, pulling them and dragging them along from here to there, asking them to leave one place to come to yours, advocating disloyalty and condoning instability. Congratulations to the Lady Phoenix for achieving success while practicing good moral values.

From: jay boogie
Date: Monday, July 18, 2005
Time: 3:51 P.M.
Message: RE: Not a peep!
the number of hatas is growing every day. lets not forget it was a old lady phoenix player that started that fight.

LET HIS WILL BE DONE

Wednesday, July 20, 2005 – 2:03 P.M.

Velvet sat with the choir looking around the church. Sheila was sitting next to her, and Velvet clutched her hand as she stared into the faces of the fifty or so people scattered in small groups in the first few rows of the middle aisle. The first row consisted of only Beverly, Melinda, Carlene, Juanita and T.J. All of the other Lady Phoenix players from the junior and senior teams occupied the next two rows. Sam Pernell and Glen Ford sat several rows behind them, and Velvet didn't know anyone else. This was a small sendoff, but not one anyone present would ever forget.

"And it has been said that the good die young, but their spirits live on in our hearts forever," Reverend Scott said as he stood behind the podium on the pulpit. "As we bid farewell to our friend, our colleague and a loving father, we wish him well as he stands in the presence of the Almighty. And he wishes us well in the world of the living and leaves this praise for God's Surpassing Greatness for his daughter Beverly, his fiancée Carlene, her daughter Melinda, and to all of the loved ones. This is Psalms 150. Indeed, this is a message for us all.

"Praise the Lord! Praise God in His sanctuary; praise Him in His mighty firmament! Praise Him for His mighty deeds; praise Him according to His surpassing greatness! Praise Him with trumpet sound; praise Him with lute and harp! Praise Him with tambourine and dance; praise Him with strings and pipe! Praise Him with clanging cymbals; praise Him with loud clanging cymbals! Let everything that hath breath praise the Lord! Praise the Lord!'"

When Reverend Scott stepped away, the choir stood up and Sheila stepped forward. She always loved the Gospel Keynotes singing the song "I'm Going to a Place" and thought it would be the ideal song for her to sing for Burton. She practiced with the choir five hours the previous day, and she sung it with fire and passion, all the while keeping her eyes closed and wearing a slight smile. She was rejoicing Burton's departure from this world and his arrival to a better place—her baby's as well.

RISE OF THE PHOENIX

As everybody stood and rejoiced with Sheila, most swaying with their hands in the air and tears streaming, Beverly sat still in her black pantsuit and her hair in Shirley Temple curls with dry eyes and a blank look on her face, staring straight ahead. She wasn't looking at her father lying in the casket. She wasn't looking at Sheila and Velvet singing with the choir. She was remembering. She recalled something her mother said to her: *"Hey, baby. You know we gotta take care of your daddy, right? He needs us more than he'll ever admit. He's strong emotionally, but weak physically. We have to do whatever it takes to make sure he doesn't get overworked or stressed out."* She then thought about why her father ended up in the hospital. It was tearing her up inside.

T.J.'s face didn't show sorrow or grief, he appeared to be angry. But a bawled up face was his way of displaying hurt, sadness, disappointment or any type of discomfort. His mind was racing and his migraine flared. He kept asking himself over and over, "What are we going to do now?" He was worried about what was going to happen to Beverly. He was upset that Velvet was leaving. Most of all, he couldn't understand why so many misfortunes were falling upon him and everyone he cared about. He started blaming himself. He figured that if he was more focused he would've been able to tend to what ever was troubling Tabitha better, more aware of Mildred's actions, able to deal with Velvet better, and been in touch with his wife's needs.

When Sheila finished her song, the choir continued with a dirge as the mourners, which included some of Burton's clients and members of the PTA from Beverly's middle school, lined up in concession to view Burton's last remains one final time. When Melinda reached the casket, she began crying uncontrollably and Carlene had to hold her up to keep her from falling out. Melinda's reaction made everyone else grieve more. Everyone except Beverly, who walked by slowly with the same blank look on her face. She looked down at her father and swallowed hard. She felt a sinking feeling in her stomach just before a single tear ran down her nose.

5:48 P.M.

Everyone gathered in the recreation room at T.J.'s job at the Brownsville Recreation Center after returning from the burial. The catering was enough to feed five times as many people that were present. Beverly tried to isolate herself from everyone else by sitting in a corner in the back of the room, but Melinda would not leave her alone and sat right beside her. She knew Beverly wasn't in the mood for conversation, so she just stared off into space with her.

Carlene was also sitting alone until T.J. led Reverend Scott over and they sat with her. T.J. had been a middleman between the two in making arrangements for the funeral, so he took the opportunity to formally introduce them.

"Carlene Thompson, this is Reverend Douglas Scott, Velvet's father."

"How do you do?" Carlene said, extending her hand.

"I'm okay," Reverend Scott said, shaking her hand. "Blessed in Jesus' name."

"I brought Reverend Scott over to meet you because his church is affiliated with Children's Services, Child Welfare and The Blooming Rose foster agency," T.J. said.

"How are you?" Reverend Scott asked.

"Scared," Carlene admitted. "Very, very scared. Burt was an only child and both of his parents are dead. Beverly's only family is her grandfather on her mother's side."

"Yes, Chuck Nolan," T.J. told Reverend Scott. "He does commentaries for NBA games."

"Well, it seems the ever popular Mr. Nolan doesn't have the time to take on such a responsibility," Carlene told them. "He suggested sending Beverly to a boarding school."

"What? I can't believe that," T.J. said.

"That was the gist of the message he left on my machine last night," Carlene said. "Burton told me a lot about him and his ex-wife's families. He told me that Beverly's mother and grandfather weren't close. Her grandfather turned his back on her mother when she chose to live with Beverly's grandmother instead of him after their divorce. Burton told me that Chuck Nolan didn't show up for his ex-wife's nor his daughter's funerals when they died. Beverly never even met him."

Reverend Scott shook his head, thinking about his own family. "Well, I'm here to help anyway I can, Ms. Thompson," he said. "You let me know what steps you want to take to help get Beverly into your home, and I'll see to it that things get done."

Carlene raised her brows. "Into *my* home?" she asked. "Oh, well, I hadn't even considered that. The truth is that I couldn't handle taking on another child. Raising Melinda by myself has been challenging enough for both of us."

RISE OF THE PHOENIX

"But weren't you and Mr. Smalls planning to get married?" T.J. asked.

"That would've been different. The girls would've had two parents living in a household with two incomes. If Burton would've passed after we were married, I at least would've been his wife, and things could've worked out a little better."

T.J. and Reverend Scott looked at each other, neither of them knowing what to say. They both thought for sure that Carlene was worried about how she was going to be able keep Beverly. Never did they fathom the possibility that she wouldn't want to.

Melinda was holding Beverly's hand as her best friend continued to stare off into space. She looked over her shoulder and saw Kimberly clutching her cane and looking Goth in her black garbs and dark makeup on her light skin. She was sitting alone near the back wall looking across the room at Velvet, who was sitting at a table chatting with Trina.

Melinda took a breath and turned her attention back to Beverly. "Hey, Bev, I'll be right back, okay? Do you need anything?" Beverly slowly shook her head. "You're not hungry or anything?" Again, Beverly made the same gesture. "Okay, I'll be right back."

Melinda got up, tugged the bottom of her black dress that had risen on her wide hips, and walked over to where Kimberly was sitting. Kimberly saw her coming and rolled her eyes up, thinking that she really didn't feel like dealing with anyone's problems. She decided she'd give Melinda a piece of her mind once and for all.

"Hey, Kim, what's up?" Melinda asked as she approached.

"What's up, Melinda?" Kimberly defensively responded.

"You feeling okay?"

"Yeah, I'm chillin'. Why?"

"I don't know," Melinda shrugged. "Maybe because you're sitting over here all by yourself."

"I'm not in a very social mood, right now," Kimberly said, trying to brush Melinda off.

"Oh, okay. Well, I won't bother you too much then. I just wanted to apologize for the way I've been acting toward you. You're a cool person, and you're always nice to everybody. You and Velvet both are. I just bugged out because...you know...it took me by surprise. I never even met a gay person before, not that I know of. It's just that when you're taught certain things about people all your life, you tend to judge without really knowing."

"I know that's right," Kimberly said, now looking at Reverend Scott. She faced Melinda and looked her in the eyes for the first time. "You know I have interracial parents? My father's black and my mother's white, so I know a thing or two about prejudices. Being a mulatto lesbian—shoot, I'm destined for ridicule, I guess. You know what, though, Melinda? I wouldn't change a thing."

Melinda shook her head. "I hear you, Kim," she said, softly. "I can never get down with it, but it's your life, and as long as you're not trying to force it on anyone and you're not hurting anyone, I really shouldn't care what you do."

Kimberly heard sincerity in Melinda's voice. "Thanks, Melinda. It was cool for you to come over here and say that."

"I hope that we can be cool again."

Kimberly held out her hand. "No doubt."

Melinda gave her the Lady Phoenix handshake, and then returned to Beverly's side.

Kimberly looked across the room again. She saw Velvet glance over at her, look at her father, and then turn her attention back to Trina. Kimberly sucked it up, braced herself on her cane and made her way to join Juanita and some of her other teammates at another table.

"Dang, we're gonna have to play without you and Beverly for real this time," Trina said.

"You'll be fine," Velvet said. "We'll be there in spirit, and the spirit of this team is too strong for anybody to pull apart. Just go out there and do your thang!"

"It's different for me, Vee," Trina said. "You and I are exact opposites."

"In what way?" Velvet asked.

"You're guaranteed a scholarship in something other than basketball, but basketball is what you want. Me, I'm guaranteed a basketball scholarship, but I want one in academics. I want to study law, get into politics; become a mayor, governor, senator, or the first of the two unlikeliest people to get into the White House, an African-American female. Whatever it is, I'm going to make some differences. Everybody's gonna know the broad, six-foot-four woman with the loud mouth, who came out of the projects and shook up the world."

RISE OF THE PHOENIX

"I feel you, Tree," Velvet laughed. "Just make sure you call me to sing at your inauguration."

"Oh, hell yeah! You can count on that."

"You know, Tree, I was going to make it to Texas Tech," Velvet said to her friend. "I was going to win a championship there like Sheryl Swoopes, and then play for the Houston Comets. But, I guess God just has other plans for me."

"I would be inclined to agree under different circumstances," Trina said. "What I mean is, if somebody from Texas Tech saw you in person and decided you were not what they were looking for, that would be one thing. But you're not even going to get the chance."

"No, if it was meant to be, then nothing would be stopping me from getting there. My presence is needed elsewhere, that's all."

Trina threw up her hands. "Fine," she surrendered.

Carlene stood up from the table. "It's time I got the girls home," she said.

T.J. and Reverend Scott both stood up.

"Okay, Ms. Thompson," Reverend Scott said. "I'll have the appropriate people call you tomorrow, and we'll work on doing whatever we can to help Beverly."

"Thank you, Reverend. Thank you, too, T.J. You've been wonderful. I appreciate all your help arranging the funeral and everything else. I don't know what we would've done without you."

"Don't mention it, Ms. Thompson," T.J. said, giving her a hug. "If you need anything, don't hesitate to call me."

"Thank you." Carlene gave a cordial smile, and then walked off.

"Well, I'm going to get Velvet, and we're going to make it on home, as well," Reverend Scott said.

T.J. shook the reverend's hand. "Yeah, I'm going to wrap everything up so we all can get out of here. We have to catch a nine-thirty flight to New Orleans tonight. Thanks for everything, Reverend."

"You don't have to thank me, Coach. It was God's will for me to be here."

"I wish you were staying longer so that you can see first hand the hard work these girls are putting in to reaching their goals and achieving their dreams. They're all good girls."

"I don't doubt that one bit, Coach. You have a close-knit, family-oriented program. Unfortunately, your open-door hospitality lacked screening, so evil found its way in. The devil doesn't go where he's not invited. Put God first, Coach. Because it's Him that you all are missing."

"One of the things my mother and my grandmother constantly reminded me of as I was growing up, which is something I'm sure you know very well, is that Jesus said, 'Come as you are.' My open-door hospitality is no different from your church's. First, get them in the door, and then help them save themselves. You know it doesn't always happen overnight, though."

Nodding, Reverend Scott said, "I hear you talking, Coach, and perhaps you're right. Regardless of what anyone thinks, I don't want my daughter to be unhappy, miss out on her dreams or anything like that. She showed me something out there on that basketball court the other day. Something I didn't know she had. We'll do our family counseling, and I'll pray on it and see where God leads me. Have a safe flight tonight. I'll be praying for you all."

"Thank you, Reverend."

7:18 P.M.

"Everything is all messed up," T.J. said to Sheila as they sat on their bed changing their clothing, her into a nightgown and him into jogging pants, a long-sleeved T-shirt and his favorite pair of Adidas cross trainers. "I can't start to tell you how surprised I was when Carlene Thompson said she couldn't take Beverly in. Damn! Why is all of this bad stuff happening? First, Tabitha quits the program. Now, Velvet's father is *making* her quit. Kimberly's hurt, physically and emotionally. You ended up in the hospital. Even Trina broke up with her boyfriend. I forgot to tell you about that." He sucked his teeth in frustration. "We're not ready to go to New Orleans tonight. With all that's been going on, I forgot to check with Melva's school to see if she's doing well enough to be excused to make the trip. It's a good thing Juanita thought to do it. With Kimberly hurt and Beverly, Velvet and Melinda not going, we're only going to have seven players dressed. That saying is right. 'Sometimes when you win, you really lose.'"

"Oh, I don't think that saying is true in this case, T.J.," Sheila said. "Most of what you just mentioned would've still taken place even if your team would've lost the game. With the exception of finding out that Carlene Thompson won't take Beverly in, everything else happened before the game. Winning provided a temporary high from all the lows."

"Yeah, well, we all came down off that high real fast after finding out that Mr. Smalls died that morning," T.J. said. "I keep thinking about Beverly. God, that poor girl. She's going to be bounced around in the system and end up God knows where. When I met the Smalls, they were so happy. They had plans. Then, here I come exposing them to the madness. I took an innocent, defenseless little girl and left her alone in the midst of predators."

"T.J., stop it," Sheila said. "Why are you blaming yourself for that?"

"Because I know what I'm dealing with when it comes to people like Millie Negron and Charles Greene, and I let my guard down."

Sheila slid over close to her husband and rested her head on his shoulder. "When I was in the hospital, something occurred to me. You and I vowed before God to be one, but instead we were being separate. You were putting basketball ahead of everything and everybody, including God and me. I brought Velvet here without talking to you. We were fighting about what church to join, for God's sake. None of that stuff is what we were supposed to be doing. We stood before the Lord on our wedding day and promised to live for Him so that He could bless this union. When we stopped doing what we were supposed to do and we stopped living right, the blessings stopped too. We went back on our word, and He let us know it. We have to get back to praying and praising Him together. That's when things will get back on the right track for us."

T.J. put his arm around Sheila and held her lovingly. "You're absolutely right. Reverend Scott was saying something very similar to me today. Let's start right now, Mama. Let's pray, beg for His forgiveness and start making strides to get back on the right road."

Sheila smiled. "That sounds like a good idea."

"Let's pray for Beverly, too. She needs some blessings right now. It would be nice if we could help her out somehow."

"Yeah, let's do that. God will make a way."

KENNETH J. WHETSTONE

NEW ATTITUDE GIRLS NATIONAL TOURNAMENT
Division I 17-Under Results
Thursday, July 21, 2005
1:30 – Jaguars(TN), 61 – Lady Gators(LA), 43
3:30 – Red Birds(MO), 54 – Lady Raiders(MD), 53
5:30 – Bridgeport Belles(CT), 68 – Lady Phoenix(NY), 51
7:30 – Lady Cougars(CA), 57 – Lady Vikings(NC), 55
Friday, July 22, 2005
1:30 – Lady Raiders(MD), 66 – Lady Gators(LA), 65
3:30 – Lady Phoenix(NY), 64 – Lady Vikings(NC), 61 OT
5:30 – Jaguars(TN), 58 – Red Birds(MO), 44
7:30 – Bridgeport Belles(CT), 67 – Lady Cougars(CA), 50
Sunday, July 24, 2005
11:00 – 7th Lady Vikings(NC), 46 – 8th Lady Gators(LA), 41
1:00 – 5th Lady Raiders(MD), 55 – 6th Lady Phoenix(NY), 52
3:00 – 3rd Lady Cougars(CA), 51 – 4th Red Birds(MO), 47
5:00 – 1st Jaguars(TN), 56 – 2nd Bridgeport Belles(CT), 49
Division I 14–Under Results
Saturday, July 23, 2005
11:00 – 7th Red Birds(MO), 45 – 8th Flamingos(FL), 36
1:00 – 5th Lady Bulldogs(VA), 38 – 6th Lady Knights(AL), 33
3:00 – 3rd Lady Vipers(MS), 45 – 4th Bridgeport Belles(CT), 42
5:00 – 1st Scorpions(AZ), 49 – 2nd Lady Phoenix(NY), 42

FUTURE OF THE LADY PHOENIX

Saturday, July 30, 2005 – 8:39 A.M.

Juanita pulled her fuchsia RAV4 into the parking lot of the International House of Pancakes on Ralph Avenue and found a parking spot next to Glen's blue BMW X5. She walked into the restaurant and saw T.J. and Glen sitting at a table near the back wall. T.J. called her over.

"Good morning, guys," Juanita said, wearing her Alex Rodriguez jersey as she sat in the booth next to her mentor.

"Hey, Nita." T.J. kissed her on the cheek.

Glen took her hand and kissed the back of it. "You're looking lovely as always."

Juanita blushed, showing off her deep dimples and a smile fit for a toothpaste ad.

Glen looked out of the window into the parking lot. "I just want to ask you one thing."

"What's that?" Juanita said.

"Why the hell you get your car painted that ugly-ass color, and then have the nerve to park it next to mine?"

Juanita quickly snatched her hand away. "Later for you, Glen!"

They all laughed. The waitress approached and they all placed their orders.

"So, what do I owe the pleasure of being invited to breakfast with the boys, and where is Sam?" Juanita asked.

"Sam has to take care of some important business this morning," T.J. told her. "I asked you to join Glen and me because we both have something to tell you."

Juanita looked at both men and shrugged. "So, tell me."

"Well, there's good news and bad news," T.J. said. "First, the bad news."

Juanita had no idea what to expect, so she braced herself to hear what T.J. had to say. She was usually able to read him very well, so she looked into his eyes and waited.

"You've done an outstanding job with the Lady Phoenix as my assistant with the senior team and as the junior team's coach. You've already won two tournaments this summer and came in second at the National Tournament in New Orleans. With all of your success over the last two years, I feel comfortable with cutting the umbilical cord and letting you go."

Juanita gasped.

"You need to do your own thing," T.J. went on. "You've proven that you're capable of being successful, so starting over fresh and venturing out on your own shouldn't be too difficult for you."

Juanita looked deeper into T.J.'s eyes, trying to see if he was putting her on. She was hoping that he was just playing a joke on her, but his eyes showed no jest. "You don't want me to be a part of the program anymore?" she stammered.

T.J. shook his head and dryly said, "No."

"Why?"

"Because of the good news," Glen answered. "I'm the new head coach at Hofstra University."

"What does that have to do with me?!"

That's when T.J. cracked, and he and Glen started laughing.

"What's going on, you guys?" Juanita asked, pleadingly.

"I want you to take over my old position as head coach at Kingsborough Community College," Glen finally told her. "I always knew you had the coaching skills, and it was confirmed when you beat the Roadrunners. Me nor T.J. could've done a better job."

Juanita put her hands on her chest and her big smile returned. "Are you guys serious?"

"Hell yeah!" Glen assured.

"I don't know what to say."

T.J. slouched back in his seat and huffed. "You'd better say yes, because I'm serious about you being fired."

"It's a part-time gig that only pays eighteen thousand," Glen informed, "unless you'd be interested in taking on an administrative position, then it'll be full-time."

"No, I just got a permanent position teaching health education at I.S. 302, so part-time would be perfect."

"You did?" T.J. asked. "Why didn't you tell me?"

"I just got the job on Thursday," Juanita said. "I was going to tell you at practice today."

"Well, that's great. This is your week."

"Yep, it's been all good."

"So, are you saying yes?" Glen asked her.

"Yes!" Juanita ecstatically responded.

"Good. I'll call the A.D. today and tell him to call you for a meeting next week."

T.J. sat up and hugged Juanita. "We're gonna miss you," he said. "But you're inheriting a good program. They just won the junior college national championship, so you're gonna have a lot of pressure on you to maintain the success with very little to work with."

"I can handle it," Juanita said, confidently.

10:17 A.M.

T.J. had all the players sit on the bleachers so that he and Juanita could talk to them. Melva wasn't there, and no one knew her whereabouts. Juanita proceeded to tell the members of upcoming events.

"The junior team will be playing tomorrow in the West Fourth Street Tournament. The game is at four o'clock, so everyone needs to meet Coach Stone here at two so he can take you there."

"Are you meeting us there, Coach Moore?" one of the junior players asked.

"No, I will be coaching both teams," T.J. informed.

Before T.J. could explain or anyone could ask why, Melva walked in with Rayna Cortez. There was a dead silence, and everyone was motionless as the two girls approached.

"Hey, sorry I'm late," Melva said. "I was waiting on Future. She wants to ask you something, Coach Stone."

"Uh...sure," T.J. said, hesitantly.

"Go on, T.J.," Juanita told him. "I'll fill the team in."

"Okay," T.J. nodded. "Come, right this way, Rayna." He led her out of the gymnasium and to his office across the hall.

"Well, girls, I have good news and bad news," Juanita told the team. T.J. looked back at her and twisted his lips, knowing she was going to put them on the way he and Glen did her.

Once in his office, T.J. pulled a chair up close to his desk. "Have a seat," he told the young point guard whom he was very fond of.

Rayna sat and crossed her legs. She wore a white nylon blouse with a gold brooch, a long, blue, nylon skirt, white sandals with thick two-inch heels, and her long, straight, jet black hair hung down behind her pinned with a single white barrette near the back of her neck. T.J. had never seen her dressed in anything other than jeans or basketball shorts with her hair tied up in a bun and was impressed at how nice she looked.

"To what do I owe the pleasure of this visit?" he asked as he took his seat behind his desk.

"I want to join the Lady Phoenix," Rayna directly stated.

T.J.'s response was a bewildered stare. Rayna grinned, expecting his reaction.

"I know what you must be thinking, so let me answer a few questions for you in advance," she said. "Yes, I'm very sure and very serious. No, I'm not looking to jump ship because y'all beat us in the championship. Yes, I intend on being committed, and I understand that I won't be coming in and taking spots or anything like that, nor do I want to. No, I will not be returning to the Roadrunners for any more tournaments, so if you don't take me, I'm going somewhere else like to the Imperial Crew or the Lady Panthers."

T.J. traced his thumb and index finger around his goatee as he continued to stare. "This is something I'm going to have to put some thought into," he told her. "I mean, well, it's because I take a strong stand against team hopping."

"I'm not team hopping, Coach Stone. I'm going to team hop. One time and that's it. When I was young I played for the Lady Tigers, but when the new coach took over and they started doing grimy sh— …uh…stuff, I couldn't be bothered anymore. I'm not into grimy people, Coach Stone. My aunt raised me better than that. That's one of the main reasons I have to separate myself from the Roadrunners, too."

"Well, you know that the Roadrunners have a strong link with your school team at Jefferson. Aren't you afraid that this decision will have a negative affect on your playing there?"

Rayna squinted her eyes and fanned her hand at T.J. saying, "Nah, are you kidding? Coach Greene don't care if I play for the Roadrunners or not. Not all of the players from Jeff play for the Roadrunners, you know."

"I know. I just thought that—"

"Look, here's my essay," she said, leaning forward to hand T.J. a folder. "There's a check for a hundred and twenty-five dollars in the inside pocket from my aunt to pay for my membership fees. Melva filled me in on what I needed. If you decide not to let me join, keep

281

RISE OF THE PHOENIX

the essay and give me back the check. If you do let me join, I'll be ready as soon as you say. We can be good for each other, Coach Stone."

T.J. stood up and walked around his desk. He kept his eyes on Rayna patiently holding her folder out while he thought about what she just told him. "I really would love for you to be a part of our program," he said. "It was just a couple of weeks ago I was telling that to someone. I've always thought you were a class act."

"Does that mean you're letting me in?" Rayna asked anxiously.

T.J. finally took the folder and looked inside, skimming the first page of the essay. "Have you discussed this with Coach Negron yet?"

"I didn't tell her what team I wanted to play for, but I did tell her that I wasn't going to play with the Roadrunners anymore."

"I'm sure she was less than thrilled."

"Yeah, but she'll get over it," Rayna shrugged. "They'll start winning tournaments again, and she won't even notice I'm gone anymore. Anyway, how she feels ain't my concern. She decided to have a little practice or whatever the day before the New Attitude championship and me, Connie, Renee and the twins were the only ones to show up. She told us we'd be the starting five, but when game time came, she let Tabitha start over Erin and Stacey start over Renee. Renee never even got into the game. She quit the Roadrunners, too."

T.J. knew exactly how Rayna felt, and it was that moment he knew he had to let her join. "Well, let's go in and make the announcement to the rest of the members."

Rayna got excited as she stood and followed him out of the office.

3:12 P.M.

When T.J. returned home from practice, Sheila met him at the door with her usual hug and kiss.

"Hey, baby, how was practice?" she asked.

"Humph, let me tell you," T.J. said as he took her hand and led her to the loveseat. "First, Juanita accepted the job as Glen's replacement. She was so happy."

"That's good," Sheila said as she snuggled up under T.J. in the chair. "She does deserve this opportunity."

"Well, also, Rayna 'Future' Cortez is now a member of the Lady Phoenix."

Sheila jumped and whipped her head around to look at her husband's face. "What?! You're joking!"

"No, I'm not," T.J. said, smiling. "Melva brought her to practice this morning."

"Melva who?"

T.J. laughed. "Melva Fields, that's who. Rayna wants out of the Roadrunners program. She said if I didn't take her she'd play for the Imperial Crew or the Lady Panthers. She was ready, too. She was all dressed up like she was on an interview and she was prepared. She had her essay, her membership dues, everything. She looked me straight in the eyes the whole time and sold herself like she really wanted the job."

"Wow, that's something else." Sheila snuggled again. "I hope it works out."

"Me too. She'll be my first left-handed point guard. Her, Danisha and Melva sharing the same position is too much talent to even think about...but I have been thinking about it."

"I'm sure you have," Sheila chuckled.

"I figure I can use Melva as a shooting guard a lot, especially until we find out what Beverly's situation is going to be."

"Oh, Beverly called," Sheila remembered. "She said she wants you to call her on her cell phone before five o'clock if you can."

"Is she okay? Did she sound okay? Did she sound like something was wrong?"

"None of the above," Sheila told him. "All she said was that she wanted to ask you something."

"Oh, okay. Excuse me, Mama."

T.J. attempted to get up, but Sheila stopped him, reached down on the side of the loveseat and handed him the cordless phone. "Here. I was just on the phone with my mother before you came in."

T.J. quickly dialed Beverly's number and waited impatiently for her to answer.

"Hello?"

"Beverly, this is Coach Stone. How are you?"

"Hey, Coach Stone. I'm doing fine."

She sounded fine, which brought T.J. some relief. "What's up?"

"Hold on a minute," she told him.

T.J. heard Beverly tell someone that she was going to sit on the porch, which led him to believe that what she wanted to ask him was personal.

"I hope to be able to come to practice soon," Beverly said, as she headed outside.

"Oh, that'll be great, Beverly. We all miss you."

"I miss y'all, too. I miss playing."

"You're going to be in for a couple of surprises when you get back," T.J. teased.

"I already know about Coach Moore and Future," Beverly told him. "Kim already called me. I talk to her and Trina every day."

"You girls don't miss a beat. That's good, though. I'm glad to hear that they're keeping in touch with you."

"Coach, this is what I wanted to talk to you about." T.J. heard a change in Beverly's voice and prepared himself to hear what she had to say. "Ms. Thompson decided to take me in as a foster child, at least for a while."

"Oh, that's great!" T.J. rejoiced.

"No, it isn't," Beverly said. "I don't wanna stay with her."

T.J. went into shock. "What?! Why not?!"

"You don't know her like I do, Coach Stone. I won't be able to breathe. She's going to treat me the same way she does Melinda, and I'll never be able to do anything, and I won't be able to play."

"But she let Melinda join—" T.J. started.

Beverly cut him off saying, "Why do you think you haven't seen us at practice? We've been ready to come back, but she won't let us."

"She told me that you needed some time," T.J. said.

"That's her talking, not me and Melinda. She's telling us that we need time. *I* wanted to go to New Orleans."

"You did?" T.J. was totally stunned now, and couldn't believe what he was hearing. "But, Beverly, you didn't seem like you were in any condition to go."

"I would've played," she said. "I wanted to. My father... He was telling me he wanted us to win so I could go. That was just before..." She got choked up a bit.

Soothingly, T.J. said, "Beverly, if I would've known I would've said something to Ms. Thompson."

"It wouldn't have made a difference. That's the way she is. Please, Coach, I can't stay here. Can't you do something to help me go somewhere else?"

"I know how you must be feeling, Beverly, but if you stay there, at least you'll be with people you know and you and Melinda will still be together."

"But I'd be smothered," Beverly complained. "She makes us hold hands in the street and stupid stuff like that. I know things would've been better if my father was here and they would've gotten married or whatever, but with him gone, she's already back to her usual self. You probably will never see Melinda at a practice or a game again. I'm telling you, Coach, I'mma go crazy if they make me stay here."

T.J. rubbed his forehead, somehow thinking it would keep his headache from coming. "So, Beverly, what do you want me to do?"

She was glad he asked. "How about if you and your wife applied to be my foster parents?"

"What? You want to live here?" T.J. asked like he was surprised, even though he knew that was what Beverly was leading up to. Sheila heard and her face lit up.

"Yes," Beverly replied. "Velvet always talked about how cool it was living with you. Well, she said your wife, but I know she meant you, too."

T.J.'s face wrinkled. "Very funny," he said, sarcastically. Then he got serious again. While in thought, he made a few popping sounds with his lips before he said, "The truth is, Beverly, that I would love to have you here." He looked at Sheila's face, which he knew would lighten up the way it did. "I know we both would. We're going to talk about it and see what we can do."

"Please, Coach?"

"We'll do our best, Beverly."

"Thank you."

T.J. hung up and looked at Sheila again. She was staring at him with stars in her eyes.

"Well, Sheila, Ms. Thompson doesn't really want Beverly there, and Beverly really doesn't want to be there. Can we really be foster parents? Is that something we can do?"

"Of course it is," Sheila said. "I think we could even eventually go all the way if the foster thing works out."

"Fine, then," T.J. agreed. "Let's do what we need to do and get the ball rolling."

WHAT GOES AROUND, COMES AROUND

Saturday, August 13, 2005 – 4:06 P.M.

It was a good day for basketball to be played outdoors as the temperature dropped to a breezy and comfortable eighty-four degrees. The "Just Say No to Drugs" league was played on the upper west side in a sub-level playground at the Frederick Douglass Community Center and had been going strong for the past three weeks. The two present teams both stood at 3–0 with three more games to go after their match-up that was about to begin.

T.J. stood in front of his team's bench waiting for the 4:15 P.M. start of his game against the Roadrunners. He watched the eight players of the opposing team dressed in their burgundy with white print league-issued T-shirts doing their pre-game drills directly in front of him. Stacey Conyers, Renee Imes nor the two girls from Staten Island were among them. They did have three new players, though, two from Jefferson that used to play for the Lady Panthers and one girl who usually played for the Ravens.

Another player missing from the Roadrunners was Rayna. T.J. struggled with the idea of letting her play with the Lady Phoenix that day, being so soon after she joined and against her former team. He didn't want to be viewed as being anything like the Mildred Negrons of the world. But Rayna had done everything that was expected of every member of the Lady Phoenix program, including attending all four practices that week, both tutoring sessions, and volunteering with Trina and Melva to show up at his job seven o'clock that morning to help set up the gymnasium for a play that the drama club was putting on that afternoon. Also, she fit in well with her new teammates, and they welcomed her with open arms. T.J. ended his struggle, realizing he was nothing like his adversary. He accepted Rayna after *she* came to *him*.

He looked down on the other end of the court at his own players— also dressed in league-issued T-shirts, theirs royal blue with white print— who were also doing their pre-game drills. They seemed loose and relaxed, smiling and chatting as they went through their routine. Kimberly's ankle was wrapped, but she appeared to be moving much better. T.J. was just as happy to have her back in action as she was to be back.

Mildred Negron was watching the Lady Phoenix players as well. She had a serious look on her face as she sat with her elbows resting on her knees and her hands folded while watching each player take their lay-up. None of them, including Rayna, looked back in her direction.

Charles Greene was sitting in the bleachers on the other side of the court. He was leaning back with his legs crossed, and he had a disinterested expression. He and Rayna spoke privately when he arrived in the park. T.J. let it be. The girl they called "Future" walked away from the conversation smiling. Charles Greene didn't.

Trina left her team on the court and sat on the bench next to her coach. "You okay, Coach Stone?"

"Yeah, of course," he said. "Don't I look okay?"

"Oh, you look fine," Trina cooed. "But you always look fine to me."

"Yeah, well, I don't always feel fine. I've been feeling better lately, though."

"Yeah, so have I," Trina related, and then shared, "I miss Velvet, Coach. I'm not used to not having her around."

"Me, either. It's been a long, eventful summer, but it'll be over soon, and we can all start focusing on school again."

Trina nodded. "Yeah. You heard—Melva's gonna pass all her summer school classes."

"Yeah, well, she shouldn't have needed to take them," T.J. said bitterly. "She's your best friend, so you'd better keep your eye on her and make sure she doesn't screw up anymore. If she does, I'm going to hold you personally responsible."

Trina laughed. "Fine, put the onus on me, I can handle it. It's not gonna be hard because she's a lot more focused now. She's got something to prove."

"So, what about you, Trina?" he asked her. "What are you going to do for yourself?"

"I'm going to get that Ivy League scholarship, Coach. But...I want to go on *one* visit for basketball. I got stuff in the mail from a few schools, and one of them was from Stanford."

"That's good, Trina. You know you can apply for an academic scholarship there if that's what you prefer to have, right? I'm sure if you can get into the Ivy Leagues, you can get into Stanford, too."

"That's true. Either way, it'll be cool to go there if Velvet's there."

"And going to Southern State University or Hofstra University is out of the question?" T.J. threw in.

Trina twisted her lips. "I not feelin' those schools, Coach. They're okay, but they don't fit into my plan, you know what I'm sayin'?"

T.J. grinned. "Yeah, I hear you."

"Send me your captain, please, coaches?" the official requested, calling out from the center circle on the court.

"That's your cue," T.J. told her.

Trina stood up and started out onto the court. Then, she turned around and looked back at T.J., feeling the desperate need to finally get a weight lifted off her heart. "I love you, Coach Stone!" she called out to him.

T.J. turned up a flattered smile and innocently responded, "I love you, too!"

5:20 P.M.

The scoreboard read 49–42 as the Lady Phoenix defeated the Roadrunners for the second straight time. The players all lined up to show their sportsmanship. Rayna and Connie hugged when they reached each other. T.J. and Mildred trailed their respective lines, and when they reached each other, Mildred turned and walked away. T.J. laughed it off to himself and gathered his players to have their post game meeting.

Charles Greene left the park with thirty-one seconds left in the game and the Roadrunners fouling to try and stop the clock, hoping the Lady Phoenix would miss free throws so they'd be able to get back into the game. It was too little too late.

As the Lady Phoenix players followed their coach around the fence into the children's playground, where T.J. always talked to them beside the monkey bars, Melva tapped Trina on the shoulder.

"Yo, check it out, dawg," she said, tilting her head back toward the court.

Trina turned around and saw Daquan walking down the ramp that led into the park from West 104th Street. She looked at Melva with raised brows and a surprised expression. "What is *he* doing here?"

"That's what I was about to ask you," Melva said.

"How would I know, I haven't seen him in weeks."

Just then, they saw Erin walk over to Daquan, and they hugged and kissed before heading back up the ramp hand-in-hand. In total shock, Trina and Melva both watched with hanging jaws. Finally, Trina grinned and shook her head.

"You know what that's all about, don't you?" Melva asked. "He's just trying to make you jealous."

"I don't give a damn about what he does," Trina honestly stated. "If he thinks that's going to bother me, then he's a bigger fool than I thought."

"You think he's bangin' her?" Melva crudely asked.

"Most likely," Trina responded. "He wouldn't be hanging around her if he wasn't."

Melva looked her friend up and down. "You sure you don't care?"

Trina returned the same look. "I don't give a *dayum*!"

They laughed and proceeded to join the team.

6:33 P.M.

T.J. arrived at the Waverly Restaurant on Sixth Avenue in Greenwich Village after Sam Pernell called him and insisted they needed to meet there right away. He got a booth by the window, ordered some coffee and waited for Sam to arrive. Soon after, Sam walked in with Terry Gonzalez.

"What's up, T.J.? Thanks for coming on a spur of the moment."

"It's cool, Sam. What's going on?"

"This is Terry Gonzalez," Sam said, as they both sat across from T.J. "Terry owns an employment agency. He works closely with government programs, job training programs, getting people jobs who've been on welfare, and the like."

T.J. extended his hand. "How are you doing?"

Terry smiled and shook his hand. "Fine, thanks. I'm pleased to meet you."

"Terry has some very interesting information to share with us," Sam happily announced.

"What about?" T.J. asked.

"About my ex-fiancée," Terry told him. "I was in a relationship with Millie Negron for four years. We recently broke up because she got angry that I wouldn't help her cheat for Charles Greene."

T.J. raised an interested brow. "Really?" He checked out at the person sitting next to Sam, with the wavy hair combed back into a short

RISE OF THE PHOENIX

ponytail, wearing a Calvin Klein business suit and dark shades. "You've got my attention."

Terry looked at Sam for a confirmation. Sam gave an encouraging nod. "Well," Terry said. "My job allows me to work closely with several state and government agencies such as the Department of Social Services and some others. Because of my connections with these agencies, Millie wanted me to use my influence for Dawn Conyers, Stacey Conyers' mother, to receive public assistance and Section 8 to get her some money and an apartment. Ms. Conyers has a job working security, but the plan was to get her to move to the city from Long Island, get her on public assistance for a month or two, and then get her a better job as a case worker after she settled in."

T.J.'s face lit up. "I knew it! I knew they were up to no good!"

"There's more," Terry said, and then placed a CD-ROM on the table. "These are some files Millie left on my computer when she moved out of our apartment. She deleted them but forgot to empty the recycle bin. I went in to retrieve something else and found them. They show that she and Charles have been paying people off to let their kids travel long distances to attend Jefferson."

"I knew it! Does it show where they're getting the money from?" T.J. wanted to know.

"Yes," Terry said. "Every player pays five hundred dollars a year each to play for the Roadrunners, even if the athlete isn't a permanent member or only plays in certain tournaments. They charge every Jefferson player an additional two hundred dollars to cover expenses for *their* trips during the school season."

"Well, making the kids pay for their trips and tournaments isn't illegal," T.J. said.

"It is if they're not using the money for those things," Terry told him. "The players shouldn't have to pay anything at all with all of Millie and Charles' resources, but they use the kids' money they aren't pocketing to pay off whomever they need to: parents, tournament directors, etcetera. I personally went out of my way and got sponsors that bought all the Roadrunners supplies and equipment and paid for all of the local tournaments they participate in. I got them money from the community board and from local businesses. Of course you know that Charles got their Nike connection, but he also got money from Jefferson's PTA, who raised over seven thousand dollars for them last season. Millie told me that the PTA raised the money to send the players to the Lady Ballers basketball camp in Atlanta, but I found out that all the kids received scholarships to go that camp."

"Son-of-a...!" T.J. said, angrily.

"Wait, there's still more," Sam told him.

"Charles also gets money from the Jefferson's Alumni Athletes Association," Terry continued. "Jefferson has a bunch of former athletes who've gone on to become professionals making millions of dollars, and they all give generous donations every time one of the varsity teams or their club teams competes for a championship."

"That explains why they participate in so many of the small local tournaments," Sam said.

"Yeah, all except the small *free* ones," T.J. figured out. "That's why they didn't participate in the City Housing League, because it's financed by the city, and they can't solicit money from their sponsors to participate in it."

"That's right," Terry confirmed. "But here's the kicker. These files also prove that they've been getting other people to take the S.A.T. for some of the players. And they're not doing this simply for the sake of pushing their athletes through, it's because the more kids that pass and get into college on scholarship, the more money they get from their sponsors, as well. Also, the community board set up a specific fund to support student-athletes who live or go to school in the neighborhood to get scholarship money if they maintain a 3.0 GPA and score over a thousand on the S.A.T."

"I never heard of a program like that before," T.J. said.

"It's real," Terry said. "I know because I wrote the proposal to start it three years ago."

"But you said it's a community program, which means it's open to anyone and not just the Roadrunners, right?"

"That's right. It's for anyone in Thomas Jefferson High School's district. But of course, Charles and Millie do everything they can to keep people from finding out about it."

T.J. was outraged. He slouched back in his seat and used both hands to brush his locks back. "I'm gonna get their asses," he grumbled.

"I want you to know that I didn't come to you with this to get revenge on Millie for leaving me," Terry told T.J. "I came to you to save her from doing anymore wrong...and from Charles Greene."

"Terry has proof of everything, T.J.," Sam told him. "But you have to promise to use it under one condition."

"It depends on the condition," T.J. said smartly.

"I don't want to see Millie get into any serious trouble," Terry said. "I just want her back. I'll show you all the evidence I have if you can you give me your word that you'll use your resources to bring Charles Greene down, *only*, without dragging Millie's name through the mud. She'll hurt enough when her team loses all the backing that Charles and I were responsible for. Can you do that?"

T.J. looked out of the restaurant window, clutched his fists and shook his head at the same time, and then cut his eyes back at the two people sitting opposite of him. Sam was nodding encouragingly and Terry was patiently awaiting a reply.

"Yeah, sure," T.J. muttered.

Terry slid the disk across the table to him. "It's yours. I've already given the sponsors I was associated with just cause not to support the Roadrunners anymore, so my part in this is over. I erased the files from my computer, and I don't have any copies. My work here is done."

"Thank you," T.J. said. "I appreciate this very much. You did the right thing."

Terry nodded, and then got up and left the diner.

"This is it," Sam said, excitedly. "We got him good! Stealing money, paying parents off, cheating on the S.A.T., he's going down for sure. And Millie won't have a pot to piss in or a window to throw it out of."

"Now, just hold on a second," T.J. hesitated. "I'm not sure I want to go these routes. If it comes out that parents accepted money or gifts from Charles to let their kids go to Jeff, or that kids weren't taking their own tests, it may cause some of them to lose their eligibility. What if a kid whose parents he paid off is in college already? How many people will that have an effect on?"

"I figured you might say something like that," Sam said. "But what if we could get him for misusing the money without revealing on who or for what. Since Millie and Charles are so into pulling strings for people, I figure it's time we pulled a few strings of our own."

"What are you getting at, Sam?"

Sam leaned forward, motioned for T.J. to do the same, and spoke quietly. "Well, this is really sort of Terry's idea, but I was thinking that with Sheila's help down at the IRS, we could check on a few things."

T.J. jerked back in his seat, raised his hands with the palms down and shook them a little. "Ooh, Sam, I don't know about that."

"C'mon, man..." Sam said.

"I'm not feelin' that idea, Sam."

"Look, T.J., if you're going to do this without dragging Millie's name through it like we promised Terry and without bringing down any of the athletes, you *gotta* let Sheila investigate him, or get her to get someone to do it. We can probably get Charles fired for misusing funds. Without Charles and without Terry, as we now know, Millie won't be able to hold her own to keep the Roadrunners running the way it is for too long."

"Even if Charles isn't coaching at Jefferson, it doesn't mean he won't support the Roadrunners. He may want to be more involved with them. He'd have more freedom and fewer rules to follow. Think about it, Sam, he could actually do more harm if he did leave."

Sam shook his head and leaned back in his seat. "No. Nobody would trust him enough to sponsor him if he got in trouble for misusing funds, which is why I say we get Sheila to act on this right away."

"Well, let me take a look at this disk and see how much proof is on here and if it's enough to do something with without involving her."

"Yes, you do that," Sam said. "Call me once you've seen them so we can nail this bastard!"

T.J. sat and thought about his options. He really didn't want to involve Sheila, but he knew that he might not have a choice. He was at the point where if it meant bringing Charles Greene *and* Mildred Negron down, he'd do just about anything.

7:06 P.M.

Sheila was sitting up in the bed talking on the telephone when T.J. walked in. She smiled and patted the bed, gesturing for him to sit beside her.

T.J. did what Sheila wanted, all the while still debating with himself if he should take Sam's advice and ask for her help. During his drive home, he was practicing ways to ask her or to bring it up to her if indeed he was going to do it.

"It's Velvet," Sheila said to him. "She wants to speak to you."

T.J. took the telephone. "Hey, Velvet, how are you?"

"I'm good, Coach." She sounded like her usual, pleasant self. "How are you and everybody else doing?"

"I'm fine, and everybody's doing okay. We beat the Roadrunners again today in the 'Just Say No to Drugs' tournament."

Sheila heard and quietly applauded her husband.

"Way to go," Velvet cheered. "What was the score?"

RISE OF THE PHOENIX

"Forty-nine to forty-two. I'm sure you've heard that Future is playing with us now."

"Yeah, I heard. How did she do?"

"I only played her about ten minutes or so, but she had three points, four assists and a couple of steals. Danisha played so well, just like she did in New Orleans, that I didn't have to play Future so much, and I didn't play Melva at the point at all. You know what else? Kim played today, too."

"Yeah? How did she do?"

"She hit a three and a couple of free throws, caused havoc on defense—her usual game. Keisha was the one who carried us, though. She scored twenty-five."

"I'm glad you are all doing well," Velvet said. "I wish I was still playing, but I have to say that things have been good since I got to California. I'm in Beverly Hills right now with my sister-in-law and my niece. They're showing me around and taking me shopping. I'm glad I'm able to spend some time with family whom I haven't seen in a long time."

"Have you had time to talk with your mother?"

Velvet paused and her voiced softened. "Not really. She's in Cleveland right now with the tour. When she gets back we'll have our counseling sessions and see where things go."

"Oh, okay. Well, best of luck with that. I'm glad to hear you're doing okay."

"Yeah, you too, Coach. I'll be home in a few weeks, and I'll see you then."

"Okay, take care. Here's Sheila."

"I'll talk to you later, girl," Sheila said after taking the phone. "Remember, if you run into Morris Chestnut, tell him to holla."

"Okay, I will," Velvet laughed. "Bye."

T.J. twisted his lips. "Morris Chestnut, eh?"

"You jealous?" Sheila teased.

"Yep," he shamelessly told her.

"Good," she said. "Mission accomplished."

"You're a mess." T.J. grabbed Sheila, pinned her down and started kissing her neck.

"Ooh, baby, you know that's my spot. You're not playing fair."

"Mmm, now who do you want to holla?"

"Nobody but you, Daddy. Say my name, say my name."

T.J. sat up and joked, "Nah, you don't deserve the kind of passion and lovin' that I can give. You don't appreciate me."

"I do appreciate you, you know that." She pulled him back down to her. "I love you. You complete me. You're my world. There's no me without you, and on and on…"

"Okay, Mama, I get it," he laughed. "I love you, too. So much it burns to the point where I feel like I'm going to burst into flames whenever I'm near you."

"Me too, baby. I feel like that all the time." Sheila looked into T.J.'s eyes and saw that something was bothering him. She cupped his face in her hands and brushed his eyebrows with her thumbs and asked him, "What's wrong, baby? You look like you have something on your mind."

"I do," T.J. admitted, and then got up and took the disk out of his backpack. "I got this from Millie's ex today. It's supposed to have files that prove that she and Charles have been embezzling money from Jefferson and the Roadrunners and using it to pay off players, parents and whomever else in addition to lining their own pockets."

"Are you serious?"

"I haven't looked at it myself yet, but that's what I was told. It's also supposed to have proof that they had other people take the S.A.T. for some of their players and all kinds of stuff."

"Wow, T.J. So, what are you going to do with it?"

"Well, Terry Gonzalez—that's Millie's ex—made me promise to use it to bring Charles down without bringing Millie down with him, figuring that without Charles the Roadrunners will fold and Millie will be forced to give the team up."

Sheila covered her mouth in shock. "Whom did you say you got this disk from, Millie's ex?"

"Yes."

"Is it that woman we used to see her with all the time last summer?" Sheila inquired.

"Oh, yeah," T.J. recalled. "I forgot about Millie's old sidekick." He laughed. "Her name was Rose Armstrong or Armstead or something. She's an assistant coach up at Central, I think. Oh man, a lot of people thought that woman was Millie's lover. But no, Terry's a guy: one of those Fabio or Rico Suave-type dudes. Sam told me he said he and Millie had been together four years."

Sheila's face lit up like she'd just heard some juicy gossip.

T.J. digressed and gave Sheila a serious gaze and spoke passionately. "Mama, you know how much I want to be the one to pull the plug on Millie's and Charles' operation, and that's what I want to talk to you about. I'm gonna need your help to do it so that I can keep my word to Terry Gonzalez, and so I won't get any kids in trouble."

Sheila shrugged. "Sure, baby. What can I do?"

KENNETH J. WHETSTONE

NEW YORK DAILY NEWS
Friday, September 9, 2005
HIGH SCHOOL SPORTS

Jefferson Girls' Hoop Coach Resigns
BY PEARL McBRIDE
DAILY NEWS SPORTS WRITER

THE ANNOUNCEMENT came yesterday on the first day of classes for New York City's high schools. Charles Greene, Thomas Jefferson High School's girls' basketball coach, decided to retire and move to Hawaii. Jefferson's athletic director, Mary McIntosh, told the media yesterday that Greene, 55, who taught at the Brooklyn high school for last six years of his thirty-one year tenure, accepted his retirement effective immediately in lieu of original plans to wait.

McIntosh said that Greene told her last June that he would retire from teaching in 2006, but wanted to continue coaching the girls' basketball team until 2008. But after visiting Honolulu this past summer, Greene changed his mind, saying that he wanted to move there for good and couldn't wait to do it. Greene, who won the last four public schools championships and the last three state championships, will formally announce his retirement and resignation as coach on a date to be determined when he returns from closing the deal on his new Hawaiian condominium.

THE FINAL CHAPTER

Friday, September 9, 2005 – 8:07 A.M.

Charles awoke to the sound of his doorbell ringing out of control. He dragged himself out of bed shouting, "Just a minute!" as he made his way to the door. He looked through the peephole and grunted, "Oh, shit," when he saw Mildred's face. When he finally unlocked and opened the door, Mildred stormed inside and slammed a newspaper into his chest.

"What the hell is this?!" she roared.

Charles stumbled back a couple of steps and fumbled to keep the paper from falling apart. "What are you talking about?"

Mildred snatched the newspaper back from him and pointed to the article she wanted him to see. "I'm talking about this right here. Is this true? Are you quitting as coach so you can retire and move to Hawaii?"

"It's in the newspaper?" Charles asked, surprised.

"It's right here, Charles." Mildred stabbed her finger at the article.

Charles quickly read as Mildred stood before him tapping her foot with her hands on her hips.

"Wow," Charles said, finally. "Well, that's it in a nutshell. You know they hired Christine Caputo as my replacement? She's the damn volleyball coach, for crying out loud. What does she know about basketball? Er…no offense."

"Fuck you!" Mildred retorted. "And fuck Christine Caputo, too. What do you have to say about this article?"

"What do you want me to say, Millie?"

"How could you do this without telling me?"

"I was going to tell you before I left. Hey, I did invite you to come live with me. That offer still stands."

"I don't want to go anywhere with you!" Mildred shouted. "I'm fine right where I am! I just want to know how you can just up and leave, knowing that we still have things to take care of! How am I supposed pay off the Roadrunners' debts and maintain the current status without the money we were getting from the connections at Jefferson?!"

Charles grinned. "There aren't anymore connections at Jefferson, at least not for me. All of my connections and resources have been exhausted."

"What?! How could that be? What happened?"

"T.J. Stonewall is what happened," Charles said.

"T.J.?" Mildred squinted her eyes, paced away and back with her hands on her hips. "What the hell does *he* have to do with this?"

"He came to me with some very interesting documents," Charles explained. "He had files of both the Roadrunners' and Jefferson's budgets, where we got our financial backing from, everyone we paid off, and he even had records of all the people we got to take the S.A.T. for some of the players. He threatened to get his wife on me, who, by the way, is an agent for the IRS. Did you know that? She was about to have me and everybody in every program on those files investigated. How do you like that?"

The anger on Mildred's face immediately turned into perplexity and worry. "Oh, no. How could he have gotten a hold of that stuff? I'm the only one who kept records."

"Oh, is that a fact?" Charles sarcastically asked.

"Wait, I know you don't think I gave him that information," Mildred asked, defensively.

Charles threw his head back with laughter. "Don't be ridiculous. I know you wouldn't have done such a thing. Ruining me means ruining yourself, and you're much too full of yourself to risk taking any type of a loss. No, I know you didn't give him that information, but I know who did and so do you."

"No, I don't, Charles. I have no idea."

"C'mon, Millie, you're an intelligent woman. Don't get stupid on me now."

"I swear. You and I are the only ones who've ever seen those files. I've never even shown them to…" That's when it hit her. "Terry? You think Terry did this?"

"Who else?"

"That's not possible. I deleted all of the files from his computer the day I left."

"You sure about that? Are you absolutely sure?"

"Yes!" Mildred insisted. "I copied each file, and then deleted…oh, wait…"

Charles nodded and rolled his eyes. "Uh-huh."

RISE OF THE PHOENIX

Mildred turned her anger on herself. "Aw, fuck, I was rushing! No! How could I be so stupid?"

"Hey, at least you still got your looks," Charles quipped.

"Fuck you, Charles! This is not the time for jokes. I can't believe Terry would do such a thing."

"A broken heart knows no reasoning," Charles told her, "and you did break Terry's heart. Just make sure you watch your back. T.J. is sure to come after you, too. I'm sure he hates you more than he does me."

"I'm not afraid of T.J., and I'm not going to run away with my tail between my legs. I'll deal with him, and I'm definitely going to deal with Terry's ass."

Charles waved his hands, shooing the situation away. "I just don't need the extra headaches, Millie, that's all. Whether or not what T.J. and Terry are doing has any weight to it or not, I don't need the bullshit in my life, right now. Not over some girls' high school basketball team, especially when I can retire on the hush-hush as a winner and with my name untarnished. I don't need a bunch of negative publicity when all I really care about is lying up on a beach, anyway. As for the sponsors, the alumni, the school, the kids, their parents, and everybody else, fuck 'em all!"

"What about me, Charles?" Mildred asked. "I thought you said you were doing it for me."

"I was, but you've got to know that I wasn't going to forever. You read the article. Three more seasons and I was out of here, regardless. I know I could've kept things going at Jefferson for at least that long, and by then I'd have you running things without me. I was willing to do that for you, but not at the expense of all of this. It just isn't worth it, Millie. Not for either of us. If you continue with the Roadrunners, you're always going to have people like T.J. breathing down your neck, and your team is never going to be able to live up its reputation of the last few years."

Thinking about what Charles said, Mildred tightened her lips and shook her head. "No," she said. "You're wrong. I have enough support and backing to stay alive and to stay on top. I'll reach out to those people and get things done. No two-bit jealous coach or strung-out ex is going to ruin what I have and bring me down. I'm going to be fine. You go ahead to Hawaii and lay up on the beach. I hope your little pale ass gets sunburn, skin cancer and die!"

With that, Mildred turned and marched out of Charles' apartment. Charles locked the door behind her, looked at the newspaper again and laughed out loud.

6:27 P.M.

There was a sinking feeling in Terry's stomach stemming from the fear of coming home and finding the door to his condo unlocked. He entered to see the place ransacked. He immediately snatched his cell phone from off his hip and dialed 9-1-1. While describing what he'd discovered to the dispatcher, he heard a noise coming from the bedroom. He placed the phone down on a nearby counter and pulled his .22 from the ankle holster. He could see the light coming from his bedroom and moved through the apartment cautiously, holding his gun out in front of him with both hands, ready to take aim and fire if need be. With his back against the wall, he moved slowly from the dining area to the short hall that led to the bedroom. There was a loud crashing sound, like his lamp was knocked over or thrown down.

"Who's in there?" he called out. The sound of footsteps marching across the room caused him to backpedal and lift his weapon up to firing position. "Wait! Be careful, I have a gun! Come out slow with your hands out in front of you!"

The footsteps stopped, and then there was no movement and no sound.

"The police are on their way! They'll be here soon!" Terry shouted. Perspiration caused strands of his wavy hair to fall over his face and cover his left eye. He dared not brush it away in fear of removing either hand from the gun.

"So, which is it, Terry? Are you going to shoot me or have me arrested?" asked the intruder from inside the bedroom.

Terry recognized the voice. "Millie? Is that you?"

When Mildred stepped out of the room into the hall area, Terry gasped at the sight of her. Her copper complexion was so flushed from her anger it appeared to camouflage her crimson Roadrunners tanktop. The muscles in her arms flexed as she stood clutching her fists covered in a pair of workout gloves. She wore black biker shorts, revealing her long, muscular legs, and a pair of running shoes. Her hair was pinned up and wrapped in a bandana. There was no doubt what her intentions were.

RISE OF THE PHOENIX

"How could you do it, Terry?" Mildred asked through clenched teeth as she peered at him. The whites of her eyes had turned a fiery red from her rage and all the crying she had done.

"Do what?" Terry asked innocently, even though he knew exactly what she was referring to.

"Don't play stupid! You know what the fuck you did!" Mildred screamed as anger engulfed her and she charged toward the man she once loved, swinging her arms, not caring that he was still pointing a gun right at her.

Mildred's sudden lunge wasn't something Terry expected and his reflexes caused him to squeeze the trigger as her right fist landed just above his left eye. It was by the grace of God that he forgot to take the safety off and the gun didn't fire. The gun fell from his hand as Mildred's onslaught of punches came down on his head one after the other.

A moment after taking countless hits to the face and head, Terry was able to shield himself with his arms enough to charge at Mildred, overpower her and prevent her from hitting him anymore. He grabbed her swinging arms and maneuvered past her kicks to make his way around her and put her in a bear hug from behind. They stood in that position several minutes while Terry tried to calm Mildred down. She was relentless in her struggles and fought to free herself until they both heard the police radios of two uniformed officers getting off the elevator.

"The police are here and the front door is open," Terry whispered into Mildred's ear. "You can either calm down, or go to jail. Which is it going to be?"

"Fine," Mildred grumbled. "I'm calm. Now unravel the flesh." Her struggles stopped and her breathing slowed, so Terry unwrapped his arms and quickly bent down, picked up the gun and shoved into the side pocket of his nearby briefcase.

It was a long while after the police arrived that Terry and Mildred were able to convince them that everything was all right and no charges would be pressed. When they finally left, Terry walked over to his favorite chair and plopped down. Mildred stood a moment staring at him, and then walked over and sat in the exact spot as Sam Pernell during his visit.

"Where are the files, Terry?" Mildred asked softly. "Just give them to me, and I'll leave."

"Oh, so that's what you tore up my apartment for," Terry said. "I don't have them anymore. I erased them from the computer and turned over the only copy I had."

KENNETH J. WHETSTONE

Mildred sighed hard. She looked over at the man she agreed to marry five months earlier and knew he was telling the truth. He always did. "If you weren't going to help me, you should've just left me alone. Why was that so hard for you to do?"

"Because I love you!" Terry exclaimed, throwing up his hands as if to ask why didn't she get it. "That's what people do when they're in love; they do whatever it takes for the person they're in love with."

Mildred twisted her lips and rolled her eyes. "We've always told each other throughout our four years together that we'd always have each other's back no matter what. You said you'd do whatever it takes to make me happy, and you reneged on that promise."

"Come on with that, Millie. You know good and well I wasn't talking about anything illegal or immoral. I would never ask you to cross those lines for me."

Mildred cast her eyes down in disappointment. "Well, I guess it doesn't matter now."

"It does matter," Terry said. "You don't have to do the things you're doing with the Roadrunners. Eventually, you're going to get caught and get into some serious trouble. I don't want to see you get into any kind of trouble. Charles Greene is the one who doesn't care about you, but you do whatever he wants whenever he wants. He's got you doing all the dirt. While everyone viewed him as Mr. High Profile High School Coach, you were just his lowly puppet dangling on a string doing his bidding. I couldn't sit around and watch him use you like that. Since you were too blind to see it for yourself, I had to bring things to light."

"I was so glad I found those files you left. It was just what I needed to use to separate you from that loser. You can be successful without Charles' help or negative influence. I'll help you! I'll be the positive influence on you so that you can be a positive influence in the kids. They don't need a coach that'll spoil them to death and not make them earn anything. They need someone to care for them enough to make them realize that they're not going to be spoon fed all their lives, and that hard work and discipline is what's going to help them get ahead."

Mildred slouched back on the coach and rolled her eyes some more. She shook her head saying, "So, now T.J. Stonewall is your friend? You sound just like his bitch ass. I can't believe you're an ally with my enemy."

"Never!" Terry shouted. His eyes widened as he leaned forward to make himself clear. "I would never, ever betray you like that. What I did was for your own good. I used him to help me get Charles out of your life, that's all. I made him swear to keep your name out of it, and he gave me his word. Up to now he's kept his word. Charles is leaving, and your name hasn't been mentioned once."

"And it better not ever be," Mildred said. "I'll have both your asses if it is. I swear to you, Terry, I'll make you pay!"

"Trust me, it won't," Terry assured her.

"Good," Mildred said as she stood up ready to leave.

Terry sprung up from his chair and started toward her. "Where are you going?"

"I'm leaving. I have shit to take care of. I'm going to show you and Charles that I'm nobody's puppet, and I don't need either of you to do jack shit for me. I can run my team and keep them on the highest level without you or him. And I'm going to show T.J. Stonewall's sorry, wannabe ass that his little reign is just a temporary thing. I already got something lined up, and you're all gonna look like fools!"

"Are you going to do those things legally?" Terry asked.

"Stay out of my affairs!" Mildred barked. "Stop caring so much about what I do! Our relationship is over! ¡Nunca me estoy volviendo a usted! Accept that and move on!"

"Fine," Terry said, taking her by the arms. She stared coldly into his eyes, but she didn't resist. "So you don't love me anymore, and I'm going to have to come to terms with that. Eventually I will, I'm sure. I just want to know who you're going to turn to now? Is Rose Armstead going to help you the way you helped her?"

Mildred broke free of Terry's hold and stood back. "You've been all up and through my business, haven't you?"

"So you did knowingly aid and abet a pedophile. How could you, Millie?"

For the first time, Mildred looked remorseful about something. "Look, I just wanted that chick away from *me*. She's the daughter of one of Charles' friends from college. She's from a rich and successful family with a lot of connections, which is why we needed her around. But when we found about the things she'd been accused of, we both knew it would be bad for business if we kept her around. I told her she had to leave and why, but she denied the accusations and promised to buy us a bus and finance our trip to Orlando for the team's vacation last year if I'd let her stay around and prove herself. After we won the Pro Bound National Championship last year, she took us all to Disney World."

Terry's heart started to race as he was hardly able to believe what he was hearing. "But didn't some of your players complain to you that this woman had made advances toward them? Didn't you catch her in the act with one of your players?" he asked dolefully.

"It was one of my player's brother," Mildred muttered with tears running down her cheeks. "I'm not proud of what I did, or what I let her get away with. I just needed her to get the hell away from me, so I did what I had to."

"You should've gone to the authorities and told them what you saw. That would've gotten her away from you. You could've helped put a pedophile behind bars, but instead, your selfish ass did what benefited you."

Mildred's sorrowful face hardened as she became angered. "You got some kind of nerve, Terry. You did the exact same thing I did."

Terry brows wrinkled in bewilderment. "What are you talking about, Millie?"

Mildred walked up on Terry with her face barely an inch away from his. Her watery, red eyes were two inches higher as she cast them down to meet with his looking up. "Why didn't you just take the files you found and give *them* to the authorities?" she asked, and then went on without waiting for an answer. "It was your selfishness, that's why. You did compromise your morals and integrity, the very things you proclaim to be so sacred to you, because you thought that you could get me to come back to you. You went out of your way, using people in the process, to have a chance at getting what you wanted. You talk about my aiding and abetting someone to get away with something just for my personal gain, but you did the exact same thing. How do you feel about that, Terry?"

Terry stepped back and nearly stumbled over as Mildreds words hit him like a wrecking ball. Beads of sweat gathered on his forehead and his mouth got dry. He opened his mouth to speak but Mildred cut him off.

"Don't say shit, Terry," Mildred ordered. "There's nothing for you to say anyway because we're just alike." She watched as Terry fell back into his chair and looked up at her pleadingly. She walked up and stood over him pointing her finger. "For the last time, I'm telling you to stay out of my business and out of my life. I don't want to ever see you again, because if I do, I promise you you'll regret it for the rest of your life."

RISE OF THE PHOENIX

NYC GIRLS BASKETBALL WEBSITE
MESSAGE BOARD
From: Coyote
Date: Wednesday, September 21, 2005
Time: 12:18 P.M.
Message: New Coach; No Team
Just as I suspected (and I think most people knew this), now that Charles Greene is no longer coaching at Jefferson, the Roadrunners have practically folded. Coach Greene is enjoying his retirement in Hawaii and all three of Jefferson's all-star freshmen transferred to other schools (2 to Paul Robeson and the other to Boys & Girls) and the Roadrunners have lost some of their best players as well. It's the third week of the Slam Jam fall tournament, and the Roadrunners are 2–3, losing by 14 to the Imperial Crew, 17 to the Lady Phoenix and 8 to the Lady Panthers, who all have former Roadrunners playing for them. How's that for karma? I do hope that the new coach at Jefferson does a good job and keep them winning because I'd hate to see the talented players that are still there suffer with the same lack of guidance and knowledge of the game they've been dealing with. I've never been a Jeff supporter before, but it was because of the coach not the players.

From: Mighty Isis
Date: Wednesday, September 21, 2005
Time: 12:46 P.M.
Message: RE: New Coach; No Team
Being that I have a niece who plays for Jefferson and used to play for the Roadrunners, I can relate to what Coyote is saying. I thought that because Jefferson and the Roadrunners where always winning, the coaches must've been doing a good job. I realize that isn't true now because my niece has learned so much in the short time she's been with her new program. We heard a lot of good things about Jefferson's new coach, so we're both much happier now.

From: Roadrunners Fan
Date: Wednesday, September 21, 2005
Time: 1:11 P.M.
Message: We'll Be Back!!!
The Roadrunners have suffered some minor setbacks, but they'll be back to running this city and to being one of the best teams in the country in no time. There are too many supporters that'll back them financially and any other way for them to suffer for too long. As soon

as things get back on track all the best players will come running back, and the Roadrunners will rule again!

From: CrossOver
Date: Wednesday, September 21, 2005
Time: 2:30 P.M.
Message: RE: We'll Be Back!!!

I guess Roadrunners Fan didn't hear that after the Roadrunners lost to the Lady Panthers last Sunday, Coach Negron withdrew the team from the tournament. She told the director of the tournament that it was because of a family obligation she was committed to, but we know the real reason—she can't deal with losing. They beat the Ravens by five on Saturday and then lost on Sunday, but they only had six girls both days. Only Connie, Angela and the twins showed up both days, and they had Brittany and Illyana on Saturday and Jennifer and a girl I've never seen before (who wasn't that good) on Sunday. The Roadrunners were scheduled to play the Long Island Tide next Sunday, and Coach Negron knew Stacey Conyers was going to give them the business. I think this is the beginning of the end for the Roadrunners, and I'm so happy.

From: Coyote
Date: Wednesday, September 21, 2005
Time: 2:39 P.M.
Message: RE: We'll Be Back!!!

That's something else, CrossOver. I guess Roadrunners Fan will have to find another bandwagon to jump on, and you and I will have to change our screen names. I think my new moniker will be "Tiger Tamer" so I can bring the heat down on another cheater. Hey, has anyone heard from jay boogie? LOL

From: jay boogie
Date: Wednesday, September 21, 2005
Time: 3:08 P.M.
Message: RE: We'll Be Back!!!

here I am and i'm sitting back laughing at coyote and crossover and all the other roadrunners hatas cause your going to cry later when coach negron gets back on top. i know she already got the scope on something that's gonna make you all shut your mouth.

EPILOGUE

Saturday, December 24, 2005 – 7:17 P.M.

T.J. was about to get ready for his Christmas Eve party when he got a call from his mentor, David Martin. The Jewish Stuyvesant High School coach didn't celebrate Christmas, so he decided to wash some clothes, knowing that he'd probably have the laundry room all to himself. He did want to touch bases with his favorite protégé while he was home—being that T.J. seemed to be so busy as of late.

"So, what's the story?" David asked, holding his cellular phone to his ear while taking is laundry down to the basement.

"I heard Millie Negron got another money connection to support the Roadrunners," T.J. sadly replied from the other end of the line as he lay back on his bed with his feet hanging off the side.

"Yeah? Who?" David asked.

"Well, the grapevine says that she's hooking up with a high school coach in New Jersey, Newark I think, who has connections with Nike and a few other corporate sponsors. I guess that means she'll be doing her dirty work in New Jersey now since Charles is gone."

"People like her just don't give up because you set them back for the moment, not anyone with a team with players like the Roadrunners have had. What you did only got Charles to leave and abandon Thomas Jefferson's program with all the money he stole. You may have made him look like a jerk, but you made people feel sorry for Millie."

"No, David, I doubt that."

"Are you kidding? Half the people on the website are crying for her and offering support."

T.J. raised his brow. "The website? Please, you know I don't read the garbage on that message board. Those people don't even count as far as I'm concerned."

"Well, half of them should, because they agree with *you*. The problem is that the half that's on Millie's side are vocal Roadrunners supporters. The half that on your side aren't Lady Phoenix supporters, they're just anti-Millie."

"What are they saying about Future leaving the Roadrunners to join the Lady Phoenix?" T.J. asked.

"No one has said anything, which surprised me a lot," David said. "But I'm guessing that probably made them all feel sorry for Millie, too."

"I can't believe people are so stupid."

David laughed at T.J.'s remark. "Them? What about you?"

"What do you mean by that?"

"You know, you and Terry Gonzalez were both fools for thinking Millie would just go away. By doing what Terry wanted and not exposing everything that Millie was doing, all people see is her getting the short end of the stick, somehow. Again, they're going to feel sorry for her, especially when they think she's God's gift to girls' basketball."

T.J. huffed as he moved the telephone receiver from his right ear to the left. "I would've had to reveal everything about everybody involved, and I didn't want naïve players and parents to have to pay the price."

"Well, it's true that you can't really blame the kids because coaches like Millie and Charles will offer them the world and any kid will take it. But if the parents aren't smart enough to see that they're being suckered, it's their own fault and they deserve whatever comes back on them, especially the ones accepting payoffs."

"That's not going to do anything for the kids, though," T.J. said. "It's still going to be them who'll end up suffering. Now, when the kids get to college and they do something like accept payoffs or merchandise, they're old enough know better and accept the consequence for their actions."

David laughed. "You're joking, right? How much difference is there between a high school senior and a college freshman? About ten months, that's all."

"Well, I'm not going to worry about it because Charles is gone and Millie is somewhere else."

"So sending the problem someplace else is good enough for you?" David stopped shoveling clothing into the washer and leaned against the machine. "What's the difference between that and running drug dealers off your block just so they can go set up shop around the corner? The problem is still there. It's just not directly in your face. So the way I see it, Millie taking the Roadrunners over to Jersey just opens doors here for teams like the Lady Tigers. What's stopping someone who uses illegal players from going further and doing everything that

RISE OF THE PHOENIX

Millie did now that she's out of the picture in New York? You drive one drug dealer off your block just to have a bigger, badder dealer come in and set up shop. This is the same thing. You end up jumping out of the frying pan and into the fire."

T.J. moaned in disappointment. "I thought you wanted Millie and Charles out of the picture. I got them out, and you act like I've done something wrong."

"No, it's just that you didn't get rid of them or the problem. All you did was sweep the dirt under rug, which means the floor is still dirty, so the problem is still here. Don't you see that nobody's going to get it? In their eyes, you're just someone who's jealous you can't offer the players and their parents all the material things that Millie and Charles were giving them. People want glamour and instant gratification. They don't want to hear that you're taking your time to help teach *their* kids about what it takes to be dedicated, loyal, and responsible functioning adults with integrity and good moral values, nor do they care. They see the Roadrunners' bus, their fancy gear, sneakers, trips and trophies and it gives them something to get on that stupid website and brag about. You're a religious guy. Why don't some people believe in God?"

"Because they say they can't see and feel Him," T.J. replied.

"That's right. Why should they believe people like you and me who're offering a better life at a later time when they can enjoy the glamour and instant gratification right now? It's just a temporary fix, but they don't understand that, and some don't care."

"I hear what you're saying, David. I'm still going to do what I do, though."

David resumed putting his clothes into the washing machine. "I just want to warn you that it's going to get harder and harder. There are lots of people like Millie and Charles who are lurking in the shadows, waiting for people like you and me to spend all of our time developing kids just so they can come around and offer them things they know will draw them away. Take Melinda Thompson for instance. Look at how fast she's developing."

"I know," T.J. said. "She was sitting in the stands at Baruch High School's Thanksgiving tournament wearing a Lady Phoenix sweatshirt, and someone from the Ravens asked her to play for them."

"You think that's bad? We played St. Joseph's a few weeks ago—at *our* school—and one of their assistant coaches was talking to my center about transferring. Now, the coach of the Lady Tigers is trying to recruit the point guard from Philippa Schuyler Junior High School, who has already been accepted into Stuyvesant, to go to South Shore...and her mother is considering it! Now you tell me, why would any parent whose child gets into a school like Stuyvesant even think twice about letting them go to any other public school?"

"I really don't know," T.J. muttered.

"C'mon, T.J., isn't it obvious? The coach at South Shore is using the Lady Tigers as their farm team, following in Charles' footsteps at Jefferson. In fact, the Lady Panthers and the Ravens are also recruiting players for high school teams. The Lady Tigers' coach is South Shore's assistant now. So, guess what? Millie Negron and Charles Greene are still here in spirit."

"Damn!" T.J. shouted.

"Getting mad ain't helping either," David told him. "If you don't tell people what you know about what Charles Greene and Mildred Negron have done, you're just as guilty for what's happened and what's going to happen as they are."

"What about what I promised Terry Gonzalez?"

"What about what you promised your players and their parents?" David returned. "What about what you promised yourself? One of those promises is going to get broken. Which would you rather it is?"

T.J. didn't respond. David put the last of his clothing into the machine and started it. "Hello?" he said, loudly.

"I'm here."

"Look, it's something for you to think about..."

"No, you're right," T.J. told his mentor. "I wasn't looking at the big picture."

"Damn right, you weren't."

"I gotta go, David. Thanks."

"What are you gonna do, T.J.?"

"Right now, I'm going to take a shower and join my Christmas party. On Monday, I'll get up after having a good Christmas, and I'm going to do the right thing."

"Okay, T.J., make sure that you do."

"Merry Christmas, David." T.J. hung up the phone.

RISE OF THE PHOENIX

7:25 P.M.

Beverly came into the living room carrying a picture frame and knelt in front of the Christmas tree. She looked at the picture of her father and started talking to him.

"I miss you so much, Daddy. You would've been so proud of me. You really would be proud of Miss Thompson, too. She let Melinda join the basketball team at her school, and she's going to come back to the Lady Phoenix. You should see Melinda now, Daddy. She's gotten so much better. She even made the winning free throw in one of her games. She's been working real hard on her game. She's the second person off the bench at school. Oh, and I got the public school's player of the week again. That's three straight weeks."

Sheila came out of her bedroom and quietly walked up behind Beverly.

"Coach and Sheila have been so good to me," Beverly continued. "It feels like a real home here, and I feel like this is my real family. I wanted to ask you something. They want to make this family official and adopt me. Is that okay with you? If it is, you need to show me a sign. I hope you show me a good sign, because I would really like for this to happen."

Sheila put her hands over her mouth to keep from crying out loud with joy.

"I hope Mommy understands," Beverly went on. "Is she there with you? I'm sure she is. It's good the two of you are back together again."

Sheila walked over and placed her hand on Beverly's shoulder. "Hey, baby, are you okay?"

Beverly stood up and smiled. "Yes, I'm fine. I was just talking to my daddy."

"Yes, I heard. I love you, Beverly. I'm so glad you're here."

Beverly threw her arms around Sheila. "I love you, too."

At that moment, the doorbell rang and Sheila opened the door for Carlene and Melinda followed by Melva, Trina, Danisha, Tracy, Monica, Tanya, Kimberly and Rayna. They were all shouting "Merry Christmas!" and carrying gifts.

"Where's Coach Stone?" Trina asked.

"He's in the bedroom talking to Beverly's high school coach on the phone," Sheila told her. "He'll be out in a minute."

Trina, Kimberly and Rayna sat on the couch, and Melva walked straight to the buffet table.

Trina nudged Rayna. "Look at her, going straight for the food."

"What? I just wanna see," Melva said, innocently.

"Don't worry, Melva," Sheila said. "We're going to eat as soon as Juanita and her fiancé get here."

"Excuse me, everyone," Beverly said. "I'll be back. I just wanna put this away."

"What's that, Bev?" Trina asked.

Beverly held up the frame for her to see. "It's a picture of my father."

"Why are you putting it away? Why don't you leave it on the table so he can enjoy the party, too?" Kimberly suggested.

"That's a good idea, Kim," Melinda agreed, and then walked over and took the picture from Beverly and placed it on the table. "Here, where he can be a part of the party and everyone can see him."

The doorbell rang again.

"Oh, that must be Juanita," Sheila said, and got up to go answer it.

Melinda sat on the couch next to Kimberly and Tracy. "You know our first game after the holiday is against your school, Kim?"

"Yeah, I know," Kimberly said. "I know it's gonna be a tough game, but we'll be ready."

Melinda hesitated at first, and then asked, "Kim, have you heard from Velvet?"

Kimberly responded with a quick and dry, "No."

"Velvet's chillin', y'all," Trina told them.

"Yeah," Melva chimed in, "she came to our game against Boys and Girls High last week. Ain't nothin' changed. She's still a diva."

"She's going through some stuff, y'all," Trina said. "But she's strong, and she's hanging in there."

"So, what's up with Tabitha?" Melinda asked Tracy.

"Yeah, how's Miss Attitude doing?" Melva asked. "She's still throwing her jerseys at people?"

"She doesn't talk to me anymore," Tracy said. "I used to try to be friendly with her, but she acts like *I* did something to her. She just walks around school mad at everybody all the time."

"Is she even playing ball?" Trina wanted to know. "I never see her name in the newspaper or anything."

"Yeah, she's on the team," Tracy said. "She hasn't been playing up to her potential, though. She only scores four or five points a game, and

RISE OF THE PHOENIX

she doesn't always hustle. She does crazy stuff, too, like coming to a game with her hair full of beads. Then she cursed at the ref when she was told she couldn't play unless she took them out."

"Tabitha knows that already," Trina said.

"She's trippin'," Tracy said. "The coach is threatening to cut her from the team."

Trina shook her head in pity. "That's too bad. She does have potential…"

"Yeah, right!" Melva interjected. "She's a scrub! I told her that weak little jump shot wasn't gonna get her over."

"She does have potential, Mel," Beverly said. "Her jump shot is dangerous when she's on."

"Yeah, but her attitude is more dangerous than anything," Rayna commented. "And she's only hurting herself."

Sheila came back into the apartment followed by Juanita and her fiancé, both carrying decorative shopping bags, smiling cheerfully and shouting, "Merry Christmas, Lady Phoenix!"

T.J. came into the living room. It was noticeable, however, by the blank look on his face, that he wasn't as festive as everyone else.

"Hey, sweetheart, is everything all right?" Sheila asked, going to her husband's side and taking his hands.

T.J. let go of a half smile and a shrug before kissing Sheila's cheek and greeted everyone.

"Hey, everybody, I'm sorry if I seem a little out of it. I'm really fine, and I'm glad you're all here. I thank you all for coming. This is really very nice. Wow, this is great because it feels so warm and so much like a family in here. This has got to be the closest team I've ever coached."

"You know how we do, Coach Stone," Melva said. "It's all one love. We're tight like that."

Fellow Lady Phoenix members all agreed.

"We *are* tight, Melva," T.J. said. "And we have to stay that way. We are who we are because of our closeness. A lot of people don't expect much of us or give us the respect we deserve. But we don't need them to give us respect because we work hard for it, and we'll earn it, just as the Lady Phoenix has always done. That's why the Lady Phoenix has the highest grade point average of any of the AAU or club teams in this state. All of our members get into college, and we have more business executives, entrepreneurs, teachers and coaches than anyone else over the past five years.

KENNETH J. WHETSTONE

"But the most important thing is that I feel confident that we will never again fall prey to the materialistic, spurious charlatans lurking around like sharks in the water. We learned a lot from our experiences last summer. There are a lot of negative influences out there. There are people who just want to use you. They're not interested in you until after someone else spends all of their time helping you develop. Don't let those people use you, girls. You don't need to travel with a specific team or go to a well-known school to get a scholarship. Being a good student and a good athlete will get you what you deserve no matter where you play. The recruiters will find you if you play for a team on the moon, just as long as you have what it takes. The Bible says, 'Train a child in the way he should go, and when he is old he will not turn from it.' I'm doing my best to show you all the right way to go; to let you know that no matter what happens we're all in this together. The good thing about being in the Lady Phoenix program is that we know we have each other to lean on. We will reach our goals and excel…as students, as athletes and in life."

RISE OF THE PHOENIX

NYC GIRLS BASKETBALL WEBSITE
FRONTPAGE

The following is a list of high school seniors from the New York City area and their basketball commitments for college. Listed are the student-athlete, height, position, hometown, high school and AAU or club team, with the college commitment listed below in **bold**:

Shaniyah Banks, 6–0, F, Staten Island, NY, Curtis HS, S.I. Angels
Bethune-Cookman College

Lissette Cruz, 6–2, F, New York, NY, Murry Bergtraum HS, Roadrunners
Queens College

Jennifer Davis, 5–9, G, Brooklyn, NY, Thomas Jefferson HS, Roadrunners
Kingsborough Community College

Melva Fields, 5–8, PG, Brooklyn, NY, Paul Robeson HS, Lady Phoenix
Kingsborough Community College

Renee Imes, 6–0, F, Jamaica, NY, Christ the King HS, Lady Panthers
St. John's University

Ramona Beau, 5–11, F, Hempstead, NY, Hempstead HS, L.I. Tide
Hofstra University

Connie King, 6–4, C, Rosedale, NY, Thomas Jefferson HS, Roadrunners
Baylor University

Tara Serrano, 5–9, G/F, So. Ozone Park, NY, St. Francis Prep, Lady Tigers
University of Bridgeport

Juliet Phillips, 5–5, G, Brooklyn, NY, ENY Family Academy, Imperial Crew
University of Massachusetts-Lowell

Illyana Santana, 6–1, F, Riverdale, NY, St. Michael's Academy, Roadrunners
Central College

KENNETH J. WHETSTONE

LaTrina Smith, 6–4, C, Brooklyn, NY, Paul Robeson HS, Lady Phoenix
Columbia University
Sylvia Swanson, 5–10, G, Bronx, NY, St. Joseph's HS, Imperial Crew
Rutgers University
Jillian Thorne, 5–9, PG, Staten Island, NY, McKee Tech, S.I. Angels
Hofstra University
Kelly Wharton, 5–4, G, Bronx, NY, Stuyvesant HS, Ravens
Emmanuel College
Malaika Williams, 5–9, G/F, New York, NY, Lab Museum United, Ravens
New York University

ABOUT THE AUTHOR

Kenneth Jerome Whetstone was born and raised in the Brownsville and East New York sections of Brooklyn, NY, moving back and forth between the communities to spend time living with his mother and grandmother. Mr. Whetstone, the proud father of four daughters and one son, is still a Brooklyn resident, where he attends the Christian Cultural Center. A former high school and college women's basketball coach, he is now a certified men's and women's basketball official and works as a Human Service Professional for YAI:NIPD, as well as a sports instructor for the Children's Aid Society. He founded the Imperial Crew girls basketball program in 1986, which he evolved into the New Attitude Basketball Program in 1989, and then took a step further in 1992 to form the New Attitude Sports Association Phoenix and Lady Phoenix programs.

Mr. Whetstone grew up an aspiring artist. He loved to draw and won scholarships to programs at the Brooklyn Museum, Pratt Institute and Parson's School of Design. He also dabbled in the music industry in the late eighties and early nineties as a rapper, songwriter and producer. Additionally, he was a slow jams mixed tape DJ with the moniker "The Mighty Romancer."

Mr. Whetstone is now working on two more novels, including *Daddy Says*, the family drama which is the story of the Scott/Fuller family as told by the *Rise of the Phoenix* character, Velvet Fuller. He will also be working on *She's the One*, a romantic story based on his erotic short story, "Lady Baller" from the *Stories to Excite You* anthology.

You can reach Mr. Whetstone at **kennethwhetstone@yahoo.com** for information on his online groups and book clubs.

RISE OF THE PHOENIX
2006 Publication Schedule

January

A Lover's Legacy
Veronica Parker
1-58571-167-5
$9.95

Love Lasts Forever
Dominiqua Douglas
1-58571-187-X
$9.95

Under the Cherry
  Moon
Christal Jordan-Mims
1-58571-169-1
$12.95

February

Second Chances at Love
Cheris Hodges
1-58571-188-8
$9.95

Enchanted Desire
Wanda Y. Thomas
1-58571-176-4
$9.95

Caught Up
Deatri King Bey
1-58571-178-0
$12.95

March

I'm Gonna Make You
  Love Me
Gwyneth Bolton
1-58571-181-0
$9.95

Through the Fire
Seressia Glass
1-58571-173-X
$9.95

Notes When Summer
  Ends
Beverly Lauderdale
1-58571-180-2
$12.95

April

Sin and Surrender
J.M. Jeffries
1-58571-189-6
$9.95

Unearthing Passions
Elaine Sims
1-58571-184-5
$9.95

Between Tears
Pamela Ridley
1-58571-179-9
$12.95

May

Misty Blue
Dyanne Davis
1-58571-186-1
$9.95

Ironic
Pamela Leigh Starr
1-58571-168-3
$9.95

Cricket's Serenade
Carolita Blythe
1-58571-183-7
$12.95

June

Cupid
Barbara Keaton
1-58571-174-8
$9.95

Havana Sunrise
Kymberly Hunt
1-58571-182-9
$9.95

2006 Publication Schedule (continued)

Love Me Carefully
A.C. Arthur
1-58571-177-2
$9.95

July
No Ordinary Love
Angela Weaver
1-58571-198-5
$9.95

Rehoboth Road
Anita Ballard-Jones
1-58571-196-9
$12.95

Scent of Rain
Annetta P. Lee
158571-199-3
$9.95

August
Love in High Gear
Charlotte Roy
158571-185-3
$9.95

Rise of the Phoenix
Kenneth Whetstone
1-58571-197-7
$12.95

The Business of Love
Cheris Hodges
1-58571-193-4
$9.95

September
Rock Star
Rosyln Hardy Holcomb
1-58571-200-0
$9.95

A Dead Man Speaks
Lisa Jones Johnson
1-58571-203-5
$12.95

Rivers of the Soul-Part 1
Leslie Esdaile
1-58571-223-X
$9.95

October
A Dangerous Woman
J.M. Jeffries
1-58571-195-0
$9.95

Sinful Intentions
Crystal Rhodes
1-58571-201-9
$12.95

Only You
Crystal Hubbard
1-58571-208-6
$9.95

November
Ebony Eyes
Kei Swanson
1-58571-194-2
$9.95

Still Waters Run Deep –
Part 2
Leslie Esdaile
1-58571-224-8
$9.95

Let's Get It On
Dyanne Davis
1-58571-210-8
$9.95

December
Nights Over Egypt
Barbara Keaton
1-58571-192-6
$9.95

A Pefect Place to Pray
I.L. Goodwin
1-58571-202-7
$12.95

RISE OF THE PHOENIX

Other Genesis Press, Inc. Titles

A Dangerous Deception	J.M. Jeffries	$8.95
A Dangerous Love	J.M. Jeffries	$8.95
A Dangerous Obsession	J.M. Jeffries	$8.95
A Drummer's Beat to Mend	Kei Swanson	$9.95
A Happy Life	Charlotte Harris	$9.95
A Heart's Awakening	Veronica Parker	$9.95
A Lark on the Wing	Phyliss Hamilton	$9.95
A Love of Her Own	Cheris F. Hodges	$9.95
A Love to Cherish	Beverly Clark	$8.95
A Risk of Rain	Dar Tomlinson	$8.95
A Twist of Fate	Beverly Clark	$8.95
A Will to Love	Angie Daniels	$9.95
Acquisitions	Kimberley White	$8.95
Across	Carol Payne	$12.95
After the Vows (Summer Anthology)	Leslie Esdaile T.T. Henderson Jacqueline Thomas	$10.95
Again My Love	Kayla Perrin	$10.95
Against the Wind	Gwynne Forster	$8.95
All I Ask	Barbara Keaton	$8.95
Ambrosia	T.T. Henderson	$8.95
An Unfinished Love Affair	Barbara Keaton	$8.95
And Then Came You	Dorothy Elizabeth Love	$8.95
Angel's Paradise	Janice Angelique	$9.95
At Last	Lisa G. Riley	$8.95
Best of Friends	Natalie Dunbar	$8.95
Beyond the Rapture	Beverly Clark	$9.95
Blaze	Barbara Keaton	$9.95
Blood Lust	J. M. Jeffries	$9.95
Bodyguard	Andrea Jackson	$9.95
Boss of Me	Diana Nyad	$8.95
Bound by Love	Beverly Clark	$8.95
Breeze	Robin Hampton Allen	$10.95

Other Genesis Press, Inc. Titles (continued)

Broken	Dar Tomlinson	$24.95
By Design	Barbara Keaton	$8.95
Cajun Heat	Charlene Berry	$8.95
Careless Whispers	Rochelle Alers	$8.95
Cats & Other Tales	Marilyn Wagner	$8.95
Caught in a Trap	Andre Michelle	$8.95
Caught Up In the Rapture	Lisa G. Riley	$9.95
Cautious Heart	Cheris F Hodges	$8.95
Chances	Pamela Leigh Starr	$8.95
Cherish the Flame	Beverly Clark	$8.95
Class Reunion	Irma Jenkins/John Brown	$12.95
Code Name: Diva	J.M. Jeffries	$9.95
Conquering Dr. Wexler's Heart	Kimberley White	$9.95
Crossing Paths, Tempting Memories	Dorothy Elizabeth Love	$9.95
Cypress Whisperings	Phyllis Hamilton	$8.95
Dark Embrace	Crystal Wilson Harris	$8.95
Dark Storm Rising	Chinelu Moore	$10.95
Daughter of the Wind	Joan Xian	$8.95
Deadly Sacrifice	Jack Kean	$22.95
Designer Passion	Dar Tomlinson	$8.95
Dreamtective	Liz Swados	$5.95
Ebony Butterfly II	Delilah Dawson	$14.95
Echoes of Yesterday	Beverly Clark	$9.95
Eden's Garden	Elizabeth Rose	$8.95
Everlastin' Love	Gay G. Gunn	$8.95
Everlasting Moments	Dorothy Elizabeth Love	$8.95
Everything and More	Sinclair Lebeau	$8.95
Everything but Love	Natalie Dunbar	$8.95
Eve's Prescription	Edwina Martin Arnold	$8.95
Falling	Natalie Dunbar	$9.95
Fate	Pamela Leigh Starr	$8.95
Finding Isabella	A.J. Garrotto	$8.95

RISE OF THE PHOENIX

Other Genesis Press, Inc. Titles (continued)

Forbidden Quest	Dar Tomlinson	$10.95
Forever Love	Wanda Thomas	$8.95
From the Ashes	Kathleen Suzanne Jeanne Sumerix	$8.95
Gentle Yearning	Rochelle Alers	$10.95
Glory of Love	Sinclair LeBeau	$10.95
Go Gentle into that Good Night	Malcom Boyd	$12.95
Goldengroove	Mary Beth Craft	$16.95
Groove, Bang, and Jive	Steve Cannon	$8.99
Hand in Glove	Andrea Jackson	$9.95
Hard to Love	Kimberley White	$9.95
Hart & Soul	Angie Daniels	$8.95
Heartbeat	Stephanie Bedwell-Grime	$8.95
Hearts Remember	M. Loui Quezada	$8.95
Hidden Memories	Robin Allen	$10.95
Higher Ground	Leah Latimer	$19.95
Hitler, the War, and the Pope	Ronald Rychiak	$26.95
How to Write a Romance	Kathryn Falk	$18.95
I Married a Reclining Chair	Lisa M. Fuhs	$8.95
Indigo After Dark Vol. I	Nia Dixon/Angelique	$10.95
Indigo After Dark Vol. II	Dolores Bundy/Cole Riley	$10.95
Indigo After Dark Vol. III	Montana Blue/Coco Morena	$10.95
Indigo After Dark Vol. IV	Cassandra Colt/ Diana Richeaux	$14.95
Indigo After Dark Vol. V	Delilah Dawson	$14.95
Icie	Pamela Leigh Starr	$8.95
I'll Be Your Shelter	Giselle Carmichael	$8.95
I'll Paint a Sun	A.J. Garrotto	$9.95
Illusions	Pamela Leigh Starr	$8.95
Indiscretions	Donna Hill	$8.95
Intentional Mistakes	Michele Sudler	$9.95
Interlude	Donna Hill	$8.95
Intimate Intentions	Angie Daniels	$8.95

Other Genesis Press, Inc. Titles (continued)

Jolie's Surrender	Edwina Martin-Arnold	$8.95
Kiss or Keep	Debra Phillips	$8.95
Lace	Giselle Carmichael	$9.95
Last Train to Memphis	Elsa Cook	$12.95
Lasting Valor	Ken Olsen	$24.95
Let Us Prey	Hunter Lundy	$25.95
Life Is Never As It Seems	J.J. Michael	$12.95
Lighter Shade of Brown	Vicki Andrews	$8.95
Love Always	Mildred E. Riley	$10.95
Love Doesn't Come Easy	Charlyne Dickerson	$8.95
Love Unveiled	Gloria Greene	$10.95
Love's Deception	Charlene Berry	$10.95
Love's Destiny	M. Loui Quezada	$8.95
Mae's Promise	Melody Walcott	$8.95
Magnolia Sunset	Giselle Carmichael	$8.95
Matters of Life and Death	Lesego Malepe, Ph.D.	$15.95
Meant to Be	Jeanne Sumerix	$8.95
Midnight Clear (Anthology)	Leslie Esdaile	$10.95
	Gwynne Forster	
	Carmen Green	
	Monica Jackson	
Midnight Magic	Gwynne Forster	$8.95
Midnight Peril	Vicki Andrews	$10.95
Misconceptions	Pamela Leigh Starr	$9.95
Montgomery's Children	Richard Perry	$14.95
My Buffalo Soldier	Barbara B. K. Reeves	$8.95
Naked Soul	Gwynne Forster	$8.95
Next to Last Chance	Louisa Dixon	$24.95
No Apologies	Seressia Glass	$8.95
No Commitment Required	Seressia Glass	$8.95
No Regrets	Mildred E. Riley	$8.95
Nowhere to Run	Gay G. Gunn	$10.95
O Bed! O Breakfast!	Rob Kuehnle	$14.95

RISE OF THE PHOENIX

Other Genesis Press, Inc. Titles (continued)

Object of His Desire	A. C. Arthur	$8.95
Office Policy	A. C. Arthur	$9.95
Once in a Blue Moon	Dorianne Cole	$9.95
One Day at a Time	Bella McFarland	$8.95
Outside Chance	Louisa Dixon	$24.95
Passion	T.T. Henderson	$10.95
Passion's Blood	Cherif Fortin	$22.95
Passion's Journey	Wanda Thomas	$8.95
Past Promises	Jahmel West	$8.95
Path of Fire	T.T. Henderson	$8.95
Path of Thorns	Annetta P. Lee	$9.95
Peace Be Still	Colette Haywood	$12.95
Picture Perfect	Reon Carter	$8.95
Playing for Keeps	Stephanie Salinas	$8.95
Pride & Joi	Gay G. Gunn	$15.95
Pride & Joi	Gay G. Gunn	$8.95
Promises to Keep	Alicia Wiggins	$8.95
Quiet Storm	Donna Hill	$10.95
Reckless Surrender	Rochelle Alers	$6.95
Red Polka Dot in a World of Plaid	Varian Johnson	$12.95
Reluctant Captive	Joyce Jackson	$8.95
Rendezvous with Fate	Jeanne Sumerix	$8.95
Revelations	Cheris F. Hodges	$8.95
Rivers of the Soul	Leslie Esdaile	$8.95
Rocky Mountain Romance	Kathleen Suzanne	$8.95
Rooms of the Heart	Donna Hill	$8.95
Rough on Rats and Tough on Cats	Chris Parker	$12.95
Secret Library Vol. 1	Nina Sheridan	$18.95
Secret Library Vol. 2	Cassandra Colt	$8.95
Shades of Brown	Denise Becker	$8.95
Shades of Desire	Monica White	$8.95

Other Genesis Press, Inc. Titles (continued)

Shadows in the Moonlight	Jeanne Sumerix	$8.95
Sin	Crystal Rhodes	$8.95
So Amazing	Sinclair LeBeau	$8.95
Somebody's Someone	Sinclair LeBeau	$8.95
Someone to Love	Alicia Wiggins	$8.95
Song in the Park	Martin Brant	$15.95
Soul Eyes	Wayne L. Wilson	$12.95
Soul to Soul	Donna Hill	$8.95
Southern Comfort	J.M. Jeffries	$8.95
Still the Storm	Sharon Robinson	$8.95
Still Waters Run Deep	Leslie Esdaile	$8.95
Stories to Excite You	Anna Forrest/Divine	$14.95
Subtle Secrets	Wanda Y. Thomas	$8.95
Suddenly You	Crystal Hubbard	$9.95
Sweet Repercussions	Kimberley White	$9.95
Sweet Tomorrows	Kimberly White	$8.95
Taken by You	Dorothy Elizabeth Love	$9.95
Tattooed Tears	T. T. Henderson	$8.95
The Color Line	Lizzette Grayson Carter	$9.95
The Color of Trouble	Dyanne Davis	$8.95
The Disappearance of Allison Jones	Kayla Perrin	$5.95
The Honey Dipper's Legacy	Pannell-Allen	$14.95
The Joker's Love Tune	Sidney Rickman	$15.95
The Little Pretender	Barbara Cartland	$10.95
The Love We Had	Natalie Dunbar	$8.95
The Man Who Could Fly	Bob & Milana Beamon	$18.95
The Missing Link	Charlyne Dickerson	$8.95
The Price of Love	Sinclair LeBeau	$8.95
The Smoking Life	Ilene Barth	$29.95
The Words of the Pitcher	Kei Swanson	$8.95
Three Wishes	Seressia Glass	$8.95
Ties That Bind	Kathleen Suzanne	$8.95
Tiger Woods	Libby Hughes	$5.95

RISE OF THE PHOENIX

Other Genesis Press, Inc. Titles (continued)

Time is of the Essence	Angie Daniels	$9.95
Timeless Devotion	Bella McFarland	$9.95
Tomorrow's Promise	Leslie Esdaile	$8.95
Truly Inseparable	Wanda Y. Thomas	$8.95
Unbreak My Heart	Dar Tomlinson	$8.95
Uncommon Prayer	Kenneth Swanson	$9.95
Unconditional	A.C. Arthur	$9.95
Unconditional Love	Alicia Wiggins	$8.95
Until Death Do Us Part	Susan Paul	$8.95
Vows of Passion	Bella McFarland	$9.95
Wedding Gown	Dyanne Davis	$8.95
What's Under Benjamin's Bed	Sandra Schaffer	$8.95
When Dreams Float	Dorothy Elizabeth Love	$8.95
Whispers in the Night	Dorothy Elizabeth Love	$8.95
Whispers in the Sand	LaFlorya Gauthier	$10.95
Wild Ravens	Altonya Washington	$9.95
Yesterday Is Gone	Beverly Clark	$10.95
Yesterday's Dreams, Tomorrow's Promises	Reon Laudat	$8.95
Your Precious Love	Sinclair LeBeau	$8.95

ESCAPE WITH INDIGO !!!!

Join Indigo Book Club©
It's simple, easy and secure.

Sign up and receive the new releases every month + Free shipping and 20% off the cover price.

Go online to www.genesis-press.com and click on Bookclub or
call 1-888-INDIGO-1

Order Form

Mail to: Genesis Press, Inc.
P.O. Box 101
Columbus, MS 39703

Name _____
Address _____
City/State _____ Zip _____
Telephone _____

Ship to (if different from above)
Name _____
Address _____
City/State _____ Zip _____
Telephone _____

Credit Card Information
Credit Card # _____ ☐ Visa ☐ Mastercard
Expiration Date (mm/yy) _____ ☐ AmEx ☐ Discover

Qty.	Author	Title	Price	Total

Use this order form, or call 1-888-INDIGO-1

Total for books _____
Shipping and handling:
   $5 first two books,
   $1 each additional book
Total S & H _____
Total amount enclosed _____
Mississippi residents add 7% sales tax

Visit www.genesis-press.com for latest releases and excerpts.